FIGHTING FOR YOU

THE WRIGHT HEROES OF MAINE
BOOK 8

ROBIN PATCHEN

CHAPTER ONE

Noah Aylett preferred the hour before dawn to any other slice of the day.

The world was as close to silent as it would get, only interrupted by the whoosh of his rowing machine, the thump of weights, the whistle of his breath. Unlike the rest of his life, these were predictable things. Things he could wrestle into order.

He racked the barbell—a clean, hard clank—then rolled his shoulders and checked the time. Twenty till five. He had at least another hour before Charlotte woke, before the slow, sticky business of fatherhood—unclehood, in his case—turned his orderly existence into chaos. Time enough for one more set.

He had just settled on his weight bench, hands spreading wide to grip the bar, when a shriek pierced his peace.

It was so out of place that it took him a moment to realize what it was. The burglar alarm.

Then his phone was vibrating, and his lungs filled with dread.

He stood, swiping to answer.

A woman's voice. "We have an alarm sounding—"

"Yeah. I know. Let me check." Noah crossed the basement workout room, phone pressed to his ear. "Can you turn it off?"

"Sir, if you didn't set it off accidentally—"

"Turn it off!" He hadn't triggered it, but maybe Charlotte had woken up early and opened a door, looking for him.

That would be a first, but there was a first time for every-thing. Thinking of all the *firsts* this year, his heart thumped in a way that had nothing to do with his punishing workout.

Mercifully, the alarm silenced as he hurried up the stairs to the first floor.

The quiet allowed him to hear heavy footsteps thumping toward the back of the house. Footsteps that couldn't be his niece's.

He hurtled the last few steps, shouting into the phone, "Intruder!" He hit the main floor and bolted toward the noise.

One of the rear French doors stood wide open. It had been locked.

It was still dark, but a shadow moved on the far side of the backyard. Noah rushed onto the patio, ready to give chase.

Then stopped.

He needed to check on Charlotte. Surely the intruder hadn't had time to get upstairs.

The shadow disappeared into the hedge—if it'd ever been there in the first place, not a phantom born of fear. If that *was* a person, they were getting away. Climbing over the fence, headed for the beach or even a boat.

He stood frozen, listening. The sharp scents of salt and wet fern drifted in, along with the distant slap of waves. No childish screams.

Noah lifted the phone. "Get the police here."

"They're en route."

He ran back inside, anxiety crawling up his throat. He had to get to her.

"Can you confirm everyone in the residence is accounted for?" the voice on the phone asked.

"Working on it."

He bolted toward the staircase, fear plucking his nerves. He hit the bottom and looked up.

Charlotte was halfway down, eyes wide. She rarely sucked her thumb outside of bed these days, but it was in her mouth now, her ratty crocheted blanket dragging on the steps behind her.

Relief washed over him. "Hey, Charlie-Bear." Somehow he kept the panic out of his voice.

Through the phone, the woman said, "Sir?"

"We're both fine. Thank you." He tossed the phone onto the table inside the entryway. "That alarm was loud, huh?"

Charlotte took a few more steps down, frowning. "Is it a monster?" The words were muffled, coming out around her thumb.

At least she'd spoken. It'd taken her weeks to open up to him, weeks during which he'd wondered if his four-year-old niece had learned to put together sentences.

He climbed the few steps and picked her up, heart still going wild under his ribs. "No monsters." Not the mythical kind, anyway.

Noah carried Charlotte to the back door, which he'd left open in his rush to get to her. He closed it, then triple-checked the lock. He pressed her close, letting the soft feel of her push back his fear.

The cops would come. Nosy neighbors would see the cruisers and gossip. He didn't care. All that mattered was Charlotte, healthy and in his arms.

He turned on the outside lights, peering through the glass doors to see any hint of what had happened. The flower beds, so pretty in the daylight, looked ghostly in the darkness, the foliage shivering in the sea breeze. Aside from that, nothing moved.

He hadn't imagined the thump of footsteps. Someone had been in his house.

Charlotte clung to him, and he tucked her blanket around her. Despite his assurance that they were safe, terror wafted from her, stronger than the scent of baby shampoo.

"No monsters, I promise. We're safe."

Charlotte didn't relax at all. She didn't trust him yet. Didn't trust that the world could be a secure place with grown-ups who stuck around and protected her.

"Let's just make sure." He turned on the sunroom lights.

"No monsters in here." He let her get a look, then moved into the dining room—also empty—and the kitchen. "Monster-free."

Her gaze fixed on the closed pantry door.

"Good point," Noah said, as if she'd vocalized her fear. "Maybe there's a monster in there eating all your cereal. What do you think? Cheerios?"

She scrunched her little nose in disgust.

He chuckled. Apparently, Charlotte's grandmother hadn't worried about healthy eating. When Noah had taken Charlotte to the grocery store, she'd pointed out all her favorites—the kinds of cereal that had more sugar than grain. He'd chosen one he'd loved as a kid.

It had not gone over well.

He yanked the pantry door open and shouted, "Boo!"

When no boxes of food responded, Charlotte grinned around her thumb.

"Yay! Your Cheerios are safe!" He continued the search throughout the first floor, checking under every piece of furniture and in every closet, making a game of it.

By the time they were on their way upstairs, Charlotte was giggling.

A sharp knock sounded on the front door, and her eyes popped wide.

"It's okay. It's the police." He kept his voice low and soothing. "They're going to double-check and make sure we're safe."

She wrapped her skinny arms around his neck, her legs around his torso, and clung like a barnacle.

Her fear seemed to be of much more than monsters. He angled back to see her face, but she wouldn't look at him, wouldn't lift her head from where she'd buried it in his neck.

"Charlie-Bear, you're safe here." And then he realized what she was afraid of. "I promise, nobody's going to take you away from me. This is your home. You'll always be safe here." His heart squeezed for this poor child. She'd finally started to feel secure with him, and now this.

"You promise?" The words were so faint, he wasn't sure he'd really heard them or just felt them, soul-deep.

"I promise, sweetheart. You're home now. This is where you belong."

And it was, even though Charlotte wasn't his, and the promise wasn't his to make.

One battle at a time.

He waited for some reaction, but she didn't speak again and didn't let up her grip on him.

The next time he saw his brother, he was going to punch him square in the face.

Noah carried Charlotte down to the foyer, which was now lit by flashing red and blue lights coming through the windows, and opened the front door.

A cop stood on the porch, another at the bottom of the steps. Two more were shining flashlights into the bushes in the front yard.

Noah was thankful they'd come, though he could've lived without the patrol car's strobe-lighting the neighborhood.

"It's Noah, right?" The officer at the door was a stocky guy with a buzz cut. He looked vaguely familiar. "I went to school with your brother. I'm Mason Pike."

"Right." Noah didn't recognize him, but then he and Jasper hadn't run in the same crowd. "Thanks for coming."

"I didn't hear you had a kid."

"Long story."

Mason stayed quiet as if waiting for Noah to share. After a moment, he asked, "What happened tonight?"

"The patio door opened and set the alarm off. I'm guessing the wind blew it open."

Mason's eyes narrowed.

There was very little wind, so Noah's theory made no sense. He glared at the cop, a look intended to say, *Keep your opinions to yourself.*

The last thing he needed was to scare Charlotte even more.

Mason shifted his weight, angling to look beyond Noah down the center hall. "Can we sweep the inside? It's best to be sure."

"Of course."

Noah carried Charlotte back into the house and settled on an antique rocking chair in the sitting room while Mason and his partner looked around.

Charlotte was smaller than a typical four-year-old, maybe due to genetics. More likely because of neglect. She was small enough to fold atop him, knees digging into his ribs. Noah rocked, humming a hymn his mother used to sing to distract her from the low but serious voices carrying from down the hall.

Charlotte had relaxed by the time Mason's partner stepped into the living room, hovering near the doorway. He was a younger guy, looked barely out of high school, with a tired smile.

He focused on Charlotte, whose head rested on Noah's shoulder. "Hey there, little bit."

She hid her face in the crook of Noah's neck.

He smoothed her hair. "She's wary of strangers."

"Just wanted to be sure you're both doing all right. Did you notice anything missing or out of place?"

"Haven't looked. If it's all clear, I'll put her back to bed."

Charlotte tensed but didn't object. He was learning to read her body language, and right now, he read *I don't wanna go to bed.*

"It's practically the middle of the night, Charlie-Bear." Fortunately, most of the blinds were closed so she couldn't see how the sun was already brightening the eastern sky. He carried her up to her room. The cops had left every light on, which might've comforted Charlotte, but it only reminded Noah that nothing was as it should be.

Her things were undisturbed—her storybooks, the princess lamp he'd bought when she'd first come to live with him, the mountain of stuffed animals she arranged all around her at bedtime every night. Maybe their plush presence made her feel less alone.

He tucked her in and perched on the edge of the bed. "Shall we say prayers again?"

She shook her head, then changed her mind and nodded, wearing a grave look no child should wear, like she was weighing some private equation. Had this event destroyed the trust he'd spent months building?

He held her hand, and she bowed her head. He gave her a moment to speak if she wanted to, then said, "Dear Jesus, please protect little Charlie-Bear and help her sleep." *And help her trust me. And help me keep her safe.*

He kissed her forehead. "I'll be downstairs. All the doors are locked. You're safe. I've got you."

She placed one tiny palm on his cheek and studied his face while he tried to convey so much with his look—that he loved her, that he'd protect her, that he would never let anybody hurt her.

And then she curled onto her side and tucked her little hands beneath her cheek.

He tugged her ratty crocheted blanket—the only thing she'd brought with her when she'd come to live with him—up over her. "See you in the morning, beautiful girl." Before he left, he slid the curtains closed in front of the blinds, hoping that, if no light peeked in, maybe she'd sleep later than usual. She needed the rest.

God willing, today he'd find a nanny to help him take care of her.

He crept out, leaving the door open a crack, and headed downstairs.

Mason and his partner were on the patio beyond the French doors. Mason was crouched but stood when Noah neared. "You want to look?"

Deep down, Noah had held out hope that he'd imagined those footsteps. That the shadow moving in the garden had been nothing. That the doors had opened on their own. If not wind, then...ghosts, maybe. Somehow, that seemed less menacing than the alternative.

But he stepped outside and crouched down.

"Looks like someone picked the lock." Mason angled a flashlight so he could see.

Noah had no idea what he was looking for. He'd take the expert's word for it. He stood and faced the cop. "Have there been other break-ins in the area?"

"Burglaries, sure. But not robberies or home invasions. Nothing when people were home."

"What's your theory?"

Mason shrugged. "Don't have one. Do you? Anything valuable in the house? Anything worth risking prison for?"

Those were two different questions. Yes, there were valuables. Mom's silver, Dad's rare coins. But only Noah and Jasper knew about them, and Jasper had a key.

Anyway, it didn't matter how much their possessions were worth. None of them seemed valuable enough to risk prison.

"Where'd the girl come from?" Mason asked.

Since it wasn't his story to tell, he said, "Is there anything else?" He understood the gossip mill well enough not to dump his news into it.

"I'm not trying to get juicy tidbits to share at the barbershop, Noah." Mason's use of his first name—as if they were friends—grated on his nerves. Mason's friendship with Jasper didn't raise the man's stature in Noah's book. Exactly the opposite, as a matter of fact. "There were footprints in the dew. Someone broke into your house while that child slept upstairs. If you have any idea—"

"You think I wouldn't tell you? I have no idea who it was."

"Maybe it has something to do with the kid."

"Maybe it does. Again, I don't know."

"If you tell me who she belongs to—"

"Why don't you talk to your old friend about it?"

That had Mason's eyes widening, then narrowing. "Okay, gotcha." The words came slowly, as if he were processing the information. "What about her mother?"

Noah sighed. "My understanding is that she doesn't want anything to do with her." He wasn't about to tell Mason that Charlotte had been taken away from her mother.

The whole town didn't need to know the ugly details, and he didn't trust anyone to keep his private life private.

"Don't you think this was a robbery attempt?" Noah asked. "Why do you think it's anything else?"

Mason looked up from his notebook. "Just covering the bases. Let us know if you hear from the mother or if anything seems amiss." He nodded toward the yard, where the sun was turning the darkness into gray. "The footprints aren't pronounced enough for us to tell if they were made by a man or a woman. Could've been a kid, even. I'll write up a report. Let us know if you discover anything missing."

"Will do."

After the cops left, Noah locked the doors, checked all the windows, then made a sweep of the house.

Nothing was missing. Did that mean the intruder hadn't been a thief but something else? Or just that he or she had been scared off by the alarm?

The lack of an answer didn't rest easily.

Noah's parents had had the first-floor doors and windows wired to the alarm years before. Noah would be adding to the second-floor windows. He'd do whatever the alarm company recommended.

This wasn't supposed to be Noah's life. He was the stable one, the guy who got up at four to exercise, the guy who was at his desk by seven, the guy who'd turned his dad's small software business into a multimillion-dollar enterprise by predicting what would happen next and getting there first.

Nothing about his life made sense anymore, nothing except the little girl sleeping upstairs, who'd turned everything upside down, including his heart.

CHAPTER TWO

Delaney Wright pressed her face deeper into the pillow, willing herself back into the dream. She'd been home in Shadow Cove, where her bedroom smelled like sea salt and her mother's lavender sachets. Reality smelled like stale tobacco and unwashed bodies.

A harsh cough from one of the beds across the room shattered the last wisp of her peace.

Delaney pushed herself upright on the thin mattress, springs creaking as the familiar weight of dread settled on her. Sunlight filtered through the dirty windows, casting dappled shadows across the worn linoleum. A few days in this place and already she could feel it trying to claim her—the despair that clung to the peeling wallpaper, the resignation that echoed in every conversation.

But today would be different.

She swung her legs over the side of the bed, her bare feet touching the cold floor, and checked the time.

Then checked it again.

She hadn't slept past six thirty since she'd moved in here. But it was an hour after that. Why hadn't her alarm gone off?

It didn't matter.

What mattered was that she had forty-five minutes before she had to leave for her interview, forty-five minutes to transform herself from a down-on-her-luck shelter resident into someone worthy of caring for a precious child. Someone who deserved a chance.

Delaney pulled her robe around her shoulders and hurried down the hall. The night before, she'd pressed her outfit and hung it in the laundry room, since the closet in the bedroom she shared with two other residents was too packed with stuff to hang anything.

She hadn't brought a lot with her when she'd left Maine, but she'd thought to pack clothes suitable for an interview—a navy blazer, matching slacks, and a cream blouse. They made her look professional and competent, like someone who belonged in the stately homes that lined Driftwood's old-money neighborhoods.

She reached the laundry room and stopped cold in the doorway.

Her slacks were on the hanger, but her blazer and blouse lay on the floor in a heap, wrinkled beyond recognition. The acrid smell of cigarette smoke hung thick in the small room despite the no-smoking sign plastered on the wall.

Two women sat on folding chairs near the open window, sharing a cigarette between them, blowing the smoke outside. As if that worked.

"Sorry," one of them said, glancing at her crumpled clothes. "They were like that when we got here."

Delaney's throat was too tight to respond. She bent to retrieve them, her hands trembling as she shook out the blazer. Aside from the wrinkles, it was unharmed.

The cream blouse bore a brown stain across the front—coffee, maybe, or something worse. The careful plans she'd made, the confidence she'd tried to build up since she'd gotten the call from the agency about the position, crumbled like the cigarette ash flicked onto the floor.

She wanted to scream. Wanted to demand an explanation, to insist her housemates show some basic respect. But the words would do no good. If she didn't get the job, she'd have to come back here, have to keep living with these people.

Lord, please give me favor.

"You okay, honey?" The second woman's voice carried a note of genuine concern, though she made no move to put out her cigarette.

Delaney didn't trust her voice. Of course she wasn't okay. She was a thousand miles from home with exactly forty-seven dollars in her wallet and clothes that now looked like she'd pulled them from a donation bin.

But she didn't say any of that. Instead, she swiveled and hurried back to her room.

One of her roommates was still sleeping, so she quietly spread the blazer across her narrow bed and tried to smooth the worst of the wrinkles with her palms. Maybe she could press them out.

She held up the blouse near the window, hoping the stain might look better in natural light. It didn't. The dark splotch fell right across the front.

She took the blouse to the bathroom and tried to scrub the stain out. No luck. Now it was stained *and* wet.

Back in the bedroom, she dug through her clothes, trying hard not to look at her purse, sitting on the cardboard box that served as her nightstand. The check from her father was practically pulsing inside. Ten thousand dollars. *"Come home when you run out of money."*

Cashing that check would prove she couldn't handle life on her own. Cashing that check would mean defeat.

Delaney found nothing in her bureau that would work with the suit. She covered her face with her hands and whispered, "Lord, I know You have a plan. I know You brought me to Driftwood. What do I do now?"

"Tell me you ain't praying again. Don' you know God don' care about people like us?"

She lowered her hands to see that her sleeping roommate was awake after all. And watching her.

"He *does* care." She hated how her voice trembled. If Delaney knew nothing else, she knew God cared. "You should try asking for His help."

"That what you did that landed you here in this Taj Mahal?"

At least Delaney wasn't sleeping in her car anymore. This place might not be fancy, but it was an answer to prayer. She'd grown up in luxury. In the last few months, she'd learned to appreciate a bed where she could stretch out her long legs and a shower where she could clean herself up in private.

"Today's the day, right? The interview?" Linda's voice was gravelly from years of smoking.

"Yeah, the nanny position."

"You got a shot?"

"I have experience. I've worked as a nanny since I graduated from high school." Except for a few months at a desk job in Boston, months Delaney had tried to scrape from her memory.

That brought a hard laugh. "High school. What was that, five minutes ago?"

Almost a decade, but she didn't say that.

Linda propped herself up on one elbow. "You try washing out that stain?"

She must've been awake longer than Delaney realized. "It's not budging. I bet a good dry cleaner could get it out." But not in time.

"What size are you? Four? Six?"

Delaney's pulse quickened. "What I am is flexible. You have an idea?"

"I might." She swung her legs over the side of her bed, pulled a battered suitcase out from underneath, and opened it on the floor, where she rummaged through it.

Delaney hadn't expected kindness from Linda, who'd made it clear what she thought of her faith.

"Here." Linda pulled out a white button-down shirt. "I had a waitressing gig with a catering company. Job didn't last, but I got to keep the shirt. It's nothing fancy, but it don' have no stains."

The shirt was cheap polyester, but that made it wrinkle-free. It was a little dingy, the collar crumpled, and it was at least a size too big. But it would work.

"Linda, I—thank you." The words were thick with gratitude.

"Geez, with the tears." But Linda's gruff tone had softened a fraction. "You seem like a decent kid. Someone's gotta look out for you."

Delaney was trying very hard to look out for herself, but so far all she'd done was prove she couldn't manage.

She clutched the shirt to her chest, feeling something loosen in her throat. God worked through unlikely angels sometimes. "I'll wash it and get it back to you as soon as I can."

"You better. You never know when my ship's gonna come in. That's the fanciest blouse I own." Linda settled back onto her pillow. "Now go on. I need a few more hours of beauty sleep." She yawned and rolled over.

Ten minutes later, Delaney stood before the cracked mirror in her room, adjusting the collar that didn't want to sit right. The shirt bunched up where she'd tucked it in. But the white looked crisp against the navy blazer. It wasn't perfect, but it would work.

Surely, the cigarette smell would lessen during her walk across town. All she needed was a little time in the cool sea breeze.

She'd pulled her dark-blond hair into a bun and applied her makeup, going for a natural look.

Professional and competent. Someone who could be trusted with a child.

~

The walk through Driftwood helped settle Delaney's nerves. The October morning was crisp, and the salt-tinged air reminded her of home. Leaves crunched beneath her sensible flats as she made her way from the shelter's rundown neighborhood toward the historic district where the grand houses stood.

In Maine, the coastline jigged and jagged in rocky cliffs. It was smoother here in Virginia, more gentle.

She found the address on Magnolia Street—a three-story Victorian painted sage green with white trim. Wraparound porches adorned both levels, and climbing roses, though past their summer bloom, still clung to the latticework. The property was protected by a thick hedge. She could imagine happy children playing in the yard, stability and love behind leaded-glass windows.

Delaney stopped at the foot of the porch steps, tucking in the front of Linda's borrowed shirt one more time. This could be the chance to prove to her family that she wasn't incompetent, that she could make it on her own.

"Lord, please let her like me."

Delaney climbed the steps. Taking a deep breath, she pressed the doorbell, and it chimed somewhere deep inside the house.

Footsteps approached—heavy, purposeful strides across what sounded like hardwood floors.

The door swung open, and Delaney found herself looking not at a woman but at a man. A man whose appearance made her forget every word she'd practiced on her way.

He was taller than she was by at least four inches and had blond hair that looked like he'd been running his fingers through it. His pale-blue dress shirt was wrinkled, the sleeves rolled up to reveal forearms dusted with dark hair. But it was his eyes that stopped her—the gray of the sky an instant before dawn.

She'd expected a woman, a harried mother. She had not expected *this*.

She smiled and stuck out her hand. "You must be Mr. Aylett." She forced confidence into her voice. "I'm Delaney Wright. The agency sent me." When he didn't respond—or react—she added, "For the nanny position?"

He didn't shake her hand, his gaze taking her in. His expression shifted from curiously polite to worried to...angry? His jaw tightened. "I'm sorry. This isn't going to work."

Her arm fell to the side, her hopes plummeting much further. "I don't understand. Has the position been filled?"

"My apologies." With no more explanation, he slammed the door.

Delaney stared at it.

Had that really just happened? She'd barely gotten three sentences out before he'd dismissed her completely.

Heat flooded her cheeks as she replayed the moment. The way his eyes had swept over her, taking in her carefully applied makeup, her slightly wrinkled jacket, and Linda's too-big shirt. Had the stale cigarette stench followed her?

Whatever the reason, he'd taken one look and found her lacking.

She raised her hand to knock again, then let it fall. What

would she say? That she didn't usually stink like cigarettes? That she had nicer clothes back home? That she'd grown up in a bigger house than this one and she belonged here, even if she didn't look the part?

Those facts didn't qualify her for the job, and anyway, he already knew her qualifications. The agency must have sent them along.

It wasn't her experience. It was...her.

She simply wasn't good enough.

The walk back to the sidewalk felt endless, each footfall echoing her humiliation. She'd known she might not get the job, but she hadn't considered that she might not even make it through the front door.

She turned to look again at the beautiful Victorian that she'd believed, for a few glorious seconds, could be her home. A live-in position that might solve all her problems.

A curtain twitched in an upstairs window, and a child peered down at her. The curtain fell back into place before Delaney was able to get a good look.

By the time she made it to the corner, tears streamed down her face, hot and angry and filled with frustration and shame.

Now what was she going to do?

CHAPTER THREE

Noah stared at the closed door, his hand still gripping the brass knob with enough force to leave impressions in his palm.

The potential nanny had reeked of cigarette smoke. He wasn't about to let someone who smoked anywhere near Charlotte.

But potential nanny's smell hadn't been his only problem, and Noah knew it.

The real problem was his own outsized reaction. Those wide eyes, pale blue like clear water, the way her teeth had caught her lower lip when he'd rejected her, the curve of her waist beneath that fitted blazer...

Sheesh. What was he doing?

Delaney Wright was exactly the kind of woman who could ruin his life.

Marianne's face flashed through his mind—another beautiful woman. The divorce two years before had been messy and public, and the rumor mill still swarmed with stories of things he'd never done, never thought to do. The rumors hadn't been

Marianne's fault, but she could've trusted him. She might have if she'd cared more about their marriage than her potential settlement.

Noah hadn't met a female he could trust since Mama died.

After the break-in that morning, he needed someone reliable, someone with integrity. In his experience, young, single women were the opposite of trustworthy.

The sound of footsteps on the stairs had Noah spinning.

Charlotte froze halfway down, eyes wide as if he might shout at her. She'd changed into her favorite T-shirt—the pink one with the sparkly butterfly—and stretchy pants, her blond curls sticking out at odd angles.

"Hey, Charlie-Bear. You're awake." He kept his voice low and steady, as he'd learned to do with his jumpy niece.

She continued down on bare feet, her hand trailing along the banister. "Who was the pretty lady?"

He kept his smile in place. Charlotte hardly ever spoke. And now she'd wasted words on the nanny he'd sent away.

"Nobody important."

Charlotte's lower lip pushed out in the expression that often preceded tears. "She looked sad."

Noah hadn't watched Miss Wright leave—had forced himself to turn away from the windows beside the door the moment he'd closed it. The last thing he needed was to have the image of her walking down his front steps burned into his memory.

"You must be hungry." He moved toward the kitchen. "How about breakfast?"

Charlotte's small hand slipped into his.

"Apple sandwiches and eggs?"

She shrugged. He knew she'd prefer a bowl of sugary cereal and milk, but he'd refused, and she didn't argue like an ordinary four-year-old might. She was compliant, as if she feared... something.

He had no idea what. His goal was to be the father figure she'd never had, to make her feel safe and secure in his home. Soon, God willing, he'd be able to spend more time with her. But not until he completed the merger he'd been working on for months.

The familiar routine of scrambling eggs helped steady his nerves. Once they were cooking, he pulled an apple from the bowl on the granite countertop and began slicing it.

The mundane task should have calmed him, but his mind kept drifting back to the nanny he'd rejected.

He'd been rude. Unforgivably rude. His mother would have threatened to box his ears.

She'd threatened that punishment a thousand times during his childhood, and to this day, he had no idea what it would feel like.

Charlotte had climbed onto one of the barstools and was watching him, her little eyes squinted with worry.

Oops.

He'd been chopping the apples into chunks instead of the thin slices she preferred. "Sorry, Charlie-Bear."

After stirring the eggs, he started over with a fresh apple, forcing himself to concentrate on turning the fruit into wedges, then smearing them with peanut butter. Apple sandwiches, an Aylett family tradition. Until Charlotte had come to live with him a few months before, she'd never even heard of apple sandwiches.

The smallest of Jasper's many failures as a father.

In the foyer, the grandfather clock chimed quarter after nine, reminding Noah of the conference call he was supposed to join in fifteen minutes. Plus, he had to review documents before the afternoon meeting. And he still hadn't returned a call from his attorney.

Somewhere in there, he'd have to call Jasper. Again.

Instead of taking care of all that stuff, he fixed a late breakfast and tried not to think about a beautiful creature who smelled like cigarettes and looked like every mistake he'd ever made.

He needed to find Charlotte a nanny—today. Things had been spinning out of control ever since she'd come to live with him. As if he hadn't already been busy enough, he now had an intruder to deal with and a security system to upgrade.

Food prepared, he settled Charlotte in her seat at the kitchen table, then sat beside her, munching the chunks of apples he'd cut accidentally and trying not to think about his to-do list.

Noah's phone vibrated, a staccato buzz on the table.

Seeing his brother's photo on the screen, Noah stood and grabbed the phone before the second ring. He swiped to answer. "You're alive."

"Shut up." Jasper's voice sounded rough, as if he'd only just remembered that *morning* was a thing that happened to other people. "You texted like it was DEFCON one."

Good thing Noah hadn't needed his brother for anything, considering he'd texted hours before, right after the cops left.

"Hold on a second." He kissed Charlotte on the forehead. "I have to take this. Can you finish your eggs, please? Then come find me and we'll decide what to do next, okay?"

She nodded, the only response he expected.

He stepped out of the kitchen and toward his office at the front of the house. "What time is it where you are?"

"Early," Jasper said. "What's going on?"

He didn't have time for Jasper's hangover or whatever he'd gotten into, wherever in the world he was. "Someone broke into the house." He kept his voice low so Charlotte wouldn't hear. "Any idea who might do that?"

"Whoa. What?" A rustle sounded through the phone, probably Jasper dragging himself out of bed. "Someone broke in? A burglar? Did they steal anything?"

"The alarm scared them off. But it was four thirty in the morning. We were home."

"Aw, man. Poor Charlotte. That must've scared her to death. Is she okay?"

Noah sat at his desk. He was already having a bad day. Adding a conversation with Jasper didn't help.

He gave his brother a rundown of events. "I wondered if you had any idea who might've done it. Enemies? Former friends? Or maybe someone who thinks we have valuables?"

"I'm not an idiot."

He managed to swallow a dark chuckle. Any man who abandoned a little girl to gallivant around the world was worse than an idiot. "What about"—he lowered his voice even more—"Violet?"

Jasper made a sound, a sharp laugh that bordered on a cough. "No way. She's in New York—last I heard, anyway. She promised to stay away."

"Maybe she wants to see her daughter."

"If she did, she'd contact me, not break in."

"Unless she wants her back." He couldn't imagine how she'd ever get custody legally. Maybe she knew her only shot was to kidnap her.

"She doesn't," Jasper said. "She only had the kid to get money out of me."

"Charlotte." Noah ground out his niece's name through gritted teeth. "Her name is—"

"I know her name. I'm just saying, her mother doesn't care

about her. She just wanted cash, and I gave her as much as she's ever getting."

His brother's photo should be on a billboard outlining all the reasons not to have one-night stands with strippers.

"I'm trying to cover all the bases," Noah said. "Have you heard from her lately?"

"Not a peep since she lost custody. What did the cops say?"

"Someone picked the lock on the patio door. They checked the yard, found footprints, but no sign of who it was or what they wanted. Whoever it was took off when the alarm sounded. I assume he—or she—hopped the fence. I just need to know if I should be watching for Violet or...anyone else. Maybe an enemy, or—?"

"I don't tell people where I'm from."

That was a strange thing to say, and why would Jasper hide his past?

Not only that, but Jasper sounded tired. Not the kind of tired that came from too much bourbon and not enough sleep. More...weary, which didn't make any sense. The guy spent his life hobnobbing with the rich and famous, hopping from party to party, yacht to yacht. What could he possibly have weighing him down?

"Are you okay, Jaz?" Noah asked, practically against his will. He didn't appreciate Jasper's life choices, but he was still his little brother. "You don't sound like yourself."

Jasper laughed, the sound hard. "Don't worry about me, bro. I'm fine, and nobody's coming for her."

That last sentence landed too heavy. Until a few months before, Noah hadn't known Charlotte existed. Nobody had cared about her at all. At least Jasper had brought her home, even if he wasn't doing his part as a father.

"You'll call if you think of anyone who might—"

"I'll call. And Noah?" All humor and irritation seemed gone from his voice. "Take care of her."

Right.

Noah jabbed his phone to end the call, irritation spiking.

What did Jasper think he was doing? Noah was killing himself trying to take care of Charlotte.

He was the only person in the world who could be bothered.

CHAPTER FOUR

A week had passed since that horrible moment on Magnolia Street, a week with no prospects at all.

Delaney crossed the town's main thoroughfare and entered the park in the center of downtown Driftwood, phone pressed close to her ear, trying to hear the woman from the agency over the traffic.

"...to say there's nothing right now."

Delaney's hopes blew away on the breeze. "I'm flexible." She hated how desperate she sounded. "Anything part-time or weekends, or even—?"

"Sorry." The woman's voice carried a note of genuine sympathy that somehow made it worse. "There aren't many in these parts who can afford a nanny, and most folks hire people they know."

Wasn't that how Delaney had gotten her jobs back in Shadow Cove? Her first employers had been friends of her parents. After that, her reputation had grown naturally. She'd never wanted for clients in a town where the Wright name was well-known and well-respected, a town where she'd proved herself capable over and over.

Nobody in this little hamlet in Virginia knew her or her family. To them, she was a stranger, an outsider. A Yankee, to boot. She tried to ignore the suspicious looks she got from shoppers and clerks at the local grocery store every time she opened her mouth.

"We just don't have any other placements available at the moment," the woman said. "I wish we did."

Delaney moved aimlessly, deeper into the park. She'd walked a few blocks into town that morning to search for a job, but she hadn't seen a single help-wanted sign. The call from the agency had given her a surge of hope.

Now, she felt more dejected than ever.

"How long before something might open up?"

"Could be a week, could be a month. You know how these things go."

She didn't, not really. She'd always had a waiting list of potential clients.

Maybe it was time to give up and go home. Or worse, cash Dad's check.

"You'd probably best find something else for the time being, except... It's a small community, Ms. Wright, and times have been lean."

Translation: *Move along, Yankee. You're not welcome here.*

"Thank you for calling." Delaney ended the call and stumbled toward the closest bench, where she sat and stared at nothing. *Lord, what do I do now?*

A chilly wind rustled leaves, casting dappled shadows across the grassy park. She'd fallen in love with Driftwood when she'd first come here. The park sat in the center of town, surrounded by shops on three sides. The fourth was lined with trees and bushes. This park reminded her of the town common back in Shadow Cove. This morning, the oaks and pines seemed to be looking down on the outsider who didn't belong.

She was out of money. A church was funding her stay at the shelter, but she couldn't rely on them indefinitely. The most pathetic part? She didn't even have enough cash to fill her car with gas.

She'd come to Driftwood seeking a fresh start. It felt ironic, and slightly cruel, that when she was finally ready to give up her dream, she couldn't even afford to leave.

Looking up past the canopy that shaded the park, she gazed into the bright blue sky. "Lord, what are You doing? What am I doing here?" She'd been so certain when she'd arrived in town after wandering down the East Coast for months on end, burning through her savings. This place felt like the Virginia version of Shadow Cove, the closest thing she'd found to home since she'd left Maine in July.

But she didn't belong here, and apparently, she never would.

"I want to go home. Please?"

The Lord didn't give her the go-ahead to give up her quest for independent living. He'd led her on this crazy adventure, but had she missed a turn along the way? Done something to disobey Him? Because this couldn't be what He had in mind.

Not that going home felt like the right answer, either. She hadn't gone back because she wanted to prove she could be independent like her confident and accomplished sisters. She wasn't like them, though. She wasn't smart or well-read or talented.

All she'd proved so far was that, away from Shadow Cove and her family's good name, she couldn't even land a job.

She slipped her phone into her purse, gaze drifting to a nearby playground, where children's laughter carried on the sea-scented breeze. She watched mothers push their toddlers on swings. A father knelt at the bottom of a slide, catching a little boy as he squealed with delight.

Sitting here was only making her wish for things she might never find. She stood, brushing off her slacks, and turned toward the street. She needed a job. She'd just have to go into every shop and restaurant in town until she had one.

Movement at the edge of the playground caught her attention. A little girl with blond curls had wandered past the safety of the mulched bark of the play area to the hedge that stood between the park and the road. The child looked to be about three years old—far too young to be exploring alone.

Delaney glanced around, expecting to see a parent hurrying after her, but no one seemed to notice. The little girl continued along the hedge line, getting closer to the park's exit and the busy street.

Delaney's pulse quickened. She left the paved path and jogged across the grass, her flats sliding on leaves damp from an overnight rain.

"Hey there, sweetie." She kept her voice gentle as she approached, not wanting to startle her. "Are you looking for something?"

The little girl turned, revealing the brightest blue eyes Delaney had ever seen. She stuck a thumb in her mouth and pointed with her other hand toward the street, where an orange tabby disappeared behind a parked car.

"What a cute kitty cat. Is it yours?"

The child shook her head.

Delaney knelt to her eye level. "I think we should get you back to the playground where it's safe. Are you here with your mommy?"

When the child didn't respond, Delaney stood, took her hand, and tugged her toward the park.

The girl didn't budge.

The back of Delaney's neck prickled, and she suddenly had the strongest sense that she was being watched.

She turned, and sure enough, a few yards away, a figure stepped behind a tree. Like someone was trying to avoid being caught. She hadn't seen a face, just a shoulder an instant before it disappeared. She didn't even know if it'd been a man or a woman. Whoever it was, he or she didn't emerge on the other side of the tree.

Was someone watching this child?

Delaney's heart pounded, fear coiling in her stomach, but she pasted on a smile. "What's your name?"

The girl stared at her for a long time, as if assessing her trustworthiness. Finally, she spoke around her thumb. "Charlotte."

"That's a pretty name. I'm Delaney."

"Hi."

"You want a piggyback ride?"

She grinned, showing her baby teeth.

Delaney took that as a yes. She turned and crouched down enough that Charlotte could climb on.

Once she was on and steady, Delaney stood and walk-bounced toward the playground, eliciting giggles all the way.

When they arrived at the kids' area, she looked around, again searching for someone who might've lost a child.

Nobody seemed alarmed.

She lowered herself, letting the child slide from her back to the ground. "Who are you here with?"

Charlotte shrugged, then lifted her arms in the universal sign for *pick me up*.

Delaney did and propped Charlotte on her hip. "Your mommy? Your daddy?"

No response.

"Your grandparents?"

The question only seemed to confuse her, as if she'd never heard of such a thing.

"A nanny?"

That brought a shrug, and the girl's eyes scanned the people sitting on benches along the edges of the play area. They landed on an older woman who was absorbed in her phone, thumbs flying across the screen. The woman looked to be in her sixties with graying hair pulled back in a ponytail.

Delaney pointed. "Is that her?"

Charlotte nodded.

It worried her that the child wasn't more vocal, but at the moment, she was mostly concerned about the woman who hadn't looked up from her phone, hadn't noticed that the girl she was supposed to protect had wandered dangerously close to traffic.

And had caught the eye of a stranger.

What kind of caregiver was so distracted that a preschooler could disappear without her knowledge?

Delaney marched toward the woman, Charlotte still balanced on her hip. The closer they got, the tighter the little girl held on. And the angrier Delaney became.

The woman glanced up as they approached, her eyes widening slightly. She shoved her phone into her purse and stood quickly.

"Charlotte! There you are, sweetie." Her voice carried the artificial brightness of someone who'd been caught.

"I found her on the opposite side of the park," Delaney said. "She was almost to the road."

"Well." The woman *tsked*, shaking her head. "I was just wondering where you'd gone off to." The lie rolled off her tongue naturally. "You were supposed to stay where I could see you. It was very naughty to wander off like that."

"Don't blame her for your negligence." Delaney kept her voice low, not wanting to frighten Charlotte or attract attention. "Her safety is your responsibility."

The woman's face flushed bright red. She squared her shoulders. "How I care for my charge is none of your business."

"The well-being of a child is everyone's business." Delaney usually avoided confrontation like a toddler avoided nap time, but some things were more important than her feelings. "She was following a cat toward traffic while you were on your phone. She could've been hit by a car." The thought of the person who'd been watching Charlotte filled her stomach with acid. "She could've been snatched by a stranger while you checked your Instagram feed."

"How dare you? Give her to me." The woman held out her arms. "Time to go, sweetheart."

Charlotte didn't squirm to get down or shift to move into her nanny's arms. Instead, she turned and wrapped her arms and legs around Delaney, koala-style, burying her face against her shoulder.

The woman's expression hardened. "Charlotte, come here. Now."

"She doesn't want to go with you," Delaney said quietly. What kind of caregiver inspired this level of resistance?

"She's not your kid." The woman dug in her purse for her phone, then stepped closer, her voice rising. "Put her down or I'll call the police."

Her shout drew the attention of curious onlookers, whose gazes darted between Delaney and this distractible caretaker. Moms and dads and babysitters, all looking at Delaney as if she were in the wrong. All but one woman, whose expression held nothing but compassion when she met Delaney's eyes.

Maybe Delaney had an ally, one in a sea of angry faces.

Getting arrested would certainly slam the final nail in her Driftwood coffin.

But Charlotte wasn't letting go. And Delaney didn't want her to.

There was nothing for it now. Delaney wasn't going to leave this precious child with an inept, and now angry, nanny. "Go ahead, and after you do that, call her parents. They should know what kind of woman they trusted their child to."

"You think I won't?" The woman started tapping on her phone. "You're gonna end up in jail, lady."

Maybe, but if it meant Charlotte was safe…

The child's tight grip suddenly eased. She spoke over Delaney's shoulder. "It's the pretty lady."

Delaney had no idea what she was talking about, but the nanny's eyes widened, and her flushed cheeks paled.

"I was just about to call you, sir."

Someone approached from the side and stopped a few feet away.

Delaney glanced and realized with a sinking feeling that it was Mr. Aylett, the man who'd taken one look at her and decided she wasn't worth five minutes of his time.

And then relief washed over her. He must've been the one watching Charlotte. Odd that he'd hidden, but at least he took his daughter's safety seriously.

He wore a business suit and tie, his gray eyes sweeping the scene: Charlotte clinging to Delaney, the nanny clutching her phone, the small crowd of onlookers pretending not to stare. When his gaze landed on Delaney, something flickered across his features, gone before she could name it.

"It's the pretty lady," Charlotte said again. She was no longer clinging to Delaney, but still, she hadn't done the kid-wiggle that said she wanted down.

Mr. Aylett squared off with the nanny. "Explain."

The woman took a few brave steps toward him, her artificial smile back in place. "Thank goodness you're here. This woman"—she gestured toward Delaney—"snatched Charlotte right off the playground. I was trying to get her back when—"

"That's not what happened." Delaney's voice came out strong despite her anxiety.

Charlotte's father turned to look at her. "Go on."

The nanny said, "Sir—"

"You had your say." Mr. Aylett nodded at Delaney. "Please."

Seemed he was *capable* of being polite, despite how he'd treated her at their first meeting.

"Charlotte wandered toward the street while her caregiver was focused on her phone. I brought her back to keep her safe."

Mr. Aylett's piercing gaze held her eye contact for a long moment before shifting back to the nanny. "To this, you say...?"

"She's lying."

The man's expression shifted to a glower. "Unfortunately for you, Mrs. Dechambeau, I saw the whole thing."

Cheeks bright red, the nanny shook her head. "I was watching—"

"You're fired."

"What? For one little mistake?"

"You consider putting Charlotte's life in danger a *little* mistake?" He didn't raise his voice. In fact, his volume lowered as the intensity of his words increased. "Perhaps next time you'll take better care of a child in your care—assuming you ever get another position. I can assure you it won't be in this town."

"But... If you would just—"

"You're dismissed."

"My things—"

"I'll have them packed and delivered to the agency." He turned away from her, though she stared at him with wide eyes and open mouth.

But he was, apparently, done with her. He stepped closer to Delaney and held his arms out for the child.

Charlotte shifted into them.

He settled her on his hip, his focus on Delaney. "Thank you."

The tension that had been wound tight since she'd spotted Charlotte lessened.

But standing this close to Charlotte's father made her stomach flutter in a way that had nothing to do with the confrontation.

"You're welcome." She smiled at Charlotte, nodded at Mr. Aylett, and took a step back, needing distance from those smoky eyes. She swiveled and walked away, forcing herself not to run. She'd probably slip and face-plant on the sidewalk.

"Wait!"

His voice followed her, but she didn't slow down.

She might be jobless and penniless and...hopeless, but the rude Mr. Aylett didn't know any of that.

Delaney needed a job. What she did not need was to linger and chat with a man who'd already judged her and found her wanting.

CHAPTER FIVE

Noah caught up with Miss Wright, his longer strides eating up the distance between them despite Charlotte's weight in his arms.

"Please, can we just…?"

She turned, cheeks flushed, eyes narrowed. Gone was the stench of cigarettes, replaced with a hint of coconut that reminded him of the beach, swimming with his brother while Mom and Dad lounged nearby.

That, plus the way the afternoon light caught the gold in Miss Wright's hair, not to mention the way she'd secured Charlotte, fought for Charlotte…

They all scrambled his thoughts.

"Did you need something, Mr. Aylett?" Her voice carried that gentle quality he'd noticed when she'd stood on his porch, though that same voice had been steel when she'd confronted Charlotte's former nanny.

She was an enigma, this one.

"I owe you an apology," he said. "My behavior at our first meeting was inexcusable." He sounded too formal, as if he were speaking to his old headmaster, not a woman he'd insulted.

"When you came for an interview, I—" He ran a hand through his hair, feeling insecure in a way he hadn't in years. "I was rude."

He expected quick forgiveness, considering the difference in their stations.

That thought had him wincing. *Stations?* He sounded like his late grandmother, who'd been far too concerned with that kind of thing, as if their wealth made them not just better dressed, but better people.

Miss Wright wore jeans and a pretty sweater, her dark blond hair blowing in the breeze. She couldn't be more than twenty-one or twenty-two, far too young for him.

Not too young for *him*, too young to be a nanny. Too young to trust with his niece. Except the more mature one he'd hired had been incompetent.

Miss Wright straightened her shoulders. "I agree," she finally said. "You were."

Noah was so surprised by her answer—by everything about her—that he was speechless. He shifted Charlotte to his other hip, buying himself a moment to come up with a decent reply.

"It wasn't about you," he said finally. "I mean, it was a little. Hiring someone like you—"

"Someone like me?" Her chin lifted. "What does that mean? You don't even know me."

What was wrong with him? He navigated boardrooms and high-society functions with finesse, but he couldn't get through a single conversation with this woman.

"I meant..." He cleared his throat, acutely aware of Charlotte's curious gaze bouncing between them. "A young, unmarried woman living in my home. Surely you can see how people might interpret that. I have reasons for needing to avoid scandal right now, and—"

"Are you saying I'm...scandalous?" Her lips twitched, and

he couldn't tell if she was amused or insulted or something else entirely.

"No, of course not. But you're..." He gestured toward her, taking in her tall, shapely form. He regretted that move when her eyebrows rose. "That is, you're clearly...attractive, and I'm a single man, and people talk."

Now, her eyes narrowed and flicked to Charlotte. "You're a single father?"

"The agency didn't tell you?"

"Only that you were looking to hire a nanny. I didn't know..."

He guessed by the way her lips pressed together that she was taking in all the information she'd learned and working the problem. "So, based on my looks alone"—her words came out slowly—"you dismissed me out of hand and hired an inept grandmother instead?"

How he wished he could argue with her conclusion.

Mrs. Dechambeau had come with zero references, but she was mature, and she'd babysat her grandkids for years. A sixty-three-year-old widow, she'd posed no threat of wagging tongues.

"Yes, well..." He cleared his throat. "The 'inept' part was, admittedly, less than ideal." He'd been so focused on protecting himself from scandal that he'd failed to protect his niece from real danger.

Charlotte tugged on his shirt collar and whispered in his ear. "I like the pretty lady better than the mean lady."

He looked down at his niece, whose blue eyes were fixed on Miss Wright with obvious adoration. "Was Mrs. Dechambeau mean?"

She shrugged one shoulder but didn't elaborate.

So far, he was doing this parenting thing all wrong.

Miss Wright smiled at his niece, and in that moment, all her defenses seemed to fall away. She was beautiful, yes. And kind and tenderhearted. If she weren't so attractive, she'd be perfect.

But this wasn't about him.

"If you would consider—"

"I'm sorry. Of course I accept your apology." Her gaze shifted back to Charlotte. "It was nice to meet you, Charlotte." She swiveled and walked away.

"Daddy, please."

Daddy?

The word was a gut-punch. He needed to correct her, remind her that he wasn't her father. And he would, later.

His niece's plea got his feet moving. He fell into step beside the stubborn, beautiful woman.

She slowed, glancing his way. "Did you need something else?"

"I'm guessing you already found another position." When she didn't respond, he continued. "Whatever they're paying you, I'll add twenty percent."

That brought her up short. "You want to hire me? Even though I'm scandalous?"

"I never said…"

"Please." Charlotte's little voice was barely audible.

His niece never spoke to strangers. She hardly ever spoke to him.

This woman had somehow connected with her in a way he'd seen nobody else do.

If Miss Wright didn't agree, Charlotte would be crushed. And he would do anything, even risk scandal, to avoid that.

"Is it still a live-in position, even though I'm…" Her voice faltered, and for the first time, he picked up a hint of insecurity.

"Attractive?" he prompted. When she just blinked those large, innocent eyes, his rogue body went a little haywire. "We'll just have to be very careful not to give off any vibes."

"I see." She looked at Charlotte again, eyes sparkling. "We must promise to have no vibes. We must be vibe-less, Charlotte. Completely vibe-less."

Charlotte giggled. She put her hand on Noah's cheek and said, "Can you be vibe-less?"

She'd spoken a complete sentence.

He swallowed a rise of hope. In a few minutes, Miss Wright had gotten closer to his niece than Mrs. Dechambeau had in days.

"I'll do my part." He focused on Miss Wright again, speaking the words with a confidence he didn't feel.

He was going to have to trust somebody, and his first instinct had been way off. Delaney Wright had already proved her ability to not only care for Charlotte but also to draw her out.

He'd have to trust her, despite the definite existence of vibes —even if they were only on his part.

____

CHAPTER SIX

The next morning, Delaney woke in her new room at the Aylett house, still coming to terms with the events of the day before. She'd gone from depressed and despondent, ready to give up her dreams...to this.

The bedroom felt like a sanctuary from another time. She ran her fingers along the ornately carved bedpost, admiring the rich mahogany that glowed in the sunlight filtering through lace curtains. The four-poster bed dominated the space, its matching dresser and armoire pushed against walls painted a soft sage green.

An area rug in muted blues and greens covered most of the hardwood floor, its intricate pattern pulling the room together. Her toes sank into it as she padded across to examine a small writing desk nestled in the corner by the window.

Back in Shadow Cove, her bedroom had been all whites and pastels, filled with modern furniture with clean lines. She'd wanted a simple space so that the focal point would be the view from the window—the rugged Maine coast.

This room was nothing like that, with its antiques and character, yet it felt more like home than anywhere else she'd stayed since she'd left that summer.

On the dresser, a collection of silver-framed photographs caught her attention. Delaney moved closer, drawn to the smiling faces. A striking brunette woman stood beside a tall light-haired man with Noah's jawline and serious eyes. His parents, she guessed. In another frame, a teenage Noah stood with his arm slung around a younger boy, who looked enough like him to be his brother. Maybe this was Charlotte's father. Mr. Aylett still hadn't explained how exactly he'd become her guardian, but Charlotte had called him "Uncle Noah" a few times the night before.

Delaney picked up the third photo, this of the older couple and the two boys, though they were younger here, perhaps ten and seven. The photo had been taken in the living room—the one she'd seen when Mr. Aylett had shown her around when she'd first arrived. In the photo, there was a Christmas tree in the corner, a few mugs of hot chocolate or coffee on the tables, and used wrapping paper strewn across the floor.

The family looked...happy. Just plain happy.

Where were Noah's parents? Where was his brother?

What events had transpired from the Christmas in that photo to today?

She set the frame down and moved to the window, where she shifted the curtains aside and peered out. By the time she'd gotten here the night before, the sun had set. This morning, she saw that her second-story room looked over a small yard hemmed in by a hedge of evergreen bushes. On the other side was a narrow road that separated the property from a sandy beach and, beyond that, the Atlantic, shimmering gold beneath the sunrise.

Though Delaney was far from Maine, those waters were as familiar as her reflection. The Atlantic made her feel at home. It was why, in the previous few months, she'd never ventured far from the coast, even though the cost of living was so much higher than if she'd gone inland. Somehow, it felt like, if she stayed near the ocean, she would stay connected to her sisters and her parents. She longed for them, but the homesickness was a little lessened today. Today, she had a higher purpose than just keeping herself alive.

Delaney showered and dressed in jeans and her favorite soft lavender turtleneck. She arranged her hair into a low ponytail and hesitated in front of the mirror.

Though the bed had been comfortable, she hadn't slept well, which showed in the dark smudges beneath her eyes.

In her reflection, Delaney didn't see her sister Alyssa's stubbornness or Brooklynn's cheerfulness. There was no trace of Cici's determination or Kenzie's thirst for adventure.

None of her sisters' admirable traits stared back at her. All Delaney saw was a woman nervous to walk downstairs and face her new employer. She and Charlotte were already friends, but Mr. Aylett was intimidating, exacting, and demanding. The day before, she'd watched him fire Charlotte's former nanny on the spot.

Would one misstep cause her to suffer the same fate?

Certainly not for the same reason. Delaney was more watchful of the children in her care than that so-called caregiver had been. She understood what the slightest distraction could cost.

She was great with kids. It was adults she had a problem with, especially intimidating ones like her new employer.

She took a deep breath and blew it out, trying to blow her fear away with it. "You can do this."

Her reflection smirked at her as she headed for the door.

A small, octagonal window at the end of the hall let in enough light for her to make her way to the staircase. The banister, floors, and molding all gleamed with the patina of age and dignity.

Mr. Aylett had given her a quick tour the night before. Charlotte had accompanied them, her quiet presence distracting—and worrying. Delaney needed to know more about her, but Mr. Aylett had seemed reluctant to say much in front of her.

After the tour, he'd told Delaney to meet him in the kitchen "first thing," and then retreated to his office to work.

How was she supposed to know what time "first thing" was? Better early than late. He didn't seem the type of man to sleep in.

She reached the foyer, flanked by a sitting room and an office, and headed down a wide center hallway lined with black-and-white photographs of people from past generations.

A dining room on her left boasted a long, heavy table with carved legs surrounded by twelve matching chairs. In the center of the table, a vase overflowed with blue and lavender silk hydrangeas. An empty crystal decanter and matching glasses stood on a side table against the far wall. She crossed to it and lifted one of the glasses to see the bottom. Sure enough, there was that distinctive mark...

"...did you think was going to happen?"

The angry tone had her spinning

Mr. Aylett was walking down the hallway but must've seen her out of the corner of his eye. He stopped, then backed up and stepped into the doorway. He wore only gym shorts and tennis shoes, a towel wrapped around his neck, his phone pressed to his ear.

The man had broad shoulders and defined muscles in his chest and abdomen. His hair was damp, his skin flushed and healthy.

He was beautiful. And eyeing her like he'd caught her casing the place.

He spoke into the phone. "I'm blocking your number. Stay away from me." He ended the call and glared at Delaney. "What are you doing in here?"

His voice held the same angry intensity.

Hadn't he told her the night before to make herself at home?

She set the glass down. "Just looking." At least her voice didn't shake. "These pieces are similar to..." Her words trailed at the flash of fury in his gaze. "Is something—?"

"Similar to what?"

"My mother has glasses like these. I was looking to see if they were the same."

"Those are antique Waterford passed down from my great-grandfather. They're incredibly valuable."

Annoyance pricked her skin, but she kept her tone even. "Unless they were custom made for the Aylett family, it's possible they're the same." She nodded to the phone he held in a white-knuckled grip. "Everything okay?"

"It's none of your business," he snapped. Then took a breath. "Sorry. It was just a former colleague. She took me by surprise, and..." He shook his head. "Once again, I have to apologize for my rudeness. My mother would be appalled."

His abrupt shift was jarring, but nothing like the sight of her employer without a shirt on. She tried to focus on his face, but her gaze kept flicking downward.

The crystal was pretty, but this man was a work of art. That thought had her cheeks burning.

He pulled the towel from around his neck and shook it out. It wasn't a towel but a T-shirt, which he slipped over his head. Maybe he'd read her thoughts. How mortifying.

"I was working out. There's equipment downstairs, if you ever want to use it. I mean, except between four and six a.m."

"Gotcha." This was starting out as the strangest first day of any job she'd ever had.

He spun and headed down the hall. "Coming?"

She followed him to the kitchen at the back of the house—a large open space housing the living room on one side, the kitchen on the other. The kitchen had modern white cabinetry and a gray granite-topped island. This was the only room that didn't seem hemmed in by the house's original Victorian layout. Walls must have been removed to create this modern look. Floor-to-ceiling windows displayed the porch and, beyond that, the grassy yard she'd seen from upstairs. She glimpsed the ocean between the bushes.

Mr. Aylett rounded the island to where a coffee maker stood on the far counter, its carafe already filled with dark brew. "You want a cup?"

"Sure."

He filled a mug and slid it across the island. "Cream, sugar?"

"If it's no trouble."

He retrieved a carton of cream from the refrigerator, then slid it and a sugar dish—pale blue with pink flowers—across the counter.

"Thank you." She doctored her coffee while he filled a glass with water.

She sipped the warm drink, and he sipped his cold one. Neither of them said anything.

They hadn't spoken much the night before, either.

She said, "I suppose we should—"

"—Charlotte usually wakes—"

He stopped, a tiny smile tugging at his mouth. "Ladies first."

"I was going to say that we should talk about Charlotte's

schedule and what you expect from me." Ordinarily, those things would be covered in the interview. Nothing about this job so far had been ordinary.

He leaned back against the far counter. "Have a seat if you want."

She chose one of the barstools and pulled her phone from her pocket to take notes.

"First, you might have realized already, but Charlotte is not my daughter. She's my brother's child. He asked me to take her in a few months ago."

She couldn't imagine how disruptive that must've been to a single man. "Had your brother been caring for her? Did he not feel up to the job?"

"Charlotte's mother had her for the first five months. Then child services stepped in, and she went—"

"Wait, sorry. Why did child services step in?"

His brows crinkled, and she guessed her question had annoyed him. Before he could tell her, once again, that it wasn't her business, she added, "If I'm to take care of her, then I need to understand what she's been through."

He licked his lips, gaze shifting toward the windows. "I don't know exactly, but I think she's a drug addict."

That knowledge had Delaney's heart dropping. Poor Charlotte.

"Do you know if she was sober during her pregnancy?"

"As far as I understand, she was. That's what Jasper said, anyway, and her doctor sees no sign of fetal alcohol syndrome or...whatever it's called when a mother uses drugs during pregnancy."

One bit of good news. Maybe the woman had intended to be a worthy parent. And then...what? Decided she could take care of an infant and use drugs?

"Jasper was out of the country at the time, so CPS placed

Charlotte with her maternal grandmother. She was still a baby. The courts forbade the mother to see her. When my brother returned earlier this year, he visited Charlotte and realized the grandmother wasn't fit."

"In what sense? Was she also an addict? Or abusive?"

"Neglectful. At least that's what he told me. That's when he brought her to me."

How sad for little Charlotte. No wonder she was so quiet.

"What about Jasper? Where is he?"

"Not in the picture, and neither is the mother. They're both..." He shook his head. "Suffice it to say, Charlotte's stuck with me, and I'm doing my best. But what do I know about a four-year-old girl?"

"She's four?" That information was almost as shocking as the rest. "She's so small."

"Yeah." He sipped his water, then took a deep breath, and she got the sense he was still reeling from everything that had happened, maybe trying to rein in emotions he didn't want to show. They flickered in his eyes. Anger, frustration. But why did he feel those things? Because he was stuck with Charlotte? Or was he angry at the child's neglectful parents?

She couldn't exactly ask, but she figured Mr. Aylett's true feelings would come out sooner or later.

"The doctor calls it 'failure to thrive,'" Mr. Aylett said. "Before she came here, she was malnourished, which affected her development. I have her on a high-calorie, high-protein diet —which she hates, by the way. But it's very important that we feed her healthy foods, more so than with other children."

Delaney hated to think what little Charlotte had gone through before she'd come here. And now she was stuck with an uncle who hadn't even known her before.

At least he was trying to do right by her.

"Is she in therapy?"

"No." His shoulders sagged as if the weight of the world rested there—and had just become a little heavier. "I need to do that, but I haven't found anyone suitable yet."

"Suitable meaning...?"

"It's a small community. We have therapists, but I've been told she needs a well-trained play therapist, and I haven't found one close by. And with my work..."

"I understand." Delaney tapped a note into her phone. "I'll compile a list, and we can find one together. I'll make that my first priority. You might need to attend some of the sessions, but hopefully, I'll be able to take her most of the time."

"Okay, good. That would be very helpful. I'll be there if I have to, but it'll be hard for the next few weeks, maybe a month. My schedule should open up after that, and I'll be able to devote more time to Charlotte. Do you have a car seat?"

"I need to get one."

"I'll take care of it. That Toyota you drive—that belongs to you?"

"I'm not in the habit of stealing cars—or crystal, for that matter."

"I never thought..." He shook his head, and maybe her remark amused him, but it was hard to tell. "I thought maybe the car belonged to a friend or a boyfriend or something. What year is it?"

"It's ten years old, but it's in good shape, if that's what you're worried about."

"Not worried, just..." His voice trailed. Then he said, "It has Maine license plates."

"I didn't want to register it until I was settled." And until she was certain she wasn't going to have to go home.

"I don't want Charlotte to get attached to you if you're not planning to stay."

"I agreed to stay on at least until she starts kindergarten next year." They'd talked about this the night before. "I'll honor that commitment. And she should get attached to me. She needs to trust me."

Mr. Aylett stared at Delaney for long enough that it started to feel awkward. She waited for him to argue or clarify his position.

Instead, he said, "You're okay with driving Charlotte in your car?"

"Of course." Delaney tried to sound lighthearted, but she'd gotten here on fumes the night before. It was less than two miles from the shelter, yet she was lucky she'd made it. "It's just that..." She steeled her courage. "I hate to ask, but I need to fill up my tank, and—"

"Not a problem. I'll provide you with a credit card to cover your expenses."

Wow. He was worried she was going to take off with the Waterford, but he was going to give her a credit card?

She couldn't figure this guy out.

"I was thinking we should get Charlotte involved in some activities," he said, "like...dance or...I don't know." He shrugged. "I have no idea. If you think she'd enjoy lessons of some kind, feel free to arrange it."

"I grew up with four sisters. Among the five of us, we did pretty much every activity you can imagine. I'll feel her out, see what she might like. I assume she likes the park. Is it all right if we do that?"

He nodded, then added, "All I ask is that, for the first few weeks, you let me know where you are so I don't worry."

"I'll share my location with you."

They exchanged numbers, and she did that, which reminded her...

"Yesterday, when I stopped Charlotte from running out into the street." She put her phone away. "That was you, wasn't it?"

He narrowed his eyes. "What are you talking about?"

"I saw someone duck behind a tree. At the time it made me nervous. I thought maybe it was a kidnapper." She'd laugh at her own paranoia if he weren't giving her such a serious look. "I assumed when you showed up—"

"I was behind you. I saw Charlotte and was running to intercept her, but you got to her first. Once I knew she was safe, I wanted to see what her nanny would do. Not that I would have kept her on, but if she'd been horrified at taking her eyes off Charlotte, if she'd been repentant, I would've offered her severance—a week's pay, anyway."

"She blew that." But the rest of what he'd said registered. "Wait. Then who did I see?"

"I have no idea. Someone was watching Charlotte?"

Delaney thought back to that moment, to the glimpse of a person ducking away. "I could have imagined the whole thing."

"Either you saw someone or you didn't."

"I did." The words came slowly as she remembered the moment. "I just had a weird feeling, that's all. That doesn't mean the person was doing anything wrong."

He seemed to take in that information. "It sounds like you have good instincts."

Her? She had terrible instincts, but she wasn't going to tell her new employer that.

"If you ever get that feeling again," he said, "or see something suspicious, tell me right away."

"Okay." The discussion reminded her... "You said last night that you're upgrading your security system." He'd mentioned it as an aside when he told her the code. "Did something happen?"

"We had a break-in a few nights ago. It was the same morning as your interview. Not that that excuses my rude behavior."

"You were home?"

"We were."

"Any idea who did it?"

"It might've been random. Whoever it was, the alarm scared him away."

"If it wasn't random, who could it have been?"

"I don't know."

"Are you sure? Because if it affects Charlotte..." She wasn't in the habit of arguing with her employers, but it had to be said.

"If I learn anything else about the break-in, I'll let you know. Meanwhile, the additional sensors should alert us if whoever it was comes back."

It wasn't the security she had at home, but then Mr. Aylett wasn't as paranoid as her former CIA-agent father. Also, presumably, he didn't have the same kinds of enemies. "Does she have any regular activities?"

"No. I thought about putting her in preschool, but it seemed too soon after she came to live with me."

"Allergies, medical issues? I'll need her doctor's phone number and your medical insurance card, should anything come up."

"I have those." He pulled a clipboard out of a drawer and slid it across to her. An insurance card was clipped to it over a piece of paper with the information she'd requested, along with names and numbers of emergency contacts.

When she looked up, he said, "What else?"

"Dislikes? Quirks?"

"Charlotte needs structure. She needs to know you can be trusted. I know things happen, but please do your best to make good on your commitments. A lot of people in her life have failed to do that."

"I understand. My goal is for her to trust me, to know she can count on me. That's a vital part of my job."

He dipped his head, a quick acknowledgment. "She enjoys being with kids, but she needs to be able to step in or step out if she gets overwhelmed. I think she shuts down when there's too much chaos, but that's just a theory. I will say that when there are a lot of people around, she tends to wander off."

"Like yesterday?"

"Exactly like yesterday." By the dark look that crossed his features, he was still angry with the former nanny.

"My sister was like that," Delaney said. "I'd tell her to stay here or go there, and...she wasn't disobedient, just easily distracted. I learned from Kenzie that kids need to be watched all the time."

"Okay, good. Let's see..." He stroked the short whiskers on his chin. "Oh, she doesn't like pizza."

"Really?"

"Go figure." His lips quirked at one corner. "She's been through...a lot." His gaze flicked to the ceiling, then back to Delaney. "I want her to make friends and be happy. I'm just... I'm in the middle of this thing at work. I'm finding it hard to balance that and parenting."

"It's not easy. I'm sure you're doing great." Delaney had worked for enough families to know it was hard for two parents who worked to take care of their kids. How would a single man do it? A man who wasn't even the child's father?

"I guess that's about..." His voice faded, and his serious expression morphed into a smile aimed beyond her.

Delaney turned one second before Charlotte collided with her. She didn't say anything, just held up her arms.

She lifted the precious girl, who was far too light for her age. Her hair was a mop of messy curls, her pink pajama pants twisted around her waist.

She was adorable.

The thought brought her mind back to the stranger in the

park, who may or may not have been watching her. And the intruder who'd set off the alarm.

There had been a time when Delaney would have brushed away her worries, but between Dad's horrifying stories and everything her family had been through in the last couple of years, she knew trials and danger could strike anywhere.

Lord, protect this little one. Help her uncle and me to keep her safe.

CHAPTER SEVEN

On any other morning, Charlotte would have walked to Noah, arms up, silently requesting her morning hug. Not today. The little traitor had barely glanced at him before going to Miss Wright, looking up with wide, expectant eyes.

His niece and her nanny were already bonding. It'd taken him weeks to break through Charlotte's defenses when Jasper had first brought her here. Noah hadn't hired a nanny right away, knowing Charlotte needed to understand that she could trust him to be available for her in a way no adult had been before.

He'd spent time with her, played with her, hugged her tiny little body, and cursed her selfish parents for all the neglect she'd already endured. He'd stayed up late after her bedtime every night to get his work done, choosing to spend the bulk of his waking hours with her. He'd talked to her and joked with her and gone for walks with her. It'd still been warm enough to swim in the ocean when she first came, and he'd given her swimming lessons at the beach.

Noah had no idea how to be a father, but he was learning. He was trying.

He figured good fathers didn't get jealous when their kids bonded with other people. Charlotte hadn't been like this with Mrs. Dechambeau. The former nanny hadn't been nearly as sweet as Miss Wright.

He shook himself out of his stupor and started breakfast. Bread in the toaster, eggs out of the fridge.

He took his time breaking them, whisking them, pouring them into the warm skillet while the nanny bent over a book with Charlotte at the kitchen table.

He eavesdropped on their conversation.

"Is that the one you like best?" Delaney asked.

"Uh-uh." She was sitting at the table, swinging her legs.

"Which one is your favorite?"

Charlotte indicated a picture in the book.

Catty-corner from her, Miss Wright studied whatever she'd pointed at, giving her the kind of attention Noah reserved for financial reports.

She didn't seem to be performing for him, or if she was, she had perfected the art. She pointed at something in the book. "What about that one?"

Charlotte shook her head and pointed at something else.

"I love his curled tail," Miss Wright said. "That's called an Akita."

Oh. They were looking at the dog book.

Charlotte must've said something because Delaney said, "You'll have to ask your uncle."

For an Akita?

Right. Because nothing said "family pet" like a Japanese attack dog.

Noah regretted having checked out the library book that

described all the different breeds. He'd found it interesting. His niece treated it like a catalog of possibilities.

"That one." Pointing again, Charlotte's eyes went dreamy.

"I think that's a wolf. Wolves are...tricky." Miss Wright tapped her nose theatrically. "Do you think your uncle would let a wolf into the house?"

Charlotte's little shoulders drooped. For the first time since she'd walked in, Charlotte looked at him. "Uncle Noah doesn't like dogs." A full sentence, spoken in front of the new nanny, loudly enough for him to hear.

That was progress.

"I never said I didn't like dogs." He turned down the fire under the eggs. "I don't have time to train a dog."

"We could, right?" The question was directed at Miss Wright.

The nanny's gaze flicked to him, her wide eyes pleading for him to answer that question.

She was the new favorite. Let her crush Charlotte's hopes and dreams.

Miss Wright must've guessed his answer because her expression shifted to a sickly-sweet smile. "That's up to your uncle. I'll do whatever he says."

The toast popped up, and Noah focused on buttering it so she couldn't see his smile. She was a shrewd one. But also, despite her obvious youth, she knew a lot about kids.

He'd spent the last decade in boardrooms and attending business functions, cultivating a poker face and a reputation as someone who did not get ruffled, even under pressure. But standing in his own kitchen, listening to his niece and her new nanny plot canine insurrection, Noah felt his world spinning out of control.

He'd never been a dog person. Or a kid person, for that

matter. He loved Charlotte, obviously, but kids should come with an instruction manual. And a self-cleaning mode.

He fixed three plates and set them on the table before grabbing his coffee and a glass of orange juice for Charlotte.

His niece took a bite of eggs, scrunching her little nose.

She wasn't a fan, but she needed healthy protein. Sometimes he added cheese and chunks of ham, which she seemed to like better. This morning, he'd been distracted, too focused on *not* watching the new nanny.

"Thank you," Miss Wright said. "It's tasty." Her voice was soft. "I can cook breakfast in the future, if you'd like."

"I don't mind making breakfast, but if you could help with dinners..."

"Sure. Do you have certain kinds of foods you prefer over others? Or anything I should avoid?"

"I'll eat whatever you make. I'm not picky." If Miss Wright cooked, he'd take whatever she made. It was no easy task coming up with a well-balanced meal every night.

He worked on his eggs, ravenous after his workout. "Do you want juice?" He'd filled Charlotte's glass but hadn't thought to ask Miss Wright if she wanted some.

"I'm good with coffee, but thank you." She ate a few bites of her eggs, checking on Charlotte often.

His niece was, as usual, quiet, but not solemn—a nice change.

His phone rang, and he glanced at the screen, then pushed away from the table, ignoring the twinge of regret that his breakfast would get cold. "Excuse me. I need to take this."

"Of course," Miss Wright said.

She was very agreeable. Worse than that, the flash of attraction he'd felt for her when he'd first seen her on his doorstep hadn't been an anomaly. Something about her drew him like metal shavings to a magnet.

He needed to be very careful to keep her at arm's length.

He connected the call, stepping out the back door onto the patio. The cool morning air was tinged with the scent of rain. "Hey, Richard."

"Have you seen the latest issue of *Coastal Virginia?*"

"Sure, sure." Noah leaned against the railing, watching a seagull soar against the bright sky. "I was clipping recipes and tearing out decorating ideas last night. You know how I love the ladies' magazines."

Richard chuckled. "I sort of figured you didn't know."

"Didn't know what?"

"They've named you the region's 'Most Eligible Bachelor.' Congratulations," he deadpanned. "Your picture's on the cover —that photo from the charity gala last spring."

Heat crawled up Noah's neck. He'd gotten a call about their annual feature, but he'd declined the interview.

"I thought they'd respect my wishes and leave me out of it."

"They're reporters. Your refusal probably just made them more interested. There's a whole sidebar about how you're raising a child alone. I assume that's part of the allure since nobody knows who Charlotte is. You can imagine all the juicy gossip going around."

Through the kitchen window, Noah watched as his niece spoke to Miss Wright, who seemed engrossed in the conversation.

Charlotte hardly ever spoke to anyone. How had the nanny done that?

Something about the scene—the domesticity of it, the way they already looked like they belonged together—made his heart do weird things.

"That's not all," Richard continued. "I heard there was police activity at your place the other day. What happened?"

"Who did you hear that from?"

"You know how news travels around here. Folks love a scandal."

That last word plucked Noah's spinal cord like a guitar string. "There's no scandal. Someone broke in but was scared off by the alarm."

Even as he said it, he remembered those footsteps. Whoever it'd been hadn't been too scared to take at least a few steps into the house. What had they been after? What had they deemed worth the risk of getting caught?

The most precious treasure in the house was sitting at the table eating eggs right now. Surely, nobody was after Charlotte.

"Must've been jarring," Richard said.

"Nothing was taken."

"You didn't mention it when we spoke yesterday."

"I didn't realize you needed to know."

"I'm your attorney, and you're in the middle of a huge deal. I need to know everything. But the intruder makes me wonder..." Richard's tone was pensive. "Did you know Lena Monroe is back?"

Just the sound of the woman's name had acid pooling in Noah's stomach. "She called me this morning."

"Just up and called you like you were old friends?"

"Like nothing ever happened. Like she hadn't ruined my life."

The older man blew out a breath. "She's three pickles shy of a quart, that one. But I still say she did you a favor."

Noah wasn't going to admit that, not even to Richard.

"You don't s'pose it was her in your house the other night, do you?"

Lena? His home invader? The woman had some bizarre idea that the two of them belonged together, but breaking and entering? "To what end?"

"No telling with someone like her," he said. "Whoever your

invader was, the board got wind of it…all of it. The article, Charlotte, the cops. It's causing some…disruption."

Noah pinched the bridge of his nose. The merger of Noah's company, MidAtlantic Analytics, with a logistics company out of Norfolk was supposed to be straightforward. Noah's new AI integration would be customized to work with Tidewater's existing infrastructure. The merger would fortify Tidewater's position in the market and secure MidAtlantic's place as an innovative leader. And, more importantly for Noah, provide him enough margin in his life to raise a four-year-old without risking his father's legacy.

"What kind of concerns?" he asked. "None of this has anything to do with MidAtlantic—"

"The board's wondering if you're more interested in being in the spotlight than running a company."

As if he'd ever craved the spotlight. That had been Marianne's obsession, not his. "By 'they,'" Noah guessed, "you mean Lowell, right?"

"His voice is loudest, but he's not the only one expressing doubt. Nadine suggested you've been really distracted lately. Now that they know about Charlotte, at least I can explain that away."

"I don't want you using my niece as an excuse."

"She's not an 'excuse,' Noah. She's a reason, a very sound reason, for why you haven't gotten them everything they've asked for."

They'd demanded financials going back years. He was working on compiling all the information they required, but between caring for Charlotte and running his company…

"Lowell convinced the board to look at other AI companies before committing."

Noah stifled his frustration. "He's been looking for any excuse to call it off." Lowell Jeffries used to be Noah's best friend. Just one more person he'd lost when his life had blown up a couple of years before. "I hired a new nanny, and I think this one's going to work out. But is it too late? Do I still have a shot?" Noah's tone was steady, even if his nerves felt anything but.

"If they call it off, I have no doubt Lowell will give you the news himself."

Noah covered the speaker and blew out his fear. *Thank God.*

Let this merger happen, please.

"Just don't feed the rumor mill, stay out of the paper, and keep your head down until we get those papers signed."

"That's what I've been trying to do."

"I know most of this has been out of your control."

The understatement of the year.

"Please, just...do what you can."

Noah desperately needed the merger to go through, to save his family home and his father's legacy—so he could focus on being a good parent to a little girl who had nobody else.

CHAPTER EIGHT

Maple leaves crunched beneath the bag Delaney dragged toward the growing pile, Charlotte's delighted shriek echoing across the backyard as she flew headfirst into the freshly raked mound.

The little girl who'd suffered bouts of melancholy that first week Delaney had lived here—occasionally retreating into herself—had slowly opened up. She still rarely put more than two sentences together at a time, but she smiled more. She laughed a lot.

Delaney loved seeing her personality emerge.

Now Charlotte popped up, leaves clinging to her curls like nature's confetti. "Again!" She jogged to the far side of the yard.

Delaney raked to pile the leaves, and Charlotte got a running start and dove headfirst, sending all Delaney's work flying.

Delaney brushed dirt from her jeans, surveying the yard. There were oversized trash bags bulging with leaves at every corner. She needed to fill one more, and they'd be finished.

She hoped to surprise Mr. Aylett by completing this task, giving him one less thing he needed to do. He'd mentioned more than once his plan to get back here, but he'd been so busy. Though he was home for breakfast and dinner every night, she'd seen him in his office many times before breakfast and after he kissed Charlotte good night—after being gone all day long. He'd apologized once during that first week for heaping so much responsibility onto Delaney so quickly.

"It's just this merger," he'd said. "As soon as it's completed, I'll be around more."

Delaney hoped that was true, but she wouldn't count on it. Her own father had always had excellent excuses for not being with the family. Giving him the benefit of the doubt, maybe Dad had truly believed that as soon as *this* assignment was over, or *that* business deal, he'd spend more time at home. Whether he'd believed it or not, it was never true. Dad always seemed to have somewhere more important to be than in Maine with his wife and kids.

In Mr. Aylett's case, he was doing his best to make room for a child in his life who wasn't his. She couldn't imagine her father making half the effort her employer did for someone else's little girl.

Charlotte sat in the middle of the pile and threw leaves over her head.

Delaney grinned at her. She'd been clingy when Delaney had first come to work for the family, and overly compliant, as if she'd feared that, at any sign of disobedience, Delaney might abandon her. Three weeks later, she talked more, laughed more, and trusted more. She was also less quick to obey.

It was good, though. The new therapist warned her that Charlotte would start testing boundaries. *"She wants to know if you'll stick around, no matter what."*

Delaney didn't plan to leave anytime soon, but what would it do to Charlotte when she went home to Maine?

She wasn't about to risk her little heart, not after everything she'd been through.

Charlotte rolled in the leaves, undoing all of Delaney's hard work.

"Sweetheart," she said, "the goal is to gather the leaves, not scatter them."

Charlotte had other ideas about leaf management. Giggling, she stood, lifted an armful, and threw them in the air, shouting, "Scatter, scatter!"

Delaney laughed. "One more jump in, then we need to get these bagged up before your uncle gets home." She raked them close and formed a pile.

Charlotte backed up, then plopped into it.

"Silly girl!" Delaney reached in after her, ostensibly to pull her out. Instead, she found the child's sweet spot—under her arms—and tickled.

Charlotte's giggles were contagious. And who cared about the yard, anyway?

Delaney fell in with her, eliciting a fresh bout of laughter.

Charlotte popped up, then jumped on top of her, knocking her over and earning even more tickles.

Finally, Delaney caught her breath.

"We should really clean this up before—"

A tree's worth of leaves fell on her head, covering her and Charlotte completely.

What in the world?

She pushed her way out and looked up.

Mr. Aylett was standing over them, holding an empty trash bag, grinning. He'd shed his tie—something he did the moment he walked in the door. The first button of his shirt was undone, and with the afternoon sun shining behind him, he was practically glowing.

"Daddy!" Charlotte screeched. "Play with us."

Delaney had heard Charlotte call him that. He usually gently corrected her.

She took the lead this time. "Uncle Noah's in his dress clothes. Maybe he shouldn't—"

"No way you're keeping me out of the fun." He plopped down in the pile, lifted an armful of leaves, and threw them in the air.

Leaves fluttered down, catching in Delaney's hair and landing on her shoulders. She couldn't help laughing. "This is starting to feel counterproductive."

"Is that so?" His eyes twinkled as he scooped Charlotte up and pretended to bury her in the pile.

"No fair!" Charlotte squealed. "Miss Laney, help me!"

Delaney joined the fray, showering a handful of leaves over Mr. Aylett's head. His gray eyes caught hers for a moment, and something electric passed between them.

Whoops. She looked away, reminding herself they were supposed to be *vibe-less.*

Three weeks she'd worked for Charlotte's uncle. He was handsome, but also busy and distracted and completely professional. They'd had countless conversations about Charlotte, but nothing personal. Nothing playful. Even then, it was impossible not to notice what a handsome man he was.

What a *good* man he was.

Delaney shifted out of the pile to put distance between them. "We were trying to clean these up for you," she said, gesturing at the scattered leaves and the bags she'd managed to fill before their play had taken over.

Mr. Aylett shook his head, sending leaves flying from his blond hair. "Why would you do that when leaves are clearly meant for fun?" He threw another armful over his head.

Charlotte danced in the raining leaves.

"Stop that!" But Delaney was laughing too hard for her admonishment to sound convincing.

Three weeks at the Aylett house, and she'd never seen her employer this relaxed. His usual serious demeanor had given way to something lighter this evening, something more carefree.

It suited him.

Charlotte flopped onto her back, making leaf angels. Delaney reclined beside her, the damp earth soaking through her jeans. She didn't care. The late October air felt refreshing against her flushed cheeks, and Charlotte's laughter was worth every bit of dirt she'd have to scrub from her clothes later.

Mr. Aylett stood and extended his hand to help her up. His palm was warm and firm against hers as he pulled her to her feet. A tingle shot up her arm. They'd been careful not to touch in the weeks she'd been working for him. She realized now what a good policy that was.

She brushed leaves from her clothes to hide her reaction. "I should get dinner finished. It's almost ready."

"Don't leave on my account," Mr. Aylett said, back to burying his niece in leaves. "You two were having fun."

Delaney took a step back, needing space from the man who was making her heart do strange things. "The pulled pork has been in the slow cooker all day. It just needs to be shredded and served."

"Smelled delicious when I walked through. Let us know when it's ready."

"Will do." She retreated to the kitchen, berating herself for her attraction. She'd vowed on her first day to keep a professional distance from Mr. Aylett, yet here she was, flustered by a simple touch.

After scrubbing her hands, she shredded the pork with two forks, the tender meat falling apart easily. Through the open windows, she could see Mr. Aylett and Charlotte still playing, their voices carrying on the evening breeze. The sight made her yearn for something she didn't want to name.

This wasn't supposed to happen. She'd been so careful to keep things professional and maintain appropriate boundaries. The little girl had stolen her heart from day one, and the man was proving far more complex than his initial rudeness had suggested.

Had she ever heard him laugh like he had just now? Not the polite chuckles he offered during their careful conversations over breakfast and dinner, but real, unguarded laughter? Like his niece's, his laugh was contagious.

She arranged the pulled pork on a platter and set buns, pickles, and barbecue sauce on the kitchen table. The green salad she'd prepared earlier went beside it, along with the baked potato chips she'd found at the local market.

"Dinner's ready!" she called.

They trooped inside, both covered in bits of leaves and grass, their cheeks flushed. Charlotte's curls were a tangled mess, creating a wild halo around her face.

Mr. Aylett looked younger somehow, his usually perfect hair mussed, his expensive shirt wrinkled.

"We should wash up." He plucked a leaf from Charlotte's hair. "We look like we've been rolling around in the yard."

"We have been rolling around in the yard," Charlotte said.

"Oh, yeah." He lifted her and headed for the bathroom.

Delaney was struck by how natural he was with her. He'd been more awkward before, more guarded around both of them. Today, he seemed comfortable in his role. Not just comfortable, but content.

Two very attractive qualities.

They returned, and the three of them settled around the kitchen table.

When Delaney had started working here, she'd offered to

take her meals separately, but Charlotte and her uncle had both insisted she join them for the dinners she prepared. At first, it'd felt uncomfortable, like trying to fit into someone else's clothes. But they'd settled into a natural rhythm.

Charlotte chattered about their leaf fight while Mr. Aylett built her sandwich, then his own. His gaze fell on the bowl of baked chips, and one eyebrow lifted. "Those look...different."

"They're healthy," Delaney offered.

"I see." He picked up one of the golden chips and bit into it, his face thoughtful. "They taste...healthy."

She ducked her head to hide her smile. He was teasing her. "I'd thank you." She met his eyes across the table. "Except that wasn't a compliment, was it?"

"Not even a little bit." But his smile took any sting out of the words.

Grinning, Charlotte looked from one of them to the other like she was watching a tennis match.

The rest of dinner passed with easy conversation. Charlotte told her uncle about her new friend at dance class, and he asked questions, trying to draw her further out.

Delaney found herself relaxing in a way she hadn't before in his presence.

When Charlotte's plate was empty, Mr. Aylett stood. "Bath time for you, leaf monster. You've got half the yard in your hair."

"Can Miss Laney read with us tonight?" Charlotte's voice held a wheedling tone that sometimes worked on her, but never on Mr. Aylett.

"Miss Laney has been busy all day," he said gently. "She deserves some time to herself."

Wow. Most of her previous employers had expected her to be available around the clock. "I don't mind—"

"Go relax." He lifted Charlotte from her chair and threw

her over his shoulder like a bag of rice. "We've got this covered, don't we, Charlie-Bear?"

Charlotte's giggles faded as he carried her down the hall and up the stairs. Delaney stared after them, the warmth of the moment lingering even after they'd gone.

A few minutes later when the kitchen was spotless, she headed upstairs and changed out of her dirty, leaf-specked clothes. She donned clean yoga pants and a sweatshirt and then headed down the hall toward the staircase. The door to Charlotte's room stood partially open, spilling warm light onto the hardwood. Delaney paused and peeked in.

Mr. Aylett was reading Charlotte's favorite story. His voice shifted with each character—gruff for the bear, squeaky for the mouse, deep and measured for the owl.

Charlotte's giggles punctuated his performance.

Delaney leaned a shoulder against the wall, transfixed. This wasn't the buttoned-up businessman who hurried out the door each morning for work and returned haggard and stressed. This was someone else entirely—someone warm and playful.

A father figure, not an uncle trying to learn how to raise someone else's child. The transformation she'd seen in both of them was remarkable, and watching it made her long for things she had no business wanting.

Stop it.

This was exactly what she'd promised herself she wouldn't do—develop feelings for her employer. But standing in the darkened hallway, listening to him bring storybook characters to life for Charlotte's delight, something shifted inside her.

Mr. Aylett must've felt her gaze because he glanced toward the doorway. Their eyes met, and heat flooded her cheeks at being caught. She offered a small wave and mouthed "sorry" before retreating toward the stairs.

Embarrassed, Delaney slipped out the front door onto the

wraparound porch, hoping Mr. Aylett would go straight to his office so she wouldn't have to face him tonight.

She settled onto the wooden swing that overlooked Magnolia Street, the chains creaking softly as she pushed off with her toes.

The salty breeze carried the scent of the ocean, reminding her of home. She missed her sisters desperately—their laughter, their constant chatter, even their arguments. She missed her parents and the familiar rhythms of life in Shadow Cove.

But she didn't miss the suffocating feeling of being the Wright daughter who could never measure up.

She might not have any friends yet, but she was making a life for herself apart from them. If she wanted to stay here, she needed to make a few friends.

And she needed to control her rogue thoughts about Noah.

Mr. Aylett, she berated herself.

Her boss. And nothing more.

CHAPTER NINE

Today had been a good day.

Noah kissed his niece goodnight and stepped out of her bedroom, then headed to his own room to change out of his suit. He'd need to take it to the dry cleaner's tomorrow, but it'd been worth it.

He'd attended the Tidewater board of directors meeting to address all the "scandals" they were concerned about. He'd outlined the details of the break-in as if it were nothing serious.

He hoped that was true. There was no evidence that his intruder was, as Richard had theorized, Lena Monroe. Noah had blocked the woman's number after she'd called him, and he hadn't seen or heard from her since that day three weeks before. Maybe she'd finally taken the hint.

Too bad he hadn't gotten through to her before she broke up his marriage.

Noah had explained to the board that Charlotte was not his daughter but a family member who needed a home, which was true, if not the whole truth. They'd pressed for more information, but it wasn't his place to name Jasper as her father, not when Jasper was barely willing to face the fact himself.

"For now, that's all the information I'm willing to share," he'd said. "I'd like to believe that taking on the responsibility for someone else's child would be a mark in my favor."

"And we're supposed to believe you?" Lowell snapped. "That you didn't father this kid when you were cheating on my sister."

He'd met his ex-brother-in-law's eyes. "I can show you the court papers assigning me custody, if that would put your mind at ease."

"But you're not willing to take a paternity test." Lowell's gaze had scanned the rest of the board members. "Which tells us everything we need to know."

Noah had known Lowell would fight dirty—former friends made the worst enemies—so he'd anticipated that. "I'm happy to take a paternity test."

Nadine, another board member, said, "That won't be necessary. I assume you have an explanation for the magazine article?"

"I refused the interview, but I have no control over what they choose to write."

As if any intelligent man would ever want to be named "Most Eligible Bachelor." Noah couldn't even go to the market these days without some woman sidling up beside him, batting her eyelashes. He'd thought taking Charlotte along would discourage them. He'd been wrong. Apparently, single women loved children, or, if not, they were good at pretending they did.

The board had agreed—all but Lowell—that Noah did seem to be trying to avoid scandal. Fortunately, the subject of Charlotte's new nanny hadn't come up. Miss Wright was attractive enough to raise eyebrows, but apparently, none of them had seen her.

Thanks to today's meeting, the merger was back on track. Noah needed to coordinate the finishing touches on the software his employees were customizing to work with Tidewater's system and finish collecting all the financials. Then Richard and Tidewater's attorney would put the paperwork together.

After all the stress of the previous few weeks—not to mention the months of preparation before that—the merger should come together soon. When it did, Noah would have more time than he'd had in years, time to spend with the little girl he loved.

The little girl who kept calling him Daddy.

It was enough to make a man's heart melt.

He liked it. He liked taking care of her. He liked being with her. He'd never considered himself good with kids—he was nothing like Miss Wright—but he'd fallen head over heels in love with Charlotte. The thought of her real father taking her away from him... He couldn't stand it.

Did Jasper even miss her? Did he care? He sure didn't call very often, and when he did, he rarely asked to talk to her.

Charlotte needed a daddy who loved her completely. She needed one who'd make sacrifices for her.

She needed...Noah. And Noah needed her.

He pulled on his favorite pair of jeans and a T-shirt, then stared at himself in the mirror.

What was he thinking? He couldn't keep Charlotte, no matter how much he wanted to. Was he really going to challenge his own brother for custody? Their relationship was strained enough.

But Charlotte was more important.

Noah didn't know what to do. He'd pray and follow God's lead. That was his only choice.

Putting the idea out of his head for now, he headed downstairs. Normally, he'd go to his office to put in a couple hours of work before bed, but he didn't have it in him tonight.

The front door was open, letting in the telltale creak of the swing.

Before he could talk himself out of it, he pushed through the screen door and stepped onto the porch.

The sun had set, Magnolia Street only lit by moonlight, and for a moment, he saw into the past. Mom and Dad, cuddled up like smitten teenagers, sharing secrets and ice cream. Noah used to enjoy seeing them in moments like that, together and in love. There was something so comforting about those times. They'd made him feel secure.

That was back when he was too little to understand how quickly security could unravel like threads on a cheap sweater.

The image faded, replaced by Miss Wright staring into the darkness. He could envision her face when he'd caught her watching him read to Charlotte, and he still couldn't name her expression. Or maybe he just didn't want to acknowledge it.

If he were smart, he'd turn around and go back inside.

But this was a day for celebrating. Today was for playing in the leaves in his suit and reading stories with silly voices.

Not the day for being smart.

"Mind if I join you?" He kept his voice soft, not wanting to disturb her if she didn't welcome his company.

"Sure." She scooted over to make room.

The swing dipped under his weight. He pushed off with his foot, and they rocked in silence, the squeak of the chains and the distant surf creating a soft symphony.

"She's asleep. Hopefully, she'll stay that way."

"I heard her cry out the other night."

"Mmm." His niece had night terrors, something he'd never even heard of before she came to live with him. Though she seemed to be improving in other areas, the night terrors had not only not stopped, but they seemed more frequent.

"If you ever want me to handle it—"

"It's okay," he said. "You need to sleep."

"So do you. You've been burning the candle at both ends—and maybe holding a match to the middle."

He chuckled. "Don't worry about me. Besides, she's not usually even awake when she does it. Once I go in there and hold her for a bit, she goes right back to sleep." He hated thinking about what caused those terrors, but there was something sweet about how she relaxed in his arms. It mattered that she trusted him.

He'd do everything in his power to never betray that trust.

"Maybe she'll sleep through tonight," Miss Wright said. "She played hard today."

"She does everything with her whole heart." Charlotte reminded him so much of her father. Jasper had been like that, passionate and determined. But that was before. Noah didn't understand the man his brother had become. "I never thought I'd be raising a child alone. Certainly not my brother's."

"You're really good with her, you know." Miss Wright's gaze flicked to his, but she quickly averted it. "She adores you."

Pleasure washed over him at her words. "It's mutual. I'm figuring it out as I go. Some days are better than others."

"All parents can say that. That's part of parenting."

"Is it?" He shifted for a better look at her, needing to know if she was being genuine or just trying to placate him.

"Of course. Did your parents always have it together?"

He looked forward again, shrugging. "Seemed like they did."

"I've worked for my share of families, and they all have issues. I haven't met the perfect one yet."

"That makes me feel better, I guess. Except I was sort of hoping I'd figure it out."

"Oh, you will. As soon as you do, she'll change." Miss

Wright uttered a small laugh. "I don't think it's supposed to be easy."

"Hmm. S'pose not." They rocked for a few moments. Despite the fact that he was sitting with his child's nanny—a woman he barely knew—he felt comfortable. He settled back on the swing.

"What brought you to Driftwood?" He didn't know what prompted him to give voice to the question he'd been wondering about since he first met her. Even before he'd seen her license plates, he'd known she was a Yankee, thanks to her distinctive accent.

"I just needed to get away."

He guessed there was a story that she didn't want to tell him, and he didn't push. Everyone had secrets.

"And you picked Driftwood? Of all places?"

A small smile played at her lips. "When I was a kid, we had family friends who lived near here. We'd visit sometimes in the summer, so it's not completely unfamiliar to me. And being close to the Atlantic...I grew up on the coast. It reminds me of home, in a way."

"Same ocean, different view," he said. "I can see why that would be comfortable."

"Exactly." She looked at him, her expression both pleased and surprised. "That's it exactly."

He pushed off the porch floor gently to get the swing going again. Not wanting its stopping to give her an excuse to get up and go inside. "Most of my friends left after college. Headed to Richmond or DC or New York. Bigger dreams, I guess."

"But not you?"

"Dad was gone. Jasper rarely came home. Mom was still with us. I didn't want her to be alone."

"She must have been happy to have you close."

"She was." Noah felt a familiar pang at the memory of his

mother. "You would have liked her. She had all the"—he gestured vaguely toward the door—"home stuff figured out. The cooking, cleaning, baking, and doing it all with grace while she took care of two rowdy boys. I realize now how much work it was, but Mom made it look easy. Like you do."

"Oh." The surprised sound escaped Miss Wright's mouth. "That's a nice thing to say. Thank you."

He forced his gaze forward. "I think Mom wished Jasper had stayed too." He watched an unfamiliar SUV cruise slowly down Magnolia Street, its headlights sweeping across the darkened lawns. Odd at this time of night. Most of his neighbors were older, the ages his parents should have been if they hadn't passed so young.

"Is that why he left?" Miss Wright asked. "Because he felt pressured to stay?"

"No." Noah's jaw tightened. "Jasper left because that's what Jasper does. He leaves." Bitterness hardened his voice.

"Maybe he has his reasons, but..." She shook her head. "I will never understand how a person can *not* treasure their own child. Does he ever call?"

"Occasionally." When Noah called him first.

"But to check on Charlotte...?" When Noah didn't answer—and what defense could he make for his wastrel brother—Miss Wright said, "At least you know he trusts you to look after her."

Maybe. Or maybe he just didn't care.

Silence fell between them again, the swing's gentle motion filling the space. "Your brother leaves"—her tone was thoughtful—"and you stay. That's what *you* do."

He hadn't thought of it that way before. "I like it here. For me, Driftwood is home."

"What is it for Jasper?"

"Shame." The word slipped out before he'd considered it. Before he'd ever really thought about it.

Miss Wright looked at him, the question clear in her expression.

"It's a long story," he said.

She looked forward again, her profile soft in the dim light. "It's a beautiful town."

He was grateful she didn't push for more information.

All those eager bachelorettes who flirted at the market and the park had nothing on the kind and graceful presence of this woman.

There was a thought he needed to banish.

"Similar to where you grew up?" he asked.

"To Shadow Cove?" Her head tilted to the side as she considered his question. "In some ways, yes. It's about the same size, probably settled around the same time, back when the locals were still happy subjects of the crown."

"Early eighteenth century," he said of Driftwood.

"Close," she said. "Shadow Cove was settled not long after Portland, late sixteen hundreds. It's got a long fishing history, but nowadays the economy revolves around tourism."

Noah tried to picture it—a quaint coastal village, cold winds blowing off the North Atlantic, rocky shores instead of sandy beaches. A place that had shaped the woman beside him.

"Are you planning to go back?"

"I don't think I could've left if I'd thought I'd never go back." She tucked a strand of hair behind her ear, peeking at him. "I needed to prove to myself I could survive on my own."

"Why?"

She shrugged.

The worry that had been gnawing at him since he'd hired her surfaced again. "Charlotte's getting attached to you."

"I know." Her voice was soft but steady. "I'm attached to her, too. But my family's there. My sisters. I miss them. By next fall, I'll have been gone for over a year."

He hated to think of how her leaving would break Charlotte's heart. "You mentioned sisters. Are you the oldest? Is that why you're so good with kids?"

She laughed, the sound adding melody to the rhythm of the surf. "I'm the fourth of five. My little sister's four years younger than I am."

"You mentioned her once. Kenzie? The runner?"

"That's right." She sounded pleased that he remembered. "I was often tasked with keeping an eye on her. She didn't make it easy." Miss Wright shot a look his way. "Kenzie can be a handful. She was always climbing or jumping or just wandering off. A little adventurer. We're all thankful she survived her childhood."

"Did she settle down?"

"Hardly. She's a sailor."

"Like...in shipping, or for the Navy?"

"She captains yachts, often sailing them from one port to another for owners who prefer to fly but want their boat at their next destination."

"Interesting job."

"I guess. We don't even know where she is half the time."

"She and my brother would get along famously."

"Maybe we should introduce them."

He laughed. "I wouldn't do that to my worst enemy."

Miss Wright smiled, but it faded. "Too bad he doesn't know how amazing his daughter is."

"Yeah. Well, that's Jasper."

Noah clamped his lips shut. He'd been badmouthing Charlotte's father to the nanny. Talk about unprofessional. He'd never been one to air family grievances to strangers.

But she didn't feel like a stranger.

"I've known her less than a month, and I already dread walking away from her."

He loved how devoted Miss Wright was to Charlotte. Yet again, fear dogged him. What would happen when she left?

Noah pushed his foot against the porch boards, setting the swing into motion again. The night air carried the scent of sea salt and late-blooming roses.

She shivered beside him.

He should suggest they go inside where it was warm. That would be the sensible thing to do. But it would also put an end to the best conversation he'd had in a long time.

Instead, he blurted, "Why did you really leave Maine?"

Her body stilled, all sense of relaxation gone.

"I'm sorry," he said quickly. "That's none of my business."

"No, it's okay." She exhaled. "I was with this guy. We were talking about getting married."

"Married? You're so young."

She looked at him, eyebrows hiked.

"I mean, aren't you?"

She smiled. "How old do you think I am?"

She looked about nineteen, but she had to be older than that, based on all the jobs she'd listed on her résumé.

"Twenty-one?"

"You're off by six years. And before you guess again, I'm not fifteen."

She was twenty-seven? He'd never have guessed it. Still too young for him, and it wasn't just her youth. It was her innocence. Her naivety.

Not that any of that mattered. She was the nanny. That was all the reason he needed to keep his distance.

She was watching him, so he gestured for her to continue. "You were an appropriate age to be talking about marriage, and then…?"

"I discovered he was working for a smuggling ring. He shot a man. Didn't kill him, thank God. When he confessed, he claimed he was trying to earn enough money to buy me a ring."

"Wow. Obviously, he hid that side of himself from you."

Miss Wright's head tilted to the side, a curious expression on her face. "Everyone else, when they hear the story, reassures me that it wasn't my fault, as if I might blame myself."

"Why would you?"

"I wouldn't. I didn't tell him to commit a felony. I didn't tell him to shoot my sister's boyfriend."

That sounded like some story. "You don't strike me as the type of person who'd care about the size of a diamond."

"Thank you. Anyone who knows me knows that about me." She faced forward again, shaking her head. "That wasn't what had me questioning everything. I just...I still can't figure out how I missed it. His true nature."

"Maybe you didn't. Maybe he was acting outside of his true nature when he got involved with the smugglers, and he couldn't figure out how to get out."

"Yeah. Maybe. But the point remains. I had no idea."

"What do you think that means?"

"That I'm a fool. That I need to be more careful. That I need to trust my judgment less."

"You're being pretty hard on yourself."

She shrugged.

"That day in the park when you confronted Charlotte's nanny? You showed very good judgment." He thought of the wonderful therapist she'd found. Miss Wright had narrowed the list, then interviewed each one before recommending the one they'd landed on. The therapist had done wonders for Charlotte. As had Miss Wright herself, always knowing when to push his niece and when to give her space. "You've shown excellent judgment the entire time you've lived here."

"You're very kind."

"Well, sure." He lifted his hand in a *what else would you expect* gesture. "As you know, 'kind' is my fallback position."

That made her laugh, which was what he'd been going for.

He really enjoyed the sound.

He enjoyed everything about this woman.

Another SUV—or maybe the same one—drove by, snapping him out of his trance.

This was his employee. His niece's nanny. They were supposed to be keeping their distance from one another. *Vibeless*, as Delaney...Miss Wright had put it.

Who had seen them sitting together on this porch swing?

He was definitely feeling some vibes.

He could hear the echo of Richard's voice in his head after this afternoon's meeting.

"The merger's on track. Just stay out of trouble."

Everything about Miss Wright spelled trouble.

He pushed himself to his feet abruptly. "Sorry. I just remembered something I need to do." The something being *to avoid this exact situation.* "I'll see you in the morning."

He headed into the house before he did something stupid.

Like kiss his niece's nanny.

CHAPTER TEN

The weight of someone's gaze prickled at the back of Delaney's neck as she walked with Charlotte toward the park. She glanced around. A mom pushing a stroller. A teenager on a bike. An older couple strolling hand-in-hand toward them.

Nobody was paying Delaney or Charlotte any attention. She must've imagined the feeling.

Charlotte skipped beside her on the sidewalk, golden curls bouncing with each step.

The bright blue sky was dotted with cotton-ball clouds, the sea breeze fluttering the autumn leaves.

But Delaney was churning over the night before. Had she said something wrong? One minute, she and Mr. Aylett had been having a lovely conversation, sharing bits of their lives, and the next, he was practically running away from her. His excuse about remembering something important had rung hollow.

"Miss Laney, look!" Charlotte pointed to a squirrel darting up a tree trunk, its cheeks bulging with acorns. "He's funny."

"He's getting ready for winter. Squirrels have to store enough food to last until spring."

"Really?" Her eyes widened. "Maybe we should help." She slowed, gaze on the ground. She started collecting acorns, displaying a level of generosity Delaney had rarely seen in a four-year-old. The child's own cheeks had filled out, her complexion pinker than it'd been before. She was gaining weight, too. She was thriving.

"God will take care of the squirrels' needs. He takes care of His whole creation."

Charlotte touched a finger to her mouth, her little head tilted to one side as if she were contemplating what Delaney had said. After a moment, she opened her hand and let the acorns fall. "Okay."

God would provide for the squirrels, as He'd provided for Charlotte, though from the child's perspective, it probably hadn't felt like it for a long time. Yet she was healing, despite all the adults who'd let her down.

They continued on the sidewalk, and Delaney replayed her conversation with Mr. Aylett again. The way his voice had sounded when he spoke about his mother. The genuine concern in his eyes when he'd asked why Delaney had left Maine. The moment when he'd seemed truly surprised by her age.

And then that strange, sudden withdrawal.

Charlotte veered off the sidewalk to catch a particularly vibrant red leaf, adding it to the small collection she'd been accumulating in her pocket. Older, dried leaves crunched pleasantly beneath their feet.

Delaney suddenly felt it again—that odd sensation of being watched. She glanced over her shoulder and spotted a dark sedan parked along the curb about a block behind them. They'd just walked by that spot, and that car hadn't been there.

"Miss Laney, come on!" Charlotte called.

She hurried forward and took Charlotte's hand. When they turned at the corner toward the playground, Delaney casually looked back again. The same car was rolling slowly toward them.

Her pulse quickened.

They crossed the street and entered the park. Delaney was eager to get there, where they'd be surrounded by kids and their parents and caregivers. "Race you to the swings!"

Giggling, Charlotte took off running, giving Delaney the perfect excuse to hurry.

Charlotte got there first and settled on the only empty one. "Push me!" she called, her little legs getting her moving.

"Hold your horses, love."

Charlotte grinned like she always did when Delaney called her that.

Delaney shifted to stand in front of her, hoping to see that the sedan had moved on.

But it hadn't.

It was now parked on the far side of the street, across from the playground, too far away for Delaney to see inside and get a glimpse of who had followed them.

Assuming she wasn't being completely paranoid.

Swallowing a rise of nerves, she smiled at her charge. "I'm going to take your picture." She crouched down, ostensibly to take a photo of Charlotte. Instead, she zoomed in on the sedan.

"Lemme see!" Charlotte demanded.

"One more. Smile." This time, she took Charlotte's photo, then showed her the image.

Charlotte seemed satisfied. "Now, push me, pleeeeease."

Delaney moved behind Charlotte, which put her back to the parked sedan. Playing it cool. She didn't want them to know she'd spotted them.

"Higher!" Charlotte squealed, kicking her legs out.

Delaney gave another gentle push, keeping her voice light

despite her bubbling anxiety. "We don't want you to fly all the way to the moon."

"I could go to the moon and bring back cheese!"

Delaney forced a laugh.

"Well, hello there!"

She startled, spinning to find a woman approaching them with a friendly smile. She was familiar, but it took Delaney a moment to place her. It was the one who'd looked sympathetic during her confrontation with Charlotte's former nanny a few weeks earlier.

"Hi."

"I'm Heather." The woman extended her hand. She was about Delaney's age with dark curly hair that she'd pulled into a messy ponytail. "Heather Brown," the woman added with a warm smile. "I remember you from that day with the nanny." She glanced at Charlotte. "Looks like things worked out for you."

"Delaney Wright." She shook her hand. "I wasn't trying to take her job, but God has a way of working things out."

Heather's eyebrows scrunched together. "Hmm. Maybe He just likes you." There was something in her tone—not quite mockery, but definitely skepticism. Her head tilted to the side. "You okay? You jumped out of your skin a minute ago."

Heather was practically a stranger, but it had been weeks since Delaney had had a real conversation with anyone besides Charlotte or Mr. Aylett.

"Charlotte, love, I'm going to sit on the bench for a minute. Stay where I can see you, okay?"

Charlotte nodded, gaze averted, thanks to the stranger who'd joined them. But she didn't argue, just pumped her legs like Delaney had taught her to keep her swing moving.

Delaney led Heather to a nearby bench and sat, her gaze focused on Charlotte—and not missing the sedan still parked across the street. "This is going to sound silly," she began, "but I think someone might be following us."

"Seriously?" Heather's eyes widened, scanning the area. "What makes you think that?"

Delaney explained, and Heather glanced casually toward the street. "That car?" At Delaney's nod, she said, "Could be anything. A delivery driver on break, some guy waiting for his girlfriend. But I totally get it. Between the news and all the creepy stuff I watch on TV, I can find *scary* in everyday moments."

Delaney didn't watch those kinds of movies. Her family had been through so much in the previous twelve months that the last thing she needed was fictional danger.

But Heather had a point. Having someone see what she saw and explain away her concerns made them seem smaller, more manageable. "You're probably right."

"Now, tell me about Charlotte's hunky father. What do you know about him?"

Hunky? That wasn't the word Delaney would use to describe Mr. Aylett. He was so much more than that.

She recalled him covered in leaves the evening before, making Charlotte giggle, playing with abandon.

The man was more than hunky. He was beautiful.

Delaney wasn't about to discuss her employer's appearance with a woman she barely knew, especially when her own feelings were so confusing.

"He's not her father," Delaney said, feeling a strange protectiveness toward both Charlotte and Noah. "He's her uncle. Her parents are...not in the picture."

"Uncle, huh? I didn't see a wedding ring, so that's even better." Heather's eyes lit with interest. "No baby-mama drama."

Heather had noticed his lack of ring? What did that say about her?

Delaney shifted uncomfortably on the bench. This conversation was veering into territory that felt inappropriate. "I really shouldn't discuss my employer's personal life."

"Sorry. My parents always said I was too nosy for my own good." The words were tinged with amusement. "If there's nothing between you and Uncle Hottie, you must be lonely, working as a nanny. I mean...I guess I'm just assuming you don't have a lot of friends around here. You certainly don't sound like a local."

"I'm from Maine," Delaney said. "Charlotte's good company."

"Do you live in the house with them? I bet it's nice, one of those mansions."

Charlotte's delighted giggle gave Delaney an excuse to avoid the question. She watched her charge leave the swing and climb the ladder to the slide, her curls bouncing with each step. She was urging on a boy who looked a little younger than her as he climbed up behind her.

The car Delaney had feared was following her was gone, telling her she'd probably overreacted.

"What about you?" she asked, eager to shift the focus away from herself. "Is one of those kids yours?"

A shadow passed over Heather's face, but she pressed on a smile. "No kids. I work as a bookkeeper at an accounting firm nearby. Nothing exciting, but it pays the bills." Heather's hair blew in the breeze, and she tucked a strand behind her ear. "I come here when I need a break from the monotony. Something about kids laughing—it just makes everything better, you know?"

Delaney did know. Children's laughter had always been a

balm to her soul. Even on her worst days, the children she cared for brought her joy. "It's like a reset button."

They were chatting about nothing important when Charlotte stepped off the mulched play area and wandered toward the woods.

"Looks like I need to run." Delaney stood, never taking her eyes off Charlotte.

"What do you say we meet up here again? Maybe Thursday midmorning? Give us both someone to talk to besides four-year-olds and stuffy bosses."

The prospect of having a friend—even a casual one—made Delaney's heart lighten. She was moving toward her charge but said, "I'd like that."

"Great! See you then!"

Delaney ran toward the little escapee, pleased with herself.

She had a job, a place to live, and now a new friend. Not only was she living away from home, she was practically thriving.

She thought of the check her father had given her, still uncashed in her purse.

Maybe, for the first time in her life, she could actually make him proud.

CHAPTER ELEVEN

T he glass-walled office felt more like a cage than a sanctuary as Noah stared out at the Driftwood town square two stories below, searching for a glimpse of Charlotte and her nanny through the canopy of autumn oaks.

They probably weren't there anymore, since Charlotte had dance class in half an hour, but he searched anyway, as eager to catch a glimpse of Miss Wright as he was of Charlotte.

The admission knotted his gut. Just what he needed, an attraction to the too-young, too-naive nanny to add to all his other problems.

"You hear what I said?" Richard asked behind him.

Noah needed to be present here, now. He turned to face his office and the man on the far side of his desk.

Twenty-plus years his senior, Richard was tall and broad with gray hair thinning at the crown. He'd been Dad's lawyer and dearest friend, and in the years since Dad's death, he'd become more than a mentor. He was the closest thing to a father figure Noah had.

Unfortunately, Richard had brought bad news today.

The Tidewater merger, the one Noah had worked for months to orchestrate, the one he'd thought the night before was all but sewn up, was in even more jeopardy than it'd been before.

"Lowell's all for this new company," Noah guessed.

Richard shifted in the leather visitor's chair. "I can't say for sure, seeing as how I haven't talked to anyone on the board about it, but that's a good bet."

"What do you know about this rival company?"

"It's Hayes Industries, run by Frederick—"

"Hayes. I've met him." Noah sank into his chair, a holdover from when MidAtlantic Analytics had belonged to his father. He'd replaced a lot of the furniture, but there was something about sitting in Dad's chair that grounded him.

Sometimes.

But today, the creaking leather made him feel like he was in someone else's seat, living someone else's life. Exhaustion pressed behind his eyes—not the good kind that came from honest work, but the bone-deep weariness of fighting battles on too many fronts. Battles that weren't meant to be his.

Raising a child who belonged to his brother.

Building a business that belonged to his dad.

"What do you know about him?"

Noah considered the stories he'd heard about the man. "I've heard he's tough, plays dirty."

"Yeah." Richard sat back with a sigh. "I heard the same, but I've never done business with him."

"Why did Davis tell you?" Noah wouldn't call the president of Tidewater Logistics a friend, but they'd been acquaintances for years. He seemed like a good guy, but he'd shared something outside the company he'd been asked not to share. Not that Noah minded, but he was curious.

"He prefers MidAtlantic. He doesn't want to change horses midstream. I'm sure he doesn't like the idea of backing out of a commitment, even if it was only sealed with a handshake. And maybe"—Richard shrugged—"maybe he figures a little competition will bring a better product in the end." He leaned forward and squinted, the crinkles around his eyes deepening. He didn't say anything for a long moment, but Noah felt his scrutiny.

"What?"

"Do you mind if I pry?"

"Since when do you ask?"

Richard sat back. "I know the merger is really important to you, but I don't understand why. Business is good, right? You've taken what your dad built and turned it into something amazing, something he'd never have imagined."

"Artificial intelligence wasn't a thing when he died."

"Even so, you've done wonders with MidAtlantic. He'd be proud of it. Of you."

Would Dad be proud, though? What would he say if he knew how Noah had failed to rein Jasper in? His little brother had pulled a prodigal, selling his shares in MidAtlantic, taking his portion of their inheritance, and brushing the dust of Driftwood off his shoes. He'd rarely returned since Mom's death, just for the funeral and then, a few years later, to dump a daughter Jasper had never told him about. Sure, there'd been visits—an hour here, a day there. But while his body had been in Driftwood, his mind had been very far away.

Noah had tried and failed to get Jasper to change his behavior, though it hadn't been Noah's job to instill a sense of responsibility into his younger brother.

Noah *had* been responsible for who he'd chosen to marry. Noah's short, disastrous marriage had cost him half his assets.

After what Jasper had cashed out and what Marianne had

taken, Noah needed this merger to secure their family's home—a legacy passed down from his great-great-grandfather—for the next generation.

Meaning Charlotte. At this point, unless Jasper accidentally fathered more children, Charlotte was the only heir.

Noah had lost everything else that really mattered to him. His dad, his mom, his brother. He was not going to lose the property entrusted to him.

He blew out a breath, feeling overwhelmed and defeated. He didn't want to talk about any of that. He didn't want to remind his mentor how his failures had risked Dad's legacy. He didn't want to share his desire to be a good father figure to the little girl who desperately needed him, and he didn't want to confess that, unlike generations of Ayletts before him, he couldn't figure out how to care for a family and run a company at the same time.

So he avoided the question. "Any advice on how I should play this?"

Richard's lips slipped into a smirk. After a moment, he said, "As my daddy used to say, 'All you can do is the best you can do.' Just keep showing up and putting in the work. They have the financials now, which prove you've run your business well. Davis—and the honest ones on the Tidewater board—know that nobody else has a product as good as yours."

But what if Hayes could compete? Noah was proud of what he and his team had built, the first fully comprehensive AI assistant for nautical logistics companies. MidAtlantic was in a class of its own.

Or so he'd thought.

"I'll deal with it." He checked his watch, surprised to find it was already after three. His entire day had vanished into meetings and problem-solving.

The weight of all of it—the merger, Charlotte, the still-unsolved break-in, even his inconvenient attraction to Delaney—pressed down on his shoulders. He needed air and space to think.

He stood. "I should get going."

"You're leaving work early?" Richard's eyes widened as if he'd never heard of such a thing.

Noah gathered his keys from the desk drawer. "Charlotte asked me to come to her dance class today. I promised I'd try, and to be honest, I need to get out of here for a while."

Richard's expression softened. "Go on, then. Little girls don't stay little forever." He pushed himself to his feet with a groan that spoke of aging joints. "Don't let this business get to you. You've got a great product and a great team, and there are a few on the board pulling for you."

"Appreciate that." But Lowell had it out for him. If Noah had to guess, he'd been the one to alert Hayes to the opportunity. He'd do whatever he could to get revenge.

Noah didn't want to think about the damage Lowell could do to this merger and to his company.

He and Richard took the stairs to the first floor and faced each other on the sidewalk. Richard's hand clamped his shoulder in that paternal way that always made Noah miss his dad.

"Give that little girl a hug from me," the older man said.

"Will do. Thanks for the heads-up."

Noah walked down the block and cut through the narrow cobblestone alley lined with a boutique and a tea shop, where locals sat at wrought iron tables beneath colorful umbrellas.

He nodded to a shopkeeper and an older woman from church, their familiarity both comforting and suffocating in a town where everyone knew the Aylett name.

The alley opened onto another street, giving him a view into the parking lot behind his building. Before Charlotte had come to live with him, he'd walked to work on nice days, but now it felt wiser to have his car close in case she needed him.

At least he could count on Miss Wright to handle emergencies. She'd proved competent over and over, and every day that went by, he relaxed a little more, knowing she could manage Charlotte and all her needs.

The October sun glinted off the cars in the lot, and he quickened his pace, already calculating the time it would take to reach the studio. When he'd told Charlotte he'd try to make it, he'd already been composing excuses to give when he failed. But Richard was right. Charlotte wouldn't stay little forever, and she needed to know somebody was willing to make sacrifices for her.

He stopped short when he reached his sedan.

A woman was leaning against his car.

Lena Monroe pushed away from the vehicle when she spotted him, her red lips curving into a smile that had once seemed sultry but now just looked calculating. She wore a fitted black dress that hugged every curve, her dark hair falling in waves around her shoulders.

"Noah," she purred. "I was hoping to catch you."

The sight of her sent him into fight, flight, or freeze mode.

Fight won.

"What are you doing here, Lena?"

She seemed unfazed by his cool tone. "Is that any way to greet an old friend?"

"We're not friends." He kept his voice level, though he hummed with anger that simmered beneath the surface. "We used to be, and then you destroyed my life."

"I made a mistake." Lena stepped closer, her perfume—something floral and cloying—assaulting his senses. "Marianne didn't deserve you. The way she bought my story so easily... Honestly, some would say you owe me."

"Nobody sane would say that." Noah took a step back, putting distance between them.

"You and I, we belong together."

"There was never anything between us, Lena. And there never will be."

"Aren't you ever going to forgive me?" Her voice softened, taking on a wounded quality he didn't believe for a second.

"I forgive you," he said flatly. Because that was what God expected. Maybe someday, with the Lord's help, his heart would match his words. "But that doesn't change anything."

Lena's eyes narrowed, her entire visage changing. "You moved on from me fast enough."

"Moved on from *you*? You and I were never together." As the words were coming out, he realized what she was implying.

"Your young new girlfriend has that same sweet look about her that you fell for in Marianne, and you know how that worked out. You'd think you'd learn."

The comment hit like a splash of ice water. He took a step toward Lena, glaring down at her. "I don't have a girlfriend. What are you talking about?"

"Oh." She blinked, and her countenance changed again. She became a picture of innocence. Did she have an authentic side, or was she just one facade after another? "I assumed. I happened to be in your neighborhood last night and saw you two on the porch swing. Seemed cozy."

So it had been Lena's car crawling down Magnolia Street. She'd been watching. She'd seen him with Delaney.

"Stay away from my home."

"It's a public road, and I have—"

"And stay away from my family." He moved past her toward his car door.

She didn't budge. "Family? Is that what you're calling her and your bastard kid?"

He froze, turned slowly, and moved into her space.

She must've seen the fury in his expression because she took a step back.

"Pay very close attention, Lena." His heart was thumping like a war drum. "You and I were never together. We aren't together now, and we will never be together. You faced no consequences after you broke up my marriage. If you come after me again, if you so much as blink at Charlotte or her nanny, you will be sorry."

He wasn't sure what he'd expected, but he hadn't expected her to smile the way she did, to reach out as if she were going to touch him.

He retreated just in time.

"Fate can only be put off for so long, darling. I'm willing to wait."

He'd never feared a woman, but this one had already proved dangerous—maybe not to him physically, but in every other way. She was manipulative and determined and, obviously, walking a few blocks off Reality Road.

He didn't want to think about what lengths she'd go to fulfill her bizarre notion that they should be together, that he could ever love her.

With Lena Monroe back in the picture, Noah needed to be very careful.

~

Halfway to the dance studio, Noah was still brooding about Lena when his phone rang through the speakers. His brother's name came up on the screen.

"Thanks for calling me back." Noah worked for a neutral tone, though he'd called his brother three days before.

"Yeah, sorry." Jasper's words came out weary, with a touch of defensiveness. "I didn't have service."

"Where are you?"

"Long story. How's Charlotte?"

"She's doing exceptionally well, actually. Her new nanny has helped pull her out of her shell. She's been seeing a play therapist, working through some trauma, and—"

"What kind of trauma?"

"You'd know better than I would. I don't know what she's been through."

"Doesn't she tell the therapist?"

"She's four, Jaz."

"Right. Yeah." He blew out a breath. "I'm glad she's getting help. Thanks for doing that. And, you know..."

When his brother didn't finish, Noah said, "I wanted to float something by you." Anxiety pooled in his stomach. He'd prayed about adopting Charlotte that morning, and it felt so...right. He didn't think that feeling was just his own desires telling him what he wanted to hear. He thought the Lord had given him the go-ahead to mention it to his brother.

"I've got two minutes. What else did you need?"

Two *whole* minutes to talk to the man raising his daughter? His brother's attitude solidified Noah's resolve.

"Charlotte's been calling me Daddy sometimes. I always correct her, but since I'm the one taking care of her..." He paused to give Jasper a chance to say something. To act sad or hurt or surprised or angry.

Jasper didn't say anything.

Here goes. "I want to adopt her."

The silence on the other end of the phone could have meant anything. Noah waited, praying his brother would see reason.

"She's *my* daughter." Jasper's words were hard and angry.

"And yet, somehow, I'm her dad."

"No."

No?

Just...no?

Noah tamped down all his arguments. He wasn't going to fight his brother, the only family he had left. He had Charlotte now, and he'd need to be content with that.

The answer should have brought a level of peace, but all he felt was hollow.

"I'm going to come home." The hardness in Jasper's voice had shifted. Now he sounded almost desperate. "I am, I swear. I want to be there for her. I just have to take care of—"

"What? What could possibly be more important—?"

"I can't talk about it, but as soon as I finish—"

"Then something else will come up, and something else. She's four years old, Jaz, and you haven't spent more than, what? A week with her? I'm raising her. I *love* her."

"I'm doing my best."

Fury had his body trembling, his hands gripping the wheel so tightly they hurt. He eased up on the gas when he realized he was going twenty over the speed limit. The last thing he needed was to wreck on these winding roads.

He didn't know what to say. There were no words to explain to his useless brother everything he was missing, everything he was messing up.

He was almost to the dance studio. And he was done with this conversation.

"You know what, Jaz? Your best sucks." He pressed the button to end the call and pulled into the parking lot.

The dance studio was located in a converted Victorian home with a wraparound porch painted ballet-slipper pink. The lot was filled with minivans and SUVs—mom vehicles that made his black BMW stand out like a tuxedo at a barbecue.

His heart was still thumping after the confrontation. Confrontations, plural. One with his wastrel brother, and before that, with his...

Stalker.

It was the only word that made sense.

He parked and sat, watching parents and children emerge from cars with dance bags slung over shoulders and water bottles in hand. Through the large front windows, he could see small figures in leotards and tutus moving around inside.

His frustration eased slightly. Charlotte was in there, face bright with the joy that still surprised him every time he witnessed it. When she'd first come to live with him, her smiles had been rare, tentative things. He'd started coaxing her, proving she could trust him, and she'd become comfortable with him.

Certainly not her father, who'd done nothing for her but dump her with Noah.

Lord, help me forgive him. Help him figure it out. Charlotte needs a real father, and soon.

Because if it wasn't going to be Noah, then her heart was going to break all over again when Jasper took her away.

She'd flourished in the last few months. Her new nanny deserved some of the credit for her transformation.

Delaney.

Even thinking her name sent an unwelcome jolt of attraction through his system. And then dark fear.

Lena had seen them together. They hadn't done anything untoward, but the woman wasn't exactly sane. She wouldn't tell people about Noah and the nanny, would she?

One more supposed scandal and the Tidewater board would fully shift to their new option. He'd been stupid to join

Delaney—*Miss Wright!*—outside. Stupid to let even a hint of anything pass between them where someone might have seen.

No. To let anything pass between them, full stop. Because nothing could happen with the nanny. She was his employee, nothing else.

As far as he knew, the only person on the board Lena knew was Lowell. If she told him what she'd seen, that would give him the ammunition to destroy the merger.

But Lowell believed Noah had had an affair with Lena. He hated her almost as much as he hated Noah. She wouldn't dare approach him.

Probably.

With that less-than-confident thought, he made his way to the door.

Inside the studio, he was hit with the faint scent of sweat and the sound of music coming from far away. The reception area buzzed with activity—mothers clustered in conversation, younger siblings sprawled on the floor with coloring books, and the occasional father scrolling through his phone.

"Mr. Aylett!" A woman called out to him. It was Mrs. Moffett, the studio owner. She approached with a warm smile. "Charlotte will be so happy you made it."

"Where should I—?"

"Right through here." She gestured toward a set of double doors, where moms and kids sat on folding chairs that faced a window overlooking one of the two dance floors. "The girls just finished warming up."

Noah stepped inside and peeked through the window. He spotted Charlotte immediately, standing in the front row of a group of four- and five-year-olds. She was by far the smallest child in the class. Also, the cutest, in his very jaded opinion.

He scanned the chairs and spotted Miss Wright in the front row, an empty seat beside her. She was watching Charlotte with such obvious affection that something shifted inside him. Had any woman ever looked at Charlotte like that? Probably not her negligent mother nor her neglectful grandmother.

No wonder the child was smitten with her nanny. They adored each other.

Maybe Miss Wright felt his gaze because she glanced toward the door, then looked again, her face splitting into a gorgeous smile.

She gestured to the empty chair beside her, and he made his way over, nodding politely to the other parents who glanced his way with varying degrees of curiosity.

"You made it. Charlotte kept asking me if you'd be here." Miss Wright's voice was soft as he settled into the folding chair. The scent of coconut and vanilla drifted from her, and he forced himself to focus on the girls through the window rather than the way the nanny's hair fell in soft waves around her heart-shaped face.

"I promised I'd try." On the far side of the glass, Charlotte executed a twirl, her form enthusiastic if far from perfect. "How's she doing?"

"She loves it. Look at her."

Charlotte's face was radiant with joy. She was happy and safe. He wasn't messing this up too badly.

"The studio is planning a recital for Christmas," Miss Wright said. "Her class will all be snowflakes."

He pictured his niece in a white tutu, arms outstretched like delicate ice crystals. The image made him smile.

"She's very serious about it," Miss Wright said. "She asked me to help her practice her snow dance at home."

The casual way she mentioned home, as if it were as much hers as his, sent another unwelcome jolt through him. She'd settled so naturally into their lives, into Charlotte's heart—and if he were honest, into his own thoughts far too often. What would happen when she left for Maine?

What had Lena seen the night before? Had his inappropriate affection shown in his expression?

He needed to stop thinking such thoughts about the nanny. Or at least, when that proved impossible, do better at hiding them.

The music stopped, and the instructor gathered the girls into a circle. Charlotte plopped down cross-legged next to a little redheaded girl, who whispered in her ear.

"That's Shanyn," Miss Wright said. "Her new 'favoritest' friend."

"This was a good idea. Thank you for signing her up."

"She likes it."

The girls stood again, fanning out across the room to practice a series of arm movements that looked utterly random.

"Oh." Miss Wright shifted, pulling out her phone. "I'm glad you're here. There's something I wanted to show you." She found her photos, then held the screen toward him. "I took this earlier. It was probably nothing, but I got the feeling... It seems silly now."

Noah studied the image, taken at the park, which showed a dark sedan with tinted windows parked along the road.

Not the SUV he'd seen the night before. Did Lena have two cars?

There was no front license plate, a red flag. "What happened?"

"Nothing, really. I saw it on Magnolia Street, then on Cedar, then again there, across from the playground."

"You were followed?" His heart thumped erratically.

"Maybe?" She shrugged one shoulder. "Or maybe I was being paranoid." She tucked a strand of hair behind her ear, a gesture he was beginning to recognize as nervous. "A friend I met at the park—"

"What friend?"

Miss Wright's eyes widened.

"Sorry, I don't mean…" He took a breath to calm down. "Of course you can meet friends at the park."

"Um, okay." Her tone shifted back to that insecure one she'd used a lot when she'd first moved into his house. "I'd seen her at the park before, and we got to talking. I told her about the car, and she suggested it could be a delivery driver or something. The car was gone when we left, so maybe—"

"You should have told me right away."

The woman on Miss Wright's other side glanced in his direction. He needed to lower his voice.

Miss Wright was more careful, speaking at one click above a whisper. "I know you don't like to be bothered at work, so—"

"I never said that."

She blinked. "Oh. I guess I just…assumed."

"Don't make assumptions about what I want. I told you to let me know if you had any suspicions. I meant it."

She faced forward again. "You're right. I just talked myself into believing it was nothing."

"Maybe it was." His heart was racing. This day was going to send him into cardiac arrest.

He didn't recognize the car in the photo. It probably hadn't been following her. It probably hadn't been anyone who had anything to do with Charlotte or himself or Miss Wright.

But there'd been someone watching Charlotte the day he'd hired Miss Wright, or so she'd thought. And there'd been that break-in.

Lena had called the morning after that. And she'd shown up this afternoon.

Keeping his voice low, he asked, "What's your new friend's name?"

"Heather."

"What does she look like?"

"Dark, curly hair. Attractive. About my age."

That could describe thousands of women in Virginia alone. Or it could describe Lena.

He pulled his phone from his pocket, navigated to Facebook, and found Lena's profile. He clicked on her photo and showed it to Miss Wright. "Is that her?"

She studied the photo, then shook her head. "No. Heather's hair is naturally curly. That woman's curls come from an iron."

"How do you know?"

She smiled. "I have four sisters, Mr. Aylett. Trust me, I know my way around hair. Besides, Heather's much more down-to-earth looking than"—she glanced at the screen—"Lena Monroe. Less sophisticated."

"You're sure."

"Completely. But if you want to see for yourself, I'm meeting her at the park on Thursday morning. Feel free to come check her out. It's not like it would be the first time you've 'accidentally' been there at the same time as us." She made quotes with her fingers.

Ah. And here he'd thought he'd gotten away with checking up on them. "Sorry, I—"

"I get it, especially after your former nanny's behavior. It's a weighty thing to be responsible for a child."

"You're right, it is." He was so thankful that Charlotte had a nanny who understood. He watched the little girls on the dance floor, debating. Decision made, he leaned toward her. "That woman whose photo I just showed you?"

"What about her?"

"She's kind of a"—he felt stupid saying the word aloud but

forced it out—"stalker. She thinks she and I are…fated to be together." He glanced Miss Wright's way, confirming that he had her full attention. "If you ever feel like you're being watched again, please let me know immediately. And don't be afraid to call the police."

"I will."

"And if you ever see Lena, assume she wants trouble, and keep your distance."

Miss Wright looked at him and held his eye contact. "Do I need to be worried?"

"Just watchful, please." He'd do enough worrying for the both of them.

CHAPTER TWELVE

The music stopped, and the studio door burst open like a dam breaking, releasing a flood of tutu-clad little girls into the waiting area.

Delaney followed Mr. Aylett out of the viewing area to meet Charlotte.

She emerged from the chaos, her eyes scanning the room until they landed on her uncle.

Her face transformed—not into the reserved smile Delaney had grown accustomed to, but into something brilliant and unguarded. She didn't run to him, didn't call out his name, but her entire being seemed to vibrate with joy as she made her way slowly, as if afraid sudden movement might make him disappear.

"Uncle Noah," she whispered when she reached them, and though her voice was barely audible, it carried more emotion than Delaney had heard from her in weeks.

Mr. Aylett crouched to his niece's eye level. "Hey there, Charlie-Bear. You looked beautiful out there."

She ducked her head, watching him through her eyelashes, pleased at his compliment.

A redheaded girl bounced over, her freckled face bright with excitement. "Charlotte, is that your daddy?"

Charlotte's fingers gripped her tulle tutu. "He's my uncle."

"I'm Shanyn," the redhead announced, extending a small hand toward Mr. Aylett.

Mr. Aylett shook her hand with grave formality. "It's a pleasure to meet you, Miss Shanyn."

The girl dissolved into giggles.

A woman with the same fiery hair and freckles as Shanyn approached, grinning at her daughter's boldness. "I'm Lisa." She extended her hand to Delaney first. "Shanyn talks about Charlotte all the time. They've become quite the pair."

"Delaney Wright." She shook the woman's hand. "I'm Charlotte's nanny."

"Noah Aylett." He shook her hand as well. "Her uncle."

"We're heading to Dockside Burgers for an early dinner. Would you like to join us?"

Mr. Aylett glanced down at Charlotte. "What do you think? Do you want to go get burgers?"

Charlotte's eyes widened, her shy grin suddenly wide. She nodded, then looked up at Delaney expectantly.

That was just the kind of family outing she would love.

And the kind she must avoid. The last thing Mr. Aylett needed was to be seen eating with his nanny.

And there was the stalker to worry about now too.

"I'd love that, Charlotte, but sadly, I need to run to the store." She looked at Mr. Aylett. "Anything I can get for you while I'm there?"

"No, but..." His brow furrowed. "You need to eat."

"I'll grab something while I'm out." Delaney smiled at Charlotte, whose face had fallen. "You have fun with your uncle and Shanyn. Tell me all about it later, okay?"

Charlotte gripped her hand, tears hovering in her eyes.

Oh, dear.

Delaney crouched in front of her, ignoring the others. "I'm going to go to the store, and then I'll be home."

Her little lip trembled. She leaned in and whispered, "You promise?"

Delaney backed up and took Charlotte's little face in her hands. "Beautiful girl, I promise I will come back tonight. And I'll bring you some of those yummy peanut butter bars you like."

The child studied her as if looking for lies. After a moment, she said, "Okay."

"Love you, sweet girl." She kissed her on the forehead, then stood and addressed Lisa. "It was nice to meet you." To Mr. Aylett, she said, "Text if you think of anything you want me to get while I'm out."

"See you at the house."

The late afternoon air had cooled considerably, and Delaney zipped her jacket as she walked to her car. She'd meant what she said about needing to go to the store. Her toothpaste tube had been rolled within an inch of its life, and she was almost out of shampoo. Now that she had a few weeks' pay in her checking account, she felt confident stocking up on personal products she hadn't wanted to add to Mr. Aylett's grocery bill.

She pulled out of the parking lot, checking her mirrors more carefully than usual. The man had a stalker. So strange.

Fortunately, no one followed her as she drove the few miles to the superstore on the outskirts of town.

Her list wasn't long. She'd made a mental note to pick up a few things they were running low on—bread, eggs, and fresh fruit. She'd add those peanut butter bars to the list. Anything to see that sweet smile when she returned home.

Home. The word rooted in her heart. When had the Aylett house begun to feel that way? It wasn't hers, but for now, it was the only home she had.

Delaney took her time in the personal care section, scanning the shelves for her favorite shampoo. Now that she had a steady income, she could finally replace the travel-sized bottles she'd been rationing.

In the clothing section, she shopped for sweaters and a jacket. She'd left home in the middle of summer, and though it wouldn't get nearly as cold here as it would in Maine, she'd still need a few things to get her through the winter months. She took her time picking out items, not eager to go home to an empty house.

Her phone vibrated, a text from Mr. Aylett.

> Charlotte wanted me to make sure you're really coming back.

Delaney's heart squeezed. After everything the little girl had been through, of course she worried about abandonment. Delaney dug through her cart, found the peanut butter bars, and took a selfie with them. She tapped a reply.

> Tell her I promise.

She sent the photo and the note.

Three dots appeared, disappeared, then reappeared before his reply came through:

> Thank you. Drive safely.

Strange how those four words warmed Delaney's insides.

The total at checkout made her wince. Her bank account wasn't flush, but she wasn't destitute either. She was surviving.

Her phone buzzed again, and she glanced at the screen. A text from her mother simply read,

> Please consider coming home for Christmas.
> We'll cover the cost.

The words were followed by a travel website.

Home for Christmas?

The thought of going home filled her with equal parts joy and dread.

She wanted to see her sisters, to hug her mother. To give her father back his you'll-never-make-it check.

But was she ready to face them? Or to face the townspeople and their judgment after learning she'd been dating a criminal?

Nobody cared that much, not really. But she did.

She stared at her phone for a few moments, at the dancing dots that told her Mom was either typing or waiting for her to respond.

She tapped the best answer she could give at the moment.

> I'll think about it.

After paying for her purchases, she rolled her cart to the fast-food restaurant inside the superstore's entrance. The smell of fried food made her realize she was hungrier than she'd thought. She ordered a chicken sandwich and ate it at one of the high tables near the window, watching the parking lot as daylight faded into dusk.

The lot wasn't empty when Delaney stepped outside, but it felt that way. The distance between her small SUV and the store entrance stretched farther than it had when she'd arrived. She saw only one other person, a person ducking into a vehicle a few aisles away.

By the time Delaney loaded her purchases, full darkness had settled. She pulled out of the parking space, her headlights sweeping across the rows of empty spaces.

The drive back to Driftwood took her along the winding two-lane highway that cut through farmland and patches of forest. During the day, the route was scenic. At night, it felt isolated. Her headlights carved a tunnel, illuminating the yellow center line and the reflective markers that dotted the shoulder.

She'd driven this route dozens of times now, but tonight something felt different. When she pressed the brake pedal as she approached a stop sign at a crossroads, it felt mushy beneath her foot.

Weird. But the car stopped normally, so she continued toward town.

The road was mostly flat with one exception, a hill that bordered the valley where Driftwood was nestled among the pines. When she crested the hill, the little town's lights shone in the distance.

Her SUV picked up speed as she headed down. She pressed the brake pedal. It mashed all the way to the floor.

But her Highlander didn't slow.

Her heart lurched as the car gained speed down the incline. She pumped the brake frantically, but the pedal offered no resistance, no response. She sped around turns that seemed to get sharper the faster she went.

"No, no, no!" The yellow center line blurred beneath her headlights.

A sharp curve loomed ahead, marked by reflective yellow signs. She yanked the wheel into the turn, tires squealing as she fought to keep the SUV on the asphalt. The vehicle fishtailed, and she feared she'd spin.

She managed to straighten out, but another curve was coming fast.

The emergency brake. She yanked it up. The car shuddered, slowing slightly, but not enough. The acrid smell of burning brake pads filled the cabin.

Another curve. She took it too wide, her tires hitting the gravel shoulder before she wrestled it back onto the road.

Lord, help!

The road continued to wind, curve after deadly curve between the dark trees. At this speed, she'd never make them all.

Her heart pounding in her throat, Delaney spotted a small turnout ahead. She remembered the abandoned strip mall on the hill, having seen it on other trips to the store. It was her only chance. She steered onto the gravel, bracing as her Toyota lurched over the uneven ground.

It skidded on loose stones, careening toward the trees that bordered the pullout.

Delaney yanked the wheel hard to the left, trying to avoid a head-on collision with a tree. She failed. The front of her car rammed into the trunk with a sickening crunch of metal and glass.

The impact jerked her forward against her seat belt as the airbag deployed, knocking the wind from her lungs. But at least the car had stopped.

The headlights cast eerie shadows into the forest.

She shifted into Park and shut off the car, as if the thing might suddenly drive on its own. For several moments, she sat frozen, hands still gripping the wheel, the only sound her ragged breathing and the tick-tick-tick of the cooling engine.

"I'm alive." The whispered words caught in her throat. "Thank you, Lord."

She fumbled for her phone and called AAA, relieved to find her membership was still active. The operator's calm voice helped steady her as she explained what had happened.

"We'll send someone right away, ma'am. Are you injured?"

"Nothing serious." At least, she didn't think so.

"Okay, just stay with your vehicle. Our technician should be there in about thirty minutes."

Thirty minutes.

She needed to call Mr. Aylett and let him know she'd be late, if only to reassure Charlotte that she would keep her promise and come home. She'd do that when she thought she could talk without bursting into tears.

It was just a car accident, and she'd survived. But adrenaline still coursed through her veins.

Delaney stared into the darkness beyond her windshield. The turnout was deserted, the only light coming from her damaged headlights. Even the distant glow of Driftwood was hidden behind trees.

She tried to steady her breathing. How had her brakes failed? Had she done something to cause that? She hadn't been good about getting her oil changed, but that wouldn't affect the brakes, would it? Maybe the fluid was low. Wouldn't there have been a warning light or something?

Delaney unbuckled her seat belt and climbed out of the car. She stretched, carefully checking herself for injuries. Her chest ached from the belt or the airbag, and her neck felt stiff. But nothing seemed broken. At least outside, she could breathe fresh air, away from the airbag dust.

Headlights appeared, approaching slowly from the direction she'd come. Thank goodness. She wouldn't have to wait alone in this dark place until the tow truck arrived.

But the vehicle didn't pull up beside her. Instead, it stopped at the entrance to the turnout, high beams suddenly flashing on, blinding her.

She lifted her hand to shield her eyes, thinking the driver would get out or call through the window to ask if she needed help.

But nobody stepped out. Whoever was in that car just sat there, engine running, lights blazing.

Delaney's relief curdled into unease. If they hadn't stopped to help, why not move along? Why stop at all?

The car idled. The driver watched.

Delaney took a step back toward her damaged Toyota. Was this the same car she'd seen following her and Charlotte earlier? The glare made it hard to tell.

Mr. Aylett's warning echoed in her mind. Could this be his stalker? The woman who thought she and Noah were "fated" to be together?

Delaney slid back into her SUV and locked the doors. The stranger's high beams illuminated the steam still rising from her crumpled hood, turning it into ghostly fingers reaching toward the night sky.

Whoever that was behind her...it wasn't a friend.

And she was all alone and defenseless. She was no longer careening along the narrow highway, but the situation suddenly felt just as dangerous.

CHAPTER THIRTEEN

Noah walked with Charlotte toward the car, the scent of french fries following them from Dockside Burgers. Charlotte's small hand swung his arm back and forth, her fingers warm against his palm.

The dinner with Lisa, her husband, Wilt, and their daughter had been incident-free—the kind of evening that made him believe he might actually be getting the hang of this parenting thing. Charlotte had eaten her chicken fingers without complaint and even giggled at something Shanyn's father had said. It was the most relaxed he'd seen her in public.

Noah's conversation with Wilt had been refreshingly ordinary—talk of business, fishing spots, and coastal weather patterns. No probing questions about Charlotte's parentage, no sly mentions of magazine articles naming him the region's most eligible bachelor. Just guys talking about guy stuff.

"Did you have fun with Shanyn?" He glanced down at his niece.

"Uh-huh." She nodded, her blond curls bouncing.

"I'm glad we came then." His attention snagged on a man emerging from a black Cadillac sedan parked next to Noah's

BMW, all well lit by the lights brightening the parking lot. Noah recognized him immediately. Frederick Hayes, owner of Hayes Industries, MidAtlantic's rival in the Tidewater merger.

Frederick Hayes was tall and imposing in his custom-tailored suit that had probably cost more than what most people in Driftwood made in a month. His steel-gray hair was perfectly styled, not a strand out of place despite the wind.

Noah had met him only once before, but he'd heard enough about him to tighten his grip on Charlotte's hand.

"Noah Aylett." Frederick spoke over his shiny car, his voice carrying a polished, boarding-school cadence that grated on Noah's nerves. "What a pleasant surprise."

"Frederick. Bit far from home, aren't you?"

Hayes's smile widened as he approached, revealing teeth that were too perfect, too white. "Business brings me to all sorts of places these days. The coastal towns have such...charm." His gaze drifted down to Charlotte, who had partially hidden herself behind Noah's leg. "And who might this be?"

Noah didn't want Frederick anywhere near Charlotte. His phone rang in his pocket, giving him an excuse to avoid the question.

He pulled it out. "I'd better get this." He tugged Charlotte away from Hayes and toward his car, thankful for the distraction.

Charlotte tugged at his sleeve as he checked the phone screen.

"It's Miss Laney," he told her, hiding his flicker of concern. She rarely called him, generally texting if she had a question about Charlotte.

"Hello?"

"I'm sorry to bother you"—her voice was high and panicked —"but my brakes failed and I crashed my car and now there's someone—"

"Slow down." Worry crawled up his spine. "Are you hurt?"

"I don't think so. I'm at an abandoned strip mall and there's a car just sitting there with its high beams on me. They won't leave or help or anything. They're just…watching."

Lena. The woman was unhinged, but was she dangerous? He picked up Charlotte and carried her to his BMW. "Call 911. Right now."

"I already did. The police are on their way."

"Good, good. Stay in your car. Lock the doors. Don't get out for anyone except the police or me." He opened the rear door of his sedan as his phone dinged. After he settled Charlotte in her seat, he checked the pin she'd sent marking her location. "I'll be there in ten minutes."

"Okay. Thank you." She ended the call.

Noah buckled Charlotte quickly. His niece sensed his urgency, her eyes wide and solemn.

"Is Miss Laney okay?"

"She's going to be fine." He hoped to God that was true. "She just needs a ride."

He pulled out of the restaurant parking lot faster than he should have, his mind racing. The abandoned strip mall was on the highway leading out of town—isolated, dark, the perfect place to corner someone.

His phone rang through the car's speakers. Richard's name appeared on the dashboard display.

"Not now," he muttered, declining the call.

He made the ten-minute drive in seven.

Flashing red and blue lights cut through the darkness as Noah turned onto the gravel driveway. Two police cruisers flanked Delaney's Highlander, which was wrapped around a thick oak tree, the hood crumpled like an accordion.

Noah's stomach dropped. She could have been killed.

"Uncle Noah?" Charlotte's voice was barely a whisper from

the backseat. Even so, he heard panic in it. "I don't wanna go with them. I wanna stay with you."

"Charlie-Bear, nobody is taking you away from me. I promise."

"What about Miss Laney?"

He shifted the car into Park, stepped out, and unbuckled his niece. "She had an accident, that's all. She's okay."

He didn't want her to get a better view of the damaged car, but Charlotte's fear of the police, fear that they'd take her away, had him unclipping her from the car seat.

With Charlotte clinging to him, he approached the cluster of people, scanning the faces.

There she was. She stood beside a uniformed officer, clutching a blanket wrapped around her shoulders.

"Miss Wright?" He kept his voice gentle as he approached.

She turned, and her shoulders relaxed. "Thank God you're here."

That reaction did something wonky to his body, and suddenly, the urge to pull her into his arms had him keeping his distance. "Are you hurt?"

"Just shaken up. The airbag deployed." She touched her sternum, the action defying her casual remark.

One of the cops shifted, and Noah realized it was Mason, Jasper's old high school friend.

"It was probably just someone who wanted to make sure you were all right." He must be continuing a conversation from before Noah arrived.

"Then why not get out and ask?" Her voice was low and tentative. "Why sit there and watch me?"

The cop seemed to consider that. "My guess, when you got out of the car, the driver realized you were okay and took off."

"He didn't take off, though. He sat there, and then..." Miss

Wright sighed. "No, you're probably right. I guess that makes sense."

"No, it doesn't." Noah faced the cop. "Did another call come in about a wreck tonight?"

"Not as far as I know, but I can check."

"You do that. And while you're at it, check on Lena Monroe. She was outside my office this afternoon and made some...concerning remarks."

"Like...?"

Noah shifted Charlotte in his arms, trying to convey everything he couldn't say right now. "She drove by my house last night. She saw Miss Wright and me having a conversation on the porch swing."

Mason's eyebrows lifted, his gaze flicking from the nanny to him. "I didn't realize you and Delaney were—"

"We're not anything," Miss Wright said quickly. "I'm Charlotte's nanny. Mr. Aylett and I were just talking. Sort of a normal thing to do."

Noah was thankful for her quick explanation. "My point is, Lena was watching my house. And now"—he nodded to the car—"this freak accident. Too many coincidences."

Mason's expression shifted from skepticism to concern. "I'll look into it. What kind of car does Ms. Monroe drive?"

"She used to drive a black SUV." Noah glanced at Miss Wright. "Was it an SUV behind you?"

"I think so." She tugged the blanket tighter. "I only saw the silhouette of it when it drove away, but it was too big to be a sedan, and it wasn't a pickup."

Charlotte's fingers dug into Noah's shoulder as she buried her face against his neck.

"It's okay, Charlie-Bear." He rubbed circles on her small back. "Miss Laney is safe, and so are we. We're going to go home soon. All three of us." His words seemed to soothe her a little.

A wrecker pulled up, and the police moved their cruisers so it could get close to the Toyota.

"Mr. Aylett?" Miss Wright's voice came from right beside him. "Will you help me get the things I bought tonight?"

"Of course. You and Charlotte wait in my car, and I'll take care of it."

He didn't hand his niece to her, unsure about her injuries, just settled Charlotte back in her car seat.

Miss Wright climbed in beside Charlotte, understanding without being told that she was traumatized.

He shifted her purchases to his trunk, then grabbed her purse and cell phone from the passenger seat and gave them to her, earning a slight smile and a quiet thank-you.

As if he'd done anything for her except drag her into his crazy life.

An accident was bad enough, but then to feel threatened by some unknown lurker. He prayed Miss Wright wouldn't be so frightened that she would run all the way back to Maine, leaving Charlotte alone again.

CHAPTER FOURTEEN

Every breath sent pain across Delaney's chest. She winced as she pulled a loose sweater over her head, careful to avoid touching the tender skin on her forearm where the airbag had left its mark—an angry red abrasion that stung under even the gentlest touch.

Sleep had come in fitful bursts, her body unable to find a comfortable position, her mind replaying the terrifying moment when her brakes failed. The car careening down the hill, the sickening crunch of metal—it had all rushed back each time she'd closed her eyes.

She moved slowly down the stairs toward the familiar sounds of breakfast being prepared. Thank God, Mr. Aylett cooked in the mornings. She'd have to figure out something to serve for lunch and dinner that didn't require heavy pans.

When she entered the kitchen, he glanced up from the stove where he was flipping pancakes, a treat he only allowed because of the protein powder he added to the batter. His brow furrowed.

"What are you doing up?" His voice was gentle but firm. "I told you to sleep in."

"You need to go to work." She wasn't about to let her negligence affect him. Whatever she'd done—or failed to do—to her car, that shouldn't be his problem. In fact... "I wanted to apologize. I'm so thankful Charlotte wasn't in the car with me, but she could've been."

"It was an accident, Miss Wright." He slid a pancake onto a growing stack. "No need to apologize. Do you want to eat before you go back to bed?"

"I'm not—"

"I'm working from home today." He gestured toward the table with the spatula. "And you're taking the day off. Doctor's orders."

"Did you go to medical school between last night and this morning?" She attempted a smile.

"Don't need to be a doctor to know you need rest."

Noah's kindness made something surge inside. The man had enough to worry about without adding her recovery to his list, yet here he was, taking care of her like she mattered.

"If you really don't mind, that sounds wonderful." She should argue, insist that she could push through to do her job, but the thought of crawling back into bed, of letting someone else handle the morning routine, felt like a gift.

She skipped breakfast and retreated to her room. The bed welcomed her aching body, and she fell into a deep sleep.

~

"Miss Laney?" Charlotte's voice was barely above a whisper through the door, pulling Delaney from sleep.

She shifted, the pain in her sternum sharp. "Come in, sweetheart."

Charlotte peeked around the door frame, her blue eyes wide

with worry. "Uncle Noah says you have to come downstairs. There's people here."

The anxiety in the child's voice had Delaney pushing herself upright despite the discomfort. "What kind of people?"

"Police people." Charlotte's lower lip trembled.

"I see." She patted the bed beside her, and Charlotte climbed up, snuggling close. "The police just want to talk about my accident last night. Sometimes when people have problems, the police help them figure out what to do. That's the only reason they're here."

Charlotte nodded but didn't look convinced. Her small body remained tense against Delaney's side.

"Everything's going to be okay." Delaney smoothed the child's curls. "Your Uncle Noah is downstairs, isn't he?"

"Uh-huh."

"Then you're safe. He won't let anything bad happen to you." The words came easily. Noah Aylett's devotion to Charlotte was absolute.

Charlotte slipped off the bed and waited while Delaney slowly pulled herself upright, changed into jeans and a sweater, and pulled a brush through her hair. Even that simple movement sent pain to her chest, but she didn't let it show, not wanting to add to the child's fears.

She walked beside Charlotte down the stairs, one hand gripping the rail, the other resting lightly on her little shoulder.

The small living room felt crowded with three men in it. Mr. Aylett stood near the entry while two others occupied chairs in the seating area. She recognized the uniformed police officer from the night before and nodded at him.

The other wore slacks and a button-down shirt.

Both stood when she and Charlotte walked in.

Mr. Aylett's eyes found hers immediately. "Sorry to get you out of bed."

The mantel clock told her she'd slept nearly three hours. "It's not a problem. Thank you for the extra rest."

He nodded to the man she hadn't met. "This is Detective Norton."

He was a Black man in his forties with kind eyes and graying temples. "Ms. Wright, I'm sorry to hear about your accident."

Delaney settled into a chair, Charlotte immediately climbing onto her lap. Her small body pressed against her bruises, but she wrapped her arms around her anyway.

"The mechanic looked at your car this morning," Detective Norton said. "He called me with some concerning news."

Mr. Aylett moved closer to Delaney, his jaw tightening. "What did he find?"

Detective Norton barely spared Mr. Aylett a glance. "It wasn't mechanical failure or normal wear and tear. Your brake line was cut. Someone deliberately sabotaged your vehicle."

The room seemed to tilt. Charlotte's weight against her chest made breathing difficult, but not as difficult as processing what she'd just heard. Someone had tried to hurt her...or worse?

"You're sure?" The words came out as barely a whisper.

"Clean slice through the brake hose," Detective Norton confirmed. "The mechanic said it was done with a sharp knife or razor blade. Would have taken less than a minute if someone knew what they were doing."

Mr. Aylett's hands clenched into fists at his sides. "I told you something wasn't right about last night." His voice was sharp, directed at the uniformed officer who'd told her to call him Mason. "This wasn't random."

Mason shifted uncomfortably. "We're taking it seriously now."

Mr. Aylett looked like he wanted to say more, but he clamped his lips shut, glancing at Delaney.

He looked again as if to register what he was seeing. "Come on, Charlie-Bear." He took his niece, relieving the pressure on Delaney's chest. "Miss Laney needs you not to climb on her for a few days." He settled her on a barstool in the attached kitchen and set her coloring book and crayons on the bar. "You sit here and color while we talk, okay?"

"'Kay."

When he returned, Delaney gave him a grateful smile.

"Can you think of anyone who might want to harm you?" Detective Norton asked. "Any disputes, arguments, threats?"

Delaney shook her head, the movement making her sternum hurt. "I've been in Driftwood not even two months. I don't really know anyone except..." She gestured vaguely around the room.

"You've lived in this house all that time?" He pulled a notebook and pen from his breast pocket.

"I've lived here a little over three weeks."

"What about before you moved in here?" The detective's pen was poised to take notes. "Where were you living?"

"I...um." Her gaze flicked to Mr. Aylett, and his eyes narrowed as if he read her reluctance to say. He'd never asked where she'd been living, and she'd never volunteered the information. There was nothing for it now. "I was staying in a women's shelter in town."

The detective's eyebrows hiked. "Are you running from someone? A husband or boyfriend, or—"

"Nothing like that. I met someone at the church that runs the place and asked if they knew somewhere I could rent for cheap. They said I could stay there until I found a place to live or someone else needed to move in."

"I see." Detective Norton made a note, and she assumed the nice people she'd met at the Cedar Shoals Bible Church would be getting a call.

She chanced a glance at Mr. Aylett, finding that not only did he not seem shocked or worried about her admission, but he was nodding as if he'd just discovered a missing puzzle piece.

"Did you make any enemies there?" the detective asked.

"At the shelter? No. I mean, I didn't make any lifelong friends, but I didn't have conflicts with any of them."

Mr. Aylett moved closer and perched on the edge of the couch. "Did you ever let any of them borrow your car?"

"No. Never."

"What about the people at the store yesterday?" Mason asked. "Did you see anybody following you?"

"No, but I was focused on shopping, not on the people around me."

"How long were you there?" This question came from the detective. All three of the men watched her closely. Though she knew they were trying to help, she felt like she was being interrogated.

"At least an hour. I shopped and then grabbed dinner in the store."

"The brake line must've been cut while you were shopping," Detective Norton said, making another note. "The brakes wouldn't have held all the way from Driftwood to the superstore if they'd been cut before you left."

The realization sent a chill down Delaney's spine. Someone had crawled under her car while she browsed shampoo and sweaters, deliberately sabotaging her vehicle, knowing she'd be driving on that winding road in the dark.

Someone had wanted her to wreck. Someone had wanted to hurt her. Maybe kill her. But why?

"Where did you park?" Mason asked.

Delaney grabbed a throw pillow and hugged it to her chest. It helped the pain a little and gave her a shield from the barrage of questions. "It was about halfway back from the entrance, in front of the grocery side, under one of the lights."

"Good," Mason said. "I'll check if they have security cameras. Maybe we'll get lucky."

Mr. Aylett's face had darkened. "You should look into Lena Monroe. Maybe. She's been sort of stalking me."

"I spoke with Ms. Monroe this morning." Detective Norton's tone remained neutral. "She claims she was home all night."

Mr. Aylett pushed to standing. "And you believe her?"

"I don't take people at their word," the detective said evenly. "We'll look for evidence."

Mr. Aylett seemed to accept that, settling on the couch beside Delaney.

The detective turned back to her. "Where are you from?"

"Maine, a small coastal town called Shadow Cove."

"And you came all the way down here because...?"

"I needed a change." She kept her explanation vague, unwilling to share her entire history with these strangers. The pillow against her chest felt like inadequate armor.

The detective studied her for a moment longer before turning to Mr. Aylett. "What about you? Besides Ms. Monroe, can you think of anyone who might want to harm your employee?"

"No one specific, but there's a business deal I'm working on. A merger. Another company is trying to edge mine out."

"You think someone would target your nanny over a business deal?" Mason's tone held disbelief.

"I have no idea. It's possible someone might try to destabilize my life to derail the merger." He ran a hand through his hair, a gesture Delaney knew meant he was frustrated. "There's a board member who's actively working against me."

"Name?"

He seemed reluctant to say, lips pressed closed. Finally, he said, "Lowell Jeffries."

"Your ex-wife's brother?" Mason's eyebrows hiked.

Delaney blinked, surprised at this new information. Mr. Aylett had been married?

"He has reason to dislike me."

The detective asked, "Reason to try to hurt you?"

"He thinks so." His gaze flicked to hers but didn't hold. Instead, he focused on Mason, who had information Delaney did not. "Which brings us back to Lena Monroe."

Mr. Aylett's stalker, but what did she have to do with this Lowell character?

And what would Lena do if she thought Delaney was standing in her way?

CHAPTER FIFTEEN

Noah watched through the kitchen window as Charlotte chased a butterfly across the backyard, her delighted giggles carrying on the breeze, but his attention kept drifting to the woman seated on the porch in the wicker love seat.

Delaney hugged a throw pillow, her face pale despite the afternoon sun. Every few minutes, she'd shift, wincing at some movement that sent pain through her bruised sternum. Her discomfort sent a familiar surge of rage through his system—white-hot and useless.

Mason had called an hour before to tell them what he'd learned from the security footage. The cameras at the superstore had captured a figure crouching beside Delaney's Highlander, all right—someone in baggy clothing and a baseball cap pulled low, face never visible to the lens. Could have been anyone. Male, female, tall, short—impossible to tell. And there was no footage of Lena's car anywhere in the parking lot that evening.

She could have killed Delaney—and she would have gotten away with it.

The coffee in Noah's hand had gone cold while he stood

there, wrestling with the impossible choice that had been eating at him all day. He should send Delaney away. Back to Maine, back to safety, back to a life that didn't include psychotic stalkers.

But Charlotte had been through too much loss already. Her mother, her grandmother, her useless father... Everyone who was supposed to protect her had abandoned her. She'd found safety with Noah, but she'd bloomed under Delaney's care. How could he rip that away from her?

Who was he kidding? He didn't want Delaney to leave either. In three weeks, she'd become more than Charlotte's nanny. She'd become the steady presence that made their house feel like a home. The woman who made him laugh in leaf piles and whose coconut scent lingered in rooms after she'd gone.

His phone rang, jolting him from his brooding. He checked the screen and answered. "Hey, Richard."

"Did you get my message?"

"I haven't listened to it, but I saw that you called. We had some excitement around here last night." He explained about Delaney's wreck and the SUV whose driver had watched but never offered to help. "It wasn't an accident." Noah stepped away from the window, afraid his voice would carry through the glass. "Someone cut her brake line."

"You're sure?"

"Cops told me."

Richard was quiet for a moment. "Any guesses—?"

"My guess is Lena Monroe. She was waiting for me at my car yesterday after I left the office."

He sighed, the sound weary. "I was afraid she wasn't gone for good. Are the police looking for her?"

"There's no evidence it was her. They have nothing to charge her with."

"Okay, well... I'm sorry you're going through that. I've got more information about Frederick Hayes."

"Tell me."

"My friend was representing a company in a merger about ten years ago. The details aren't important, but the morning the contract was to be signed, his client backed out. Understand, by not signing, he lost millions.

"My friend found out later that someone had threatened the client's wife."

The bottom dropped out of Noah's stomach.

"There's no proof it was Hayes," Richard said. "Apparently, his wasn't the only company that stood to lose if that client signed the contract, and Hayes and his family were out of the country at the time, but he's always believed Hayes was behind it."

"Do you know why?"

"I guess because his company won the contract. I've been doing some digging. Hayes has a reputation for finding pressure points and exploiting them. Personal scandals, family secrets, business vulnerabilities—it seems nothing's off-limits if it helps him close a deal."

Pieces clicked together. "Wait. Do you think he could've been behind what happened to Delaney?"

"I don't know," Richard said carefully. "I wouldn't rule it out."

"He threatened the wife, presumably with violence." Noah peeked out the window again. Charlotte and Delaney were safe.

"Between the break-in at your house"—Richard seemed to be choosing his words carefully—"this stalker situation, and now your nanny's accident... It doesn't sound like Hayes's usual playbook. His methods are more subtle. Financial pressure, damage to reputations, that sort of thing."

Noah did not need more damage to his family's reputation.

The divorce and the rumors that swirled around it had been bad enough. Add Jasper's infamous behavior, and now the child Noah was raising. The Ayletts had kept the rumor mill well fed for years.

Through the window, Noah watched Charlotte abandon her butterfly chase and skip toward the porch where Delaney sat. Delaney's expression brightened. She set aside the pillow to study the treasure Charlotte showed her.

"I'll see what else I can learn," Richard said, pulling Noah's attention back to the call. "In the meantime, keep your head down and your family safe."

Family. The word floated in his mind and heart. He hadn't been part of a family in a long time. Six months before, he hadn't known Charlotte existed. Now he'd do anything to keep her safe.

And then there was her nanny, who elicited the same rise of protectiveness in him, an inconvenient fact he didn't have the energy to face today.

"Thanks for the information, Richard. I'll do my best."

"That's all anyone can ask, son."

After ending the call, Noah stepped outside, the screen door's screech announcing his arrival.

Charlotte had settled beside Delaney and was showing her a dandelion she'd picked. "Look what I found, Uncle Noah!" Charlotte held up the weed like a precious gem.

"That's beautiful, Charlie-Bear." He lowered himself into the chair beside them.

Delaney's eyes met his, and her head tilted to the side. "Bad news?"

"Just business." He forced a smile. "Nothing for you to worry about."

Her gaze lingered on his face a moment longer, as if she could see through his reassurance. "Charlotte, why don't you go find more flowers for a bouquet? Stay where I can see you."

"Okay!" She slid off the love seat and bounded across the yard, her curls bouncing.

"She took off on me at the playground yesterday." Delaney grabbed the pillow and hugged it. By her amused expression, she'd had the situation under control.

"How far did she get?"

"I never lost sight of her, but only because I moved to keep my eye on her. I'm trying to teach her to always be checking to make sure she can still see me."

"How's that working?"

She laughed. "Well, she spends a lot of time in her own imagination, and she's four, so..."

He grinned. "Right. Thank you for trying."

"She'll get there. I think she's never had anyone watch her so closely before, at least that's my theory. And the therapist said she could be testing me, wanting to see if I care enough to come for her." Delaney turned to him. "You want to talk about it?"

He studied her face—the way she held herself so carefully, the concern in her eyes despite her own pain. She'd endured a nightmare the night before, yet she was worrying about him.

"I'll deal with it. It's nothing for you to worry about."

"After what the detective said this morning, I wonder if maybe your business stuff is related."

Right. He didn't want to believe it, but it was possible. "I just got a call from my lawyer—and friend—about the merger. He told me the company we're competing against is owned by a man who plays dirty. Richard says he's the kind of man who'll go to extremes to win."

Her grip tightened on the pillow. "You think it was him?"

"My money's still on Lena. Apparently, Hayes's methods are more subtle."

"So I have to watch out for your stalker and your business rival." Her voice held a note of dark humor. "I wasn't this popular in high school."

"This isn't funny, Delaney." Her name slipped out. He'd been so careful to maintain professional distance, but knowing someone had tried to hurt her—or worse—because of him made it feel impossible.

She blinked those wide, innocent eyes. "I need to find some humor in it or I'll fall apart." She glanced toward Charlotte, who was now examining something in the grass. "I need to be vigilant. And try not to scare her."

Noah felt himself leaning toward Delaney...

Miss Wright.

He straightened and dropped his elbows on his knees.

Charlotte ran to the corner of the yard close to the house, and Miss Wright angled forward to keep her eyes on her.

"I think it would be best if you two stay close to home until this merger is finalized," he said.

Delaney's shoulders tensed. "For how long?"

"A few weeks at most. After that, things should calm down."

She nodded, though he could see she didn't like the restriction. "I'm supposed to meet my friend at the park tomorrow." She forced a smile. "It's fine. I'll cancel. Or...I don't have her number, but I'm sure she'll understand."

He hated for her to cancel. She didn't have any other friends in town. The park was public and crowded, but even so, he didn't like the idea of Charlotte and Delaney going there alone. "I'll take you."

"You probably would have spied on us anyway." Now, true amusement sparked in her eyes.

"Might as well just join you and meet your new friend."

"Thank you for doing that. What about Charlotte's dance class? We'll need to get an Uber."

"I'll be your chauffeur for a few weeks."

"I hate for you to—"

"Miss Wright, by hiring you, I've put you in danger."

"You didn't cut my brake line," she said. "Whoever did that is responsible, not you."

"Nevertheless, you wouldn't be a target if not for me. It's all right if it causes me a little inconvenience."

What if he was wrong about Lena being behind last night's wreck? What if Hayes had orchestrated it? If so, then Delaney could be collateral damage in a business war. But how would Hayes even know about Delaney, unless he had spies watching them?

Or was he working with Lena?

That thought sent a whole new fear churning inside him.

Either way, the danger circled back to him.

He needed to get this merger finalized and at least eliminate the war on one front.

Then he'd figure out how to deal with Lena.

All while keeping both Charlotte and her beautiful nanny safe.

CHAPTER SIXTEEN

The Thursday morning sun was deceivingly bright, considering the cool breeze that chilled Delaney's skin as she walked beside Mr. Aylett toward the park, Charlotte a few steps ahead of them. Her purse was ready with snacks and water, and he carried his laptop. Delaney's sternum still ached, but it was improving.

This should've been a relaxing outing, but the tension in Mr. Aylett's shoulders belied the peaceful surroundings. Every few steps, his gaze swept the area like he expected danger to emerge from behind the oak trees or the picnic pavilion. He reminded her of her bodyguard-cousin, Grant. No matter the surroundings, he was always on the lookout for threats.

They reached the playground, and Charlotte started to run.

Delaney grabbed her hand. "Wait. We need to go over the rules." She crouched to her eye level. "You have to stay where I can see you, within the playground." She pointed to the border between the soft mulch under the equipment and the grassy expanse beyond it. "Don't leave this area without my permission. Understand?"

Charlotte nodded solemnly, as if she had every intention of obeying. But Delaney knew better.

"Do you remember what happens if you disobey?"

The little girl's shoulders lifted and fell.

"We have to go home. So stay in the play area where you're safe, and we can play for a whole hour, okay?"

"Okay!" She ran for the swings, claimed one, and started pumping her legs.

Noah stopped to watch. "I didn't know she could do that."

"We've been working on it."

"That's amazing." He grinned at her. "It never occurred to me that she was old enough for that."

"I've been around kids more than you. Honestly, it makes my life easier when I don't have to push."

"I bet." He looked around, and she did, too, but Heather wasn't there yet.

"We're a little early," she said.

They walked to the bench closest to the play area and sat, watching Charlotte.

A question had been humming in Delaney's brain for a while. "What does her father do for work that keeps him away?"

"Jasper?" Noah's lips pinched closed. "Nothing."

"He must do something."

Mr. Aylett's scoff told her otherwise. "Mom and I did our best to try to straighten him out, but after Dad died, he just...fell apart. And then Mom died, and I tried to rein him in, but I... failed."

She was confused. "How old was he when your parents died?"

"He was fifteen when Dad died, twenty-two when Mom died."

"You're not that much older, right?"

"Three years."

"So you were...eighteen and twenty-five? Why did you feel like you were responsible for straightening him out?"

Mr. Aylett watched Charlotte swing for a few beats before he shrugged. "I've always felt responsible for him, even when we were little. Once, when he was five or six, I guess, we were at the beach. He had on those arm floats, you know what I mean?"

"I'm familiar."

"Anyway, he got too far out, and the tide was carrying him further. I was already out there, so I swam to him and pulled him back." Noah glanced her way.

"Impressive."

"It wasn't a big deal, but my mom went on like I'd saved his life. And my dad..." There was a pause, a sigh. "He took my shoulders and crouched down to meet my eyes and told me he was proud of me for protecting my little brother. That this was what big brothers did."

"Sure, when Jasper was five. When he was fifteen, you were only eighteen. It wasn't your job to save him. And certainly not when he was in his twenties. He was an adult."

"Still my brother."

"Well, yeah." She considered her words carefully, not wanting to offend him. "I used to take care of Kenzie a lot. But if I still felt responsible for her...I can't even imagine."

"It's not so easy to turn off."

Delaney watched Charlotte jog from the swings to the slides. "Children need to be protected. You've got to trust grown-ups to figure out their own lives."

"It's different with Jasper." Mr. Aylett seemed to be working through something, so she didn't argue. After a few moments, he continued. "We were on the boat, celebrating his fifteenth birthday. Dad was letting him pilot. He and Mom had gone belowdecks to make lunch. Jasper was a good sailor, but his friends were there, so he started showing off. He lifted the main sail. It was windy, and we started flying. I wasn't paying attention. I'd invited this girl, and she had on this little..." He sighed. "Doesn't matter. The point is, I should've been paying attention. Dad must've felt the speed because he came charging up the stairs, yelling at Jasper. Right when Jasper was shifting the boom."

"Oh, no." Delaney didn't know much about sailing, but she knew enough that worry pooled in her midsection.

"Yeah. Dad got hit. He wasn't wearing a life jacket. He went over and just...sank."

She gripped his arm. "I'm so sorry."

He looked at her hand, and she pulled it away, embarrassed that she'd touched him.

"Jasper blamed himself." Mr. Aylett sighed, the sound seeming to come from deep inside. "I blamed him, too, at first. But it wasn't Jasper's fault. Dad didn't follow his own rules— always observe the deck before you move, always wear a life jacket. Dad let his anger distract him, and it cost him his life."

Her heart hurt for what Mr. Aylett and his family had gone through. "But all that logic didn't change how Jasper felt."

"No." He stretched his legs and shifted, moving a few inches away from her. "He's never been the same. And yeah, what happened after that is partially my fault. I should never have said the things I said."

"You were a kid."

"I was eighteen."

"So, a kid. And you were grieving too. You can't take responsibility for everyone."

"I should've—"

"Noah." She hadn't meant to use his first name, but it slipped out.

He faced her, a thousand emotions playing in his eyes, there and gone before she could name them.

"At some point, Jasper has to be responsible for himself and his own choices. That's not your problem."

His gaze drifted back to Charlotte, so hers did too.

A group of kids had come, their shouts and screams a cacophony disturbing the quiet.

"I told him I wanted to adopt her."

Delaney whipped her attention back to Mr. Aylett. "Wow. That's quite a commitment. But, let's face it, you're already her father. You definitely should."

"He shut me down. Swears he's going to figure it out."

"Oh." She turned back to the playground, disappointed for Noah and the sweet little girl who loved him so much. She was about to ask what Jasper's plan was, but Heather was rushing toward them.

"Sorry I'm late!" She reached the bench, her gaze flicking to Mr. Aylett. "You brought reinforcements."

"This is Charlotte's uncle, Noah Aylett." Delaney gestured between them. "Mr. Aylett, Heather Brown."

He stood and extended his hand. "Nice to meet you, Heather."

"Likewise."

"Are you from Driftwood originally?"

"Baltimore, actually. I moved here this year."

"Why Driftwood?"

She looked around, her gaze taking in the pretty park and the charming downtown area. "I needed a change. The city wasn't...good for me."

He nodded as if that made perfect sense. "It's a nice community." He turned to Delaney. "I'll sit at that picnic table." He nodded to the closest one, maybe thirty feet from the edge of the play area, where he could work and keep an eye on the crowd.

"We'll let you know if we need anything."

He walked away, and Heather took his seat on the bench.

"What's up with him?" her friend asked, voice low as if he might hear.

"I was in a car accident a couple days ago, so he came in case I needed help."

"Oh, no. What happened?"

"I had some trouble with my brakes and ended up hitting a tree." Delaney didn't want to go into the details. "I'm fine, just a little bruised. Speaking of, I thought I might have to cancel, but I didn't have your number."

They traded contact information. When Delaney was finished tapping Heather's number into her phone, she looked up to see her friend watching Mr. Aylett, who'd opened his laptop but was looking around.

"Kind *and* handsome," Heather said. "Not a bad combo."

He was both, but Delaney didn't want to talk about that, either. "How about you? Dating anyone?"

Her friend's cheeks pinked. "I have been seeing this guy. He's so sweet."

Happy to have the conversation off of herself, Delaney leaned in and matched Heather's lowered volume. "Tell me about him."

"He's so handsome and just..." She sighed, her eyes taking on a dreamy quality that reminded Delaney of childhood conversations with her sisters. "He's older than I am, but I don't care about that. I just care that he's kind and generous, and really sees me, you know? Like...I've told him about all my mistakes, and he doesn't care. None of that matters to him."

Delaney didn't know what mistakes Heather was referring to, and her friend didn't explain. "Why are we whispering?"

Heather's gaze darted around the park as if spies lurked everywhere. "He's about to be single, but he's not...technically."

"He's married?" Her heart sank. Her friend had fallen for the oldest trick in the book.

"It's not what you think. He really loves me, and he's going to leave his wife soon. Before the end of the year, he said. And then we're going to get married."

"I see. He lives here, in town?"

"Virginia City. But we usually meet outside of Norfolk, where I live. Omigosh, Delaney, he's paying for my apartment. That's how I know he really loves me. It's so pretty. I can see the water from the balcony, and the beach is right there. I can walk all the way down to this pretty golf course, where the grass is so green it almost looks fake." Her eyes were wide as if she'd never seen such a thing. "He says we can live in that apartment full-time after he leaves his wife. It's little, but I don't care."

As Heather spoke, her accent became more defined, even a little...twangy.

"I can't wait until we can go out in public together, you know?" Heather said. "Like a real couple?"

"Yeah, I'm...sure."

"I know what you're thinking." Heather's expression darkened, and her voice turned hard. "It's not like... You don't know him."

Delaney wanted to tell her friend that she was being used, that he was never going to leave his wife. That if he was unfaithful to one woman, what made her think he'd be faithful to *her*?

But Heather obviously wasn't interested in her opinion, and sharing it would only put a wedge between her and the only friend she had.

So she smiled. "How'd you meet him?"

"Through work," Heather said. "He's a client at the firm."

Charlotte's delighted squeal drew Delaney's attention. The little girl was hanging from the first monkey bar, her face scrunched with concentration as she tried to reach the second one.

"You can do it!" Delaney called. "Remember what we practiced!"

Charlotte managed two more bars before dropping to the mulch with a triumphant grin. She immediately ran back to try again.

"She's adorable," Heather said. "You like your job?"

"I do. I tried something else after college. Moved to Boston, got a job at an insurance company."

"Not for you?"

She laughed, though nothing about that time was funny. "Crashed and burned. I hated it. I was determined to stay for a year, and I quit after a few months and went back to Maine."

"Was it the city, or the job?"

"Yes to all," Delaney said. "I know being a nanny isn't like a...high-powered profession, but it's what I'm good at."

"It's also incredibly important," Heather said.

Delaney was formulating a response when Charlotte jumped down from the monkey bars and wandered to the edge of the play area. And then she took off across the soft grass.

"Sorry. I gotta—"

"Go ahead."

Delaney jogged across the play area, keeping Charlotte in sight as the little girl aimed for the woods that bordered one side of the park.

"Charlotte!" she called, but the child didn't slow down. That wasn't unusual. She had a habit of climbing into her own imagination, blocking out the real world. It was something Delaney had told her counselor about.

Delaney's chest hurt with each stride, but she pushed through the pain to keep Charlotte in view.

Charlotte reached the edge of the woods and plunged into

the undergrowth. Branches caught at her pink sweater as she disappeared between the trees.

"Charlotte!" Delaney's voice came out sharp, panic rising in her throat. She'd promised to stay in the play area. They'd talked about this.

It was bad enough she'd disobeyed, but Mr. Aylett was watching, probably horrified she'd let his niece get so far away.

She followed Charlotte into the woods, pushing aside low-hanging branches that seemed determined to slow her down. The earthy smell of decomposing leaves filled her nostrils.

"Come here, sweetheart. We need to go back to the playground."

Charlotte stopped about twenty feet ahead and crouched beside something on the ground. Delaney picked her way carefully through the uneven terrain.

"Look, Miss Laney!" She held up a cluster of fuzzy green berries, her face bright with discovery. "They're so pretty."

"Charlotte Rose Aylett." She used her sternest nanny voice. "You are not supposed to leave the play area."

Her little eyes went wide with surprise. "There was a butterfly."

Delaney reached her and scooped her up into her arms despite the pain.

"I wanna look at the berries!" Charlotte wailed, her small fists pounding against Delaney's shoulders. She wiggled to be put down. "Let me go!"

Delaney held on. She didn't attempt to reason with her or calm her down, just carried her back toward the playground.

When they reached the edge of the forest, she caught sight of Mr. Aylett hurrying toward them. She shook her head and lifted one hand in the universal sign for *Stop*. She needed Charlotte to obey her, not because he was there but because she was in charge.

He froze a good distance away.

She shifted so Charlotte couldn't see her uncle, set her on the grass, and crouched to her level.

Tears dripped from Charlotte's eyes, and her cheeks were damp and red with anger. "I was just playing."

"I know that, but you need to follow the rules. I love you, and I want you to be safe, which is why I will never let you run away. Because you disobeyed, we have to go home now."

She stood and took Charlotte's hand, not wanting to lift her again. As it was, her sternum was throbbing. But the child tried to tug away, then plopped on the ground.

Delaney bent to pick her up.

"I got her." Mr. Aylett must've jogged because he was right there. He lifted her and held her against his hip, his focus on Delaney. "Do you want me to take her home so you can finish your chat with your friend?"

"Absolutely not." She was embarrassed enough to have let Charlotte run off—and to have required help carrying her. She needed to redeem the situation. "Let me just tell Heather good-bye, and I'll be right back."

She was still a good twenty feet away from her new friend when Heather called, "We'll do it again!" She waved and headed the other direction.

At least she was the understanding sort.

There was no opportunity to apologize to Mr. Aylett on the way to the house, thanks to Charlotte's crying.

When they arrived, he carried Charlotte inside while Delaney followed. Charlotte's tantrum had subsided into sullen sniffles by the time they crossed the threshold, but her little face remained damp with tears.

"I'll take her upstairs for her nap," Delaney said, reaching for the child.

"I've got her," Mr. Aylett said. "It's time for you to rest."

Before she could argue, he headed for the staircase, Charlotte's head on his shoulder.

Delaney stood in the entryway, listening to their footsteps fade down the hallway above.

The outing had been a disaster. She'd failed to keep Charlotte contained, had needed Mr. Aylett's help to bring her back, and now couldn't even manage the aftermath of the tantrum.

She made her way to the kitchen and filled a glass with water, then swallowed two Tylenol.

She settled on a kitchen chair. A few minutes later, at the sound of Mr. Aylett's steps on the hardwood, she pushed to her feet.

"She's already asleep," he said as he entered the kitchen.

"I want to apologize. I should have watched Charlotte more carefully."

Mr. Aylett's lips quirked. "She's remarkably quick when she wants to be."

"That's no excuse. I told her to stay within the play area, but she just gets into her own world and seems to forget the rules."

"You never took your eyes off her, and the second she started running, you were running after her."

"I shouldn't have been so far away."

"Was she ever out of your eyesight?"

"No, but—"

"It was a difficult situation, and perhaps in the future, you should shadow her more closely until she learns to follow the rules."

"You're right, of course. And I hate that I couldn't carry her."

"You were in a serious accident. Of course you couldn't." He got himself a glass of water and took a sip. "How are you feeling?"

"I'm fine."

One eyebrow arched skeptically, looking pointedly at her hand, which was pressed against her chest.

"It hurts a little."

He stepped into the living room, grabbed the throw pillow she'd hugged the day before, and handed it to her. "You don't have to pretend."

She held it to her chest. She had no idea why the pillow helped, but it did, almost as much as his kindness. "You're being too easy on me."

"From where I sit, you're hard enough on yourself for both of us." He chuckled, shaking his head. "Besides, do you have any idea how many times Charlotte took off on me when she first came to live here? I lost her in that same park once for a good five minutes. Scared me to death. I had every mama there helping me look. And don't think they didn't lecture me about my failures that day, as if I didn't already know I wasn't cut out to be her guardian."

"You are, though. You're doing great."

"Well." He took a breath and blew it out. "So are you, and from where I sat, you did everything you could to keep her safe. Sometimes, all we can do is our best and then trust the Lord with the rest."

His words sent a wave of emotion through her. It was exactly what she believed, even if she didn't always apply the lesson to herself. It was the reason she was so careful to pray about her job and the kids she watched. "Thank you for your grace."

"Where would we be without it?" He drank the rest of his water and glanced toward the entry. "If you're okay to stay here alone for a few hours, I have to go to the office. The tech team wants to show me the latest updates, and then we're getting on a conference call with Tidewater."

"Of course. We don't have anywhere else to go today."

"I'll pick up dinner tonight, so don't cook anything."

"I can—"

"I know you *can*. But instead, why don't you get some rest, hmm."

Her eyelids were heavy, her body begging to lie down. The fact that her employer knew it, the fact that he'd been so kind in the face of her mistakes...

Mr. Aylett was making it very difficult to remember their deal. All the feelings she was *not* supposed to have for her boss were bubbling to the surface, and she didn't know how much longer she would be able to keep them hidden.

Delaney settled on the edge of Charlotte's bed. The child had slept less than an hour after Mr. Aylett had gone to the office, waking up with a whimper Delaney was lucky to hear as she rested in her own room.

Now, she pressed the back of her hand to Charlotte's forehead, alarm shooting through her as heat radiated against her skin. Charlotte had been fine at the park.

Now red welts dotted her cheeks and neck, spreading down her arms. Her eyes were glassy with fever as she curled into a ball on her rumpled sheets.

"My face hurts." She reached toward the inflamed patches.

"Don't scratch, sweetheart." Delaney gently caught her hands. "Let me see."

The rash was raised. Delaney lifted Charlotte's shirt and saw more on her torso.

Food allergies? But Charlotte had eaten the same lunch she always did. A reaction to laundry detergent? They'd been using the same brand for weeks. The fever made it more concerning— this wasn't just a topical irritation.

Maybe something in the woods. Whatever it was, it was serious.

Should she call Mr. Aylett? No. He'd specifically mentioned a meeting with Tidewater this afternoon about the merger. She didn't want to disturb him. And also, after all the help she'd needed that day, she wanted to prove she was competent all by herself.

She pulled out her phone and scrolled to Charlotte's pediatrician's number.

A receptionist answered with, "Driftwood Family Medicine."

"This is Delaney Wright. I'm calling about Charlotte Aylett. I'd like to speak to her doctor's nurse."

She waited not so patiently until the woman came on the line. Delaney explained the situation, then said, "I was hoping you could get her in."

"I wish we could," the woman said. "Unfortunately, this late in the day, we're booked up. The earliest we could see her would be tomorrow morning."

Delaney's stomach dropped. "What do you recommend?"

"Hold on. Let me check with the doctor."

While Delaney waited, she found the thermometer and took Charlotte's temperature.

A hundred and one, which wouldn't worry Delaney if not for the sudden rash.

The nurse came back on the line. "The doctor wants you to take her to the emergency room."

"Okay, thanks." Delaney ended the call, seeing Charlotte scratching her arms. "Don't scratch, love." She gently moved Charlotte's hands.

"It itches."

"I know. We're going to get you some help." Delaney called for an Uber, then gathered Charlotte's insurance card and a snack. She called Mr. Aylett's office and left a message with his assistant.

"I don't want you to interrupt him, but let him know I'm taking Charlotte to the ER because of a rash. It's probably nothing, so don't alarm him."

She hung up, praying she was right, that the sudden fever and rash weren't anything serious.

An hour later, Delaney sat in the emergency room waiting area with Charlotte curled against her side, her fever-warm body radiating heat through Delaney's sweater and jeans. The welts had spread, creeping up Charlotte's neck toward her jawline in angry red patches.

"I don't like it here." Charlotte's voice was barely louder than a whisper.

"I know, sweetheart. But the doctors are going to help you feel better." Delaney smoothed damp curls away from Charlotte's forehead, trying to project calm while her own anxiety spiked.

A woman across from them bounced a crying baby while a toddler climbed over the plastic chairs. An elderly man in the corner dozed, his head against the window behind him. The waiting area buzzed with the low hum of worry and pain, and Delaney prayed for Charlotte and everyone else who needed medical care.

"Charlotte Aylett?" A nurse appeared at the reception desk, clipboard in hand.

"That's us." Delaney gathered their things and urged Charlotte to walk with her.

The nurse led them through a maze of hallways to a small

examination room painted a cheerful yellow. Charlotte clung to Delaney's hand as the nurse took her vitals.

"Her temp's one oh one point three." She glanced at the rash. "That looks uncomfortable." At Charlotte's nod, she said, "The doctor will fix you right up." To Delaney, she said, "He'll be in soon."

When the door closed behind the nurse, Charlotte's lip trembled. "Where's Uncle Noah?"

"He's at work, sweetheart. I left him a message." Maybe she should have called him on his cell phone rather than calling the office. But he'd specifically told her he'd be busy this afternoon. He'd already sacrificed enough time with them that morning, and Delaney could handle a trip to the ER.

Delaney stroked Charlotte's hair, careful to avoid the red patches that now mottled her forehead. "He'll come as fast as he can."

"I want him now," Charlotte whispered, her voice cracking.

The raw need in those four words squeezed Delaney's heart. Despite all their progress, despite Charlotte's growing attachment to her, in moments of crisis, she still wanted the one person who had proved he would never abandon her.

"I know, love. I know." Delaney gently held the girl's hands to keep her from scratching.

Charlotte leaned against Delaney's side on the exam table, her small body trembling. The paper crinkled beneath them as Delaney stroked her hair, humming a hymn her mother had sung when she was sick.

"I'm sorry I ran away," Charlotte whispered, her voice small and scratchy. "I was just playing with the butterflies."

"I know, sweetheart. I forgive you."

A soft knock preceded the door opening. A young doctor with dark hair and a strong jaw stepped in, his white coat crisp over blue scrubs. "I'm Dr. Wright," he said.

"Wright? That's my last name too."

He smiled, his eyes crinkling at the corners as he extended his hand. "I'm Ethan, probably your distant cousin."

"Delaney." She shook his hand. The man seemed genuinely kind, his grip gentle and firm.

He focused on the patient. "And you must be Charlotte. I hear you're not feeling so great today."

Charlotte pressed closer to Delaney, eyeing the doctor warily.

"She was fine before her nap, but she woke up with the fever and the rash."

"Do you mind if I have a look?" Dr. Wright directed the question at Charlotte. When she shrugged one shoulder, he studied the welts on her face and neck, then those on her arms. "Anywhere else?" he asked Delaney.

"Her stomach."

He checked, then looked at her throat and ears. Delaney held Charlotte's hand throughout the examination, murmuring reassurances.

"Has she been anywhere unusual recently?" Dr. Wright asked. "Playing outside, maybe?"

"We were at the park this morning," Delaney said. "She ran into the woods."

"I wasn't s'posed to."

"I see." Dr. Wright nodded thoughtfully. "Did you touch any pretty plants?"

"Uh-huh. I found green berries with fuzzy on 'em."

"Ah." He looked at Delaney as if she should have had the same realization he just did.

"Ah...what?"

"Poison oak."

"Really? What does it look like?"

He squinted as if she'd surprised him. "Where are you from that you don't know poison oak?"

"Maine. We have poison ivy."

He studied her for so long that she started to feel uncomfortable. Then, he seemed to shake off whatever had distracted him. He pulled out his phone, tapped the screen, then lifted it to show Charlotte. "Is that what you saw?"

"Uh-huh."

He angled so Delaney could see green berries and their leafy little bushes. Charlotte had been plopped right in the middle of a big clump of those a couple of hours ago. "Poison oak?" she confirmed.

"Yup. Little Charlotte's having an extreme reaction." He focused on the child. "I know the berries are pretty, but you need to stay away from them. They're poisonous."

Her eyes rounded. "Am I gonna die?"

"Nope." He smiled to calm her. "You're just gonna be uncomfortable."

She accepted that, nodding around the thumb she'd stuck in her mouth.

"I'm going to prescribe an antihistamine to help with the itching and hydrocortisone cream for the rash. I recommend oat and baking soda baths to soothe her skin." Dr. Wright confirmed the pharmacy, then tapped into the computer at the edge of the room. "I'm also going to give her a low dose of prednisone to reduce the swelling and speed up healing. Since the reaction is so severe and she has a fever, I'll add an antibiotic as well."

Delaney nodded, feeling both relieved and guilty. She should have caught Charlotte before she'd touched those plants. On the other hand, she wouldn't have known to steer her away. "How long until she starts feeling better?"

"The antihistamines should help with the itching within an hour, but the rash itself will take several days to clear up completely." He turned from the computer. "I've sent them straight there, so hopefully you won't have to wait long. Make sure she doesn't scratch. It can lead to infection."

"I'll do my best." Delaney glanced at Charlotte, who was trying to rub her arm against the exam table.

Dr. Wright smiled at Charlotte. "The medicine will make the itching better soon, I promise. You were very brave today, but next time, stay out of the woods, okay?"

"'Kay," she said around her thumb.

"You did the right thing bringing her in," Dr. Wright said to Delaney. "With reactions this severe, it's wise to be safe."

"Thank you." She felt better knowing she'd made the right call.

He hesitated, then asked, "Where in Maine are you from? I've got distant family up there."

"Shadow Cove."

A spark of interest lit in his eyes, but he said, "Never heard of it. It's on the coast, I guess?" Odd that his words didn't seem to match his reaction.

"Yeah, near Portland."

"I'm sure it's lovely." His head tilted to the side. "Are you all right?"

She realized her hand was pressed against her sternum. "It's just a bruise. Car accident."

"Okay, well, let me know if it starts to hurt worse. We could do an X-ray." He lifted Charlotte down from the table, saving Delaney from having to do it. "I'll walk you two out."

In the waiting area, Delaney spotted a familiar figure striding through the automatic doors, his face tight with concern. Mr. Aylett scanned the room, his gray eyes finding her and Charlotte immediately. Relief washed over his features, and then his expression hardened.

Uh-oh. He was angry.

CHAPTER SEVENTEEN

"Uncle Noah!" Charlotte's voice carried across the emergency room waiting area, her small face lighting up when she spotted him.

His relief had evaporated as quickly as it'd come when he'd spotted Delaney talking to a doctor.

Noah crossed the waiting room in long strides, then lifted Charlotte into his arms. She had an angry rash on her cheeks, and she burned with fever, adding more ammunition to his irritation. She clung to him.

"I touched poison plants," she whispered against his neck.

"I see that, Charlie-Bear." He held her tightly, staring at Delaney, who was chatting blissfully with the too-young, too-handsome doctor. They'd been talking when he walked in, the doctor smiling down at her like she was the most fascinating person he'd ever met.

And why wouldn't he find her fascinating? She was beautiful, kind, and clearly good with children. Everything about her invited attention. Attention she was supposed to be giving Charlotte, not some random doctor.

As Noah approached, the man managed to drag his eyes

away from the nanny to focus on him. He extended his hand. "Dr. Ethan Wright. You must be Mr. Aylett."

Noah shook the doctor's hand harder than necessary. The guy couldn't be more than thirty. Was he even old enough to have completed medical school?

"What's going on with Charlotte?"

"Severe reaction to poison oak. She'll be fine with the medication I've prescribed." Dr. Wright's professional demeanor never wavered, but something flickered in his eyes— amusement, maybe? "The rash should start clearing up in a few days."

Amazing that the man had looked away from Miss Wright long enough to figure that out. How long had they been talking before he got there?

"She touched some berries in the woods this morning," Delaney said, her voice carefully neutral. "I should have recognized what they were."

"You're not from around here," Dr. Wright said, that same warm smile returning as he looked at her. "Poison oak doesn't grow in Maine."

How did he know where she was from? Noah felt a headache forming and realized he was clenching his jaw. Had she been sharing her life story with this stranger while Charlotte scratched her rash and burned with fever?

"The important thing is that she got medical attention quickly," Dr. Wright continued. "Delaney made the right call bringing her in."

And where did he get off calling her by her first name?

Charlotte shifted in Noah's arms, pressing her hot forehead against his neck. Her skin felt like fire, and his anger burned just as hot.

"Thank you for taking care of her," Noah forced himself to say, though the words tasted bitter. He needed to get Charlotte home, away from this place, away from the doctor who couldn't seem to stop looking at Noah's employee.

"Of course." Dr. Wright's attention shifted back to Delaney. "Take care of yourself too. Ice packs should help."

Noah's gaze snapped to Delaney, noticing the hand she pressed against her sternum. He'd been so focused on his irritation that he'd forgotten she was still recovering.

"I'm fine," she said quickly, but Noah caught the slight wince as she adjusted her purse strap.

"Well, if either of you needs anything..." Dr. Wright let the offer hang in the air, his eyes lingering on Delaney's face.

Noah turned away before he could tell the too-helpful doctor what he thought of that open offer. "We should go."

He carried Charlotte toward the exit, not bothering to check if Delaney was following. Of course she was—where else would she go? The automatic doors slid open, and the late afternoon air hit his face, cooler than the stifling atmosphere inside.

"Uncle Noah?" Charlotte's voice was small against his ear. "Are you mad at me?"

The question stopped him cold. He'd been so wrapped up in his anger at Delaney—and that doctor—that he hadn't considered how his mood might affect his niece.

"No, sweetheart. Not at you." Noah softened his voice. He pressed a kiss to her feverish forehead. "Never at you."

He glanced back and saw that Miss Wright walked a few paces behind, her face pale, one hand still pressed to her chest. His anger had nowhere to land. He couldn't be mad at Charlotte. He shouldn't be mad at the nanny. And being angry at some random doctor for finding her attractive was...absurd.

All that logic didn't make his irritation go away.

He settled Charlotte into her car seat while Delaney slid into the passenger seat.

"We need to stop at the pharmacy."

"Which one?" He started the engine.

"He sent it to the one on Cedar Street."

Noah pulled out of the parking lot, his knuckles white against the steering wheel. "I'm glad you had the opportunity to make a new friend while my niece was suffering."

The words were petty and unfair. He knew it even as they left his mouth.

Delaney's head snapped to him, her eyes widening. "I'm sorry. What?"

"Nothing." Noah merged onto the main road, his grip still tight on the wheel. Telling himself to shut up. But he wasn't listening to the right voice today. "I just found it interesting that you didn't interrupt my meeting for Charlotte's emergency, but you had plenty of time to chat with Dr. Dreamy."

"I didn't interrupt your meeting because you said it was important, and I had it managed." Her volume was low, her tone tense. "I left a message with your assistant to deliver when you were finished. Which he obviously did."

Right. He had told her about the merger meeting with Tidewater's board members. Lowell and his minions had peppered him with technical questions more suited to his team. Another reason for his bad mood.

"I'm not sure what the problem is here, Mr. Aylett."

His problem? His problem was that he was jealous, plain and simple. Dr. Wright was closer to her age, handsome, accomplished, and didn't come with baggage shaped like a traumatized four-year-old girl. He hadn't been wearing a wedding ring either, a fact Noah figured Miss Wright had already noticed.

"My problem is that you promised not to leave the house alone," he said instead. "You could have been followed. After what happened with your car—"

"It was an emergency." Miss Wright's tone was measured with an edge of steel beneath it. "I called her doctor. I was told to take her to the ER, so that's what I did. I didn't interrupt your meeting because we didn't need your help, and you didn't need to sit in the waiting room for two hours. And since we arrived in an Uber, unless someone was watching the house, we couldn't have been followed. Anything else?"

Charlotte started to fuss in the backseat, and Miss Wright turned. "You okay, love? You want some water?"

"Uh-huh."

She pulled a small plastic bottle from her purse, opened it, and handed it back. "Be careful with it."

How did she have a bottle of water in her purse? She probably had snacks in there, too, and a first-aid kit, and anything else Charlotte might need.

She was better at taking care of his niece than he'd ever be, and here he was, acting like a jerk.

"It's the pharmacy up here on the left," she said.

He flicked on his blinker, then turned into the lot and parked. "I'll be right back."

"I can—"

"I got it." He stepped out of the car and slammed the door.

In line at the counter at the back of the store, he took a few deep breaths. He needed to get over his irrational anger. He had no right to feel jealous. Miss Wright was his employee, nothing else.

Yet his insides squeezed at the thought of her spending time with the handsome doctor who shared her last name.

CHAPTER EIGHTEEN

Delaney pushed her Chinese takeout around her plate, stealing glances at Mr. Aylett across the kitchen table. He'd picked up dinner on the way home, but despite his thoughtfulness, a chill colder than a Maine winter had settled between them.

He asked polite questions about Charlotte's medicine, which Delaney answered just as politely. Meanwhile, Charlotte chattered about her itchy skin and whether the rash would be gone by dance class. The fever was already lower, though it might climb back up. At least she seemed unaware of the tension.

But Delaney felt Mr. Aylett's every measured word, every controlled response. Gone was the man who'd shown her such grace at the park that morning. In his place sat a stranger, polite and distant as a hotel concierge.

What had she done wrong?

The question gnawed at her as she prepared Charlotte's bath using a recipe she found on the internet. She'd ground oatmeal in an old food processor she assumed had belonged to Mr. Aylett's mother, then added baking soda. She stepped out when Mr. Aylett carried Charlotte in, giving Delaney a tight nod she took as forced gratitude.

What was his problem? She'd made the right medical decision—even Dr. Wright had said so.

Unless...

The thought crept in as she loaded the dinner dishes into the dishwasher.

Was Mr. Aylett jealous?

Surely not. After all, the doctor had been friendly, but not in a romantic way. He'd mentioned they might be long-lost cousins. Not exactly a pickup line.

Still, the way Mr. Aylett's jaw had tightened when he'd seen them talking together, plus his petty accusation in the car... He'd acted like he'd caught her in some sort of betrayal.

But *jealous*?

The possibility sent an unwelcome flutter to her middle. If he was jealous, that meant he saw her as more than just Charlotte's caregiver. It meant the moments on the porch swing, the way his eyes lingered on her sometimes when he thought she wasn't looking, the careful distance he maintained—it all added up to something...unexpected.

But unwelcome?

No.

Yes. Unwelcome. Even if her thoughts toward him had drifted from those of an employee for her boss. She respected him. She admired him. She *liked* him.

Most of the time, anyway.

He was a good man.

She closed the dishwasher and wiped the table and countertops.

Even if Mr. Aylett were interested, she was his employee. That power dynamic made any relationship inappropriate, not to mention the disaster it would create if things went wrong. She needed this job. And Charlotte needed stability.

Whatever was going on with Mr. Aylett, Delaney must get it out in the open—as soon as possible. Though she'd prefer to hide in her bedroom for the rest of the evening, she settled on the couch in the living room to wait for him to return after putting Charlotte to bed.

She scrolled through messages from her sisters. Cici was looking at properties in downtown Shadow Cove, wanting to open a jewelry store. Alyssa sent a picture of her future step-daughter, Peri, in her little cheerleading uniform. Normal lives in a normal place where brake lines didn't get cut and stalkers didn't lurk in parking lots and woods weren't filled with poison plants that sent children to the ER.

Delaney had ignored her sisters' messages for months, but once she was settled, she'd started interacting with them again. They didn't know where she was—they'd be on the first flight here if they did. Mom knew, and that was enough.

Delaney's chest squeezed, not just from the accident, but from homesickness. Maybe she should go back to Maine, and not just for Christmas. Maybe she should give up—and prove that her father had been right all along. She couldn't hack life on her own.

But she *was* hacking it. She wasn't willing to give up on this job because of Mr. Aylett's bizarre behavior.

A few minutes later, his footsteps on the stairs sent that acid-drop feeling to her stomach. She was going to confront him —and deal with the consequences.

He appeared in the doorway, sleeves rolled up and hair slightly mussed.

"She's in bed." His voice was carefully neutral. "The oatmeal bath seemed to help with the itching. I think the other medicine was already making her sleepy."

"Hopefully, the rash won't keep her awake." She stood and took a breath, gathering her courage, but he spoke before she had a chance.

"I want to apologize for my behavior earlier. I realize now that you did the right thing taking her, and you didn't tell me because I'd told you about my meeting. In the future, if Charlotte goes to the emergency room, please alert me right away."

The apology was practiced and formal, so different from the camaraderie they'd shared before.

She adopted a similar tone. "I apologize for not calling you directly. I'll do that from now on."

He dipped his head and looked like he was ready to walk away.

"But I was hoping we could talk..."

His phone rang, and she could swear she saw relief in his expression. He lifted it to his ear.

"This is Noah." He listened, then said, "What time?" then, "I'll be there in five." He ended the call. "There was a break-in at the office. I need to go."

He walked away. A moment later, the front door closed.

If she didn't know better, she'd wonder if he'd orchestrated that interruption to avoid the awkward conversation they needed to have.

Frustrated, she headed to her room. It would keep until tomorrow.

A scream woke Delaney from a sound sleep.

She sat up, instantly alert. Normally, when Charlotte woke in the night, Mr. Aylett tended to her, but she hadn't heard him return. She hurried down the hallway.

Charlotte was standing beside her bed, eyes wide but unfocused. She was babbling, though her words made no sense.

Delaney had dealt with night terrors in children before, so she had an idea of what to do. "It's okay. You're safe." She approached slowly and kept her voice low and soothing, not trying to wake Charlotte but just to interrupt whatever had gripped her in her sleep.

Charlotte quieted, still standing motionless.

Delaney crouched next to her and placed a hand on her shoulder. "You're safe, love. You're safe."

She moved the covers out of the way, then gently lifted Charlotte and placed her back in bed, her head on the pillow. "There you go. Go back to sleep."

Charlotte never fully woke up, just curled on her side, tucked her hands beneath her head, and closed her eyes.

Delaney sat beside her, brushing her hair away from her face. "*Turn your eyes upon Jesus...*" She sang the old hymn quietly, barely above a whisper. "*Look full in His wonderful face...*"

She continued to sing, wondering what had caused Charlotte's middle-of-the-night terror. She hated to think about the adults who'd failed to protect this precious child in the past.

Delaney would not be one of those adults.

Help me protect her, Lord. Please, don't make me leave here. She needs me...and I need her.

She continued the hymn, one her mother used to sing to her when she was afraid, repeating it until Charlotte's breathing settled into the rhythm of sleep.

Delaney rose quietly from the bed and turned toward the doorway.

A tall silhouette filled the frame, and her heart leapt into her throat.

It was Mr. Aylett, still wearing his shirt and tie. His broad shoulders filled the space.

"Sorry." His voice barely rose above a whisper. "I didn't want to startle you." He stepped aside, and she moved into the hallway, pulling Charlotte's door nearly closed behind her.

"Have you dealt with night terrors before?" he asked.

"A child I watched back in Maine had them. They're fairly common. I didn't know you were home."

"I was just walking in when she cried out. I came to check, but you had it under control. You've got a way with her."

She shrugged. "It's not too hard to calm kids down when they're already half asleep. Do you have any idea what might have led to them? I mean, sometimes they seem random. I guess they're not always the result of an event, or at least not one that they can articulate."

Mr. Aylett's expression darkened. "Her early childhood wasn't...ideal. Before she came to live with me."

Charlotte's night terrors weren't random. They were echoes of trauma, fears that haunted her even in sleep.

His face looked tortured, and she had the urge to reach out and offer him comfort. "I'm sorry she's going through it." The words felt inadequate, but she didn't dare touch him. "And you too."

"Thanks." He ran a hand through his hair, something he did when he was frustrated.

"I'll ask her counselor about it," Delaney said. "Maybe she can help."

"How, if Charlotte doesn't even remember? I mean, whatever it was must've happened a while ago."

"You'd be amazed at what a good play therapist can learn."

"That would be..." But his words trailed, his voice rough with emotion. "I'm grateful for you."

They stood in the dim hallway, the house quiet around

them. Delaney suddenly became hyperaware of her state of undress—the thin cotton of her pajama pants, the way her oversized top hung loose on her frame. She crossed her arms. "Is everything okay at your office?"

His jaw tightened. "Someone broke in and did some damage to the equipment. Nothing was stolen, just...destroyed."

"Why? Who would do that?"

He sighed, the sound long-day weary. "A rival, I think. We just got the system perfect to show Tidewater, and now..." He shook his head. "It's fine. I'll deal with it."

"Okay. Well, good night, then." She turned toward her room.

"Miss Wright?" His voice was low and smooth, and though he didn't touch her, it felt like a caress. She turned back.

The hallway seemed to shrink around them, the space between their bodies suddenly charged with something electric and dangerous.

When he didn't speak, she asked, "Did you need something else?"

"I wanted to apologize. Again. For how I acted today. At the hospital, and in the car. It was...unprofessional."

It was. But so was standing in the hallway in the dark wearing pajamas.

"You were worried about Charlotte. I understand."

"No, you don't. Seeing you with that doctor made me feel..." His eyes searched hers, vulnerability written across his face.

She had no idea what she was supposed to say. She considered a few responses before settling on a simple explanation. "He was curious about my family in Maine. He thinks we might be related. It wasn't exactly...romantic." Not that Noah had suggested it was.

"Were you...did you mind, or...?"

"I'm not looking for romance."

He dipped his head and stepped back.

"You don't have to worry. Charlotte's my first priority."

It was the wrong thing to say. His expression darkened, and he looked almost...pained. "It wasn't that. It was... It doesn't matter. I had no right to feel the way I felt. You're my employee. Charlotte's nanny. Nothing more."

His words had the most irrational feeling draping over her. Disappointment.

"Of course." She needed to put a fine point on it, to make it clear where they both stood. "I don't think Dr. Wright had any interest in me"—he definitely hadn't, but she needed to clarify—"nor I him, but if he were to ask me out, you wouldn't mind if I said yes? If I went out with him when I'm off work?"

Mr. Aylett groaned, rubbing the back of his neck. The sound was barely audible, but it conveyed everything his words couldn't.

"I'd mind," he said finally, his voice strained.

The admission hung between them, words he couldn't take back. They were a live wire, an unexploded bomb. They could be the beginning of something.

Or they could destroy everything.

Delaney's pulse echoed in her ears. She should step back, should retreat to her room, and pretend this conversation had never happened.

"Mr. Aylett—"

"Noah." His voice was rough. "Please?"

Calling him by his first name felt dangerous. But she couldn't seem to stop herself. "Noah."

Something shifted in his expression. His gaze dropped to her mouth. She saw the moment his restraint snapped.

"I'm sorry." But he was already moving forward, backing her gently against the wall. "I'm so sorry, but I can't..." He lifted his hands to frame her face, thumbs brushing across her cheekbones. "Tell me to stop, and I'll stop."

She should. She knew she should. But when she opened her mouth, no words came out. Instead, she found herself leaning in, tilting her face up toward his.

His lips met hers, a whisper of contact that sent electricity racing through her. She felt his breath catch as his hands slid into her hair. The wall was cold against her back, his body warm and solid before her, and for one perfect moment, everything else fell away.

Then he deepened the kiss. His lips moved over hers with growing urgency, the tension that had been building between them for weeks finding release. Her hands clutched his shoulders, feeling the crisp fabric of his shirt beneath her fingers as she pulled him closer.

This was madness. This was everything she shouldn't want and couldn't have.

This was exactly where she wanted to be.

When they finally broke apart, both breathing heavily, Delaney kept her eyes closed, afraid of what she might see in his expression. Regret? Dismissal? She couldn't bear either.

"I shouldn't have done that," Noah whispered, his voice rough.

Her eyes opened. His face was inches from hers, his expression a storm of conflicting emotions. But regret wasn't among them—at least, not the kind she'd feared.

"I'm your boss." His thumb traced the line of her jaw with exquisite care. "You work for me. This is…" But he didn't end the sentence, and she didn't want to name it either. Because it hadn't felt wrong.

It'd felt perfect.

He stepped back. "I'm your employer."

The formal title stung.

"That was unforgivable," he added, as if condemning himself might change his feelings. Or hers.

Delaney had feared seeing regret in his expression, but now she was consumed by it. She should have stopped him.

She hadn't, and now she'd probably lose her job. Like she'd already lost her heart.

She wrapped her arms around herself. "It wasn't," she said. "Unforgivable. Considering I didn't stop you." Kissing him back the way she had... "I was just as..." Involved. Invested.

Carried away.

It was impossible to meet his eyes, so she focused on Charlotte's partially open door.

Charlotte, the sweet, traumatized four-year-old who'd just woken from a nightmare. "She needs me."

"I know." He raked a hand through his hair. "I know." He took a step back. "Forgive me. Miss Wright."

Before she could respond, he swiveled and walked away, then disappeared into the room at the end of the hall. He closed the door softly, but the sound reverberated with the echo of their mistake.

CHAPTER NINETEEN

Noah finished shaving, having lingered over scrambled eggs with Charlotte.

Miss Wright had hurried through her meal as if she were late for a flight. Even in their short time together at breakfast, tension had stretched like a rubber band.

Two weeks had passed since that world-altering kiss, and he couldn't get it out of his mind.

He'd spent more time away than usual, thanks to the mess the vandals had made of the office. The intruders had opened client files and strewn their contents across the floor. Cubicle walls had been knocked down, desks flipped. Fortunately, most of his staff had taken their laptops home for the night, but the server had been bashed with a hammer.

The vandals had had a handful of minutes before the police arrived. They must've had a plan to inflict the maximum damage in the least amount of time.

Insurance would cover the cost of replacing the equipment, and the data was stored on an external server. He would never again tease his programmers for their obsession with backups.

The police had no solid leads. Four figures, probably men,

wearing coats and sweatshirts with the hoods up, had been caught on the security camera mounted over the door. He hadn't had cameras installed inside. Noah had felt that would be an invasion of his employees' privacy, but he regretted the decision now.

This wasn't the city. There'd be no CCTV footage of cars passing by or parked in front of or behind the row of businesses.

At this point, there were no leads beyond the words spray-painted across one wall: *Back out.*

Obviously, Hayes and his people were behind the break-in and vandalism. But Noah couldn't prove it.

And he wasn't going to be intimidated.

He finished shaving and chose clothes for the day, thinking of Charlotte.

Which inevitably brought him back to Delaney…

The sweet, innocent, alluring woman he couldn't get out of his head.

Not Delaney. *Miss Wright!*

His employee.

Somehow, though they lived under the same roof, they'd hardly interacted since their kiss, operating like the clockwork figurines in the antique clock in the foyer, moving through the same house without truly inhabiting the same space. When they ate breakfast every morning, she was thankful that he'd cooked and was always kind to Charlotte but hardly spoke to him. When he returned home in the evening, she gave a succinct report of Charlotte's day before retreating to her room.

She'd even quit eating dinner with them.

It was all very proper, very professional.

And it was driving him insane.

If anything, her careful distance had only intensified his attraction, sharpening every brief interaction into something almost painfully acute. He caught himself watching the way her hair fell across her shoulders as she bent to help Charlotte with her shoes, or how her eyes lit up when his niece made her laugh.

Noah finished dressing and checked his reflection in the bathroom mirror. The man looking back at him appeared casual and composed in his navy sweater and jeans. No one would guess his insides were tangled in knots.

"Uncle Noah!" Charlotte's voice carried up the stairs. "Miss Laney says it's time to go!"

He caught his smile in the mirror. It was Saturday, Miss Wright's day off, but he'd asked her to join him and Charlotte at the Founder's Day Festival. As the only person representing the Ayletts in town, Noah needed to be there. He had a few responsibilities today, and he didn't want to risk losing sight of Charlotte when he was distracted.

Plus, he craved Miss Wright's company, a fact he wasn't planning to examine right now. He'd use any excuse to spend time with her.

He grabbed his wallet and headed downstairs, where he found Charlotte bouncing on her toes by the front door. She wore her favorite purple dress with matching tights, her blond curls tied back with a matching ribbon.

Not only had her rash healed, she seemed to have filled out overnight. Unlike the too-small, too-thin waif who'd come to live with him, she looked like a healthy, happy four-year-old should.

Miss Wright had done that. Noah had played a part, but it was the nanny's careful attention that had helped Charlotte blossom into the vibrant, joyful child she was becoming.

"You look beautiful, Charlie-Bear."

"See my new boots?" She stuck one out, as if he might miss the pink cowboy boots.

"They're so pretty." His comment earned him a bright smile.

Miss Wright emerged a moment later, a small purse slung

across her body, her dark-blond hair swept back in a low pony-tail. She'd chosen a cream sweater and dark jeans and looked nothing like the slightly disheveled, smoke-scented woman who'd shown up on his doorstep a few months before.

This woman was effortlessly elegant, and Noah's traitorous heart swelled at the sight of her.

"Ready?" Her tone was pleasant but distant, the same careful politeness she'd maintained for two weeks.

"Let's go." He opened the door, gesturing for the ladies to precede him outside.

He and Miss Wright started down the sidewalk, Charlotte walking between them, holding each of their hands. She looked up at him. "Can I get face painting?"

"If Miss Wright doesn't mind. Remember, I have to do some boring stuff for a little while."

The November air carried the scent of wood smoke and fallen leaves. They turned the corner, heading for the park.

Downtown Driftwood had been transformed. White tents lined Main Street, and the sugary aroma of kettle corn drifted on the breeze. Families strolled between booths that displayed everything from handmade quilts to apple-cider donuts.

"Face painting sounds like fun." Miss Wright's words were overly bright, as if trying to speak over the tension.

Unlike the silence between him and the nanny, the noise of the festival increased as they closed the distance. Old friends calling out greetings, children laughing as they chased each other among booths. The local high school band was warming up near the bandstand.

This whole thing was about celebrating the heroism of Elijah Aylett, Noah's great-great-grandfather, who had spotted a ship capsizing during a storm and single-handedly rescued everyone aboard.

Generations later, the event had evolved into an excuse for

the town to gather before the holidays. It was one of the few Driftwood traditions Noah genuinely enjoyed—except for his own part in it.

"Noah Aylett!" Mayor Collins approached, hand extended, as they neared the bandstand on the edge of the park. "Right on time."

Noah shook his hand. "Mayor. Nice turnout."

"Best we've had in years." The mayor's gaze shifted to Miss Wright and Charlotte. "And who might these lovely ladies be?"

"This is my niece, Charlotte, and her nanny, Delaney Wright." Noah had asked Jasper if he minded the town learning that Charlotte was his niece. He'd replied with his typical casual attitude. "Go ahead and tell. It's not like they think I'm a saint."

True enough, and Noah was glad to squelch at least one baseless rumor.

The mayor bent down to Charlotte's level. "Well, hello there, Miss Charlotte. Are you enjoying the festival?"

Charlotte ducked behind Miss Wright's legs, peering out with wide eyes.

"She's a bit shy." Noah fought the urge to shield her from the mayor's overly enthusiastic greeting.

"No problem at all." Mayor Collins straightened and offered his hand to Miss Wright. "A pleasure to meet you as well."

"You too." Her tone was much warmer than any she'd used with Noah in the last two weeks.

"We should get you to the stage." The mayor checked his watch. "The ceremony starts in twenty."

"I'll be right there." When he walked away, Noah turned to Miss Wright. "I'll find you after the presentation. It shouldn't take more than thirty minutes."

"Take your time." She looked down at Charlotte. "We'll explore the festival, won't we? And find that face painting."

Charlotte was eyeing a booth selling cotton candy.

"No sugar until after lunch," Noah said automatically, earning an eye roll from his niece that made him smile. She'd picked up that particular expression from one of her new playmates, and while he should probably discourage it, he couldn't help finding it endearing.

"We'll stick to the crafts," Miss Wright assured him. "Good luck with your presentation."

He watched them walk away, Charlotte skipping beside her nanny, and felt that now-familiar pull in his gut. They looked like they belonged together—his family.

No. Not his, not Miss Wright. But he wanted her to be.

He'd been so focused on his inappropriate attraction to her that he hadn't fully processed the deeper truth. His desire for Miss Wright—Delaney—was more than physical. He wanted this—the three of them, together.

What was he supposed to do with that? Never mind that Miss Wright was from Maine and planned to go back there in a year. Never mind that she was too young for him—and far too innocent.

Even if both of those things weren't true, she was his employee. It wasn't...fittin', as Granny Aylett used to say.

Miss Wright and Charlotte disappeared around a corner, and he shook off his crazy thoughts, then glanced around, hoping nobody had spied him staring at his niece's nanny like some kind of lovesick teenager.

He headed for the bandstand. Rows of folding chairs faced it, most already filled.

He was just about to start up the bandstand steps when a woman stepped into his path. Long brown hair, large hazel eyes. She was attractive and somewhat familiar, though he couldn't place her.

"Noah Aylett, the man of the hour." Her words came out breathy as she tucked a strand of hair behind her ear, sending a waft of perfume his way. "You probably don't remember me, but we met at a fundraising dinner last spring."

Last spring felt like a decade ago.

"Elle Baker?" She phrased it like a question, as if she weren't sure of her own name.

He didn't remember her, but he didn't want to be rude. "It's nice to see you again, Elle. I hope you're enjoying the festival."

"Of course! It's always a pleasure to celebrate the Ayletts! What an honor to know you!"

Her enthusiasm was giving him a headache. "Well, thanks." Or something. "I'd better go—"

"Yes! You don't want to be late. I'll look for you tonight. Maybe we can dance?" She ducked her head and watched him through her eyelashes, adding, "Or get a drink?"

"Oh, uh..." He looked around, desperate for rescue, and spotted Richard in the first row.

The man seemed to be enjoying the show, based on the chuckling. No help there.

"Maybe," Noah said vaguely. "See you later."

Stupid *Most Eligible Bachelor* article. As if his life weren't complicated enough, he now had random women throwing themselves at him.

He hurried up the steps of the bandstand and took a seat in one of the folding chairs behind the podium. Several town officials nodded in his direction. The Aylett name still commanded respect in Driftwood, but it'd taken some hits in recent years. Jasper's behavior, the lies Lena had spread, and Noah's divorce had all added fodder to the rumor mill.

It was a wonder he was still welcome on this stage.

As the emcee droned through his opening remarks, Noah scanned the crowd, searching for Charlotte and Miss Wright. He spotted them toward the back, Charlotte perched on Miss Wright's hip, her face painted with a colorful design.

Miss Wright was smiling at something Charlotte whispered in her ear. She'd assured him that her sternum no longer hurt, though she still pressed her hand against it when she felt distressed.

How many times had he imagined what it would be like to have a family of his own? To be a husband, a father? Before Charlotte arrived, he'd resigned himself to the likelihood that it might never happen. After the divorce, he'd locked that part of himself away. Watching his niece and her nanny, he couldn't keep those old dreams at bay.

"And now," Mayor Collins announced, "I'd like to welcome Noah Aylett to the stage to present this year's Elijah Aylett Bravery Award."

The audience applauded as Noah approached the podium. He adjusted the microphone and cleared his throat.

"Good morning. Thank you all for coming to celebrate not just my ancestor's heroism, but the spirit of community that has defined Driftwood for generations." He delivered his speech, then presented the award to a teenage boy who'd rescued a child from drowning.

Finished with his part of the presentation, he resumed his seat and endured the mayor's speech, which took a little too long for Noah's taste. Finally, it was over and he descended the bandstand steps.

He was enjoying being out of the spotlight when a cluster of women converged on him. Elle was among them, all smiles and too-strong perfume. Another woman—Melissa something, the bank manager's daughter—touched his arm and asked about his upcoming plans for the evening.

"I'm here with my niece," he said, a polite but firm dismissal as he scanned the crowd, looking for Charlotte and Miss Wright. They'd watched his speech, but must've gotten bored. Noah's pulse quickened as he searched faces in the crowd, but

Charlotte's purple dress and Miss Wright's cream sweater were nowhere to be seen.

"Excuse me." He stepped away from the group, his height giving him an advantage as he scanned over heads and between booths.

Where were they?

Charlotte had probably dragged Miss Wright away to show her something. But after everything that had happened, he couldn't help the adrenaline rush.

He pushed his way through the crowd, attempting polite responses to people who remarked on his speech. He didn't want to be rude, but wished everyone would leave him alone for a minute.

They could be anywhere—the craft booths, the food vendors, the petting zoo set up behind the library. They weren't missing, just out of his sight. They were fine.

Except his heart was hammering against his ribs like a trapped fly.

Finally, he spotted Miss Wright near the playground. Charlotte was at the top of the structure, playing with her little redheaded friend, Shanyn.

Miss Wright was talking to a man.

Not just any man. It was that doctor from the hospital. Dr. Wright. Noah's worry morphed to something darker but no less intense.

Cousins, he told himself. Except they probably weren't.

Noah forced himself to walk, not run, down the path. The last thing he wanted was to create a scene that would fuel more gossip.

Miss Wright laughed at something Dr. Wright said. He stood close to her—too close for Noah's liking—his hands animated as he spoke. The man's body language screamed interest, from the way he angled toward her to how his gaze never left her face.

Noah's jaw clenched so hard his teeth hurt.

"Uncle Noah!" Charlotte's voice rang out from the playground. She waved frantically from the top of the slide. "Look how high I am!"

"I see you, Charlie-Bear. Very impressive." He managed to keep his voice steady despite the storm raging inside him.

Miss Wright turned at the sound of his voice, and her smile faltered slightly. Was he so easy to read? "Mr. Aylett. You did a wonderful job. You're a natural at public speaking."

"Thank you." The words came out clipped. He turned to the interloper. "What brings you here, Dr. Wright?"

"Call me Ethan." The man extended his hand. "Good to see you again. I'm working in the medical tent."

"Shouldn't you be there then?" Noah had attempted the words to be lighthearted, but Miss Wright's eyebrows drew together, telling him he'd failed.

Fortunately, Dr. Dreamy was oblivious. "I was on my way back when I ran into Delaney and Charlotte." He turned to Miss Wright. "It was nice to see you again."

"You too."

The man nodded to Noah, then headed across the park to the white medical tent.

He watched Ethan go, telling himself he had no right to be jealous. A few deep breaths, and he turned back to Miss Wright.

"Thanks for keeping an eye on her."

She looked like she wanted to say something, but then her gaze slipped away. "Charlotte asked if she could have a pretzel for a snack."

He was thankful Miss Wright was too kind to call him on

his irrational reaction. "What do you think? Didn't you bring one of those protein bars?"

"I did, but it's a special occasion. And she's so much healthier than she was. It's your call, of course."

"One pretzel," he said.

"And cotton candy? I think if she has to choose one or the other—"

"It's fine." He couldn't help but smile at the nanny, who was fighting his niece's battles for her. "But if she gets sick tonight—"

"I'll handle it," she said quickly, a tiny smile quirking at the corner of her mouth.

He had the urge to kiss that corner, to see if he could coax a full smile out of her.

He forced his gaze back to her eyes. "Fair enough."

Maybe she read his thoughts because she took a step back. "Why don't I let you and Charlotte enjoy some time together? You don't need my help now that your speech is over."

He might not need her help, but he craved her company.

"I'll need you to take Charlotte home—"

"Okay. I'll meet you back here later. You two have fun."

She practically ran away from him.

Was his attraction that obvious? And if so, was she running because she was horrified by it?

Or because she felt the same way?

CHAPTER TWENTY

Delaney hurried away from the playground as fast as she could move without breaking into a jog.

Mr. Aylett's jealousy had been so clear that he might as well have carried a placard announcing it.

She hoped and prayed her own jealousy hadn't been that obvious.

She and Charlotte had been on their way to meet him after the mayor's speech. Delaney had seen women buzzing toward him like bees to a honeysuckle vine. Beautiful, accomplished women with sweet Southern accents, all *bless your heart* and *y'all come back*. Women who belonged in his world.

Women who weren't employees.

The sight had sent a wave of jealousy so intense that Delaney had changed course and taken Charlotte to the park. She didn't want to witness the parade of bachelorettes who couldn't resist him.

She knew exactly how they felt.

Now, as she walked randomly among the booths, she admitted that all her avoiding Mr. Aylett had done nothing to change how she felt about him. If anything, her feelings had only grown since their kiss. He was kind and gentle and understanding when she pretended to be too busy to eat dinner with them. The compassion and regret in his eyes made it increasingly difficult not to give in to her desire to just be with him. To sit with him and watch him love his niece so well.

The chilly air nipped at her cheeks. Strings of lights crisscrossed overhead, already illuminated, the sun having dipped below the trees. A band played on the stage where Mr. Aylett had spoken, the music adding background noise to the conversations and laughter of townspeople who wandered among the vendors. The scent of hot dogs mingled with the salt air from the nearby bay, turning her stomach.

The whole atmosphere reminded her of home. Except... except she didn't belong here.

What was she doing? Playing house with a man who was her employer, falling for a child who wasn't hers to keep? The whole situation was impossible.

She should quit, find another job. But then she'd have to leave Driftwood. She wasn't ready to go back to Maine yet, and she had no desire to start over somewhere new. Besides, though she'd gotten the settlement for her totaled car, she hadn't purchased a new one yet. She was trapped.

And while technically that was accurate...those were just excuses.

Truth was, she didn't want to leave because she was in love with Charlotte. And maybe her uncle.

Delaney needed someone to talk to and considered her options. Mom would do anything to protect Delaney and all her girls from heartbreak. She'd also love to get Delaney to come home.

She appreciated that about her mother. It would be so easy to run home to Mom's arms. Which was why Delaney couldn't call her.

Cici and Brooklynn would be just as protective, probably worse. They'd hop the first flight to Virginia and stage an intervention.

But Alyssa...

Alyssa hadn't lived in Shadow Cove for years. She might understand Delaney's need to escape for a little while.

And Alyssa had risked everything to save a little girl's life—after she'd fallen in love with that girl's father. She might be able to sympathize with the impossible pull Delaney felt toward Noah, the way her heart constricted every time he smiled at Charlotte. She'd never planned to stay away from Shadow Cove forever, but she couldn't imagine leaving them.

Wandering past a row of retail booths, Delaney pulled out her phone and dialed her oldest sister.

"Laney?" Alyssa's voice held a note of concern. "Everything okay?"

"I'm...fine. Good, really." Delaney pressed her free hand against her sternum, a habit she'd developed since the accident. "I just need to talk to someone who won't immediately tell me to come home."

"Okay. What's going on?"

"I kissed him." The words tumbled out. "Well, he kissed me. Two weeks ago. And I can't stop thinking about it. We've been avoiding each other ever since, only talking about Charlotte, never anything personal, and today he was so jealous when I talked to another man that I thought he might actually growl. And I understood because I'd just seen him talking to some women, and..." She didn't want to admit her own jealousy.

"Just so we're on the same page, you kissed who?"

"My boss." She kept her voice low in case someone might overhear. "It was stupid, and I shouldn't have, and now I can't think about anything else."

Silence stretched across the line. Then Alyssa laughed—not

mockingly, but with genuine warmth. "Oh, honey. You've got it bad."

"It's not funny."

"I know. I remember feeling the same way about Callan. We were in hiding from terrorists when I found out about Peri. The more I saw him with his daughter, the more I fell for him. It was..." She sighed. "It wasn't the same, of course, but I'm just saying, I get it."

Which was what Delaney needed, an understanding ear. Even so, she felt exposed as she passed a booth selling hand-made soaps, the scents so overpowering that they turned her stomach. "He's my boss, Lyss. And Charlotte, his four-year-old niece... She's been through so much. She needs stability, not her nanny having a breakdown over feelings she can't act on."

"Why can't you?"

"I work for him. I live in the house with him. And I'm not... I'm not suitable."

"Says who?"

"Him." The word came out too loud, drawing the glances of a couple of women nearby. She put her head down and hurried away. "He took one look at me and declared me scandalous."

"He did what!" Her big sister's anger was palpable through the phone.

"Not like that, not really. Just..." Delaney explained their first meeting and how she'd come to work for Noah, wandering into a side street away from the festival to avoid listening ears. "I don't know what to do."

"Tell me about him."

Delaney had expected her no-nonsense sister to give her step-by-step instructions, as if she were helping her reset her router. But Alyssa was softer now that she was in love. More compassionate.

Was that what love did? Changed people for the better? All it made Delaney feel was weak and exposed.

Where did Delaney even start to explain Noah Aylett? "He's...he's not what I expected when I took this job. He's raising Charlotte for his brother, who abandoned her and took off. Noah had to figure it out. But he's so good with her. Patient in ways I didn't think men could be. He makes her breakfast every morning and remembers which stuffed animal she needs for comfort. He reads her stories every night, even when he's exhausted."

The words poured out of her, weeks of suppressed thoughts finally finding voice. "And he's kind to me, Lyss. Really kind. I was in a little car accident—"

"You were? I didn't hear about that."

"I didn't want to worry anybody." Or explain the strange events of that night. "It's not important. It's just that he dropped everything to be there. I was bruised for a few days, so he worked from home to help with Charlotte. He's...he's a really good man."

Exactly the kind of man Delaney wanted to be with someday. But not this man, not this day.

"Take away the fact that you work for him," Alyssa suggested. "What's stopping you from being with him?"

Delaney laughed, though it came out more like a choked sob. "He's way out of my league. He's smart and handsome and wealthy and—"

"You're smart and beautiful, and it's not like you come from the wrong side of the tracks."

"I know, but... He's accomplished. He's a grown-up, you know? Probably a decade older than me, divorced. He owns his own business. I'm just—"

"You're not 'just' anything, Delaney. You're amazing, and he'd be lucky to have you."

Not really, but she saw no point in arguing. "I don't think he really has feelings for me. I think it's just... I mean, we live in the same house. And now we've had that kiss. I think...I think it's just physical for him."

"What if you're wrong?" Alyssa asked. "What if he really does have feelings for you?"

The question sent hope fluttering in Delaney's stomach, quickly followed by a wave of dread. "It doesn't matter. He's made it very clear that nothing can happen between us."

"Maybe, but—"

"There's no maybe."

"Maybe there is. Let's face it, the fact that you love his niece isn't exactly a point against you. If he feels the same way—"

"He can't. I'm his employee. He's trying to avoid scandal, and I live in his house."

"So move out."

Move out?

Could she? It would be tight financially, but if she could find a room to rent nearby, then that barrier would be lifted.

If she didn't live at the Aylett house, then maybe their dating wouldn't be quite as scandalous.

Or maybe their attraction for each other would fade. Well, his for her, anyway. She didn't think anything was going to change how she felt about him.

It was an idea. But how would she even broach the subject? *I have feelings for you, so I'm going to move out so we can explore...*

Her cheeks warmed at the thought of that conversation. How would she ever muster up the nerve to say it?

What if he rejected her? What if he laughed at her?

What if he wasn't who she thought he was?

Owen had been kind to her. He'd been affectionate and attentive. And he'd been a smuggler who'd shot a man.

In a million years, Delaney would never have guessed her gentle-giant boyfriend could be capable of such a thing.

How could she know if Noah really was who he said he was? How could she trust her own judgment?

And if he knew how she felt, he might take advantage of her. He might lure her in and then crush her to pieces.

Or just fire her.

She couldn't bear the thought of leaving Charlotte. She couldn't risk it.

"Thanks for talking me through it, sis."

"Sure. Keep me updated, and keep in touch. I miss you."

"Miss you too." Delaney ended the call, disappointment making her legs feel heavy. She was a fool to have thought there might be a solution to her dilemma. Her solution was to do her job and love...admire, anyway, Noah from afar and hope he never learned the truth about how she felt.

She looked around, realizing she'd wandered onto a back road that led toward the Aylett house. The sun had nearly set, casting long shadows between the stately homes. It was darker here, away from the festival lights.

When she turned to head back, movement caught her eye—a figure half a block behind her ducking behind a bush.

A shiver slid down her spine, raising goose bumps on her arms.

Was someone following her?

Her car careening down that hill, brakes useless after someone had cut her brake line, flashed through her mind.

Yet she'd wandered off alone.

Stupid.

Unwilling to walk past the place where that shadow lingered, Delaney decided to continue to the corner and return on the parallel street. She spun.

A man was right there, not even a foot away.

She gasped and stepped back, expecting an *excuse me,* or a *sorry to frighten you.*

He looked down at her, close enough that she could smell his aftershave. He was an older, distinguished-looking man with gray hair and matching eyes. His dark expression had her taking another step back.

"Tell your friend his merger's not going to happen," he said. "It's time for him to give it up."

"Who are you?"

His lips spread into a vicious, predatory smile. He turned and walked away, stride slow and purposeful.

Delaney stared after him, heart thumping a wild beat. She waited until he'd crossed at the next street, then hurried to the corner and jogged the other direction, toward the festival.

She glanced back again but saw no one following her.

That didn't mean they weren't there.

She practically ran to the park, where she searched desperately for Noah.

She wouldn't feel safe until she was by his side again.

CHAPTER TWENTY-ONE

The memory wouldn't leave Noah's mind—the way Delaney's face had transformed from terror to relief when she'd spotted him in the crowd.

Something primal had stirred, a need to protect her from harm. He still didn't know what she'd been afraid of. When he'd asked, she'd offered nothing but a quick head shake, obviously not wanting to say anything in front of Charlotte.

The park had been transformed for the evening's festivities, with tables and chairs set on the grass. Food trucks lined the road nearby, offering everything from barbecue to seafood to tacos. People waited in lines and carried plates and drinks, looking for a place to sit. The band played a country song, and a few couples were two-stepping along the edge of the temporary dance floor.

Noah watched Delaney across the table, her face illuminated by the strings of lights hanging over the whole area. The glow softened her features, caught in the loose strands of her hair that had escaped her ponytail as she laughed at something Charlotte said.

They were beautiful, the two of them together, and that

word he'd been trying not to think about knocked on the front door of his mind again.

Family.

Except Charlotte wasn't his, and neither was Delaney. But... maybe they could be. Both of them.

Sure, Jasper had shut Noah down when he'd said he wanted to adopt her. But Jasper had proved incapable of loving his daughter.

Maybe he'd change his mind. Maybe he'd realize that the last thing Charlotte needed was for her world to be turned upside down again.

And then there was Delaney. She was off-limits, but did she have to be? If Noah weren't her boss and she weren't the nanny, could he pursue her? Could they date, maybe fall in love?

No. Of course not.

But...why not? Why couldn't he be with her? She was almost thirty, not nearly as young as she looked. A decade younger than he was, but they were both adults. She loved Charlotte, and obviously, he couldn't deny the chemistry between him and Delaney. Their kiss had proved that.

Would it be so awful if he were to pursue the nanny?

Maybe...maybe the three of them really could be a family.

They'd bought a single fried seafood platter. Even shared among the three of them, it was a lot of food. Charlotte was more interested in looking around than eating, and Delaney... Miss Wright didn't seem to have much of an appetite.

"Can I go play now?" Charlotte asked Miss Wright.

She nodded to him. "Ask Uncle Noah. He's in charge."

"Please, Uncle Noah? Shanyn and Polly are playing." Charlotte practically batted her long eyelashes at him. Were all females born with the ability to cajole men?

"Her friends are right over there." Miss Wright indicated a group of girls on the playground.

He met Charlotte's eyes. "I'll let you play, but if you wander off, then you'll have to come back here and sit until it's time to go. Do you promise to stay where we can see you?"

She considered his question, then nodded. "I promise."

"Okay, then. Have fun"

She bounded off her chair and ran to her friends. Shanyn grabbed her hand, and the girls ran for the slides.

"I should probably take her home soon." Miss Wright's focus was on Charlotte. "It's getting late."

"You're off the clock. This is your town now, too, you know. You should enjoy the festival."

Something flickered across her face, reminding him of the terror he'd seen there earlier. "What had you spooked?"

She glanced at him, then back at Charlotte. "I went for a walk, and I thought somebody might be following me, and then when I turned back..." Though she'd started strong, now her voice shook. "There was a man there, an older guy with gray hair. He told me to tell you the merger's not going to happen, that you should give it up."

Noah's jaw tightened. "Frederick Hayes."

She lifted a shoulder and let it drop. "I don't know him."

Noah navigated his phone to the Hayes Industries website, found a photo of the man, and showed it to her.

"Yeah." She looked up from studying it. "That's him."

"You should have called me immediately."

"By the time you got there, I would have been back here. I was just a couple blocks away. I felt safe once I found you."

Maybe Hayes was the one who'd cut the brake line on her car. Noah had run into Hayes at the restaurant that night. Maybe he'd hired someone else to do it? Maybe he'd been at the restaurant to see Noah's reaction to her call.

That didn't make sense, though. Noah was spinning conspiracy theories out of nothing.

"You need to be more careful, and don't wander off by your-self." He was issuing orders like he had the right to tell her what to do. "I don't care if it's inconvenient."

He waited for an argument, but she nodded, then turned her gaze to the playground, where Charlotte was climbing the monkey bars. "She's gotten so much stronger."

Noah watched Charlotte swing from bar to bar. She was laughing with her friends, so different from the little girl who'd come to live with him.

"Kids are amazingly resilient," Miss Wright said.

"You've got an impressive understanding of kids." Noah's gaze drifted back to her face.

Her lips curved into a small smile, though she barely glanced away from Charlotte. "I've been babysitting for a long time, most of my life, really. Even though I was second-to-youngest, I was often tasked with keeping an eye on my little sister. And then watching other people's children. You see a lot of different situations, different families. Some kids have been through things you wouldn't believe, but they find ways to adapt, to keep going."

She spoke with such certainty. He prayed she was right, that Charlotte would be able to heal from the difficult first few years of her life.

"Tell me about your family."

Miss Wright's gaze tracked Charlotte as she moved from the monkey bars to the slide. "My father was an agent for the CIA."

"No kidding? An actual spy?"

"I guess. I don't know much about what he did. Just that he was gone a lot, sometimes for months at a time. We usually had no idea where he was."

Noah leaned forward, putting puzzle pieces together. "That explains a few things."

"What do you mean?"

"You never let your guard down when you're watching Charlotte. And the way you handled yourself after the accident, calling 911, then locking yourself in your vehicle when that other car approached. You kept yourself out of danger. Your father must have taught you to be cautious."

Her lips quirked. "Basic self-defense, and of course, how to spot a tail, which I proved today I didn't learn very well." She laughed softly. "My sisters and I used to complain about his paranoia, but it's come in handy." Her grin faded. "I'd better not tell Dad how I wandered off by myself today. He would not be impressed."

"Nobody can be vigilant a hundred percent of the time."

"Don't tell my dad that or you'll get an earful."

"What about your mother?"

"She's amazing. She held everything together while Dad was away." Her expression softened, the change on her face lovely in the glow of the twinkle lights. "Five girls under one roof—you can imagine the crazy emotional swings in our house, but Mom was always calm and rational, always kind and gentle."

"You take after her, I think."

Miss Wright looked down. She tucked a stray lock of hair behind her ear, gazing at him through her lashes.

Oh, boy.

The urge to lean closer was nearly unbearable. He sat back instead. "Did you always want to be a nanny, or did you have goals?"

By the way her shoulders stiffened, he'd said something wrong. He thought back over his words and realized how they'd sounded. "Not that there's anything wrong with being a nanny. It's a great dream. I didn't mean that the way it came out."

"I get it." She watched Charlotte on the playground. "Most people would consider what I do a fallback, not a dream. But..."

She glanced at him but didn't hold his eye contact. "This is what I always wanted to do. Watch other people's kids until…"

Her words faded, and he guessed what she was about to say. "Until you have your own?"

"Someday, God willing."

"You'll be a great mother."

Her smile was shy and too endearing.

Charlotte and her friends were on the play fort, engaged in some game of pretend. It was getting late, but he wasn't ready for his niece, or her nanny, to leave him yet.

"When I was sixteen," Delaney said, "my parents' friends asked me to stay with their kids overnight while they went with my parents to some big event in DC."

"You were sixteen? That seems young."

"I'd had years of babysitting experience by then. They lived just down the coast from here."

"From here? You were far from home."

"I was familiar with the area. We'd visited that family a number of times. It would have been fine, except there was a tropical storm. It was forecasted to turn out to sea long before it hit Virginia, but it didn't. It turned into a hurricane and came straight at us. All of a sudden, what had been gentle rain turned heavy, and the wind picked up. Sirens went off, telling us to take shelter."

"You must've been terrified."

Her laugh was low and lighthearted. "We were inside, and I'd never lived through a hurricane, so I had no idea what could happen. We had everything we needed. We hadn't been ordered to evacuate. I figured we'd be fine."

By the tone of her voice, it hadn't been fine. "What happened?"

"The kids were seven and two, both boys. I had them in the

house, hunkered down, when a door flew open. I'd forgotten to lock it, so that was my fault."

"Could've happened to anyone,"

"Maybe. And it should've been an easy fix. But the dog ran out, and before I could stop him, the seven-year-old followed."

"Uh-oh." It was ridiculous the way his stomach clenched as if Delaney and that boy were in peril right now.

"I couldn't just leave the baby alone, and I also couldn't chase the older boy and the dog while holding onto him and fighting the rain and wind. I grabbed my phone and called 911 while I carried the baby to his bedroom and plopped him in his crib. The operator told me to wait at the house, but there was no way I could do that. I took off after Chase."

"Chase? That's the kid's name?"

"Ironic, right?" Her quick smile faded. "It took me seven minutes to find him. The longest minutes of my life." A look crossed her face, gone before he could identify it. "Almost."

He wanted to ask what she meant, but she rushed ahead.

"Anyway, it was pouring. The waves were taller than I'd ever seen, crashing against the shore. The wind was whipping debris all over the beach, blowing so hard I had to fight it. The storm was thunderous, loud enough to swallow my shout. But I kept shouting. And then I heard the dog bark.

"Chase had caught up with it, and they were hunkered down by a clump of bushes, too scared to try to get back. I grabbed Chase's hand, took the dog by its collar, and dragged them both back to the house."

Noah found his heart pounding. "I'm impressed."

She shrugged. "By the time the police showed up, we were back inside and drying off. I'd even consoled the baby, who had not been happy to be dumped in his crib. Everyone made a big deal out of it. I even got"—she waved toward the bandstand where Noah had stood earlier—"that award for bravery. My mother insisted we fly back so I could be here to accept it."

"You won the Elijah Aylett Bravery Award?"

Another shrug. "It didn't feel brave. I'd lost a kid and his dog. Nothing brave about that."

"You were sixteen, and the cops told you to sit tight. Instead, you ran into a hurricane."

"They could've been swept out to sea with those waves. What else was I supposed to do?"

He knew what Charlotte's former nanny would've done. Nothing.

He marveled at this amazing woman who, even as a child, had risked her life to protect others, not family members but kids she was babysitting. No wonder they'd trusted her to watch their boys.

He'd made the right choice, hiring her.

Even now, as he studied Miss Wright, her gaze was on his niece.

And she'd won his family's award? Maybe it was a sign. He must've been here, must've seen...

Except if she'd been sixteen, then he'd have been twenty-seven. An adult, living his own life.

As if he'd needed the reminder about how much older he was than she. As if the fact that she was the nanny wasn't reason enough he couldn't be with her.

"No matter what you say," he said, "I'm impressed."

"Don't be impressed with me." Her voice sounded almost stern with disappointment. "I'm twenty-seven years old, and this is the longest I've ever lived away from home successfully in my life. I mean, I had a few live-in positions, but all within a few minutes of my parents' house."

He snagged on one word. "What do you mean, 'successfully'?"

She returned her focus to Charlotte. Her profile glowed in the overhead string lights, her pert nose and straight chin, the hair falling out of her ponytail dancing in the slight breeze. Even seated on this uncomfortable plastic chair, her back was straight, her posture perfect. She was elegant and beautiful.

"I lived in Boston for a couple of months. Got a job and swore I was going to stay for a year, but..."

Emotion played across her face, but he couldn't read it.

"I was lonely," she finally said. "Like a little kid at summer camp, I was homesick. I couldn't do it. I quit my job and moved back in with my parents."

"And that made you feel like...a failure?" he guessed.

"Wouldn't you?"

"I don't know. I'm almost forty, and I still live in my parents' house."

"It's different. You inherited it."

"It's not different. I miss them every single day."

She turned to him then, her gaze filled with sympathy and questions. "I'm sorry. I shouldn't have... Of course you miss them."

"There's nothing wrong with loving home and wanting your family. I think those are normal things. Anybody who made you feel like they aren't didn't know what they were talking about."

She nodded slowly. "My dad. He thought my mom needed to"—she made air quotes—"'cut the apron strings.' Mom used to tell him to stay in his lane. I was one of the few things they argued about."

"That sounds like a *them* problem. You are who you are, and who you are is..."

Movement had Noah turning, then his words faltered.

He wasn't ready for their conversation to end, and definitely not because his enemy had decided to interrupt.

~

Noah stood, not willing to let his former friend look down on him when he stopped beside their table. "Lowell."

"Enjoying the festivities?" He wore a conservative navy blazer paired with crisp khaki chinos, overdressed for a festival, but he and his sister had that in common—the need to, as his mother would say, put on airs. Lowell's balding head reflected the soft glow of the string lights, and his eyes held a hint of scrutiny as they took in Miss Wright.

Noah wasn't going to pretend they were friends by engaging in small talk. "Did you need something?"

The man scanned the playground until it seemed he'd located what he was looking for. His gaze locked onto Charlotte. "If she's not yours, then I assume she's the spawn of your good-for-nothing brother."

"Be very careful how you talk about my family, old *friend.*"

"After what you did to mine?"

"I did nothing to Marianne." Noah didn't even try to keep the anger out of his voice. "Your sister married me for one reason, and she took that reason with her—in the form of half my net worth—when she divorced me at the first hint of baseless rumors. She might as well have started the rumors herself. Looks like we both have good-for-nothing siblings."

Lowell's face turned deep red. "You have no right—"

"She was my wife, so I think I do. And anyway, you should know me. You know I would never have stepped out. You know what kind of man I am."

Lowell stared at him long enough that Noah started to hope he'd gotten through to his old friend.

But then he seemed to shake himself free of any doubts about his sister. He looked at Miss Wright, whose gaze bounced between them. Lowell focused back on Noah. "Are you going to introduce me to your new girlfriend?"

He curled his hands into fists. *Do not rise to the bait.* "Miss Wright, I'd like you to meet my former friend and brother-in-law, Lowell Jeffries. Lowell, meet Charlotte's nanny, Delaney Wright."

Her smile was tenuous when she extended her hand. "Mr. Jeffries."

Smirking, he shook her hand but eyed Noah. "'Nanny.' Is that what you're calling it these days?"

Miss Wright snatched her hand away.

Noah rounded the table so fast that Lowell took a step back.

"Move along, Jeffries." He shifted forward into Lowell's space, so close he could smell beer on the man's breath. "You're not welcome here."

"Back off the merger, Aylett, before your whole life falls apart."

"Is that a threat? Because your buddy Hayes already tried that tonight. You can tell him his intimidation tactics failed. I'm not going to back off the merger, not today, not ever."

"Tidewater's going to figure out pretty quick that your business can't be trusted any more than your name can."

"Your sabotage failed," Noah said. "My business is as strong as ever, and the merger is on track."

"It's going to fall apart," he said confidently, "and when it does, I'll be popping a cork to celebrate."

Worry and anger churned in Noah's gut. What did Lowell know? Or was he just blowing smoke, trying to throw Noah off his game?

His friend-turned-enemy reached past him, snatched a french fry from their platter, and popped it in his mouth. He focused on Miss Wright. "Sorry to interrupt your date. Enjoy the rest of your evening."

She said, "He's not my—"

"Don't bother," Noah said. "He's not worth your breath."

Noah watched him leave, only the Holy Spirit's self-control keeping him from tackling his old buddy and pummeling him.

When Lowell disappeared into the crowd, Noah took a deep breath, forcing his muscles to relax before he turned back to Miss Wright. She flicked her gaze from Charlotte to him, head tilted to one side, eyes more curious than alarmed.

The encounter had left a sour taste in his mouth.

"Sorry about that." He slid back into his seat.

"It's fine." She glanced toward the playground, where Charlotte was talking to a woman. After a moment, the woman turned and waved.

When the light hit her face, he realized it was Heather, Miss Wright's friend. Something about her didn't sit right with him, though he couldn't put his finger on what it was.

Miss Wright waved back, and he had to stifle a groan. The last thing he wanted was for that stranger to join them.

But Heather said something to Charlotte, then headed toward the dance floor.

The swings were empty, and Charlotte and her friends ran that way. His niece was so much more confident than she'd been even a month ago. If only adult relationships could heal as quickly as children did.

"He seemed intent on causing trouble." Miss Wright's voice was soft, barely audible over the music and the crowd's chatter.

"That's his specialty. Lowell and I were friends once. Best friends. Then I married his sister."

"And divorced her." It wasn't a question.

"She divorced me." Noah didn't usually talk about his marriage, but something in Miss Wright's eyes encouraged him to continue. "Marianne left after rumors started circulating that

I was having an affair. Lena Monroe started the rumors, but I wouldn't be surprised if Marianne fed them."

"You weren't, though," Miss Wright said. "Unfaithful." Again, her words held certainty.

"Never. But... I don't want you to get the wrong idea. We weren't happy. Before we got married, Marianne seemed sweet and easygoing. After, she was miserable and demanding. She hated my house and wanted to completely redo it. If it had been up to her, she'd have removed all the memories of my family and replaced them with high-dollar knickknacks that held no meaning at all, except to show the world how wealthy we were. Actually, what she really wanted was to tear the house down to the studs and rebuild."

Miss Wright gasped. "Your beautiful house? She would've done that?"

"In a heartbeat. As much as my brother and I have our differences, Jasper took the hit for me, threatening to sue. After all, the house is half his. I was grateful not to have to fight that battle, anyway."

"You saw none of that before you married her?"

"None." He sighed. "I wasn't perfect. My mother was... maybe like yours. A peacemaker surrounded by testosterone. She loved our home, loved being a homemaker. Marianne...I thought she was like Mom, but once we were married, she scorned the idea of taking care of our home, of being a mother. I felt like I'd fallen for a bait-and-switch scheme with a no-return policy. She'd make these outlandish demands—"

"Like tear your house down."

"Exactly. And I...I got tired of explaining myself. And arguing about stuff all the time. I mean, literal *stuff*. Couches and carpets and cars. So I gave her a credit card with a reasonable limit and told her to get what she wanted. And then I tuned her out."

What was he doing, telling his niece's nanny all this stuff? Except she wasn't just the nanny anymore. She was a friend. "The point is, I should have made an effort to understand why it was so important to her that we look wealthy, what need she was trying to fill."

"It's possible she wouldn't have been able to answer that."

"Maybe." Noah had known from about five minutes into the honeymoon that he'd made a mistake. Marianne had never loved him. She'd loved his money and his status. She'd loved being an Aylett, having a name in town everybody looked up to. For his part, he'd fallen in love with a woman who hadn't really existed.

At least she got what she wanted in the end. She kept his last name and half of his estate. What she hadn't taken, he was struggling to keep from crumbling to dust.

Miss Wright's expression softened. "That must have been difficult." She held his eye contact for too long, then turned back to check on Charlotte.

He sipped his soda, telling himself to change the subject. But he wanted to talk about this with Miss Wright. He wanted her to know. "The divorce was a relief, though it's wrong to think of it that way. It was nothing compared to losing my friendship with Lowell."

"I can't imagine." She reached across the table and rested her palm on the back of his hand.

All the regret he'd been feeling about Marianne, all the anger toward Lowell, dissipated as warmth spread from the skin she touched, reaching clear to his toes.

She seemed to realize what she'd done and pulled her hand away, sitting back.

He'd started to reassure her that there was nothing to apologize for when he caught sight of Lowell, who watched, wearing a triumphant grin.

Miss Wright had turned her focus back to Charlotte on the

playground, hand pressed against her sternum. Her cheeks were flushed, her eyes wide. She was probably trying to look like her touch had meant nothing, but she wasn't fooling anybody who might be paying attention.

Just what he needed, more rumors flying.

Frustration had him sitting back. He turned toward the dance floor, watching friends and neighbors attempt a new line dance. A few knew the moves. The rest fumbled along, most laughing as if all were right with the world.

And then, on the far side of the dance floor, he caught sight of someone even more distressing than Lowell.

Lena Monroe was glaring...at Miss Wright.

CHAPTER TWENTY-TWO

Delaney barely noticed the chill as the temperature dropped. The evening had been magical—twinkling lights, the scents of fried food and joy hanging in the air, Charlotte's delighted squeals as she'd played with her friends.

Lowell had ruined it.

Well, he'd started the ruining process. She'd ended it with that stupid gesture. What had she been thinking, touching Noah like that? It had felt so natural to comfort him.

But she'd seen the stiffness of his posture. Even after she'd snatched her hand back, she'd felt his frustration.

Stupid, stupid, stupid.

She wasn't surprised when Noah said, "We'd better get Charlotte home."

It was already an hour past her bedtime, but of course that wasn't Noah's real reason. After Delaney's foolish show of affection, he'd wanted her gone.

While he gathered their trash, she went to the playground and coaxed the little girl down from the perch where she stood with her friends.

Charlotte only put up a little fight before climbing down and returning with Delaney to their table.

"I'll walk you both home." Noah stood as they approached. "Unfortunately, I'm expected back for the final dance."

They snaked through the park, Charlotte wedged between them, her tiny hand warm in Delaney's. The crowd had thinned since the height of the festival, but remnants of the celebration lingered—discarded napkins fluttering in the autumn breeze, the band still playing for the younger crowd who'd taken over the floor.

When they reached the sidewalk, Delaney said, "I'm sorry about that touch." Her cheeks warmed. "I shouldn't have—"

He stopped suddenly, so she did, too, finding him facing her.

"You have nothing to apologize for. If anyone should be apologizing..."

He took a breath, his gaze flicking down to Charlotte, who plopped down on the sidewalk as if too tired to take another step. She was chattering to a stuffed animal she'd won with Delaney's help.

Mr. Aylett continued. "I'm sorry about...you know." The intensity of his gaze told her what he meant, and her cheeks burned when she remembered their forbidden kiss. "You've been... You *are* amazing, and if I ever make you feel otherwise, I don't mean to. I just can't risk..."

"Scandal. I know."

His lips twisted as if he found the word distasteful.

"Delaney."

She loved the way her name sounded on his tongue. He hadn't used it since the night of their kiss.

He was watching her, his gaze intense. "I'm just going to say it. It's not nothing, this thing between us."

Her heart raced. What was he saying? That what he felt wasn't just physical? That he felt something more for her?

He continued. "The timing is wrong, that's all. But when the..." Something must have caught his attention. He glanced away, and those eyes that had held her captive narrowed.

She turned to see what he'd seen.

A block from the festival on a side street, Heather got into the passenger seat of a dark Cadillac. The car's interior light illuminated her face briefly before going dark.

"Wasn't that your friend?" Noah's tone had an edge. "What is she doing with him?"

"Do you know him? Heather mentioned at the park that she's dating someone. Maybe that was him."

Noah watched the black sedan pull away, his brow furrowed. "I'm pretty sure that was Frederick Hayes's car."

"The guy who threatened me tonight? What a weird coincidence that they're together."

He uttered a skeptical *hmm* in the back of his throat. "He's married."

"Yeah, she said that."

Noah gave Delaney a sharp look, and she lifted her hand in surrender. "I don't condone it. And I didn't know the guy's name."

"I know, of course. Sorry. It's just..." But his words faded, leaving her to wonder what he was thinking.

Charlotte was telling her stuffed bear all about their house and her bedroom. Her little voice was so innocent, a sharp contrast to the evening.

"Let's go, Charlie-Bear," Noah said.

She stood, and they resumed their walk.

They'd gone a block or so when Noah blew out a long breath, then inched a little closer to Delaney. "I need to tell you something." His voice was low. "I'm going to have to let you go for a little while."

The words hit Delaney like a slap. She stumbled on the sidewalk, and he gripped her arm to keep her from falling.

"You okay?"

She ignored the stupid question. "Are you serious? You're *firing* me?"

"Not...firing. Just...just until after the merger."

"When is that going to happen? What am I supposed to do between now and then?"

"You told me your mom wants you to go home for Christmas. I'll buy you a ticket—"

"Why?" The temperature seemed to drop ten degrees. "What did I do?"

Charlotte looked up, her gaze flicking from her to Mr. Aylett and back.

"Nothing." He lowered his voice. "You did nothing wrong. It's just, you were threatened tonight, and—"

"I'm fine. And you need someone to take care of Charlotte."

"It's just for a little while. People are starting to talk, and—"

"You'd do this to her to avoid a scandal?" Delaney let her anger mask the hurt and betrayal she was desperate to hide. How could he do this to her? How could he do this to Charlotte? "You're more worried about your reputation than your niece."

"I'm not. It's just until the merger's finalized, which should be—"

"Who's going to take care of Charlotte?" Delaney's voice cracked on the child's name.

"I am." His gaze hardened. "I managed it before. I can do it again."

"Who's going to take her to dance? Who's going to make sure she doesn't run off at the playground?" Delaney's hurt was transforming into something sharper, more dangerous. She lowered her voice to a whisper, checking on Charlotte. "I grew up with a father who always had something more important to do than spend time with us. At least we had Mom. Who will she have?"

Noah's jaw tightened, but he offered no answer.

They walked in tense silence, Charlotte's innocent chatter to her teddy bear the only sound between them.

The injustice of it burned. Delaney had done everything right. She'd protected Charlotte, loved her, helped her heal. And now Noah was throwing her away because some gossips had nothing better to do than speculate about his personal life.

"You don't understand the pressure I'm under," he said finally.

"You're right, I don't." The words came out whispered and clipped. "I don't understand how a business deal could be more important than a little girl's well-being. I don't understand how you can—"

Charlotte stopped abruptly, tugging on both their hands. "Look! A kitty!"

The same small tabby cat Delaney had seen the day she'd met Charlotte darted across their path. Charlotte veered in that direction, but Delaney took her hand and gently pulled her forward.

"Just look, love. Don't follow."

They watched until the cat disappeared into the bushes in front of a shop before turning back toward the house.

Noah froze.

Delaney followed his gaze.

A woman was standing on the sidewalk.

She held a handgun—aimed at Delaney.

CHAPTER TWENTY-THREE

Time fractured into razor-sharp fragments.

Before Noah had fully processed what was happening, Delaney stepped in front of Charlotte, her body a shield between the gun and the child. Her hands gripped Charlotte's shoulders, holding her in place behind her.

Noah positioned himself in front of both of them, desperate to call out for help, to do something. But he didn't dare take his eyes off the woman holding the gun that glinted in the streetlights.

Lena angled side to side, trying, he assumed, to see Delaney, but Noah moved with her, making his body a wall, his arms spread wide to block Lena's line of sight to Charlotte and her nanny.

What was he supposed to do here? How could he protect them?

Dear God, help!

The metallic taste of fear coated his tongue. "Lena, put the gun down." At least his voice was steady. "This won't solve anything."

"There's nothing left to solve." Her voice cracked, high and desperate in the night air. "We belong together, Noah. But she stole you away from me. She ruined everything."

Noah's heart pounded a drumbeat. He could feel Delaney pressed close behind him, could hear Charlotte's frightened whimper. Every instinct screamed at him to lunge forward, to tackle Lena. Maybe she'd fire and hit him, but at least she'd be down.

What if she dodged him? She'd have a clear shot at Delaney. It wasn't worth the risk.

There was nothing he could do. Nothing.

He was powerless to protect them. Just like he'd been powerless to protect his father that horrible day. Just like he'd been powerless to help his mother as he'd watched her life slip away. Just like he'd been powerless to keep Jasper from ruining his life.

Think, Noah. Think!

"Lena, you're my friend." He worked to keep his tone calm and reasonable. "I don't want you to get hurt. Please, just put the gun down and we can talk about this."

"Friend?" The word came out like a curse. "I'm not your friend. I'm your everything. I was there for you when that conniving little wife of yours walked out."

Lena was the reason Marianne had walked out, but Noah didn't remind her of that.

"I've waited. I've been so patient while you played house with this...this nobody."

Sweat trickled down his spine despite the cool night air. "I care about you, Lena. I do." He spoke softly, trying to reach whatever rationality remained in her mind. "But this isn't the way. If you hurt Delaney, you'll go to prison."

"I don't care! It'll be worth it to keep her away from you."

She was unhinged.

Maybe if he played into her crazy... "You'll never see me again."

"You'll visit me. You'll miss me when she's gone."

"I might miss you, but I won't visit." He tried to infuse regret into his tone, as if it would be a sacrifice.

"Never? Not even once?" Her voice had softened, childlike in its vulnerability.

"Not once." Noah's tone was gentle but firm. "This isn't the way, Lena. This isn't who you are."

Something flickered in her eyes—a moment of doubt, perhaps. But then her gaze hardened as she looked past him. "She has to go," Lena whispered. "That's the only way. You'll see."

Noah felt Delaney's hand press against his back—a silent gesture of support. Or terror. Charlotte's quiet sobs tore at his heart. He needed to end this, now. "Lena, please—"

"Stop talking!" Her voice was sharp, her eyes wild. She looked nothing like the woman who'd once worked for him, the woman he truly had considered a friend. "Please, step aside." Suddenly, she sounded rational, almost conversational. "I don't want to hurt you."

She was insane. There was no rationalizing with an insane person.

Noah sensed movement, someone creeping into his field of vision, staying low, using the parked cars as cover. He didn't dare look, didn't dare give Lena any reason to fire.

"I just want to talk to her." Lena shifted to the side. "Just move away, Noah."

He tracked with her, protecting Delaney and Charlotte with his body, making himself as large as possible.

"I said move!" Her voice rose to a shriek, the gun wavering in her grip.

The figure lunged forward. Noah recognized his brother's broad shoulders as Jasper tackled Lena from the side.

The gun exploded in the silence.

CHAPTER TWENTY-FOUR

The Aylett house felt as cold as a tomb.

Delaney stepped inside and stood in the entry, torn between her desire to run upstairs and escape the man whose presence had her emotions all jumbled and her need for a glass of water to wash down a couple of Tylenol tablets.

Behind her, Noah closed and locked the door, then set the alarm, which beeped quietly.

She couldn't help replaying that terrifying moment. She'd talked through it twice at the police station, and she'd hoped that would help her process it. But it was still broadcasting in the theater of her mind, everything that happened...and could have happened... replaying in slow motion.

She hadn't been able to see anything from her spot behind Noah. She'd done her very best to keep him positioned between herself, Charlotte, and that gun. Banking on the fact that the crazy stalker woman wouldn't shoot him.

Though Lena could have lost her patience. She could have shot Noah. She could have killed him.

That thought had kept Delaney's stomach roiling for hours.

That he might be dead.

She felt both grateful for Noah and furious with him for putting himself in danger. And for firing her. And for having a stalker, which obviously wasn't his fault.

There were a million other emotions she didn't have the energy to name.

One moment, he'd been trying to reason with Lena.

The next, he'd thrown himself on top of Delaney and Charlotte, sheltering them with his body.

She'd hear that gunshot for the rest of her life.

And Noah's strangled cry. "Jaz!" After Delaney and Charlotte were down, he'd scrambled to his feet and hurried to disarm the woman. He'd held her down, his yells frantic. "Are you hit? Are you all right?"

She could still hear the terror in his voice.

But the man who'd tackled Lena stood, unharmed. Thank God.

It could have turned out so much worse.

Delaney had shuffled Charlotte away from the chaos. They'd sat on the curb, and she'd held the terrified little girl until the police arrived.

Now she knew that the man who'd tackled the crazy stalker was Noah's brother, Charlotte's father. She'd gotten a good look at Jasper, with his striking blond hair and intense gray eyes. She wasn't sure what she'd expected after hearing Noah's description of his brother, but the man who'd saved them seemed like so much more than the "wastrel" Noah had made him out to be. He was as well-built as his brother, with a strong jawline and broad shoulders.

Charlotte's father, who'd abandoned his daughter to party. Who'd also risked his life.

Jasper Aylett was a mystery.

Which was a distraction from the fact that someone had tried to murder her.

It was crazy.

The whole thing was completely crazy.

"Hey, are you okay?"

Noah's slight touch on her elbow had her coming back to herself. She was still standing in the entry, staring at nothing. She shook off her stupor.

"Should I check on Charlotte?"

"She's asleep. Jasper texted a few minutes ago." Noah's voice was low in keeping with the house's stillness. "He stayed with her until she drifted off."

Jasper had given his statement first, then brought Charlotte home to put her to bed. Noah and Delaney had been questioned a little longer before getting a ride back from the police station.

Noah stepped in front of her and studied her with an intensity that made her skin prickle. His eyes were dark with something she couldn't quite read.

"I'm sorry about that." He nodded to her hand, which was pressed against her sternum. It had been better, but being tackled had brought the pain back.

"I'm okay."

But when he mentioned it, she felt the pain again. She needed Tylenol. She walked toward the kitchen, where she grabbed a glass, added ice and water, then shook two tablets into her hand and swallowed them. All while trying to ignore the man standing on the other side of the peninsula, watching her.

"Why would you do that?" he asked. "Why would you put yourself between Charlotte and a gun?"

Of all the questions. "I'm her caretaker." She set down her glass, the sound too loud on the granite countertop. "It's my job to keep her safe."

"Most people's definition of that doesn't include using their body as a shield." His gaze bore into hers as if he were searching for something. "Her previous nanny would have tossed Charlotte toward Lena and dived out of the way."

The words surprised a chuckle out of Delaney that sent pain through her chest. "We've already established that she wasn't very good at her job."

Noah's gaze remained intense. "You could have died tonight."

As if she needed the reminder. "You were the one with the gun aimed at you."

"It's different. Charlotte's my niece. She's no relation to you. Most people's instinct is self-preservation."

Was it? When Delaney had seen the gun, her body had moved before her mind could catch up.

She wasn't sure how to explain and didn't think it needed explanation. "Most people's instinct is to protect the innocent."

"Only truly heroic people."

His kindness threatened to dissolve her anger. She looked away from the intensity in his eyes. Danger lurked there.

Focusing on the kitchen wall, she was able to come up with a coherent answer.

"When I was eight," she said slowly, "my family was in DC to visit my dad."

"Didn't he live with you?"

"His mail was delivered to our house. But did he live there? Did he truly dwell with us? No."

"Oh. That's..." Noah seemed unsure how to finish his sentence.

"We were going to a show, but we had a little time before it started, so we stopped at this shop. It was a beautiful day—one of those perfect summer days when the sky is so blue it hurts to look at it." The memory washed over her, still vivid after all these years.

Noah leaned against the table behind him, his expression softening.

"Dad stayed at the store's entrance. My older sisters wanted to look at something, so Mom asked me to stay with Kenzie. She was five, so she and I looked at toys in the back of the store. When I saw my mom and sisters headed for the cashier, Kenzie and I followed. We were close when I told her to go to Mom."

Delaney could still picture it. Mom had been no more than six feet away. Delaney had pointed to her and her other sisters, and Kenzie had headed in their direction.

Or so she'd assumed. But she hadn't made sure.

Delaney's throat tightened. "I just wanted to look at the hair ties. Then they called me and said it was time to go. I ran after them, and we all walked away. We'd been walking for ten minutes when I realized Kenzie wasn't with us."

She closed her eyes, feeling the familiar wave of guilt. "She hadn't gone to Mom. She'd wandered off. I told my parents, and we turned back to the store. My father just... He sprinted. I'd never seen him run like that."

Tears filled her eyes, a result of bone-deep fatigue and life-long disappointment in herself.

Those were the longest minutes of her life. She'd never been more afraid.

"What happened?" Noah's voice was gentle.

"Dad found Kenzie in the store, hiding in the middle of a round rack of sweatshirts. By the time we got there, he'd coaxed her out and was holding her tightly."

He'd been sweet to Kenzie, but when he'd caught sight of Delaney, his eyes had hardened. He was furious.

"You said you were eight?" Noah asked.

"Yeah."

"Obviously, nobody blamed you."

"Dad did. When he saw me, he just...he lost it. He lectured

me on every single thing that could've happened to her, right there in the store in front of everybody."

Noah pushed off the counter. "That's just...ridiculous."

"I was supposed to watch her."

"Yeah, but..." He took a breath, then studied Delaney for a long moment. "Have you ever nannied for an eight-year-old?"

She thought about it, then shrugged. "That boy down the beach was seven."

"If you'd put that boy in charge of his little brother and something had happened, would you have blamed him?"

"I would have blamed myself." As she said the words, she realized Noah's point. "But Kenzie was my responsibility."

Noah shook his head. "She was your parents' responsibility."

Delaney felt something shift inside, like a weight she'd carried for twenty years suddenly loosening. "But I was supposed to—"

"You were supposed to be a kid. An eight-year-old kid who wanted to look at hair ties." Noah's voice was both firm and gentle. "Your father shouldn't have put that on you."

Maybe.

But Dad had started in on Delaney, listing all the terrible things that could've happened. *"She could've been kidnapped. She could've been sold to the highest bidder. She could've been murdered!"*

"Gavin, stop." Mom had pressed her hand to his shoulder. Delaney could still hear her voice.

"Calm down. Everyone's safe. It was our fault."

Their fault?

"We should have checked to make sure Kenzie was with us. It was our job."

Seeing the situation again in her mind's eye, Delaney realized Dad hadn't been angry. He'd been scared. "As a CIA agent," she said, the idea forming as she voiced it, "he knew every terrible scenario that could play out. I think...I think he was just overwhelmed at what could have happened."

"Maybe." But Noah clearly wasn't mollified. "He should have known better than to terrorize his eight-year-old daughter with those scenarios."

She'd never thought of it that way. She'd always accepted that her father's reaction was justified, that she'd deserved his anger.

"You had the right to shop, Delaney." Noah stepped around the peninsula toward her. "At eight years old, at eighteen, at twenty-eight—you have the right to pursue your own interests, to want things for yourself."

He moved closer. The words he spoke, the idea behind them, felt foreign, almost dangerous. Her whole life had been built around the belief that other people's needs came first, that her own desires were selfish.

It was as if he were speaking a language she didn't understand. "That doesn't feel true."

"It is, though." He took another step, stopping so close that she could feel the warmth radiating from his body. His eyes searched hers, and she found herself unable to look away.

"You matter, Delaney," he said softly. "Your needs, your wants, your dreams—they all matter."

The words sank into her, touching places long neglected. A lump formed in her throat. She wanted desperately to believe him.

"Even after what I said to you tonight," he continued, "you were still thinking about Charlotte first. About keeping her safe."

"I love her." Her volume was barely above a whisper.

"I know." He reached out, his fingertips gently brushing a

strand of hair from her face. The touch sent electricity racing across her skin. "You are...extraordinary."

Delaney's heart fluttered. She should step back, put distance between them, but her feet refused to move.

But he managed it, taking a step away. "That's why this is so hard. It's the last thing I want to do, you know... Send you away."

Delaney stared at him as their tender moment shattered like fine crystal. "After everything that just happened, you're still firing me." She didn't phrase it as a question, just needed him to clarify.

"*Because* of everything that happened, and you're not fired." Noah's eyes held genuine regret, which somehow made it worse. "Lena is in custody, but the merger is still hanging by a thread. What happened tonight will make the papers. I'm just... There's too much gossip, too much scandal. I need you to leave, but just until I can get the merger finalized."

She let his words roll around in her mind. He was worried about what people would say. Not worried about how she would feel or how Charlotte would feel.

Her heart squeezed for Charlotte. But if what Noah said was true, then she *did* have the right to want things for herself. She *did* have the right to think of herself sometimes. Her needs *did* matter. And he was disregarding them for the sake of his own.

Which he had every right to do.

The consequences of Noah's decisions weren't her problem.

Is that true, Lord? Shouldn't I just do what he's asking?

She loved this job. But she didn't love being treated as if she weren't valuable or needed. As if, by her very existence, she wasn't good enough.

Noah squinted, maybe trying to read her thoughts. After a

moment, he said. "It's just for a few weeks. And then you can come back."

"No."

Noah blinked. "No?"

"I'm not running away and then coming back when the coast is clear, as if I've done something wrong." She turned to dump the rest of her water in the sink. It was easier to do this when she wasn't looking at him. Her chest ached, not just from her injury but from something much deeper and more painful. "If you want me to go, I'll go. Home to Maine." She loaded her glass in the dishwasher. "To stay."

"But I want..." His words trailed, then started again. "Charlotte needs you."

She added soap. "If you were that worried about Charlotte, then you wouldn't be firing me."

"I'm not... If you would just listen to reason."

"Don't talk to me about reason." She slammed the dishwasher closed and spun to face him. "I'm not your crazy stalker. I'm not being unreasonable. I just proved I would *die* for your niece, and it's not enough for you."

"I never said—"

"I know what you *never* said." The unfairness of it all bubbled up inside her, transforming into anger. "You're firing me because you're attracted to me. That's not my fault."

Noah's jaw tightened. "I have to secure this merger. My family's home and my father's business are both at risk, and I can't lose them. They're my family's legacy. There are members of the Tidewater board looking for any excuse to vote against me, and Lowell is feeding them ammunition every chance he gets."

"There's always going to be an excuse to choose business over family. That little girl upstairs?" Delaney pointed toward the ceiling. "*She's* an Aylett. *She's* your family's legacy."

Delaney straightened, emboldened by the truth she felt in her bones. "Not this house. Not your business. Those are just your pride or some misguided sense of loyalty to dead people."

"You're reducing my parents to 'dead people'?" His volume rose. "You have no idea—"

"Right. How could I understand all the machinations of the rich and famous? You do what you have to do. I'll pray you find some ugly old woman who'll love Charlotte as much as I do." Not that he would. Not that there was any chance. She moved to walk around him, but he blocked the only way out of the kitchen.

"Delaney, I have feelings for—"

"Your feelings are irrelevant, obviously."

"No, they're..." He paused, breathing heavily. "I don't want to lose you. Please, just think about coming back."

"I don't belong here, Mr. Aylett. And you've lost my trust. Now, get out of my way."

His shoulders drooped, and he stepped back.

Heart pounding, she passed him and hurried down the hall and up the stairs to her room. She closed the door and turned the lock.

Only then did she allow her tears to fall.

CHAPTER TWENTY-FIVE

Water wasn't strong enough to wash away this kind of regret.

Noah stared into his glass, wishing it contained something that could dull the sharp edges of his thoughts. But he'd never been a drinker, not even when life had given him every reason to start.

The kitchen was too quiet. Upstairs, Delaney was probably gathering her things, preparing to walk out of their lives forever. He'd done that. He'd pushed away the one person who'd brought light back into this house, who'd somehow managed to crack through Charlotte's walls and earn her trust.

And for what? A merger that might still fall apart? But generations of Ayletts had built this family's legacy. He couldn't let it slip away on his watch.

How did Delaney not understand that?

Approaching footsteps pulled him from his thoughts. Not the light tread of the woman whose presence he craved, but heavier, a harbinger.

Jasper appeared in the doorway, looking irritatingly at ease in a faded T-shirt and plaid pajama pants. His hair was slightly damp, his skin was a burnished bronze, proof he'd spent the last six months in the sun, on beaches or yacht decks, a drink in one hand, the other wrapped around the waist of some woman whose name he probably didn't even know.

While Noah dealt with his mess.

But there was something different about Jasper—wrinkles around his eyes that Noah hadn't noticed at the police station. A heaviness in his demeanor that wasn't like him.

Holding an empty lowball glass, he leaned a shoulder against the doorjamb. "You've done a great job with Charlotte. She looks...healthy."

"Amazing what happens when a kid feels loved."

His jaw tightened. "I saved your life tonight. Maybe cut me a little slack."

Noah should, probably. But he was tired and grieving the loss of Delaney. He needed all his energy to focus on his own self-loathing. "What do you want, Jaz?"

Jasper moved past him, headed for the refrigerator. "I don't think Charlotte had any idea what happened tonight. I didn't explain it to her, obviously, just told her it was grown-up stuff and she could trust you to take care of her."

"Which I will. Just like I've been doing."

Jasper glared at him for a long moment. Then he pulled out a bottle of orange juice and drank straight from it.

"Seriously? Use a glass."

Jasper raised an eyebrow but complied, reaching for the glass he'd set on the counter. He filled it with juice. "Sorry, didn't realize I was still twelve...and you were still Mom."

The casual mention of their mother sent a fresh wave of anger through Noah. "What are you doing here? You show up out of nowhere, save the day, then put Charlotte to bed as if you care. But what happens tomorrow, huh? When you find some party that's more important than your daughter. I know what happens. You hop on the first flight and disappear until spring."

Jasper stared at him, a thousand emotions crossing his features, emotions Noah didn't recognize on his wastrel brother's face.

"I might be a useless piece of garbage—"

"I never said—

"—but at least I'm not an idiot."

Noah snorted. "Jury's still out."

Jasper finished his orange juice, then slammed the glass down on the granite countertop. "That woman upstairs is amazing. She was holding Charlotte behind her, keeping her safe. Ready to die protecting her. And you're sending her away?"

"You were listening? What are you, ten? We were having a private conversation."

"And I was having a drink in the living room. Not my fault you didn't see me."

The lights were off in the living room. Why had Jasper been sitting in the dark?

"I heard enough to know you're getting rid of her. What is she? A girlfriend?"

"She lives here."

Jasper's eyebrows rose, the expression saying, *And?*

Noah stepped back, needing distance so he didn't take a swing at him. "I wouldn't be shacking up with her under any circumstances, but certainly not with Charlotte in the house."

"I know." Jasper cracked a smile. "Just trying to get under your skin. So what's the problem with the hot nanny?"

"People are starting to talk. After what you've done..." He hated to admit his part but added, "And the rumors surrounding my divorce, there's been a lot of scandal associated with the Aylett name. It's getting in the way of a merger—"

"Oh, for—" Jaz cut himself off, probably keeping himself

from uttering some foul curse. "You're going to lose that woman for the sake of money?"

"One of us has to work. We both know it's not going to be you."

Something dark and brooding settled over Jasper's features, out of place on his usually carefree face. "You think I don't know what it's like to make difficult choices? You think it hasn't been killing me to be so far from my daughter?"

Noah stared at his brother, thrown by the intensity in his voice. This wasn't the happy-go-lucky Jasper he'd known. There was something else there—something Noah couldn't identify.

But at the end of the day, whatever choices Jasper thought he faced, he always chose wrong.

"I'm trying to save our family's legacy." Noah was too tired to have this argument again tonight. "I'm trying to save everything Dad worked for."

"You have no idea what I've done to try to make up for Dad's death."

Jasper's words deflated all of Noah's righteous indignation. He took a step toward his brother. "Dad's death wasn't your fault. He should have been more careful."

"That's not what you said at the time."

"I know." At the time of the accident, he'd called his brother an irresponsible fool. Which, to be fair, Jasper had been. He'd also been a kid.

It wasn't his fault Dad had barreled up from belowdecks when he'd felt how fast their yacht was going. It wasn't Jasper's fault that Dad hadn't worn a life jacket. It wasn't Jasper's fault that Dad hadn't heeded his own warnings, warnings he'd given the boys a thousand times, to pay attention when the ship was in full sail.

Dad had been too focused on getting to Jasper to ream him out.

Jaz had been fifteen years old. All the things Noah had said to Delaney came back to him now. He'd been a child. Yes, older than eight, but certainly not an adult. Somebody should have been watching out for Jasper.

Deep down, Noah had always thought *he* should have been watchful. That he should have noticed the speed. He'd been too wrapped up in his date in her bikini to pay attention.

The wind picked up. The sailboat flew across the waves. Dad came upstairs...

It was an accident. Just an accident.

He took another step toward his brother. "I know," he said again. "I did blame you, but I shouldn't have. It wasn't your fault. I know that now."

"Of course it was." Jasper's words were low and vehement. "And I'm trying..." He took a breath, then a step back. "The point is, Delaney is great with her. Charlotte spent our entire time together telling me how much she loves her. So I don't care what big freaking deal you're putting together, it's not more important than Charlotte."

"Said the man who's going to leave on the first flight out."

"I never said—"

"Didn't have to." Fury and frustration warred inside Noah. He should shut up now. He should go to bed, but he was too tired to dig down for self-control. "You're my brother, Jaz. And I love you. But you're the one who leaves. The son, the brother, and now the father who *leaves*. So don't tell me what I should do. I'll be the one to put Charlotte back together after you take off, after you've disappointed her—again."

The expression that crossed Jasper's face had Noah regretting his words the instant they were out of his mouth.

Everything he'd said was true. But Jasper was hurting. He'd been hurting since that awful day twenty years before.

"Look," Noah said, "I'm just saying—"

"No." Jasper lifted a hand to silence him. "You're right. I'm the one who leaves. You're the perfect big brother who's going to sacrifice everything to save a house filled with ghosts. Good luck with that."

He brushed past Noah and stalked out.

Leaving Noah to stew in his own poor choices.

CHAPTER TWENTY-SIX

T he next morning, as Delaney approached the kitchen, raised voices carried down the hallway—Noah's sharp and commanding, the other defensive and dismissive. She paused just outside the doorway, hesitant to interrupt what was clearly a heated argument.

"You're going to have to stay here until this merger is finalized. I can't risk anything else going wrong."

"I've got things to do." The other man was Jasper, the brother she'd seen the night before. His tone was casual, as if they were discussing weekend plans rather than Charlotte's care. "I plan to come home and take care of her soon, but —"

"You can sacrifice your next party to stay home with your daughter." The fury in Noah's voice made Delaney wince. "For once in your life, be responsible."

Silence fell, heavy and uncomfortable. Delaney waited a moment longer, not wanting to walk into the middle of their tension. When the quiet stretched another two minutes, she took a deep breath and stepped into the kitchen.

The brothers sat at opposite ends of the table, each nursing a mug of coffee and refusing to look at the other. The air between them crackled. Jasper noticed her first, his face transforming instantly from sullen to charming as he rose from his chair.

"Miss Wright." He extended his hand, his smile dazzling if a little forced. "We didn't meet properly last night. I'm Jasper Aylett, Charlotte's father."

Delaney shook his hand. "It's nice to meet you, Mr. Aylett."

"Just Jasper. Let me get you some coffee." He moved toward the counter, but Noah was already there.

"I've got it." He reached for a mug and fixed her coffee exactly as she liked it—with a splash of cream and a teaspoon of sugar—and handed it to her, his fingers brushing hers briefly. The warmth from his touch lingered on her skin.

Jasper noticed the exchange, his eyebrows lifting slightly as he retook his seat. "Aren't you two cozy?"

Delaney's cheeks heated. She sipped her coffee, focused on Noah. "My flight leaves just after three."

"I'll drive you," Noah said.

"I can get an Uber."

"No need. Are you hungry?" He nodded toward a pan beside the stove. "Scrambled eggs this morning."

"No, thank you." She couldn't imagine trying to eat. She'd barely slept, what with the memory of Lena's gun and knowing it would be her last night in the room she'd come to think of as hers. "I was just wondering where you put my suitcase. I need to pack."

"Right." A shadow crossed Noah's features, gone almost immediately. "I'll get it." He headed for the door, giving his brother a look she couldn't read. His footsteps were heavy on the hardwood as he walked away.

Jasper leaned back in his chair. "You're the one who's been taking such good care of my daughter."

"She's a wonderful little girl."

"She looks...amazing. Healthy and happy. When I first got

her from her grandmother, she barely spoke. Last night, she was a little chatterbox." He grinned, his face lighting up.

If he felt that way, then why wasn't he the one taking care of her?

He motioned to the table. "Have a seat."

She did, choosing the seat nearest the window where she usually ate her breakfast beside Charlotte. Chilled, Delaney wrapped both hands around her mug. "She's made a lot of progress."

"I assume I have you to thank for most of that."

"You assume wrong, Mr. Aylett—"

"—Jasper."

"Your brother is amazing with her. As busy as he is, he makes her breakfast every single day, he's always home for dinner, and he's even managed to come to her dance lessons a couple of times. He's a natural father."

"Uncle," Jasper corrected, all charm leached from his tone.

"All the more impressive, don't you think?" Delaney usually kept her opinions to herself when it came to the families she worked for, but she didn't work for this one anymore. And this... this neglectful father, this man who fought against the idea of caring for his daughter for a couple of weeks, hadn't earned and didn't deserve her respect.

He sighed, his shoulders dropping a little. "Look, I know what you think of me. It's the same thing my brother thinks. But it's complicated."

Delaney took another sip of her coffee, using the moment to study Charlotte's father. There was something in his eyes—a flicker of pain, maybe—that made her wonder if there was more to his story.

"I spend a lot of time on the water these days." Jasper's voice was softer now. "Sailing mostly. Some fishing. It's where I do my best thinking."

Where he did his best avoiding responsibilities, more likely.

She could see the resemblance to Charlotte in the shape of Jasper's eyes, the curve of his smile when he wasn't forcing it. But where Charlotte's features held innocence and wonder, Jasper's held something harder to define—worldliness, and maybe regret.

"She has your smile," Delaney said.

"You think so?"

"When she's truly happy, yes."

He nodded slowly, as if filing away this information. "Noah's an idiot for letting you go."

She wasn't sure what to say to that, so she kept her mouth shut.

"You don't look happy about it, either," he added.

Delaney wasn't about to discuss her feelings with this man she'd just met.

"Where are you going?"

"Home. To Maine."

"You don't have a car here?"

"It was totaled, and I never got around to buying another one."

Footsteps preceded Noah into the kitchen. "I left your suitcase outside your bedroom door," he said. "And I added a second one since you've bought some things since you've been here. You can just keep it." His tone was carefully neutral. "Let me know when you're ready, and I'll drive you to the airport."

"Thank you." The formality between them felt wrong after everything they'd been through.

Jasper watched their interaction with curious eyes. "So, brother, aren't you going to ask why I'm back? Or are you just happy to have a convenient babysitter?"

Noah's jaw tightened as he took his seat. "It's not called

'babysitting' when it's your own child. And I'm pretty sure I asked last night, but you refused to answer."

"There were more important things to talk about." Jasper glanced at Delaney. "I wanted to see Charlotte, of course. But also, I saw a selfie on Violet's Instagram that looked like it was taken in Driftwood. I happened to be in DC, so I thought I'd swing by, see if she's giving you any trouble."

"Violet?" Noah frowned.

Who was that? Before she could ask, Jasper explained. "Charlotte's mother." He spoke to Noah again. "I reached out to her, but she laughed me off, told me she was outside New York City. But..." He shook his head. "The leaves have fallen in New York, but in the photo, they're still in full color on the trees. Maybe she took the picture a while ago, but it looks so much like the park." He pulled out his phone and swiped through several pictures before finding what he wanted. "Here." He showed the screen to Noah. "Doesn't this look like Driftwood?"

Noah leaned forward, and his eyes widened as he stared at the photo.

"What's wrong?" Jasper asked.

"Show Delaney." His voice was tight.

Jasper handed her the phone, and Delaney's stomach dropped at the image of the curly-haired woman smiling at the camera, Driftwood's town square in the background.

"That's Heather." Her voice was barely a whisper as betrayal mixed with her few sips of coffee, souring her stomach.

Jasper's brow furrowed. "Who's Heather?"

"We met at the park." Delaney's mind raced to make sense of it. "She approached me when I was with Charlotte. She said she was new in town. I thought...I thought she was my friend."

"Remind me," Noah said. "When was the first time you saw her?"

Delaney thought back. "She was there the day you fired Mrs. Dechambeau."

"Maybe she was the person watching Charlotte."

She'd forgotten that moment, that person who'd ducked away when Delaney had caught up to the little girl wandering too near the street. "Maybe. I saw her again the first time I took Charlotte to the park after you hired me."

Noah stood and paced. "And at the festival, she was with Hayes."

"Who's Hayes?" Jasper asked.

"Frederick Hayes," Noah said. "Owner of Hayes Industries, the company we're competing with in the Tidewater merger."

Jasper seemed to take that information in. "How would Violet know him?"

"How am I supposed to know?" Noah snapped. "You're the one who knocked her up. Maybe you should have a little more information about a woman before you go to bed with her."

"Let's catalog all my faults later." His gaze bounced from Noah to Delaney and back. "What's the deal with this Hayes guy? Why is it a problem if she's with him?"

"He scared me last night," Delaney said, "a few blocks from the festival. Told me to pass the message to Noah that he should back out of the merger."

"It was a threat," Noah added. "And he's working with your..." His words faded.

"Doesn't make sense," Jasper said. "Violet's a junkie."

"If she is, she hid it well." Delaney looked at Noah. "You met her. Did you get the feeling she was using?"

"People can hide it," Noah said.

"For a little while. But she seemed...healthy, if a little haunted. Maybe she quit."

That information seemed to worry Jasper more than anything. "I don't understand."

Delaney pushed to her feet. "Whatever's going on, it's none of my business." It killed her to leave, but if she was going to make her flight, she needed to get moving. "I'm going to pack. I'll check on Charlotte while I'm up there."

"Don't wake her if she's still sleeping," Noah said.

Delaney headed for the stairs, her legs growing heavier with each step.

Heather was Violet, Charlotte's mother. She'd gotten close to Charlotte—and Delaney had let her.

Delaney had been blind to the woman's true nature. All those conversations, the careful questions about Noah and Charlotte, the way she'd appeared at just the right moments. Delaney had been so grateful for a friend that she'd missed every red flag.

Once again, she'd proved a terrible judge of character. Once again, she'd been betrayed. Twice, really, considering that Noah had betrayed her, too.

She might be great with children, but she had terrible instincts for grown-ups.

Two suitcases sat outside her bedroom door. The sight of them made this decision feel final. She was really leaving this town, this family, this little girl she'd fallen in love with.

And the uncle she'd let herself become too attached to.

Delaney continued down the hall. Charlotte was usually awake long before this time of the morning, hungry and ready for breakfast. Delaney paused outside her door and listened. Nothing. No rustling of sheets, no soft humming, no whispered conversations with her new stuffed animal.

She pushed the door open. The room was quiet.

Morning light filtered through the gauze curtains, casting soft shadows across the bed. The covers were thrown back, the sheets vacant.

"Charlotte?" She listened but didn't hear an answer. She

checked the bathroom, but it was empty, as was Charlotte's closet. Delaney checked behind the door and under the bed.

"Charlotte!" Delaney's voice carried down the hallway as she checked her own room, then Noah's, then every other room on the second floor. The guest rooms, the linen closet, even the small storage area under the eaves.

Nothing.

Delaney flew down the stairs, taking them two at a time. "Noah!" Her panic echoed through the house. "She's not here!"

Both men looked up as she burst into the kitchen, their conversation forgotten.

"What do you mean?" Noah's coffee mug clattered against the counter.

"Charlotte's not in her room. She's not anywhere upstairs." Delaney's heart hammered as she watched Noah's face.

He'd know where she was, of course. He'd know what had happened.

But she didn't see the calm she'd hoped for. His expression morphed from confusion to fear. He hurried past her toward the stairs. "Charlotte!" His voice boomed through the house. "Charlotte, where are you?"

Jasper followed, but Noah turned. "Check the basement!"

Jasper did, calling his daughter's name as he descended the stairs.

Delaney stood frozen in the hallway, her mind spinning through possibilities. She hadn't seen Charlotte since Jasper brought her home from the police station. The child had been fine. A little shaken up, but...

The men's voices were loud, shouting for Charlotte, getting more desperate by the second.

Delaney prayed they'd find her, prayed desperately. But in case they didn't, she pulled out her phone and called 911.

If Charlotte was gone, the sooner they reported it, the better chance they'd have of finding her.

CHAPTER TWENTY-SEVEN

What Noah felt went far beyond fear. He was caught in a horror movie, and against his will, he'd been given a starring role.

Scratch that. *Charlotte* had the starring role. Noah was an extra. A spectator.

He stood helplessly while Detective Norton talked to the uniformed police officer examining the alarm system keypad. An hour and a half had passed since Delaney had called 911. An hour and a half, and they still had zero leads on where his little girl could be.

It seemed obvious that Violet had taken her. But where *was* she?

"Hasn't been tampered with." The detective stepped into the living room. His weathered face held a kind of practiced neutrality that made Noah want to punch him. "No signs of forced entry, no bypassed circuits. Whoever took your niece knew the code."

"How!" Noah stood between the kitchen and the living room, wanting to tell Norton to look again, to figure out how somebody had come into their house in the middle of the night, crept up the stairs, and snatched sweet Charlotte from her bed.

Across from him, Delaney was curled into the corner of the sofa, her knees drawn up, her arms wrapped around her shins. Tears tracked silently down her cheeks, and every few seconds, her shoulders shook with a suppressed sob.

On the other side of the windows, Jasper paced in the backyard, phone pressed to his ear.

"Did you give the code to anyone?" Norton asked, pen poised over his notepad.

"Of course not."

"A repairman, delivery—?"

"I said no!" Noah hadn't meant to shout and regretted his volume when Delaney startled.

"Sorry," he muttered.

The detective's gaze shifted to her. "Miss Wright?"

She lifted her head, swiping at her eyes with the back of her hand. "I never told anyone the code. I wouldn't."

"Ma'am." The detective's tone was patient and understanding, and Noah got the feeling he plucked that chord when he thought he'd found his mark and wanted to lull them into letting their guard down.

"It's obvious you care very much about Charlotte," Norton said. "I saw you with her the day after your accident. I know you love her. And I know you want to help us find her. You're not going to be in any trouble, I promise. But you need to tell me everything, right now."

Her expression shifted from heartbroken to shocked to offended. She straightened her legs and dropped her feet to the floor, then stood. "Detective Norton, I love Charlotte with all my heart, and I wouldn't do anything to harm her."

"I'm not saying you did. But maybe someone you've been spending time with? A friend, or a boyfriend?"

Her gaze flicked to Noah, barely a glance, but the detective couldn't have missed it. He didn't say anything, just let his question hang in the air.

"The only people I know in Driftwood are Noah and Charlotte and a woman I thought was my friend. We've already told you about her."

They'd explained all about Heather/Violet when he'd arrived.

"We're looking for her now." The detective's tone was placating, bordering on patronizing. "But if there's anything else you should tell us..."

"I would do anything to get her back, detective."

Jasper stepped through the patio doors, his face grim.

"Who were you talking to?" Noah asked.

"I have some contacts. Hopefully, one will call me back soon. Violet's not answering." Jasper's face was pale, but his eyes blazed with fury.

Noah understood that. He had to focus on what was happening around him or else he'd go crazy imagining what Charlotte was going through.

The clock ticked, and every minute that passed was one more minute the kidnapper—or *kidnappers*—had to escape with her.

Detective Norton studied Delaney for another long moment, then focused on Jaz. "We've got an APB out on Ms. Bosch, and we're checking known addresses. If she's in the area, we'll find her."

"If?" Noah's voice cracked on the word. "She has to be in the area." If she wasn't...she could be anywhere.

The detective's expression remained maddeningly calm. "We don't know anything for certain yet, Mr. Aylett. We need to explore all possibilities."

Noah squeezed the bridge of his nose and concentrated on

what he'd seen the night before. "She was getting into a sedan." He looked at Delaney. "It was a Cadillac, right? You saw that, didn't you?"

"I did, yes."

Noah faced the detective. "She was with Frederick Hayes."

Jasper's cheeks flushed. "Are you saying...? You think this is about *business*?" He spat the word like one might *human trafficking* or *fentanyl smuggling*.

"Yeah, you know, *business*. Dad's business. The thing that funds your life."

"You have no idea what—"

"Stop it." Delaney marched around the sofa and stood between them, glaring at each of them in turn. "There's no time for your bickering. Charlotte's missing. Nothing else matters."

Jasper's gaze flicked from her to Noah, and then his shoulders dropped. "You're right."

"Tell me about Frederick Hayes." Detective Norton held his notebook and pen at the ready. "He's a...business rival?"

"Yeah." Noah focused on the detective. "My company was in merger talks with Tidewater Logistics out of Norfolk when Hayes got wind of it."

Via Lowell Jeffries, he would swear.

"Big deal?" Norton asked.

Noah nodded. "Millions." Not that he cared about that. Without Charlotte, none of it mattered.

If this was about that—if his choices were the deal or Charlotte, he'd pick Charlotte every day.

"Talk to Richard Whitestone," Noah said. "He's had dealings with Hayes in the past."

"Do you have an address for Hayes?"

"I think he lives in Virginia City."

"Heather mentioned Norfolk." Delaney stepped toward the

detective, a hint of hope in her tone. "She told me her new boyfriend rented her an apartment."

Norton glanced up from his notebook. "Tell me about that."

"She said the boyfriend was older, married. She said she could walk to the beach, and maybe a golf course? And...I think she said it was on an upper floor. Something about a view?"

"Okay, we'll look into it." He made a final note. "Mr. Aylett." He looked at Jasper. "Your brother mentioned you've been out of town for several months. Where exactly?"

"What difference does that make?" Noah snapped. "Jasper's Charlotte's father. If he wanted her, he could've just come and taken her."

Norton's smile was tight. "I thought you had custody."

"I do, but it's not like I'd fight my brother. She's his daughter."

That remark had the detective shifting toward him. "Do you resent taking care of her?"

"What? Are you out of your...?"

Delaney rested her hand on his forearm, her warm touch surprising him. He took a breath. "I love Charlotte, and I love Jasper. I would never do anything to hurt either of them."

The detective's eyes narrowed, and he swiveled back to Jasper. He seemed intent on finding one of them guilty, which would sure make his job easier. But nobody in this room had taken Charlotte. Noah knew that, at least.

"I was in the Caribbean." Jasper's voice was strained. "I have receipts, customs documentation, whatever you need. Have you put out an Amber Alert?"

"Yes." Norton made another note. "And the last time Charlotte was seen?"

They'd gone over all of this already. Every second they wasted here was another second she was missing. Noah forced himself to think back. "I checked on her around midnight. She was sound asleep."

Jasper wandered down the hall toward the front door.

"You're sure she was there?" Norton asked. "You didn't just see a lump under the pillows."

"I went into the room and kissed her good night, since Jasper had put her to bed."

"I see. Because you and Miss Wright were at the police station late."

Since it wasn't a question, Noah couldn't summon a response.

"Miss Wright?"

Delaney's voice was barely a whisper. "I went to bed earlier than Mr. Aylett."

Noah glared at the detective. "You need to go find Charlotte. You're wasting your time."

"I know you're worried," Norton said.

Worried. Such a common word for the feelings coursing through Noah. He couldn't even name most of them.

"We have people out looking for her right now," Norton said. "I promise, we're doing everything we can."

Which wasn't the same as "I promise we'll find her." Nobody could make that promise.

Jasper's heels thumped on the hardwood as he returned. "Someone could've watched you put the code in through the window."

"What? How?" And how had Noah's brother thought of that? Jasper was the expert at *causing* problems, not *solving* them.

"Come here," Jaz said. "I'll show you."

Noah followed his brother out the front door, where a few uniformed police officers were milling about, doing nothing useful.

He wanted to order them off his property, to order them to do their jobs. Every second they spent here was another second Charlotte was farther away from him.

Jasper led him to the hedge that separated the yard from the sidewalk and pointed. "It's hard to see right now because of the glare, but I think, from here, if you look through the window just this side of the door..."

Noah crouched and saw what Jaz had noticed, the keypad through the window. But how could someone have been here, watching, without being seen? The hedge was only waist high.

"Step away," Norton said. When they did, he crouched and poked around in the hedges. "Got it." He pulled on latex gloves before carefully extracting a tiny metal device. He held it up for them to see. It was black, cylindrical, about an inch long and no wider than a quarter. A tiny camera. "Here's your answer."

Jasper swore under his breath.

Noah's stomach dropped. Someone had been watching them. Watching Charlotte. Learning their routines, their security code, waiting for the perfect moment to strike.

"How long has that been there?" Noah's question came out in a whisper. This had happened right here, in his front yard. And he'd had no idea.

"Could be days, could be weeks." Norton slipped the device into a plastic bag. "We'll dust it for prints, but..."

"You probably won't find any." Delaney had followed them outside, her arms wrapped tightly around herself.

Noah was about to rebuke her for her negativity when Jasper added, "Professionals don't leave prints."

Ice coursed through Noah's veins. This wasn't just Violet acting on some bizarre maternal urge. Maybe Charlotte's drug-addicted mother and Noah's biggest rival were working together.

Norton stepped away to speak to one of the uniformed cops,

lowering his voice so they couldn't hear. He handed him the evidence bag, then gestured to the yard.

Noah needed to call Richard, to get him over here so he could tell the police what he'd told Noah about Hayes's tactics. He stepped away and dialed, watching the bizarre scene unfold at his house.

Police crawling all over the place, searching for clues.

His niece, missing.

None of this could be happening.

While the phone rang, Delaney approached Jasper and said something to him.

It was irrational, the rage that tiny action triggered. He knew jealousy had no place here when his niece was missing. He couldn't help his frustration that Delaney would even speak to Jaz after he'd been MIA for months. And Jasper, who'd done literally nothing to protect his daughter except dump her and then take off, was now acting like some freaking knight on a white horse.

Noah wanted to punch his brother. He wanted to punch Norton, who was chatting with his team while his little girl's life was in danger. Where was the sense of urgency?

More than anything, Noah wanted Charlotte home, in his arms.

He wanted to make sure she was safe and protected, like he'd promised her.

Once again, he'd allowed himself to get distracted by a pretty girl, and someone he loved had paid the price.

CHAPTER TWENTY-EIGHT

The vultures had arrived.

Delaney pulled back the curtain just enough to peer through the window. Three news vans lined the street, reporters gazing at the Aylett house in search of tragedy. Camera crews huddled nearby, chatting, some laughing as if this were a party instead of the scene of a kidnapping.

Thank heavens for the yellow police tape and the stern-faced officers who kept them at bay.

It didn't matter that reporters were there. What mattered was that Charlotte was missing, and Delaney was packing her bags because she had nothing else to do with her hands.

She folded another shirt and placed it in her suitcase. The house had grown crowded with people who actually belonged here—Noah, his friend Richard, Jasper, and Mason—the police officer who'd responded to her car accident and who, she'd learned, was an old school friend of Jasper's. They were all downstairs, their deep voices a constant rumble beneath her feet as they shared information and discussed strategy.

The longer the four men had talked, the more of an outsider Delaney had felt. She doubted any of them had noticed when she'd retreated up the stairs. Not that it mattered how they treated her. Nothing mattered except getting Charlotte back.

She slumped onto the side of the bed, gazing at this room she'd loved since she'd first seen it, the old four-poster, the walnut-stained bureau, the pretty chair and table by the window. It was bright and cheerful, and she'd felt at home here. Now, everything seemed to carry a pall. The very air was thick with terror, the house empty without Charlotte's pitter-pattering feet and lighthearted chatter.

Charlotte was out there somewhere, probably terrified, while Delaney sat in her bedroom feeling sorry for herself.

She closed her eyes. *Please, dear God, please save her and bring her home.*

Tears leaked from between Delaney's eyelids as she entreated the one who knew exactly where Charlotte was. *Take care of her until she comes home, Lord. You are able. Please, please...* She didn't know what else to pray but sat there a long time, begging the Lord for Charlotte's life.

When she was spent, she stood and zipped the suitcases closed. If Noah wanted her to go, she was ready, but she didn't plan to leave Driftwood until Charlotte was safe. She could get a hotel room. She had a little money saved. If she had to cash her father's check, then she would. She didn't care about proving anything to anyone.

None of that mattered anymore.

The murmur of male voices grew louder as Delaney descended the stairs and approached the living room. She paused at the threshold.

Noah stood by the fireplace, arms crossed, his face neutral but his eyes blazing with frustration and worry. Richard sat on the couch. Jasper paced. He'd run his fingers through his hair so often that it was standing on end. Mason leaned against the wall, still in uniform, his expression grim.

They were mostly quiet, as if they'd run out of ideas.

"Is someone looking at all of Hayes's properties?" Richard asked.

"All?" Jasper's volume was too high. "How many does he have?"

"I don't know." Richard's voice was almost fatherly. "He's very wealthy, so I'd guess more than one."

Mason pushed off from the wall. "Someone's following that thread. The FBI has been called in, and—"

"It's not enough!" Noah's voice broke on the last word, the raw pain in it making Delaney's stomach turn over.

Nobody seemed to know what to say.

She cleared her throat, and four heads swiveled in her direction. Noah's eyes met hers, and something flickered across his face. Relief?

She was probably projecting.

"What about the place in Norfolk?" she asked. "The one Heather...Violet told me about?"

Mason fielded that. "We're looking at real estate records for both Hayes and Bosch. If either owns a home—"

"What if it's rented?"

"That's...more difficult," he said carefully.

Noah's eyes blazed. "You have to—"

"We're looking into it." The cop's tone was reasonable with a touch of impatience. "But without more information, it's going to take some time. There's no rental database to search."

"Utility customers?" Noah suggested. "Can't they look at those?"

"They can." Again, Mason seemed to choose his words carefully. "But it takes time to do it legally. We need warrants and—"

"Who cares if it's legal?" Jasper froze, the words so loud they reverberated off the walls.

"Being the police and all"—Mason kept his tone even—"we tend to get caught up on stuff like that." He stepped closer to Jasper and clamped a hand on his shoulder. "I promise. We're doing everything we can."

Jasper shrugged him off.

It seemed Mason was trying to lean on their old friendship, but Jasper wasn't interested. He resumed his pacing.

Mason gave her a half smile. "We are looking into it, Miss Wright. It just takes time."

"I understand."

Noah stepped toward her, hands shoved deep in his pockets. "Delaney, have you packed?"

She blinked, surprised by the question. "Yes, but..."

He didn't expect her to actually leave, did he?

She glanced at Jasper, but he was paying no attention, lost in his own torturous world. Richard was leaning over a laptop. Mason had retreated to the edge of the room, observing everything.

She focused on Noah again, lowering her voice. "You don't think I'm leaving Driftwood, not now."

"It would be best if you did."

"What? Why? When Charlotte's safe, she'll want me here. She needs to know I'm not going to abandon her."

Delaney had made Charlotte feel safe. Maybe Noah didn't want Delaney anymore, but surely Charlotte still did.

Noah took her hand and tugged her down the hall and into the dining room. She hadn't set foot in here since her first day in the house. Nothing had changed. The Waterford crystal still sat where it had before, dusted by the housekeeper, who came once a week.

Noah drew her away from the door, then took her other hand. "I'm sorry. I know it's terrible. I know it's...absolutely excruciating, but you should go."

Delaney couldn't help the tears that filled her eyes. "But... but I love her. And she needs me."

"She has Jaz and me. She'll be okay."

Delaney's lips trembled. "I'll leave if you want, but I'm staying in Driftwood. I'll go to a hotel—"

"Back to Maine." His tone was even. "Please."

"What? You can't..." Her pitch rose until she sounded like a child. "I don't understand."

Noah pulled her into his arms and held her, and her barely controlled emotions burst in a sob.

She wrapped her arms around him, feeling comfort and anger and a million other emotions, too many to count. Too many to handle.

She belonged here, with him. And Charlotte. How could he not see that?

"I know, sweetheart," Noah said. "I know how hard this is for you. I don't mean to be cruel, but the news vans are outside, and—"

"Are you kidding me!" She wrenched out of his arms and stepped back. "Is that what this is about?" Her voice was too loud and she didn't care. "You're going to break my heart—and Charlotte's—because of your fear of scandal? Your niece has been *kidnapped* because of that stupid merger, and now you're worried my being here is going to...what? Cost you a little money?"

His eyes filled with ice. "You really think I care about that right now?"

"Apparently, if you're sending me away."

He pressed his lips closed so tightly they paled. He breathed in through his nose. Finally, he blew the breath out. "Delaney, do you really think so little of me?"

She didn't know what to think. She swiped her fingers

across her cheeks to remove the moisture, though her tears continued to fall.

He stepped close again and reached for her.

She crossed her arms, not willing to give in to him when he was being so cruel.

He ducked to meet her eyes. "I care about you. You know that, right?"

She'd thought so, but now, she didn't know what to think.

"What happened to Charlotte...it's killing me. It's all I can think about. But in the back of my mind, humming like a song I can't get out of my head, is the fact that I care about you, too, and everybody knows it."

"So what? Is that so awful?"

"What if they hurt you?" His voice broke. "What if they try to take you too? I can't..." He swallowed hard, staring into her eyes as if to impart some important knowledge.

Suddenly, she understood.

He wasn't trying to get rid of her. He was trying to protect her.

"Please." He gripped her elbows and stepped closer, lowering his forehead to hers. "Please go home where you'll be safe until this all blows over. If I'm afraid for your safety, I won't be able to think straight."

"But I love Charlotte too." She squeaked the words through her tight throat. "I need to be here—"

"I know you do, and as soon as she's safe and her kidnappers are in custody, you can come back. But until then, please?"

She didn't want to leave. She desperately didn't want to leave.

"Do you promise to take care of yourself?"

His lip twitched at the corner, a smile that said he knew he'd won the battle. "You know I'll try."

She also knew he'd do whatever it took to get Charlotte back, even if it meant putting himself in danger.

"I'll go if you promise to keep me updated."

"I promise." He pulled her into another hug and whispered in her ear. "I love the way you love, Delaney Wright. I love the way you...are."

Love. He'd used the word more than once. He hadn't told her he loved her, but...but was that what he meant?

Could he possibly return her feelings?

She stepped back to meet Noah's eyes. Even if this was love, now wasn't the time for declarations. "Charlotte will never be far from my mind or out of my prayers, and neither will you."

He embraced her again, and she melted against him. Yes, this was love, much stronger and deeper than anything she'd felt for Owen. Noah was a good man.

Forty-five minutes later, Delaney stared out the passenger-side window of the police cruiser. Noah had asked one of the cops to drive her to the airport to ensure she made it safely. Overkill, obviously. They approached the terminal after an uneventful ride.

The cop had been kind enough to keep the conversation light during the drive, talking about the weather and the upcoming holidays. She hadn't had much to contribute, and eventually he'd fallen silent.

She couldn't stop thinking about the apartment Violet had told her about. Based on what Mason had said, the cops wouldn't be able to find it, certainly not anytime soon.

But Delaney had resources they knew nothing about.

The terminal building loomed ahead. She watched the signage...departures, arrivals, parking, cell phone lot.

One sign jumped out at her.

A few minutes later, the officer parked by the curb in Departures. "Here we are."

They both got out, and he retrieved her suitcases from the trunk, then set them on the sidewalk.

"Thank you for the ride."

"Safe travels, miss. I'm sure everything will work out."

She wanted to ask him how he was sure, how it was all going to work out when a four-year-old girl was missing. Kidnapped, and in the hands of...

Hopefully, her mother, but her mother had lost custody of her once. She wasn't fit, and if she was working with that rival of Noah's, that Hayes guy, then who knew what he'd do to the child?

But Delaney didn't say any of that. Instead, she thanked him again, then turned and headed for the doors.

Inside the terminal, she stared at the crowd in front of the check-in desk, business travelers and vacationers, singles and families.

Delaney could get on her flight. She'd be back in Shadow Cove by evening. She could go home to her parents' house, where Mom would wrap her in familiar comfort while Noah and the others searched for Charlotte.

Or...

She thought about that other sign.

Rental Cars.

This probably wouldn't work, but she had to try.

She shifted both suitcases into one hand and rolled them toward the Arrivals area, pulling out her phone. She searched, found the contact she needed.

Was this a good idea?

Maybe not, but if she could do anything to help, if she could play any part in bringing Charlotte home...

She pressed the contact number and raised the phone to her ear.

A moment later, a man answered. "Hey, cuz. How are you? Everybody's been worried sick—"

"Michael. The girl I've been caring for was kidnapped. I need your help to find the woman I think took her."

A beat of silence, then, "Where are you? What can I do?"

Thank God. Thank God for cousins in the intelligence business.

Delaney reached Baggage Claim, spied the rental car booths, and marched that way while she explained what she needed.

CHAPTER TWENTY-NINE

Hours had passed since Delaney left, and the inaction was killing him.

Noah could feel it, his chest squeezing tighter and tighter. Was this what a heart attack felt like?

Amputees complained of pain in their missing limbs, phantom pain that no pills could deaden.

He wondered if it was similar, the empty place in his heart slicing agony through his body, a vacuum that nothing but his curly-haired niece and her beautiful nanny could fill.

At least Delaney was safe. The cop who'd taken her to the airport had returned an hour before, saying they'd had no trouble. She was probably already in flight.

He hadn't even asked her where she was flying to. Did Portland have an airport, or would she fly to Boston or Manchester? He had no idea.

His mind didn't have room for that kind of information right now. Even so, he itched to text her, to check on her. To tell her... something.

But there was no news. There was nothing to share.

He'd been sitting in his living room, listening to Mason coordinate with other officers, watching Richard refresh news websites incessantly, enduring Jasper's increasingly frantic pacing. Every tick of the grandfather clock in the hallway marked another second Charlotte was gone. Another second she was scared, alone, possibly hurt. He had to *do* something.

He stood abruptly, drawing Mason's attention from where he leaned against a wall, phone pressed to his ear.

Noah grabbed his wallet and keys from the basket where he kept them near the front door and headed for the back.

"Where are you going?" Mason's voice followed him onto the patio.

Noah turned. "I need some air."

"I think you should stay—"

He froze and faced the cop. "Am I not free to leave my own house?"

Mason stiffened. "There's nothing you can do to find Charlotte that we're not already doing. If you have an idea—"

"I don't." Not one that he was ready to share, anyway.

"I need to know where you're going," Mason said. "For your own safety."

This...this friend of Jasper's might be wearing an official uniform and a gun on his hip, but Noah didn't answer to him. If he learned anything, he'd reach out to Detective Norton.

For now, all he had was a hunch.

"I need to get out of here." That was true enough. The walls were closing in on him, suffocating him. "I'm just going to go for a ride." Also true, mostly. "I'll be back in an hour, and I have my phone if you need to contact me."

Mason's gaze was suspicious, but he didn't have the authority to stop him. "Don't do anything stupid."

He'd do whatever it took to get his niece back. He hurried to the carriage-house-turned-garage, slipped inside, then started his car's engine before pressing the button to lift the door.

He'd backed into the garage, as usual. As soon as the door was up, Noah accelerated down the driveway and careened onto Magnolia Street much faster than was safe.

A couple of reporters scrambled for their vehicles, but he had a head start. He took the first right, then another, weaving through the residential streets until he was certain he'd lost anyone trying to follow.

Noah drove through downtown Driftwood, glancing at the park where the event celebrating Noah's ancestor had been held the night before. The rental tables and chairs were already gone. The only remnant from the festivities was the bandstand. It'd looked fancy the night before, draped with banners. Now, stripped of all its adornment, it looked empty and pathetic.

Sort of like the Aylett family. All window dressing. No substance. Not since Mom's death.

All Noah had wanted to do was preserve what his parents and their parents before them had built. Was it such a sin? A sin that required this level of punishment?

Father, please. Whatever I've done to deserve this, forgive me. Don't let Charlotte pay the price.

If Delaney were here, what would she say? That this wasn't his fault. That bad things happened, and there was often no explanation.

Even so, he couldn't help but think that if he'd kept the nanny at arm's length, if he hadn't given in to his feelings for her, none of this would have happened.

It was why he'd been eager to send her away. Because when he'd been distracted by his girlfriend in high school, his father had died.

Now, he'd been distracted by Delaney, and Charlotte was gone.

So he'd sent her away. Because...because what he'd believed was true. When he wasn't vigilant, terrible things happened.

People died.

Dear God, please. Don't let that happen to Charlotte. Please.

By sending Delaney away, he was removing every distraction. And keeping her safe. The fear that she might be in danger was...

Well, just another distraction he couldn't afford.

He had to focus on the task ahead, his mind churning through everything he knew. Lowell had been feeding information to Hayes. Of that, Noah was certain. Lowell, who'd once been his best friend, who'd stood beside him at his wedding, who'd named him godfather to his firstborn, had betrayed him, a betrayal that cut deeper than Noah's failed marriage ever had.

But he wasn't a kidnapper. His former friend was bitter and vindictive, but he wouldn't hurt a child.

Would he?

One way or another, Noah was about to find out.

Lowell lived in a newer development about halfway between Driftwood and Norfolk, where cookie-cutter colonials sat on postage-stamp lots. He and his wife had chosen the development to be close to Lowell's work in Norfolk and his sister in Driftwood.

Noah hadn't been there in years, not since Marianne had packed her things and moved out.

He pulled into the driveway and parked, then sat there a minute, fumbling to make a plan.

The best he could come up with was to tell Lowell what had happened and hope the man's better self responded.

Noah climbed the front steps. Rage—just one of the feelings he'd been suppressing all day—rose inside him like lava. If Lowell had any connection to this, any part in Charlotte's disappearance...

Lord, help me here. I don't know how to do this.

He took a deep breath and rang the doorbell.

Footsteps approached, then the door opened.

Missy, Lowell's wife, smiled from the far side of the screen. Back in college, she'd been tiny, but the years and the kids had affected her figure. Even so, she was attractive, with shoulder-length brown hair pulled back in a headband. She wore jeans and a sweatshirt. "Hey, Noah. I'm glad to see you."

No matter what Lowell had believed, Missy had always been kind to him. By her casual greeting, she hadn't heard about Charlotte's kidnapping.

He didn't have it in him to explain and then deal with her emotional reaction, so he said, "Is Lowell home?"

"He's playing with Bryce. Come on in." She pushed the screen open, and he stepped inside and followed her to the back of the house.

It hadn't changed much since he'd seen it last. Missy had a talent for decorating. The dining room looked showroom beautiful, with light furnishings that matched her cheerful personality. On the opposite side of the hall, Lowell's office wasn't so airy with the mahogany desk and matching floor-to-ceiling bookshelves.

The family room, while decorated as well as the rest of the house, was far less tidy. Toys littered the floor. The Carolina Panthers football game played on the TV, but muted. Lowell sat cross-legged on the carpet, building a tower of blocks with his three-year-old son.

Noah took in the man who'd once been his friend—kind, patient, devoted to his family. A man without bitterness etched into the lines of his face.

He studied the little boy, his godson, the boy who'd been his nephew before the divorce. He and Marianne had been at the hospital when Bryce was born. Noah had held his tiny body and promised to be the best godfather ever.

He hadn't seen Bryce since he'd learned to crawl, much less walk.

Lowell looked up. The smile he'd aimed at his wife vanished when he saw Noah. "What are you doing here?" His voice hardened as he placed a protective hand on his son's shoulder.

"I need to speak with you." Noah kept his voice level despite the storm raging inside him. "Privately."

Lowell stared at him for a long moment, then spoke to his son. "Bryce, go with Mommy. I need to talk to Mr. Aylett."

Uncle Noah, he wanted to say. They were family.

Bryce protested, but Missy picked him up. "Come help me in the kitchen, buddy. I'm making cookies."

Noah expected Lowell to lead him into his office, but instead, he headed for the sliding glass doors that opened to the backyard, then stepped aside to let Noah precede him as if he feared turning his back on him.

Maybe he should.

The landscaping had grown since Noah's last visit, the saplings now sturdy young trees, the flower beds more established. An outdoor seating area was nestled under a covered patio.

As soon as the door closed behind them, Noah rounded on his former friend. "Did you know?"

Lowell's expression shifted from annoyance to confusion, his brows drawing together. "Know what?"

"Charlotte's been kidnapped." He paused to let the words sink in. "Someone broke into my house in the middle of the night and took her from her bed."

All color drained from Lowell's face. He gripped the edge of a patio chair and lowered himself into it as if his legs could no longer support him. "I would never... Of course I wouldn't be involved in something like that. She's just a child."

Noah searched for any hint of deception, any flicker that he was lying. But Lowell's shock seemed genuine—the way his hands trembled, the sickened pallor of his skin.

"I had nothing to do with it." Lowell's voice was unsteady. "You have to believe me."

Maybe. But that didn't extinguish the anger burning inside Noah. "The difference between you and me, Lowell, is that when you tell me something, I do believe you."

"But... This isn't... This is different. Marianne's my sister, and she said—"

"If Marianne believed those lies about me, then she was wrong." Noah's words were too loud, vibrating with betrayal and fury and fear. He needed to control himself. More importantly, he needed to reach Lowell to get his help. "I never had a relationship with Lena Monroe. She started the rumors because she's crazy."

"Oh, come on—"

"Right now, she's in custody after pointing a gun at us last night. She threatened to kill Delaney. Charlotte was there for the whole thing. When Jaz tackled Lena, she fired. We're just lucky the shot went wide and nobody was hurt or killed."

"Seriously?" But his expression darkened. "That doesn't mean you didn't—"

"I never slept with her!" He shouted so loudly that his words came back in an echo. He took two deep breaths. *Help me, Father. Calm me down. Give me wisdom.*

He watched his friend processing, but he didn't have time for that.

"Get it through your head, Lowell. I didn't cheat on your sister. All the things you've done to hurt me have been for nothing. Got it?"

"If what you're saying is true about Lena, then maybe she took Char—"

"She's in jail," he snapped. "Try to keep up." His heart was racing as if he'd run a marathon.

Here he'd thought having a gun pointed at him would be the most drama he'd face in a year, maybe in a lifetime.

Less than twenty-four hours later, that moment was already irrelevant.

"So you're saying somebody *else* took Charlotte?" Lowell asked. "Not Lena?" His eyes widened. "You can't think *I* did it."

"You've been feeding Hayes information about me."

"I..." Lowell sank deeper into the chair, his face ashen. "Yes, but—"

"Tell me everything you know about him."

"I don't know much." Lowell rubbed the back of his neck. "I mean, I heard he was ruthless in business. That's not a secret. And I think—" He paused, his eye contact slipping. "I know he was behind the sabotage at your office."

"I don't care about that." Noah stepped closer, looming over his former friend. "What else? What did he tell you?"

Lowell looked up at him, eyes wide. "I just know he's a dog with a bone when he sees something he wants." He blinked, looking so young, so like the college freshman he'd been when Noah had first met him. "I wanted you defeated, I admit that. I thought Hayes would stop at nothing to make the merger fail."

"You got what you wanted, then. He didn't even stop at kidnapping an innocent little girl. Now, you're involved. You have to tell him I'll back out of the deal if I get Charlotte back today. Unharmed."

"I...I'll think about—"

"Now, Lowell, or I'm telling the police you've been conspiring with him. If he's behind this, which I have no doubt he is, you'll be an accessory to kidnapping. You'll be a felon."

Noah wouldn't have thought it possible, but the remaining

color drained from Lowell's face, leaving him looking pasty and sickly.

Noah settled on the chair across from him. "Unlike you, that's not what I want for you, though God knows you'd have destroyed me if you'd had the chance."

"I believed my sister. I really thought—"

"It doesn't matter now," Noah said. "All I care about is getting Charlotte back. If I have to destroy you to do it, believe me, I will."

"Okay, I get... Okay." Lowell pulled out his phone with trembling hands. "I only have his business number. He probably won't—"

"Make the call. And put it on speaker. I want to hear everything."

CHAPTER THIRTY

With each mile marker, it felt like Charlotte slipped further away.

Delaney gripped the steering wheel of the rental car, her knuckles white as she cruised along the beachfront road in Norfolk. The November sun glinted off the water to her right, mockingly cheerful compared to the heaviness inside her. To her left, an upscale golf course stretched in manicured perfection.

This was all she knew. Violet's apartment had a view of the water and was within walking distance of a golf course. But what constituted "walking distance"? A mile, two? There were countless homes, apartment buildings, and condo complexes on this stretch of coastline. Violet could be in any of them.

Delaney did have one other piece of information, shared by Michael an hour before—the make and model of Violet's car, an older gray Honda Civic. Norton had told him the Driftwood PD had that information, but he hadn't given Noah or Delaney the details.

She'd spotted at least ten cars already that could fit the bill, none with the right plate number. For all she knew, Violet had stolen another car's plate. Or stolen a car.

"This is never going to work." How did she think she was going to find Charlotte when the police hadn't been able to?

But she couldn't stop. She wouldn't, not until Charlotte was found. Maybe Delaney would look ridiculous for thinking she could do something. That'd be a small price to pay for trying to find the child she loved.

Michael was helping. If anybody could locate Violet, he could. He'd rescued his wife—girlfriend at the time—from a heavily guarded compound in the middle of Iraq, then escaped with her and her twin through Turkey, bad guys on their tail the whole way.

She figured the story had been embellished, but even so, the man was tenacious. If he could find Leila in a desert half a world away, surely he could find Violet in Norfolk, Virginia.

That thought kept her driving, scanning every parking lot, every storefront, every flash of movement that might lead her to Charlotte.

The question wasn't could Michael do it. The question was, how soon?

Please, Father. Please lead me to her. Or the police, or anyone. Please, save Charlotte.

Her phone rang, Michael's name lighting up the screen. She searched the unfamiliar dash for the button to answer through Bluetooth, then jabbed it. "Please tell me you have something."

"Maybe." Michael's voice came through clear and focused. "Alyssa got this for me. Don't worry, I didn't tell her it was for you."

Delaney didn't care who knew what she was doing, but it would be better if her family didn't worry. "Tell me what she learned."

"She was searching utility customers. No Violet Bosch or Heather Brown, but following that pattern—"

"What pattern?"

"First name's a flower, second name begins with B."

"Oh. I hadn't noticed that."

"Most people use patterns when they're setting up aliases. It's a rookie mistake."

"Good catch."

"There's a utility customer under the name of Iris Benson. She activated the account about three months ago."

Delaney ignored the surge of hope. "Where?"

"Alyssa's still working on that. I'll get back to you. I just wanted you to know we're making progress. Don't give up."

"Thanks, cuz." Delaney ended the call, still driving, still searching for Violet's car. Maybe she'd get lucky.

One way or another, they had to find Charlotte. Delaney couldn't fathom the pain Noah and Jasper—and she herself—would feel if they didn't.

CHAPTER THIRTY-ONE

L owell's phone mocked Noah from where it sat on the patio table, Hayes's name bright on the screen. The call went to voicemail for the third time.

Noah's patience, already stretched tissue-thin, was about to snap.

"I can't force him to answer." Lowell's usual arrogance had melted away. His shoulders were hunched, his body practically doubled over as if the weight of Charlotte's kidnapping—and his part in it—were pressing him down.

Noah grabbed the phone before the screen locked and opened the text app. His thumbs flew across the screen as he typed.

GET SOMEPLACE WHERE YOU'RE ALONE
AND CALL ME NOW -NOAH

He sent the message, then stood and paced Lowell's immaculate patio with the brand-new furniture and artfully placed decor. He couldn't help the urge to kick over a potted plant.

The grass was too green. The flowers too bright. Nothing was right.

They'd discovered Charlotte missing at around eight o'clock that morning. It was now almost two thirty. Six and a half hours.

But she'd been gone much longer than that. While Noah had lain in bed sleeping, fighting nightmares about stalkers and guns and too-pleasant dreams about the nanny he couldn't have, someone had broken into his house. Crept up the creaky staircase. Snatched his niece.

He'd done nothing to protect her. Nothing.

By now, Charlotte could be hundreds of miles away. Thousands, if Violet had bought a plane ticket.

She could be anywhere.

"What if he doesn't call back?" Lowell asked, his voice small.

"He'll call," Noah snapped. Hayes had to call because if he didn't... Noah couldn't even consider it.

If Hayes didn't call, then Noah had no idea what he'd do next.

Each step was a struggle against the urge to put his fist through something, especially his old so-called friend who'd set this horror show into motion. "He wants the merger. He'll do anything for it. He'll call."

But the minutes crawled by like hours. Noah's mind raced with images of Charlotte—scared, calling for him, wondering why he hadn't protected her. He pressed his fingertips against his temples, trying to force the thoughts away.

When Lowell's phone finally rang in his hand, Noah nearly jumped out of his skin. He swiped to answer. "Are you alone?" He sounded tight and controlled despite the hurricane raging inside him.

In the background, he heard voices—multiple people talking.

Lowell stood and crossed to Noah, gaze flicking from the phone to Noah's face.

"I can't." Hayes's usual confidence was gone, replaced by a genuine note of fear.

"I told you to get somewhere you could talk." Noah's stomach, already in knots, somersaulted. If the police were with Hayes, the man would be careful about what he said. He wouldn't reveal anything useful. "Whatever you want," Noah blurted. "I don't care. I'll drop the merger, sign over my company. You can have the house. I just want Charlotte back."

There was a pause, and the background noise abated. Finally, Hayes said, "This was never my plan."

"I don't care what your plan was! Where is she?"

"The police are here. I've told them everything I know."

Noah's fingers tightened around the phone. Was this some kind of trick? "Fine." Not that he believed it. If the police had learned Charlotte's whereabouts, surely they'd have told him. "Now tell me. Where is she? Where's my niece?"

"I don't know. I swear." Hayes took an audible breath. "I hired an investigator a few months back, as soon as Lowell told me about the merger. Before I ever made a bid, I figured out who Charlotte's mother was, and I convinced her that if you were surrounded by enough scandal—if you and your nanny were caught in a compromising situation, or if she could prove that you were neglecting your niece—she'd be able to sue for custody. The courts would let her have Charlotte back."

Noah struggled to process what he was hearing. "Did you really think that would work?"

"No, not...really," Hayes admitted. "But she believed it."

"You were using her."

"I needed Tidewater to lose faith in you. I thought for sure Violet would learn something that I could use. And I figured, even if she did sue for custody, she'd lose. No harm done."

"To you," Noah spat. "But lots of harm to her. And now Charlotte has been—"

"You think I don't know?" Hayes sounded angry and defensive, but beneath that, Noah heard a hint of panic. Maybe even genuine concern, though he suspected the man was more worried about being an accessory to kidnapping than about Violet's feelings or Charlotte's safety. "She's sober now, but—"

"Is she in her right mind?"

He sighed. "I thought...I thought so. She seemed fine. You met her. You know how she was. Articulate, well-spoken. She seemed perfectly reasonable to me."

"Except that she believed she could get custody."

"Yeah." The word was drawn out, hesitant. "I think she was deceived by her own certainty that she deserves custody of Charlotte. When we first started working together—"

"Sleeping together, you mean."

A pause, then a sigh. "I've done a lot of things I regret."

"Amazing what getting caught will do to your conscience."

"I'm doing my best here, Aylett."

"You got my niece kidnapped, Hayes. Surely you don't expect sympathy."

Another sigh. "The point is, she seemed fine at first. Full of hope and totally rational. But in the last few weeks, she was getting frustrated. She hardly ever saw your nanny, and when she did, the woman didn't share any dirt. We argued last night. I knew she was losing it, but I never dreamed she would do something like this. I thought she'd just relapse or something."

"You're a real piece of work."

"I didn't mean..." The man's pitch rose. "I never meant for any of this to happen."

Noah had no time for Hayes's regrets. "What about the apartment Violet told Delaney about? Where is it?"

"I've never been there. I just gave her money to rent a place. I know it's in Norfolk, but that's all. I used to meet her at a hotel outside of town."

"Which one? Maybe she's there."

"I told the police. They checked it already."

Noah closed his eyes, his free hand clenching into a fist. The lead he'd hoped for crumbled to nothing. "That's it?" The words scraped his throat. "That's all you know?"

"I'm sorry." Hayes sounded like he meant it. "I really am. But the police are working on it. They'll find her. If there was anything I could do—"

Noah ended the call and hurled the phone onto the patio table. It skittered across the surface and clattered to the ground.

Lowell flinched but said nothing.

The rage that had been building all day erupted. Noah spun, searching for something to destroy, something to absorb the violence clawing at his chest. His gaze landed on one of Missy's carefully arranged potted mums.

Before he could think, he kicked. The ceramic pot exploded against the patio stones, dirt and yellow flowers scattering everywhere.

"Noah." Lowell's hand landed on his shoulder.

He shrugged it off. "Don't." He was breathing hard. The small act of destruction had done nothing to ease the pressure threatening to crack his skull open.

"I'm so sorry." Lowell's voice was tentative. "I had no idea—"

"*Sorry* doesn't bring her back." Noah rounded on his former friend, this man who'd once known him better than anyone, who'd helped him move into his first apartment, who'd been his best man. "You've been feeding him information about me. About my business, my life, my family. And you never once stopped to think about what he might do with it."

Lowell's face crumpled. "I thought... I was just helping him compete. Business stuff. I didn't expect something like this to happen."

Noah had never wanted to punch a man more in his life. But he had better things to do.

He pulled out his phone and called Detective Norton. The detective answered immediately.

"I just talked to Hayes," Noah said without preamble. "He admitted to everything. He's been working with Violet, but he claims he doesn't know where she is. He said he's cooperating—"

"He is. We heard everything he said to you, and he'd already told us all of that."

"How do we know he's telling the truth? Maybe he knows exactly where she is, and he just doesn't want to admit it."

"You're going to have to trust—"

"Trust him? Are you crazy?"

"Not him." Norton's words came slowly, his tone low and even. "Trust us. We know what we're doing."

Easy for him to say. It wasn't his niece who was missing. But Noah's attitude wasn't helping anything.

"You have to find that apartment. How hard can it be to track down one woman with a four-year-old?"

"Mr. Aylett, I understand your frustration—"

"No, you don't." Noah turned away from Lowell, who was picking up pieces of the shattered pot. "You have no idea what this feels like. Every second she's gone is another second she's terrified, wondering why no one's coming for her."

"We have everyone working on this, locals, state police. The FBI is involved. We're doing everything we can to find her."

The detective's calm professionalism grated against Noah's raw nerves. He wanted urgency, panic, the same desperate energy that was tearing him apart from the inside.

"I'm coming back," Noah said, not because he wanted to be cooped up at the house, but because he had no idea what else to do.

"Be safe," the detective said. "I'll call if there are any developments."

But there wouldn't be any developments. Hayes was their only link to Charlotte, and he knew nothing.

Noah couldn't help the despair seeping into every cell of his body. Charlotte was gone, and nobody knew where to find her.

CHAPTER THIRTY-TWO

Shadows stretched across Norfolk's streets as Delaney squinted at yet another license plate, her eyes burning from intense focus. The November sun hung low on the horizon, painting the world in deceptive gold while stealing away the clarity she desperately needed.

"Come on," she whispered, drumming her fingers against the steering wheel as she crawled past a row of parked cars. Gray Honda, but wrong plate. Silver sedan, not even close. She'd been at this for hours, circling through neighborhoods near the beach, checking every parking lot, every side street, every hint of a vehicle that might belong to Violet.

Her phone rang, Michael's name lighting up the screen. Her heart leapt as she pressed the button to answer.

"I've got it," Michael said without preamble. "Seaglass Towers, unit 317. It's a condo complex off Shore Drive."

Delaney's pulse quickened. "Are you sure?"

"Call it an educated guess. Iris Benson has lived there just under three months."

Delaney pulled over and typed the address into her GPS. She'd passed this place multiple times, but she hadn't been able to get into the parking garage beneath it. From where the apartment building sat, the third-floor apartments would have a view of the bay. She scanned out and saw the golf course a handful of blocks away. "I'm heading there now."

"Wait." Michael's voice sharpened. "You need to call the police."

"I will," she said, already pulling back onto the road. "I'll do it now."

"But I want you to stay away from that building, just in case."

"A little girl's been kidnapped, Michael. Would you stay away?"

"I'm a trained agent. It's my job—"

"I'm not going to charge in there. I promise. I'll call you when we've got her."

"Laney." His voice was low and filled with emotions she'd never heard from her no-nonsense cousin. That and his use of her nickname had her pausing. "Be careful. Promise?"

"I promise. Thanks."

She ended the call as she parked on the street adjacent to the apartments. She couldn't drive into the garage without entering a code on the keypad, but the ramp wasn't manned. She could duck under the gate.

She climbed out of her rental, surprised at how the temperature had dipped now that the sun was down. She grabbed her keys and phone and jogged into the parking garage.

Her phone vibrated in her hand before she could dial 911. She glanced at the screen.

Noah?

Heart pounding, she answered. "Did you find her? Is she all right?"

"No news, but you're supposed to be in Maine." By the

background noise, she guessed he was in his car. "Why do I see your location in Virginia?"

She'd forgotten she'd shared her location with him back when she'd first started working with him. But… "Why did you check it?"

"I don't know. I just…"

His voice trailed, and she understood what he hadn't said. That he missed her. She missed him too.

"What are you doing in Norfolk?"

"I was just about to call you. Well, the police, then you."

"What's going on?" His volume hiked up, more fear than anger.

Delaney scanned cars and plates as she walked through the small garage. "I couldn't get on that plane. Not when Charlotte's out there somewhere. And I think…" She didn't want to get his hopes up, but he was probably with the police right now. "I think I've got a lead."

"What are you talking about? What lead? How?"

Delaney climbed the ramp to the second level of the garage, the scents of gasoline and oil pungent. "My cousin helped me track down a possible address for Violet."

"How would your cousin—?"

"He's CIA. If he hadn't answered, I'd have called Dad. Michael said a woman named Iris Benson rented an apartment at Seaglass Towers, unit 3 1 7."

"That's not…I don't understand."

She quickly explained Michael's theory about the alias.

"Smart. But… Wait. Are you there?" His voice rose sharply. "What if she sees you?"

"I'm in the parking garage, looking for her car." She kept her voice low as she moved between the rows of vehicles, checking license plates. "If I find it, I'll know for sure she's here."

"Delaney, it's too dangerous. You need to…"

She gasped, eyeing the car that'd pulled her up short.

"What?" Noah said. "Are you okay?"

There it was, Violet's car. "I found it, Noah. She's here. I'm hanging up to call the police."

"No." The command in his voice surprised her. "Stay out of sight. I'll call Detective Norton. They need to handle this properly."

The elevator dinged, catching Delaney's attention. The doors slid open, and a woman stepped out.

Her heart stuttered.

She recognized the slight figure holding the hand of a small child with blond curls.

Delaney ducked behind a concrete pillar. "Noah." She kept her volume at a whisper. "They're here. They're heading for her car."

"What?" His voice rose. "Are you sure?"

"Call the police." She ended the call and shoved the phone in her pocket.

Heart thumping, mind racing, she ducked low and, using the line of parked cars for cover, hurried to a staircase. She slipped through the door as quietly as she could, then barreled down, hanging onto the railing to keep from tumbling and knocking herself out. She had to get to her car.

Right now, she was Charlotte's best hope. She couldn't let them disappear.

CHAPTER THIRTY-THREE

Noah yanked the wheel hard left, tires shrieking against asphalt as he executed a U-turn. There was no fast way into Norfolk from Driftwood, just dark and winding two-lane roads. But he was already halfway there, having just left Lowell's house.

He slowed to find the detective's number in his phone. As soon as it rang over his speakers, his foot pressed the accelerator. The engine roared, and his BMW shot forward.

"Detective Norton."

"Delaney found them." Noah's words tumbled out. "Violet's at Seaglass Towers in Norfolk. Charlotte too."

"How could she possibly—?"

"Doesn't matter. Charlotte's there. Delaney saw them leaving the building."

"She's sure?"

"Positive."

The detective shouted to his team, issuing commands. They'd get Norfolk PD moving immediately.

"Noah, where are you?"

"Headed that way." He checked his speedometer—sixty-five and climbing. "I'm about twenty minutes out."

"Stand down. Let the police handle it."

"If not for Delaney, the police wouldn't even know where Charlotte is." Stand down? While his niece was in the hands of a kidnapper? "Just hurry."

He ended the call and focused on the road, familiar landmarks blurring past his windows, along with miles and miles of forest.

His phone buzzed—Delaney. He answered.

"They left." She sounded breathless, as if she'd sprinted a mile.

His stomach plummeted. "They're gone? Did you see which way—?"

"I'm following. We're headed—"

"Delaney, that's too dangerous. What if she sees you?"

"I'm keeping my distance. I can't lose her, Noah. I can't lose Charlotte."

The desperation in her voice mirrored his own terror. She should back off, let the police handle it, but what if Violet changed plates or got into a different car? She could drive away and never be seen again.

Charlotte was in danger, and now Delaney was too. He hated it. But everything was out of his control now.

"Just...be careful." He swallowed hard. "Stay far enough back that she won't notice you."

"I don't think she's spotted me. We're on Ocean View Drive headed...I don't know which way. The water's on my left."

Noah slowed enough to bring up the location app on his phone so he could see where Delaney was. They were hugging the shoreline, headed east.

He forced himself to lower the phone and focus. "I'm getting closer. Just entered Norfolk city limits."

"Okay. The road is turning..." Delaney's voice was more controlled. "I just saw a sign. It's now Shore Road."

"I have your location."

"Oh, right. Did you call the police?"

"Yeah. They're on their way, but you should call them and tell them what's going on."

"You need to send me the number."

Much as he hated to stop, better him than her. He didn't want Delaney to risk losing sight of Violet. He pulled over, tapped Norton's number into a message, and sent it to Delaney.

"Got it," she said. "I'll call him now and then call you back."

"Delaney?"

"Yeah."

"Thank you. I can't...I'll never be able to..." He had no idea how to finish. There were no words.

"I know," she said. "I'll call you back."

When she was gone and only silence filled the car, Noah started praying, out loud and constant, begging God to protect the girl and the woman he loved so much.

CHAPTER THIRTY-FOUR

Delaney nearly fumbled the phone with her slick palms as she ended the call with Detective Norton and dialed Noah back.

"Everything okay?" he asked.

"The police are setting up a roadblock." She kept her eyes locked on Violet's gray Honda a few car lengths ahead. The sun was setting, the night growing darker by the second. "Norton thinks she's going to Highway 13."

"Makes sense." Noah sounded calmer than when she'd talked to him a few minutes before, almost at peace. "From there, she could go north across the bay to Maryland or south to hook up with other highways. Down to North Carolina or... anywhere, really."

Norton had said close to the same thing. He'd made it sound so simple. Local police would stop cars quietly, making it look like there was an accident ahead. Then a couple would approach Violet's vehicle from behind.

"This will work," he'd assured her. He'd sounded so confident.

But the ache in the pit of Delaney's stomach didn't agree. From where she sat, watching Violet's taillights cut through the night, the situation felt fragile. One wrong move, one moment of panic, and Charlotte could be hurt. Or disappear forever.

"God is watching over them." Noah's confidence rang despite the undercurrent of worry in his voice. "I've been praying constantly, and I know... I know He's with us, whatever happens. He's got Charlotte in His hands."

There should be peace in that. But what if God didn't see fit to rescue her? What if He let her be lost with Violet? Delaney couldn't imagine the pain of losing her, and she was just the child's nanny. How would Noah handle it? How would Jasper?

"I hope you're—wait!"

Violet's brake lights flared ahead. The Honda slowed, then turned sharply onto a narrow road. No street sign marked the intersection, just darkness swallowing the small car. "She turned. I didn't see a sign."

Delaney slowed to put more distance between her rental and Violet's Honda, then took the turn herself. The road stretched into darkness, no streetlights, no other vehicles. One side was forest. The other side was flat and, in the distance beyond a chain-link fence, well-lit. "I need to call Norton back. Or can you loop him in?"

"I think so. Hold on." The line went quiet, then she heard the ringing of an outgoing call.

"Norton."

"Detective, this is Delaney. Violet turned. We're on a side road."

Noah cut in. "I'm looking at your location. You're on Miller Shore Road. It circles the airport."

Even as he said the words, a jet sped down the runway just a couple hundred yards away.

"Maybe she's going to try to catch a flight," Delaney said.

"If she does that, she'll be even easier to catch." Norton sounded far too confident for her liking. "Norfolk Airport PD is on the lookout for her. They're ready to move in."

She prayed his confidence was warranted. Prayed this would all be over soon.

But as the thought came, Violet's taillights swung left again, away from the airport and into the thick forest.

Delaney's stomach dropped. "She turned!" *Breathe, Delaney.* They didn't need her panic. "She turned left. It looks completely deserted."

"Do not follow her." Norton shouted the command.

"He's right, Delaney," Noah added. "Just pull over. I'll be there in five."

"Are there other outlets?" she asked. "Could she—?"

"It doesn't matter," Norton said. "We know where she is. We'll find her."

Delaney approached the road slowly, her heart aching at the thought of losing sight of Violet's car. What if she disappeared? What if she got away and was never seen again?

She flicked her headlights off and took the turn.

"Delaney?" Noah said. "Stop driving."

"I will. I just want to see which way she goes."

Ahead, the headlights continued straight on the narrow road.

Delaney stopped and watched, the darkness pressing against her windows like a living thing. No houses, no businesses, just empty fields.

"Stay where you are," Norton said. "I'm redirecting the police to that area."

"Okay."

She would. But the taillights grew farther and farther away. And then disappeared.

She couldn't lose Charlotte. Not if there was a way to save her.

She pressed the gas.

CHAPTER THIRTY-FIVE

The dashboard clock ticked past nine p.m. as Noah snaked toward the area where Delaney said Violet had turned. He was getting closer.

Delaney's location dot on his phone had stopped moving five minutes before, frozen in the tangle of unmarked roads between the Norfolk airport and a neighborhood off this busy road.

Norton had hung up, but he and Delaney had remained talking, her voice tight with determination as she inched forward—headlights off, she'd said—when suddenly the line had gone dead. No goodbye, no warning. Just silence.

He'd been calling regularly since then, but his calls went straight to voicemail.

"Come on, Delaney." Noah slowed as he approached the road he'd been looking for. "Pick up."

"This is Delaney. Leave a message and I'll call you back."

Her voice, so calm and steady on the recording, made his heart constrict. "It's me again." He turned. On this end, the road was lined with homes and businesses on both sides. "I'm getting close to you. Call me the second you get this."

Not even a mile later, he was leaving the lights behind. Ahead, it was all forest, dark and foreboding, like something out of Grimm's fairytales.

Charlotte was in here somewhere.

His phone rang, and his heart lurched. Delaney?

But it was Detective Norton. Noah tapped the button to answer.

"Where are you right now?" Norton's voice carried the stern authority of a man accustomed to being obeyed.

"About a quarter mile from where Delaney's signal stopped."

"Pull over. Let us handle this."

"Are you close?"

"The police are setting up roadblocks at the major outlets."

"Then she'll take a minor one," Noah snapped. "And then she'll be gone."

"I understand your concern. We're going to find her. At this point, all you can do is get in the way."

Noah took a breath and let the detective's words sink in. The last thing he wanted was to cause the police to lose his niece. Or to put Delaney in danger.

"Noah," Norton said. "I know it's torture, but please, trust us."

He pulled over and killed his lights. "Fine. I'll stay here. Call me when they're safe."

"Will do."

Norton ended the call, and Noah sat in the darkness. Everything in him wanted to barrel into the forest and save his family. That was his job, to protect them. To keep them safe.

He'd failed. Both Charlotte and Delaney were in danger. But if he just trusted Norton...

No. It was God he needed to trust. If he did, maybe this time, God would save what Noah couldn't.

CHAPTER THIRTY-SIX

Delaney stared at the trail that was so narrow she didn't think her rental could traverse it without getting scratched by branches on both sides. If she hadn't seen Violet turn here, she'd never have known where it was.

Delaney had driven past to confirm the Honda was there, then did a U-turn about a hundred yards away and parked, watching the mouth of the trail so she could see if Violet left again. Her muscles ached from sitting motionless for so long, but she didn't dare move. Didn't dare breathe too loudly.

Forty-five minutes had passed since she'd followed Violet's car down this forgotten dirt road. There were no streetlights, just an abandoned structure way off the road. Otherwise, she observed nothing but trees and darkness and the distant sound of planes taking off and landing at the airport. Civilization was just a couple of miles from here, but it might as well have been a hundred.

The Honda's interior remained dark. No movement. No sign of Charlotte or her mother.

"Please, God," Delaney whispered, her voice barely audible. "Keep her safe."

She thought of Charlotte in that car, frightened, possibly crying, trapped with a mother she didn't remember.

It was so dark. All the kids Delaney had taken care of feared the dark, but Charlotte's fear was more acute. One night, the bulb in her little unicorn night-light had gone out, and Noah had rushed to the store to buy a new one. Until he came back, Delaney had stayed with Charlotte and kept the lamp on, anything to protect the little girl from the monsters that populated her imagination.

Did Violet know that about her daughter? Did she care?

Violet was probably the reason she had those fears in the first place.

Delaney's fingers gripped her useless phone. No service. Not even one bar. She'd tried moving it around, holding it up to the window, but nothing had helped. The dense forest surrounding them blocked any signal.

Maybe she should drive back to the main road to tell the police where she was. But if she did and Violet chose that moment to leave, she'd lose her.

Noah must be frantic. He'd probably called the police when her phone went dead, probably assumed the worst. The thought of him pacing somewhere, helpless and terrified... She hated that she'd done that to him. Maybe she should have listened to him and pulled over to wait for the police like Detective Norton had ordered.

But how could she have lived with herself if Charlotte had disappeared into the night while she sat safely on the sideline?

She couldn't have. And she couldn't sit here anymore. She needed to know if Violet and Charlotte were still here or if she was surveilling an empty car.

She reached for the door handle, then stopped. The car

must have a dome light. She found it, then flicked the switch from *Door* to *Off*.

She eased the car door open, wincing at the soft click it made in the silence. The cold bit at her exposed skin. Delaney slipped out of the car and gently pushed the door to nearly closed, afraid if she shut it properly, the sound would alert Violet that she was there.

She rounded her rental car and crouched in the woods to listen.

Nothing but the rustle of wind through the trees and the distant drone of an airplane.

Were Violet and Charlotte still in that car? She needed to find out without being seen.

She moved into the forest and crept toward the Honda.

CHAPTER THIRTY-SEVEN

The waiting was killing him.

Noah pressed the redial button for the fifth time in ten minutes, watching Delaney's name flash on the screen as his call went straight to voicemail. He ended the call before the beep, his jaw clenched so tight his head pounded.

Detective Norton wasn't answering either. Three calls, three trips to voicemail. Noah stared at the glowing dot on his phone's map app. Delaney's location hadn't changed in more than an hour. No movement. No communication. She was just a couple of miles away. Why wasn't she answering?

His luxury car's leather interior felt like a cage, the air thick and suffocating despite the cool November night pressing against the windows. Every second that ticked by on the dashboard clock was another second Charlotte remained in the hands of a woman who'd already proved she couldn't care for her.

And now Delaney was gone too.

Noah scrubbed his face with his palms, the stubble rough against his skin. He'd promised Norton he'd stay put and let the professionals handle it. But what professionals? Where were they? His niece and the woman he loved were somewhere in those dark woods, and he was sitting here like a coward while—

A sharp rap on the passenger window made him jump, his heart slamming against his ribs. He whipped around to see Jasper's haggard face peering through the glass, his brother's eyes wild and desperate.

Noah fumbled for the unlock button. The door swung open, and Jasper slid into the passenger seat, bringing with him the scents of pine and fear.

"What are you doing here? How did you find me?"

"Same way you're tracking Delaney." Jasper held up his phone, the location app glowing on the screen.

"How do you have my location?"

Jasper slipped his phone into his jacket pocket. "You gave it to me a long time ago."

Noah had, once upon a time, when he'd still had hope he and Jasper could rebuild their relationship.

Hair disheveled and jaw set tight, Jasper looked every bit the concerned father he should have been all along.

"Any news?"

Noah glanced at his phone screen again. "Delaney was following them, but I lost her an hour ago. She's not answering. No service, I assume." He hoped. Prayed. The other option was that Violet had discovered she was being followed and had done something to her. He couldn't bear the thought. "The last time I talked to Norton, he told me he was working on it and would call when they had Charlotte. I've called a couple times since then, but he just ignores me." Noah stared into the darkness beyond his windshield. He'd grown accustomed to the roar of planes passing overhead. "They're out there somewhere, and I'm just sitting here like an idiot. I have to do something."

"So let's go. What are we waiting for?" Jasper's question felt like a gauntlet, a dare.

Or maybe an assignment.

His brother blew out a breath. "It's been almost two hours since Delaney first spotted them. If the police had this under control, we'd know by now."

Reckless determination sparked in Noah's heart. No, not reckless, just...

"I'm not saying we go in guns blazing." Jasper seemed intent on convincing him. "I'm saying we get close, see what we see."

Noah was barely listening to his brother, his focus elsewhere. *Should we, Lord? Is this a good idea?*

He'd been praying for the go-ahead to do just what Jasper suggested, and so far, God had only told him to wait.

Wait. Wait. Wait.

It was making him crazy, but God knew more than he did.

Now, he heard a different answer.

Together.

"And anyway," Jasper said, "if she's not there, the cops need to know. They've got all their eggs in this basket. I'm going, so—"

"You're right."

Jasper's eyes popped wide. "Seriously? I'm not even halfway through my speech."

"I don't want to waste another second." Noah opened his door, climbed out of the car, and waited for Jasper's brain to catch up.

Jasper followed suit, slamming his door. "What happened to my never-break-the-rules brother?"

Noah knew exactly what had happened to that guy. He'd fallen in love. First with his niece, and then with her nanny.

"Try to keep up." He jogged toward the dot on his screen.

Hang on, girls. We're coming.

CHAPTER THIRTY-EIGHT

Every shadow in the forest moved, swaying in the breeze. Delaney crept toward the Honda, careful of her steps so she wouldn't alert Violet. She hoped and prayed the trees and bushes and shadows would hide her. She tried to control her breathing, to stay silent, to remain invisible.

When she came parallel to the car, she peered inside, desperate for a glimpse of Charlotte. It took a moment to make out what she was seeing. The seats, and...nothing else.

She gasped. The car was empty.

Its windows were dark, though. Delaney crept closer, praying she was wrong, searching for any sign of movement. But there was nothing. Nobody.

Where were they? Had Violet taken Charlotte deeper into the woods? Or had they been picked up by someone else? Had Violet abandoned her car here? Were they already long gone, miles away while the police set up useless roadblocks?

Delaney scanned the surrounding darkness for movement, a hint of what might have happened. She paused when a jet flew overhead, masking sounds that might guide her.

The noise faded, and she started forward again.

A twig snapped.

Delaney whirled.

Something glinted in the corner of her eye. She ducked, but not fast enough. An object whacked her temple. As pain exploded across her skull, she fell to her knees.

"How did you find me?" The voice was familiar. "Who's with you?"

Delaney looked up, disoriented from the blow. A fuzzy figure stood over her, barely a silhouette in the darkness.

"Where are they?" Heather demanded. Not Heather. Violet. *Focus.*

Nausea rolled over Delaney, but she swallowed it back.

"Tell me!" Violet sounded one notch away from sheer panic. "Who's coming?"

"Nobody." Her voice was rough and shaky, but she was slowly regaining her equilibrium.

And her vision. The figure in front of her was getting clearer. Along with the item Violet held. A gun. Pointed at Delaney's chest.

She scrambled up, backed instinctively, bumping into a tree. She lifted her hands. "Please don't... Nobody's coming. I'm alone."

Very alone. What had she been thinking, getting out of her car? She hadn't helped at all, only gotten herself caught and injured.

She was facing a crazy woman with a weapon, utterly, terrifyingly alone.

"You're lying. You wouldn't come out here by yourself."

"I'm not lying, I swear." Delaney wished she could make out Violet's features. The moon was behind her, so Delaney's face must be better lit. Another advantage for Violet, as if the gun weren't enough.

"Where are the cops?" Violet looked around. "Are they about to move in? To shoot me?"

"Do you really think they'd send me out here by myself?" She didn't know where the words had come from.

"I don't..." Violet looked around again. She seemed confused.

Delaney knew how she felt as she touched her head, her fingers coming away sticky with blood. The wound throbbed with each heartbeat.

"How did you find me?"

"I'm here for Charlotte." Delaney tried to keep her tone even, aiming for conversational. "Where is she?"

"She's mine," Violet snapped. "Not yours. She's none of your business."

Delaney needed to tread carefully. "You're right," she said softly. "She's your daughter, not mine."

Violet's stance shifted slightly, the gun lowering a fraction of an inch.

Delaney couldn't tear her eyes away from that weapon. She didn't want to die here. Everything else seemed to fade until all she could see was the glint of metal not a yard away.

Delaney needed to distract her. "She's a beautiful little girl."

"I know that."

"Of course you do. Of course you know. Like any good mother, you love your daughter."

"I...I do." Maybe she hadn't expected anyone to believe that of her.

Delaney had no idea what was going on in Violet's head, but she guessed understanding and compassion were her best options.

"Is she all right?"

"She's...fine. She's just not used to me yet."

"It'll take time."

"Yes. You're right." Violet blew out a breath. "That's all she needs, a little more time."

"Where do you plan to take her?"

The gun rose again. "You're trying to trick me! You think I'm stupid!"

"You're not stupid, Violet. You pulled this off, didn't you?"

"Yeah. I almost did it a couple months ago. Got all the way in the house before the alarm went off. I had to figure out how to get past it. I put a camera in the bushes so I could see someone plugging the code in."

"Wow." Delaney didn't want to let on that she'd already known that. Noah had assumed Hayes had been involved in the kidnapping, but Violet made it sound as if she'd acted alone.

"You're not gonna stop me."

"You're right, of course." Delaney tried very hard to keep panic out of her voice. "I'm just sad for Noah and Jasper. They're looking for her too. They're worried."

"Jasper? He's here?" Was that a note of hope in her voice?

That was information Delaney could use. She had to figure out how to play it, how to keep Violet talking. Maybe find out where Charlotte was. The child had to be nearby.

"Jasper came back to see his daughter," Delaney said carefully. "He's been frantic, searching everywhere for her."

Violet's silhouette shifted, the gun wavering slightly. "He never cared before. Not about me. Not about her."

"People change. You did, right? Change?"

"What do you know about me?"

"Nothing, really." Delaney needed to be more careful with her words. "Jasper's been out of his mind with worry."

"Right." Violet's laugh was brittle. "The party boy suddenly cares about his kid."

A faint sound came from somewhere beyond the trees—a soft cry that made Delaney's heart leap.

"Where is Charlotte?" Delaney kept her voice gentle. "Is she okay? She doesn't like the dark."

"I know that," Violet snapped, then softened. "I would never leave her alone in the dark."

"Of course you wouldn't," Delaney agreed. "You're her mother."

Violet's breathing changed, became less frantic. The gun lowered again. "I'm trying," she whispered. "Nobody will give me a chance. She's my kid. Mine."

The crying came again, louder this time. Delaney strained to pinpoint the direction, but it felt nearly impossible in the shadowed forest.

"She sounds scared," Delaney said. "Maybe I—"

"She's fine!" Violet turned her head and snapped, "Be quiet!"

Charlotte's cries cut off.

Delaney had to clamp her lips shut to keep from saying what she thought of that.

Help me, Lord. I don't know what to do.

"How did you find me?"

She tried to come up with a good answer, then decided to tell the truth. "I never had a chance to tell you this, but my cousin is in the CIA. And my sister is a cyber-investigator. They figured out what kind of car you drove, and then the apartment you rented."

"How? I didn't use my real name. Freddie told me—" She cut her words off.

"Frederick Hayes, right?" Violet didn't answer, so Delaney pressed on. "You should know, Violet. He told the police how you were trying to dig up dirt on Noah and me. About how you wanted to get custody."

Violet swore under her breath. "I should've known. Nobody can be trusted."

Hadn't Delaney had the same thought before she'd gotten out of the car? But she'd been wrong. Sure, she'd bought Violet's lies, and Owen's. But Noah had been honest with her. He was trustworthy. Everyone in her family was trustworthy. There were plenty of trustworthy people in the world.

"How did you get here?" Violet asked.

"I have a rental car"—she tipped her head toward where she'd left it—"back there on the road."

"Who's with you?"

"Nobody. Noah...ordered me away." It seemed right to say it like that, as if he'd been cruel. "He told me to get on a flight, but I couldn't leave until I knew Charlotte was okay. If you'll just let me see her—"

"C'mon, we're leaving." She flicked the gun like a pointer, and Delaney scrambled to obey. Anything to keep her from squeezing that trigger.

"Move. We're gonna get my daughter, then you're driving us out of here."

Oh, no. What had she done? If she'd stayed in the car, maybe the police would have found Violet. Instead, she was going to be the woman's escape plan.

Lord, help!

Charlotte's tiny body trembled against Delaney's chest as she stumbled through the underbrush, her arms aching from carrying her. The child's tears soaked through Delaney's blouse, her sobs muffled against her shoulder.

"Shhh, sweetie," Delaney whispered, trying to keep her voice steady despite the gun pointed at her back. "It's going to be okay."

Except it wasn't. Nothing about this situation was okay. The sight of Charlotte tied to that tree like an unwanted pet had burned itself into Delaney's memory—the rope marks on her tiny wrists, the terror in her eyes, the way she'd yelled when she'd spotted her through the trees. "Miss Laney! Help me!"

If only she could.

Violet jabbed the gun against Delaney's spine. "Keep moving." The words were a harsh whisper. Then, more softly, "Lottie, baby, it's okay. Mama's here."

Charlotte's little arms and legs tightened around Delaney's body.

Delaney bit back the furious words that threatened to spill out. This woman had neglected her daughter, lost custody, and now kidnapped her—only to tie her to a tree. What kind of mother did that?

She focused on her breathing, needing to contain her rage for Charlotte's sake.

"It's okay, honey," she murmured, stroking her tangled curls. "Just breathe with me." She tried to temper her own breaths, which were coming too fast thanks to the trek through the woods with a child in her arms and the threat of death at her back.

They were almost to Delaney's rental. When they reached it, they'd climb in and drive away. Just like that. She didn't want to think about what would happen next. Maybe she'd survive, maybe not. But Charlotte... Poor Charlotte would be stuck with this...this maniac.

Headlights swept across the road ahead.

"Stop!"

Delaney froze as the car continued past, a word emblazoned on the side bright in the moonlight. POLICE.

Violet grabbed Delaney's arm, yanking her back into the shadows. "Get down!" she hissed, pulling her into a crouch so they'd be hidden by surrounding bushes.

Delaney struggled to keep her balance with Charlotte's weight in her arms. The child's cries were growing louder.

"Keep her quiet," Violet hissed.

It was the last thing she wanted to do, but Delaney cupped the back of Charlotte's head, gently pressing the child's face into her shoulder. "Shh, honey. I need you to be very quiet right now." Her heart thumped so hard she wondered if Charlotte could feel it.

Charlotte hiccuped, her small body shuddering with the effort to control her tears. She seemed to be trying, her tiny fingers gripping Delaney's blouse.

The police cruiser's taillights disappeared around the bend, leaving them in darkness. But hope ignited in Delaney's heart. The police were here. They were looking.

Noah was close too. She knew it.

The thought of him sent a wave of longing through her so intense that it was almost physical pain.

"This is your fault," Violet snapped. "You called them."

"I told you, I was at the airport, and I got your address. I wanted to check it out. I was alone." Delaney kept her voice steady. "But they're looking for Charlotte, of course."

"Tell me the truth."

"I am. I told you—"

"You're lying." She pressed the gun to Delaney's temple.

Oh God oh God oh God. Please... Protect Charlotte.

Delaney was the child's only chance to reunite with Noah. She pressed her little head harder against her shoulder, not willing to let her see what was happening.

What do I do? What do I do!

"I called them." She squeezed her eyes closed and inhaled the sweet, sweet scent of the child in her arms. Peace came with the cool air. "When I saw you leave your apartment, I followed you, and I called the police."

"They're here, then." Violet didn't sound afraid. She sounded resigned.

Which was even more terrifying.

Delaney opened her eyes again. "I lost cell service before I saw your car. They only had a general idea of where I was."

The woman's eyes flicked around, looking for enemies or escape, but she didn't lower the gun. If Charlotte weren't in her arms, Delaney might try to disarm her, but she didn't dare risk a stray bullet hurting the innocent child.

The metal bored into her skin. Charlotte whimpered against her, and Delaney's heart shattered at the sound. This beautiful child should be protected by her mother, not endangered.

"We're surrounded." Violet's breathing turned ragged. "We're surrounded, and it's your fault." The gun trembled against Delaney's temple. "This wasn't supposed to happen. Freddie said—" She cut herself off with a strangled sound.

"Freddie betrayed you. Violet, please." Delaney's voice cracked. "Think about Charlotte. She's scared. She needs—"

"Don't tell me what my daughter needs!" The words exploded, and Charlotte flinched in Delaney's arms. "You don't know anything about being a mother!"

"You're right," she said softly. "I'm not her mother. But I love her, and I know you do too."

Violet made a sound that might have been a sob. The pressure of the gun lessened, and then she stood, aiming down at Delaney.

"Get up," Violet commanded. "We're going there." She nodded in the direction behind Delaney.

She stood and lifted Charlotte, snuggling her close, peering through the trees toward the dark structure she'd spotted earlier. It looked abandoned, a place to hide.

A place where no one would find them.

Delaney stumbled forward, Charlotte clinging to her, each step taking them deeper into danger. As they approached, the structure's weathered siding and sagging porch became clearer. They spoke of years of neglect, windows like empty eye sockets staring back at them.

But maybe someone was watching. Delaney had left her rental nearby. Maybe someone had noticed it.

Please, let someone see us. Let someone intervene before she gets us inside.

"Move faster," Violet hissed, jabbing the gun into Delaney's back.

Charlotte's tears had subsided to silent shudders, her little body curled against Delaney as if she were trying to disappear.

Delaney pressed her lips to the child's forehead, wishing she could absorb all her fear. "It's going to be okay," she whispered, praying it was true.

They circled to the back of the one-story house, where nobody would see them from the road. Wooden porch steps groaned under their weight.

"Open the door."

Delaney tried it, but the knob didn't turn. "It's locked."

"Then kick it in."

Right. Because it was that easy. She turned slowly. "Let me try the windows."

Violet seemed to consider that, lips rubbing together. "Put her down. Lottie, come to Mama."

Charlotte clung to Delaney, burying her face in her shoulder. The rejection was obvious, and Violet stiffened.

"She's just scared," Delaney said. "It's dark, and she doesn't understand what's happening."

"She understands her mother wants her," Violet snapped, her voice rising. "Do as I say."

"It's okay." Every maternal instinct screamed at Delaney not to release this terrified child. But Violet wasn't in her right mind. Delaney needed to tread very carefully right now. She tried to set Charlotte on her feet, but her little legs and arms locked around her like vices.

"No!" Charlotte wailed. "No, Miss Laney! Don't let go!"

"I have to, sweetie," Delaney whispered, her heart splintering. "Just for a minute."

Charlotte's fingernails dug into Delaney's skin as she tried to pry her loose.

"This is your fault," Violet hissed. "You've poisoned her against me."

"She's just scared of the dark. And the gun. Please, put it away."

"So you can run? Not likely."

As if she'd leave Charlotte alone with Violet. *Think.* When she crouched down, she was able to set Charlotte's feet on the boards. She took her little face in her hands. "Sweetie, I'm just going to get inside so I can open the door. It'll be warmer in there. You stay here with your mother. She won't hurt you. She loves you."

As much as she was able, anyway.

Charlotte's eyes were wide and terrified, but she let Delaney stand and step away.

Delaney descended the porch steps and tried the first window. Locked.

But the second, when she pushed hard, slid upward. She managed to get it high enough to squeeze through.

"Go on, then," Violet said. "You have ten seconds to open the door."

She didn't speak the threat, but it was clear. Maybe she wouldn't hurt her daughter, but Delaney couldn't know for sure.

She heaved herself through the window and landed hard on the dusty floor inside. The smell of mold and decay filled her nostrils as she scrambled to her feet. Her hands swept along the wall until she found a door frame. She stepped through, her eyes adjusting to the low light. It was an empty living room. She headed toward the back of the house, found the door, then fumbled for a handle.

She unlocked it and pulled the door open.

Violet stood rigid, the gun trained downward. Charlotte cowered against the railing.

"Go on, honey," Violet said, gesturing with the weapon. "Inside."

Charlotte launched herself at Delaney, who lifted her up again, the little girl's arms immediately wrapping around her neck.

Violet followed, closing the door behind them. The sound echoed through the empty house like a gunshot.

The room was cloaked in darkness.

Would anyone think to look for them here? And if someone did show up...

What would Violet do?

CHAPTER THIRTY-NINE

A voice had reverberated through the woods. Noah and Jasper had followed the sound.

On the road fifty yards away, a police cruiser's taillights disappeared around the bend. Noah hadn't dared follow it, fearing Violet would see them. Instead, he hid behind a massive oak tree, his breath catching in his throat as he watched Violet herd Delaney and Charlotte toward an abandoned house. The gun in Violet's hand gleamed in the moonlight, pressed far too close to Delaney's back.

"We have to move." He was desperate to do something.

Jasper clamped a hand on his shoulder. "She'll hear us."

He shrugged away. "We have to do something." It was killing him, seeing Charlotte clutched against Delaney's chest, his niece's hair tangled from the night wind.

"We need a plan." Jasper sounded confident, like he did this every day. "We can't just charge in. She's armed."

As if Noah hadn't noticed. He closed his eyes, fighting the urge to sprint across the clearing. Every cell in his body screamed at him to go. But Jasper was right. One wrong move, and Violet might panic.

The trio disappeared behind the dilapidated house.

Noah fumbled for his phone, but the screen showed what he already knew. Not a single bar.

"Do you have service?" he asked Jaz. "We need to call the police."

"No, and even if I did…"

Noah glared at him in the darkness. "What?"

"It's just… I'm trying to imagine what would happen if we alerted the cops."

"If? *If!*"

"They'd move in, sirens blaring, lights spinning." Jasper continued, ignoring Noah. "They'd surround the house and demand that Violet let them go."

"Right, and then…" He followed his brother's logic forward.

"That's the thing about hostage negotiators," Jasper said. "They try to rationalize with captors. But Violet is not rational. So how will it end?" Jasper watched him in the darkness, patiently waiting for Noah's thoughts to catch up with his.

"Do you think she'd hurt them, really?"

Jasper peered back at the house, where a faint light now showed through one of the windows. "The woman I knew would never have done any of this. At least, I didn't think she would."

"You didn't know her, though. Just…" He clamped his lips shut. Jasper didn't need to be reminded of his one-night stand. As awful as what he'd done was, that night had given them Charlotte.

"I didn't know her well, you're right. But after Charlotte was born, we spent some time together. I got to know her. I believed…" He shook his head quickly, like he could shake off his thoughts. "She loves Charlotte, in her own way. And she had feelings for me once too. She's just gotten in over her head. Hayes gave her hope she'd get her daughter back, and when she realized his plan wouldn't work, she took matters into her own hands. Now, she's backed herself into a corner."

"Right. And taken the two people I love most in the world with her. And a gun. Which is why the police—"

"The police are plan B."

Noah was terrified, but Jasper sounded so confident. It was...weird. "What do you want to do, then? Just sit here and hope for the best?"

"No." The word was drawn out like he was considering something. "I think...I think we need a two-pronged approach. One of us distracts Violet while the other gets in through the back."

"Don't you think the doors will be locked?"

"I can pick a lock, no problem."

Noah didn't want to think about why his brother had learned that particular skill. Was he some kind of thief?

Now wasn't the time to ask. "Fine. I'll try to talk her down while you—"

"No." Jasper turned to face him fully. "We'll look through the windows, figure out where they are. I'll pick the locks, then go inside. I'll talk to her, at least distract her. When you hear me, you go in the other door and—"

"You're not getting anywhere near that gun. Forget it."

His brother's lips tipped up at the corners. "Still trying to protect me, brother?"

"Yes." He didn't bother to deny it. "Delaney and Charlotte are already in danger. I can't risk losing you too. I'll go, and you—"

"No."

"Jaz, don't be—"

"She knows me. She used to care for me. Maybe she still does, but even if she doesn't, she'll think twice about killing me.

From her perspective, you're the man keeping Charlotte from her."

"And you're the man who abandoned her."

Jasper didn't back down. "All the more reason it should be me. Charlotte loves you. She needs you."

"You're her father."

Jaz looked back at the house. He said nothing for a few long seconds. "You're the one who's earned her trust. You and Delaney. I don't want either one of us to die, but you need to survive. You need to take care of my daughter."

A wave of terror and affection filled Noah's eyes with moisture. He gripped his brother's arm. "Please, let me."

"I'll be okay, Noah. She won't shoot me."

"You don't know that."

He quirked a smile. "Trust me. I'll charm her. It'll be fine."

His brother's cavalier attitude didn't help. But they needed to act—now.

CHAPTER FORTY

The empty house felt like a tomb. Delaney sat with her back against the wall, gaze flicking from Violet, who continually looked out each of the three windows, and Charlotte, huddled in a corner and crying softly. She'd still be in Delaney's arms, but Violet had insisted they separate.

The woman had turned off her phone's flashlight not long after she'd lit it, probably realizing it could give them away.

Now, the only light came from the moon's glow as it filtered through the filthy windows, casting eerie shadows across peeling wallpaper and warped floorboards, occasionally glinting off the gun Violet waved erratically.

They had to get out of here before the woman's last thread snapped.

Delaney mentally mapped escape routes and prayed an opportunity would present itself. She guessed this was a dining room. There were two windows that faced the road, three in the back. Interior doorways led to the hallway she'd come in through and, on the opposite side, the kitchen. She could barely make out a counter in the darkness.

"Stop crying." Violet faced her daughter. "You're fine. Just close your eyes and go to sleep."

Her demand didn't affect Charlotte's sobs at all. The little girl's face was red and swollen, her curls plastered to tear-streaked cheeks. Her gaze flicked from her mother to Delaney, eyes filled with terror.

"She's scared." Delaney kept her voice level despite the fear clawing at her throat. "Let me calm her down."

"You think I can't comfort my own kid?" Violet's eyes flashed with rage. She stepped forward, the gun's barrel glinting in the dim light.

"Of course you can." Delaney worked to keep her tone reasonable. "But right now, you're busy, and she's frightened by everything that's happening. The dark, the strange place..."

The gun, but Delaney didn't say that.

Violet glared at Delaney, but after a long moment, she dipped her head. "Fine. But don't try anything."

Charlotte started moving the instant Violet nodded, launching herself at Delaney.

Delaney held her in her lap, wrapping her in her arms to shield her tiny body from the insane woman pacing the old floors.

Charlotte trembled, burying her face in Delaney's shoulder. The sweet scent of her mixed with the musty odor of the old house—decay and neglect that seemed to seep from the very walls.

"Shh, baby." Delaney stroked Charlotte's tangled curls. "I've got you."

Violet resumed her pacing, each footstep echoing in the empty space. She paused at the front window.

"They're out there," Violet muttered. "I can feel them watching."

The police? Or Noah? She prayed Violet was right, that someone would help them.

After a few minutes, Charlotte's breathing evened out, her sobs quieting to hiccups. Delaney pressed a gentle kiss to the top of her head. How many times had she comforted this child after a boo-boo or a scare? Now Charlotte was living her worst nightmare, and Delaney felt utterly helpless.

She had to do something. She had to try to get through to Violet.

"I just met Jasper yesterday," she said, "but I can see why you were drawn to him. He's very handsome."

Violet spun, eyes narrowed. "Don't even think about trying to steal him from me. Bad enough you tried to steal Lottie."

"I'm not interested in Jasper," Delaney said quickly. "I'm in love with Noah."

The words tumbled out, an admission she'd barely acknowledged herself.

But the confession didn't calm Violet. Instead, her face contorted with rage. "You're in love with him? With Charlotte's uncle?"

"I was trying not to—"

"You lied to me." Her voice rose, shrill and accusing.

Charlotte jerked in Delaney's arms.

"If you'd told me the truth that day in the park, I could've told Freddie. He would've spun it into a big scandal, and Noah would've lost custody. Then I could've gotten her back." She gestured wildly with the gun. "But no, you had to go and lie! This is all your fault!"

Charlotte started crying again.

"Lottie, step away from her." Violet's voice dropped to a dangerous whisper.

Charlotte clung tighter, her face buried against Delaney's neck.

"Lottie, move. Now!"

Delaney's terror spiked.

Violet wanted to kill her, and the only thing stopping her was the innocent child between them.

"You need to move, sweetheart." Her voice shook, but she pressed on. "Go back to the corner and close your eyes."

"I don't wanna go, Miss Laney. Please—"

"Now!" Violet roared. "Move!"

Delaney pried Charlotte away and shoved her toward the corner, desperate to put space between them.

Protect her, Lord. Please, keep her safe.

Violet lifted the gun, and Delaney squeezed her eyes closed. *Please, Father.*

"Violet, don't."

Delaney's eyes popped open as a man stepped in from the darkened corridor.

Violet swung the gun toward Jasper, who lifted his hands. "It's me, darlin'. Don't shoot."

CHAPTER FORTY-ONE

Noah crept through the front door and slowly swung it back toward the jamb. He didn't close it all the way, afraid the sound would alert the crazy woman.

He crept into the kitchen, where he stood motionless, listening to the voices drifting from the next room.

"I know I messed up, Vi." Jasper's voice cracked with what sounded like genuine remorse. "I was selfish and awful. I was...I was just scared, you know? What do I know about being a father? So I ran like a coward. I abandoned you when you needed me most."

Jasper had missed his calling. He should've gone to Hollywood. He'd have made a bundle with that talent. And thank God for it. It might be the only thing keeping Delaney and Charlotte safe.

Noah inched forward, testing each floorboard before shifting his weight. The old house remained mercifully silent under his careful steps. He drew closer to the doorway that led to his family.

"You have no idea what it's been like." Violet sounded desperate. "The addiction took everything from me. Everything.

Even Lottie..." She choked on the name. "I thought Ma could take care of her while I got clean, but then you took her."

"I had to." Jasper's tone was regretful. "Your mother wasn't up to it. She didn't take care of our little girl like you did."

Noah reached the doorway and peeked through.

Delaney was seated with her back against the wall. Charlotte was huddled in the corner nearest to her. Jasper stood in the opening of what looked like a hallway.

All of their eyes were trained on Violet, who was out of Noah's field of vision.

"You don't mean that." Violet's voice turned hard. "You've never meant anything you said to me. You're just like her."

Noah couldn't see Violet, but by the way Delaney's eyes widened, he guessed Violet was aiming her weapon at her.

"Your fight's with me," Jasper said evenly. "This is my fault. I've been a complete jerk."

Delaney's gaze moved to Jasper, telling Noah that was where Violet had shifted her aim.

That didn't make Noah feel any better.

"I've been...awful," Jasper continued, "and I have no right to ask for your forgiveness. But I'm asking. Please, Violet, if you'll only forgive me, we can be together. You and me and Lottie."

Believe him, Noah begged. Just long enough to lower the gun.

Plan A was for Jasper to talk Violet into putting the weapon down.

Plan B was for Noah to tackle her from the side.

The police had been relegated to Plan C, except it wasn't so much a *plan* as it was a hope that they'd show up if they were needed.

Noah wasn't worried he wouldn't be able to take her down. He outweighed her and had the element of surprise.

He was worried she'd fire that weapon and kill someone he loved.

Noah inched forward, trying to get Violet in sight.

There she was, in the far corner, the wall to her back.

He shrank into the shadows again and held very still.

"You think I'm stupid?" Anger hummed in her accusation. "You think I don't know what you're doing?"

She wasn't buying Jasper's story.

Noah braced himself, ready to lunge.

He was terrified that he'd be the reason she pulled the trigger. That he'd be the reason someone died.

"I'm telling you the truth." Jasper's voice held steady, that practiced charm bleeding through even in this nightmare. "I've thought about you every day since I left. About what we could have been."

"Liar." But something in Violet's tone had shifted, uncertainty creeping in around the edges of her anger.

Delaney pressed herself against the wall as if she could push herself right through it.

"Look at me, Vi," Jaz said. "Really look at me. Do you remember that night we took Lottie to the beach? She was just a baby, remember? She was so little and perfect. You were looking up, said you'd never seen stars like that before. But I couldn't take my eyes off you and her. You two were the most beautiful sight I'd ever seen."

Silence stretched. Noah held his breath.

"You remember," Violet whispered, a hint of awe in her voice.

Delaney seemed to hear it too, relaxing a fraction.

Charlotte was a ball in the corner, her small shoulders shaking.

"I know you don't believe me," Jaz said. "I wouldn't believe me either. But I came back. I came back for you and our daughter."

This was it. Either Jasper would convince her, or he wouldn't.

Come on, Violet. Trust him.

"Really?" The word carried on a breath of hope. "You really mean it?"

Jasper took a step closer to the crazy woman. "Of course I mean it."

It was working. He was going to talk her down.

Maybe Charlotte felt it, too, because she looked up.

And locked eyes with Noah.

"Daddy!"

Violet swung her body—and the gun—toward the corner. Her eyes were wild.

Noah launched himself between the weapon and the people he loved.

The gun exploded.

A scream carried from far, far away.

CHAPTER FORTY-TWO

Everything happened in slow motion.

Violet turned, aiming.

Delaney shifted to cover Charlotte.

Noah jumped in front of Violet.

The gun went off, a deafening crack.

Somebody screamed. Maybe it was Delaney.

She couldn't breathe, couldn't think—could only watch in frozen horror as Noah collided with Violet, driving her to the ground with a sickening thud.

Jasper flew toward them. He grabbed Violet's wrist, pinning it to the floor while Noah slid off her thrashing body.

Charlotte lunged forward. "Daddy!"

"No!" Delaney held the child tightly, wrapping her arms around her and turning her away from the struggle. "Don't look, sweetie. Don't look."

She pressed Charlotte's head against her shoulder, murmuring soothing nonsense that came automatically, flowing from some deep maternal instinct, while her mind screamed a different refrain.

Noah. Noah. Noah.

Was he hit? She couldn't see past the tangle of bodies. She couldn't tell.

Charlotte sobbed against her neck, tiny fingers digging into Delaney's arms.

"Shh, it's fine, sweetheart. It's going to be okay."

Please, God. Please let him be okay.

Jasper disarmed Violet and sent the gun skidding across the warped floorboards, spinning to a stop near the wall.

Delaney kicked it into the kitchen, far from the fray.

Blood spread across the floor in a widening pool, dark and glossy in the dim light.

Noah's. It had to be.

"I've got her," Jasper shouted, holding Violet's thrashing body down with a knee between her shoulder blades. "Noah! Noah, come on! Be okay." His words broke on the plea. "Please, be okay."

Delaney started toward him, but Jasper shouted, "No. Don't let her see."

Right. Charlotte. But Noah was bleeding to death, all alone.

And then, he groaned and shifted. He turned over, slowly pushed himself up, then scooted back to lean against the wall.

Blood poured from a wound on his head.

Delaney set Charlotte down. "Stay here, sweetie. Uncle Noah's hurt. I'm going to help him, okay? Just sit here." Without waiting for a reply, Delaney crossed the room and dropped to her knees.

He looked at her, but his eyes were unfocused.

She ripped off her jacket and pressed the cloth to his wound. It wasn't absorbent, though. She yanked off her sweater, thankful she'd worn a T-shirt underneath. She pressed the sweater to his wound.

He winced but didn't say anything. He was staring straight ahead.

"Noah?" She got in front of him and met his eyes. "What hurts? What can I do?"

He looked confused, and fresh fear filled her. Was he not okay? Had the bullet done terrible damage? Was she missing a wound?

Then, his hand lifted, and he pressed it to her cheek. "You're hurt. Are you all right?"

"Yes, yes." Tears filled her eyes until she could hardly see past them. "I wasn't the one who was shot."

"Oh." Now, he reached up and touched the fabric she held to the wound. "It hurts."

"No kidding." A laugh bubbled out, relieved and hysterical. "You were shot. In the head."

"Just grazed me, I think. What happened to you?"

"Nothing." But she remembered her own head wound and the blood she'd felt. "I'm fine, thanks to you and Jasper."

That confused look was back, and then he looked past her to his brother. "Jaz?"

She turned too.

Jasper had bound Violet's hands behind her back with his belt. She was lying face down on the floor, sobbing.

Jasper knelt beside her, head bowed, shoulders heaving.

"Hey." Noah tried to stand.

Delaney gently pressed down on his shoulder. "Hold the bandage in place." He did, and she stood and laid her palm on Jasper's back. "Everyone's okay. It's okay."

He looked up at her, and all the terror he'd hidden when he was talking to Violet was displayed in his face.

"You did it, Jasper," she said. "We're safe. Everyone's safe."

He swiped at his eyes, then looked beyond her. "Hey, little bit. Come here."

Charlotte looked at him for a long moment.

And then she ran to Noah.

He welcomed her as she plopped down on his lap, snuggled up against him, and popped her thumb in her mouth. Noah kissed her head and murmured something to her that Delaney couldn't make out.

When he looked at his brother, his expression spoke of guilt, as if it were his fault she'd chosen him.

But Noah had loved Charlotte well and made her feel safe. And Jasper...hadn't.

Jasper didn't say anything, just stood and walked into the kitchen. A moment later, the door opened and slammed.

"He'll be okay." Delaney sat beside Noah and stroked Charlotte's hair. "He's just overwhelmed."

"I know how he feels."

The door opened again, and Jasper returned. He held Violet's gun, aimed at the floor. "I'm gonna empty this into a tree stump so the cops find us. Didn't want you to think I'd offed myself."

"Thanks for the warning," Noah said.

He nodded and disappeared out the door again. A moment later, the gun fired a few times.

There was nothing to do but snuggle up beside Noah and wait for help.

And thank God they were all alive.

CHAPTER FORTY-THREE

The bright hospital lights over Noah's bed made his head pound. This was taking forever. "Can't you just sew it up?"

"It's not that simple," the nurse said. "We have to be careful with head wounds. And gunshot wounds."

He winced as she pulled debris or something out of his wound, then dabbed antiseptic, the chemical burn nothing compared to the thundering in his skull.

"It just grazed me."

"Mmm." Her lips pinched closed as she tortured him a little more. "You're lucky. Half an inch to the right, and we wouldn't be having this conversation. Or any conversation."

"Not lucky. Blessed. God protected me."

Her eyes narrowed like she wasn't sure about that.

Through the open door, voices drifted from somewhere nearby—Delaney's gentle tone, Jasper's deeper one, and a woman's voice he didn't recognize.

When the nurse turned away, he sat up. Maybe not the smartest move. His vision swam.

She must've heard because she turned back. "Lie down, Mr.

Aylett. The doctor will be here to examine you, and then we'll close that wound."

He pushed to his feet and stood still through a wave of dizziness.

"Sir, sit down."

"I'll be right back. I need to check on my...daughter."

Wasn't technically true, but she didn't know that.

He stepped into the hall and made his way toward his family's voices. He found them around the corner and in a small exam space, crowded around a bed.

Charlotte lay curled on her side, thumb in her mouth. Her eyes were closed.

Delaney stood beside her, one hand resting protectively on her shoulder.

Jasper stood just inside the door, arms crossed, his face drawn with exhaustion. He shifted when he saw Noah, making room for him.

A middle-aged nurse with graying hair gave Noah a disapproving look, then continued to address Jasper. "The long-term effects of trauma can be devastating if they're not dealt with properly. Children Charlotte's age are particularly vulnerable. Night terrors, regression, trust issues."

"She's already seeing a therapist," Delaney said.

The nurse's expression brightened. "Oh, that's good to hear. Consistency is key, especially after an event like this." She made a note on her clipboard, then looked at Jasper with approval. "You're doing the right thing, getting her professional help."

Jasper nodded, but Noah didn't miss the way his jaw tightened.

"I just need to go over these instructions, and you can take her home."

Jasper heaved a sigh from deep inside. "You need to tell

him." Jasper tipped his head toward Noah, his voice rough. "He's her father."

The nurse looked confused, glancing between Jasper and the clipboard in her hand. "I was told—"

"He's her father. I'm just...not." He swallowed hard, arms tightening across his midsection as if he were holding himself together.

Noah wanted to celebrate what those words meant, but more important right now was acknowledging the sacrifice Jasper was making.

His daughter. His beautiful, precious daughter. Jasper hadn't figured out how amazing she was until it was too late.

Noah thumped Jasper on the back, wanting to pull him close like he would have the much younger, skinnier version. But the grown man beside him wouldn't appreciate that.

He angled away, then ducked out the door and disappeared.

Delaney watched where he'd gone. Her gaze found Noah's, and she smiled shyly.

Then she must've really seen him because she straightened. "What are you doing? You need to sit."

"I just wanted to make sure Charlotte's okay."

"She'll be a lot better if her uncle..." She paused. Her lips lifted in a slight smile. "Her *father* doesn't bleed to death. Come on." She urged him out of Charlotte's room and back to his own. "Do I need to sit in there with you to make sure you stay put?"

He did his best to hide his wave of dizziness. "No, ma'am."

When they entered his room, the nurse sent him a scathing look.

"My daughter's fine. Thanks for asking."

"Of course she is. I'll get the doctor. You stay put." She marched out.

Delaney watched her go. "She seems sweet."

"Oh, yeah. Regular Florence Nightingale."

The words were still hanging in the air when the door opened again. He hoped the nurse hadn't heard his remark. She already disliked him.

But it was... Noah couldn't think of his name. The only one that came to mind was his sarcastic moniker for the guy who was way too interested in Charlotte's nanny. *Dr. Dreamy.*

"How're we doing, Mr..." His words trailed as he caught sight of Delaney. "Oh. Hey."

"Hey, Ethan."

The doctor finally looked at Noah, and the smile that had filled his face faded. "They said it was a gunshot wound." His gaze flicked back to Delaney. "You okay?"

"I'm fine."

But he moved closer, eyeing the bandage on her head. "What happened?"

"Just a little cut. It's Noah—"

"Right. Sorry." He turned back to Noah and examined the wound. "You want to tell me what happened?"

"Not really." Noah was too tired to be nice, so he figured he'd better just be quiet.

"It's a long story," Delaney said.

"I bet." The doctor hummed low, then stepped back. "Looks like Nurse Nightingale did a good job cleaning it."

A chuckle bubbled from Noah's lips. "Sorry about that."

"I've met her. You're good."

Noah couldn't help but like this guy. And it was easier now that he knew which one of them Delaney loved.

"It's not that deep," Ethan said. "No need for a CT scan. I just need to close it up." He turned to Delaney. "Why don't you go check on Charlotte?"

"Uh..." She looked at Noah. "You want me to stay?"

The doctor gave him a look that told him what the answer should be.

"I'm good. Go sit with her."

"I'll get you when we're done," Ethan said.

Delaney walked out, and the doctor found a tool that looked suspiciously like a stapler.

"It'll hurt, but not as much as getting shot."

"Why doesn't that make me feel better?"

Ten minutes later, Noah wished he could have a turn with the stapler and the doctor's skull. But the wound was closed, so he ground out a thank-you before the man left.

Delaney returned a few seconds later and held his hand, gaze skimming his face. "That looks painful."

"It's just a flesh wound, which I keep telling them, but they're acting like I was—"

"Shot?"

He'd laugh, but it hurt too much. "I'm just saying..."

She bent and kissed him on the forehead. "You're going to be okay. I'll take care of Charlotte until you're a hundred percent."

"You're the best."

"I try."

She started to walk away, but he caught her hand and pulled her back. "Seriously. You saved her life."

"Not me. My cousin Michael and my sister Alyssa found her. They—"

"*You* were there. *You* found her. *You* saved her."

"So did you. So did Jasper."

He nodded. That was true. But if not for Delaney, he didn't know what would have happened.

Truth was, if not for Delaney, Charlotte wouldn't be the open, happy kid she was today. Delaney had saved her long before tonight.

"You're a wonder."

Her short laugh seemed uncomfortable. "I don't know—"

"I do. I don't deserve you. Obviously."

"That's not—"

"Let me finish, please." Because he was losing focus, and he needed to say this. "You're amazing, and you're so good with Charlotte. I love you because…" A thousand reasons that he couldn't seem to vocalize. "You're everything I want."

Her eyes widened. "You've lost a lot of blood." She was half kidding, but only half. Like she wasn't sure if she should believe him.

"I know what I'm saying." Though his words were slurring, and he wasn't saying anything well. He *had* lost a lot of blood, and the walk across the ER had taken too much out of him. "I love you. That's all. I just…love you."

"I love you too."

"Okay, then. It's settled." He wasn't sure exactly what was settled, but it felt right. Complete. Whatever that meant.

His eyes closed, but he pulled her hand to his lips and kissed it. "Take her home. Jaz can drive me when I'm done."

"Are you sure?"

"Mmm. Yes." Darkness was closing in. He was so tired, and his head was spinning.

The soft brush of her lips on his was the last thing he felt before he drifted to sleep.

CHAPTER FORTY-FOUR

Delaney had never celebrated Thanksgiving away from her parents and sisters, away from Maine.

But here at the Aylett house, she felt at home. And she had so much to thank God for.

Steam rose from the pot of mashed potatoes as Noah stirred in the butter and cream, then mashed them like they were an enemy.

"You've won the battle." Delaney nudged his shoulder with hers as she reached for the salt.

His eyes crinkled at the corners. "Just making sure there are no lumps. Charlotte hates lumps."

"Charlotte hates green beans, too, but she'll try some today." Delaney pulled casseroles from the second oven and covered them with foil.

He transferred the potatoes to a serving dish. "But it's Thanksgiving." His voice took on a whiny note, making her laugh. She loved how attuned he was to his daughter's preferences.

His daughter.

Both Violet and Jasper had waived their parental rights—

Violet had refused at first, but her attorney had advised her that doing so might help her legal case. Considering she'd be in prison until Charlotte was an adult, there was no reason for her not to relinquish her rights.

Jasper's signature on the paperwork had arrived via courier, the man himself conspicuously absent since the day after the dramatic confrontation at the abandoned house. He'd stayed just long enough to make sure his brother was going to be okay, then taken off.

The adoption wasn't final yet, but Noah's attorney assured him the state would rush it through, since he was a relative—and he'd had custody for months.

It might not be legal yet, but Charlotte was his daughter in every important sense of the word.

Delaney had stayed on as Charlotte's nanny, but she'd rented an apartment outside of town. She drove over every morning in her new car—another Highlander, like the old one—and was off the clock every afternoon when Noah got home from work, though she usually stayed to have dinner with him and Charlotte. Sometimes, Noah hired a babysitter, and the two of them went out on a date.

In the three weeks since the incident, they'd only grown closer.

She didn't know what it would mean long term, but for now, she was happy with this little family. And if she dreamed of being a part of them someday...

That was up to God. He'd taken care of her this long. He could be trusted with her future.

"The turkey's been resting long enough," she said. "Will you carve it?"

Noah wrapped an arm around her waist, pulling her close. "I'm not ready to join the mayhem."

"Mayhem? They're your friends."

"They're *our* friends, and I'm glad they're here. But that doesn't keep me from wishing for one moment alone with you."

She snuggled against him. His wound was still covered with a bandage, but it was healing, as was hers. When all was said and done, they'd have similar scars, though hers would be hidden by her hair.

Things could have turned out so differently. She thanked God every day that He'd spared them all. Even Violet, who was currently in a mental hospital while she awaited her trial.

He backed away, reached into the pantry, and came out with a grocery sack. He pulled a gift bag from it. "I wanted to give you something and...it's probably stupid, and the timing is terrible, but..." He shrugged. "I want you to have it now."

She took the bag. "Our family didn't exchange Thanksgiving presents."

"This is more of a... Just open it."

She reached in and pulled out a package of hair bows more suited to Charlotte than to her. "Wow. They're pretty." But as the words came out, they triggered her memory of that terrible day when she was eight years old and had failed to protect Kenzie.

Noah didn't laugh, just stepped closer and took the package. He tossed it on the counter next to the potatoes. "They're a symbol. I was trying to say something at the hospital, but I don't think I said it properly."

"You were a little out of it."

He took her hands and looked into her eyes. "I love the way you love my daughter, but that's not why I love you. I love you because...just you. You're everything I want. You're a great nanny, and you'll be a wonderful mother. But also, you deserve to have all the hair ties and...whatever you want." His lips pressed into a grimace. "I'm not saying this right. It's that...I love that you love her."

"And you," Delaney said.

His smile was slight. "And me, yes. But you need to know that you matter too. What you want, what you need. You matter to me. What I love about you is...you. It's not what you do. It's who you are."

"Oh." Suddenly, those were the most precious hair bows she'd ever seen. She stepped into his arms, amazed at this man who'd known exactly what she needed to hear.

They stood like that for a long moment.

"I'm so thankful for you." He tipped her chin up and tenderly touched his lips to hers.

Charlotte darted into the kitchen, took one look at them, and yelled to the other room, "They're kissing again!"

Delaney stepped away, laughing.

Noah groaned. "I need to talk to her about timing."

Lowell joined Charlotte at the door. "You two need to focus. We're hungry out here."

"Five minutes." Delaney grabbed serving spoons for all the side dishes while Noah carved the turkey.

Through the kitchen doorway, she could see Charlotte twirling among the guests in the living room, her curly hair bouncing as she showed off her new dress to anyone who would look. Her laughter carried over the murmur of conversation, a sound that still made Delaney's heart squeeze with love and relief. She was healing. It'd been traumatic, but she was a strong kid.

Ellen, Richard's wife, approached from the dining room. "The table looks beautiful, Delaney."

"Thank you." She'd spent the morning arranging autumn leaves and small pumpkins down the center of the long dining table. That first day when she'd admired the crystal on the sideboard—it felt like a lifetime ago. Back then, she'd worried about what kind of man Noah was, worried she wouldn't be able to trust him.

Now, watching Charlotte giggle as she played with Lowell's son, Bryce, Delaney felt the rightness of this home, this life, settle deep into her bones. She returned to the kitchen and ladled gravy into a gravy boat, inhaling the rich scent of turkey drippings and herbs. "Will you take this in?"

"Of course!" Ellen turned to the room and clapped. "Everybody, come help!"

Within minutes, the food had been transferred to the dining room, and everyone had gathered around the table. They'd had to bring chairs from other rooms so they'd all fit. It was tight, but worth it to be together.

Lowell had accepted Noah's invitation. It was a little awkward as Noah and his old friend worked to mend their relationship. But they were there. Lowell was trying, and Noah, wonderful man that he was, had forgiven Lowell for everything he'd done. It didn't hurt that Lowell had thrown his support behind Noah and his company. They'd signed the merger papers a week before.

Noah waited until everyone was seated, then sat at the head of the table, Delaney on one side, Charlotte on the other.

"When I was a kid," he said, "Mom used to make us go around the table and say what we're thankful for. You all know what I'm most thankful for today." His gaze skimmed to his daughter, then landed on Delaney. "Obviously, God has been" —he swallowed hard—"really good to me this year."

"Amen." Richard's deep voice resonated around the room, and the rest of them murmured similar sentiments.

Lowell cleared his throat. "I'm thankful for...forgiveness and second chances."

"Me too, my friend," Noah said.

Charlotte bounced in her seat like she was dying to say something.

"How about you, Charlie-Bear?" Noah prompted. "What are you thankful for?"

"Daddy, and Miss Laney, and apple pie!"

Her lighthearted answer had them all laughing, and then eating and talking and teasing and sharing stories.

It was...beautiful. For Delaney, it felt like home.

CHAPTER FORTY-FIVE

Noah had been warned. Delaney had told him on the flight to Maine that her family home was...how had she put it? "A little...much."

Talk about an understatement. He'd thought his house was impressive.

He stood in the grand foyer of the Wright estate, wealth practically dripping from the walls.

The irony wasn't lost on him. Not even three months before, he'd taken one look at Delaney Wright—clothes that hung loose on her willowy frame, reeking of cigarettes from, he'd later learned, the women at the shelter where she'd been living—and dismissed her as poor and desperate.

He'd been spectacularly wrong. Thank heavens, God had intervened in Noah's haughty stupidity.

Delaney stood beside him, radiant in a deep green dress that brought out the green in her eyes, her hand warm in his as her family gathered.

"Mom, this is Noah Aylett." Delaney sent him a smile, looking fully relaxed. "Noah, my mother, Evelyn Wright."

The matriarch of the Wright family was tall and slender, her silvery-blond hair swept back. She would have been intimidating, but her smile was genuine as she extended her hand.

"Noah, what a pleasure. Delaney's told us so much about you." She shifted her gaze to his daughter. "Which means you must be Charlotte."

His daughter had pressed herself against his leg the moment they'd walked through the massive double doors, but now she stepped out. "Uh-huh."

"It's a pleasure to welcome you."

Charlotte shook her hand, then dipped into a curtsy that had Evelyn grinning.

"We're going to be good friends." Evelyn sent Noah a smile, then gestured to the people who'd entered the foyer after her. "Everyone's so eager to meet you."

The next few minutes passed in a blur as Noah and Charlotte were introduced to the rest of Delaney's family. Alyssa, her fiancé, Callen, and his daughter, Peri, who looked excited to have a playmate, even if Charlotte was half her age.

Brooklynn and her boyfriend, Forbes Ballentine, the billionaire head of Ballentine Industries.

Noah shot Delaney a look, and she shrugged like it was no big deal.

Noah had figured out a few weeks ago who her father was. He'd seen the man on the Sunday morning news programs. For Delaney, it was normal.

He met Cici and her boyfriend, Asher, who looked like he could snap Noah in half without breaking a sweat. When they shook hands, Asher leaned in and spoke quietly. "They take some getting used to, but they're good people. Just beware of Gavin."

Asher backed away and gave Noah a serious look that had his gut clenching.

There was no time to worry as a woman, who must be the youngest sister, entered the room. Unlike the rest, who all wore dresses or skirts, this one wore loose trousers, a purple blouse, and tennis shoes. Her chestnut hair fell in waves around her face.

"Kenzie," Delaney said. "This is Noah Aylett and his daughter, Charlotte."

She shook his hand. "Nice to..." But her words faded as she studied his face. "Do you have a brother?"

Jasper had disappeared after the kidnapping and hadn't been answering Noah's calls or texts. Noah had no idea where his brother was.

"His name's Jasper," Noah said. "Jaz, to most people."

"I've never met the guy formally, but I've had contact with someone who looks a lot like you. Blond hair, those same eyes. Even that little..." She tapped her chin, indicating the dimple he'd inherited from his father.

Kenzie was the sailor, and Jaz liked to spend time near the water.

"Have you seen him recently," Noah asked, "in the last month or so?"

"No, not in a while." Her lips pinched. She didn't seem pleased to have discovered a connection. Jasper must have done something to offend her.

Seemed likely.

Finally, Kenzie focused on his daughter. "I'm finally meeting the famous girl!"

"I'm not famous, I'm Charlotte."

Everyone within hearing distance laughed.

Evelyn ushered them toward the large eat-in kitchen, where they shared appetizers and sipped drinks. Within a few minutes, Charlotte and Peri were playing with dolls in a corner while Delaney's sisters peppered Noah with questions.

"Leave him alone, you guys," Delaney said. "You're gonna scare him away."

"I don't know." Alyssa tapped her nose, eyeing him. "He doesn't look that fragile to me."

That was good to hear. As soon as he had the chance, he'd thank her for her part in Charlotte's rescue. But he didn't want to do it in front of her whole family. He didn't know how much she and Delaney had shared of their adventure.

The murmurs died down, and Noah looked around to see why.

The answer arrived in the form of an older man Noah recognized from the TV.

Gavin Wright walked to his daughter and pulled her into a hug, whispering something in her ear.

Whatever it was, it didn't make her smile. "Dad, don't."

But he ignored her, stepping toward Noah, just a little too close.

"What do you think you're doing with my daughter? You're way too old for her."

Noah flipped through a number of potential responses. *She's an adult, so that's none of your business.*

True, but he wasn't going to say it.

What do you think I'm doing?

Uh, no. What Gavin assumed was exactly the problem.

He realized the best course of action was the truth. "I'm falling more in love with her every day."

If he'd hoped that answer would endear him to Gavin, he'd been sorely mistaken.

The man's gaze turned fiery as he stepped even closer. "She's half your age."

"She's not." Noah resisted the urge to step back. "That would make me fifty-six. Do I look fifty-six to you?"

The man's face turned a concerning shade of red.

Evelyn appeared at his side and gripped his arm. "Gavin." She smiled as if her husband wasn't about to kill him.

The man was ex-CIA. He could do it, hide the body, and nobody would ever know what had become of Noah Aylett.

"He's ten years older than Delaney. Ten years, darling."

The man's gaze flicked to his wife. He looked skeptical.

She continued. "Which is less than twelve—"

"It's different. You were older—"

"I was twenty-four when we started dating. Delaney's twenty-seven."

He actually looked surprised by this news, as if he'd missed a few of her birthdays.

A second passed, and then he grunted.

"Gavin." Evelyn sounded disappointed. "You can do better."

He sighed, then shook Noah's hand. "Nice to meet you."

"If you say so."

The man cracked a smile and turned to Delaney, who'd watched the scene with wide eyes. "I like him. He doesn't scare easily."

"None of us does," Callan called from the other side of the room. Apparently, they'd all heard the whole thing. "Only the strong survive the Wright family."

Asher, standing a few feet away, chuckled. "You think he's scary, wait till you meet the cousins."

Oh boy. Noah wasn't looking forward to that. But he'd endure it.

Anything for Delaney.

The worn check was soft at the edges from being handled so many times over the past months. Delaney had carried it everywhere—a reminder of all she needed to prove.

She'd asked Dad if they could talk, and now they stood in the chilly sunroom at the back of the house. The rest of the family had migrated into the family room, their voices a distant hum of laughter—Charlotte's giggles among them—and conversation.

She held out the check to her father. "I want to return this to you."

He glanced at the check but didn't reach for it. "Why didn't you cash it?"

"I didn't need to." Delaney straightened her shoulders, feeling stronger. "I know you didn't think I could do it, but I made it on my own."

His eyes widened, then narrowed. "I never said that. I never doubted you." He sounded not defensive but hurt.

"When you gave it to me, you told me to come home when I ran out of money."

"I didn't mean..." He blew out a sigh and shook his head. "I really am terrible at this."

His words surprised a laugh out of her. "What?"

"Fatherhood. If that's what you thought I meant when I gave you that..." He took the check but didn't pocket it. Instead, he stared at her for a long moment. "I never doubted you'd make it, Laney. That's not why I gave you this."

"Then why?"

"Because... You're my daughter. I wanted to make sure you were okay. I wanted you to be safe." His voice cracked. "That's all I've ever wanted. To protect you. When I heard what happened..." He shoved the check into his pocket and took her hands. "You saved that child's life. You put yourself in danger to do it."

"Oh, well..." She'd told her sisters and Mom. Apparently, someone told Dad. "It's nothing you wouldn't have done."

He pulled her close. "That's true. You're like me in that way, protective. But you're like your mother in all the other ways. You're kind and caring and more...present than I've ever been." He took her shoulders and met her eyes. "I'm so proud of you. And I never doubted you. I'm sorry I'm so terrible at saying it. I'm trying harder, I really am."

She stepped into his arms again, not sure what to say. Because he *was* bad at it, but right now, he was making up a lot of ground.

After a few moments, he backed away, gave her a soft smile, then frowned at something out of her line of vision.

"I guess I'll get back to the party." He squeezed her hand, kissed her on the cheek, and left.

On his way, he nodded to Noah, who was waiting in the formal living room, sipping some of Mom's famous hot chocolate.

When Dad was gone, Noah set his mug down and stepped closer, brows lowering. He swiped his finger below her eye, catching a tear. "Do I need to beat him up for you?"

She wasn't sure if the sound she made was a laugh or a cry. Maybe a combination of both.

"Maybe not tonight."

"Fair enough." He was still studying her. "You okay?"

"Just realizing that things aren't always what I think."

"You're telling me. You, for instance, keep surprising me."

"How so?"

"Oh, your sister's been giving me an earful." He grinned. "You were quite the bossy Bess as a little girl."

"You've been talking to Kenzie. If she'd just done what I said, I wouldn't have had to boss her around."

"It's always the other guy's fault." He gazed at the snow-covered yard and rocky slope that ended with the crashing North Atlantic waves. "Your family is amazing."

"They're great. Even Dad, when you get to know him."

"I get it. I have a daughter now, so I figure I'll be a lot like that one day." He slipped his arm around her back. "Are you really okay with leaving this place? I know how much you love it."

"I do." She faced him. "But I left because I wanted to make a life for myself apart from here. And I've done that in a way I never expected."

He gazed down at her. "Delaney. You're everything I didn't even know I needed."

She smiled, her cheeks warming. She'd fought for him, and he'd fought for her, and together, they'd fought for Charlotte.

He pulled her closer. "I love you."

"I love you."

He pressed his lips to hers in a gentle kiss, then started to deepen it.

"I love you, too, Miss Laney!" Charlotte barreled into her legs and held on. She yelled to no one in particular, "They're kissing again!"

Whoops and laughter came from the other room.

Noah scooped his daughter up. "We need to talk about timing, Charlie-Bear."

Delaney grinned at the sweet little girl who'd stolen her heart. His daughter, and someday, God willing, hers too.

She kissed Charlotte on the cheek, then Noah on the lips.

Their kisses tasted like chocolate and forever.

The End...

Of this story, but of course there are two more chapters, a sneak peek into what happens in the future for Delaney, Noah, and Charlotte.

Scan or click the QR code for the *Fighting for You* Bonus Epilogue.

If you liked Delaney's story, you're going to love Kenzie's. She discovers that there's a lot more to Jasper Aylett than the "wastrel" brother he pretends to be. You'll encounter dangerous enemies in exotic ports while unraveling a twisty mystery that'll keep you engaged until the end. Turn the page for more about *Anchoring You.*

Want a free book? Join my newsletter list to download *Escaping with You,* a Wright Heroes of Maine prequel. Visit my website at https://robinpatchen.com/sub scribe/ to get your copy.

Now, turn the page for more about *Fighting for You.*

On the glittering waters of the Caribbean, a yacht captain's fight for survival forces her to rely on a man she swore she'd never trust.

A fiercely independent yacht captain, Kenzie Wright has spent her life disregarding her family's expectations. She thrives on freedom, charting her own course, and never staying in one place—or with one person—for long. But when a routine voyage thrusts her into the crosshairs of a deadly drug cartel, her carefully crafted agenda is blown apart. Her last hope to save herself and her crew is the partying playboy, Jasper Aylett.

DEA informant Jasper Aylett has spent years hunting the cartel leader known only as "the Phantom." The mission has cost him everything—his family, his reputation, and his chance at redemption. When a beautiful yacht captain gets caught in the Phantom's web, Jasper risks his life to rescue her. It's his last chance to secure the information he needs to take his enemy down—and get his life back.

Kenzie is forced into hiding with Jasper, and now two cartels want her dead. With their lives on the line, Kenzie and Jasper must work together to unravel the Phantom's network before it's too late. But the closer they get to the truth—and to each other— the more their past wounds and buried fears threaten to tear them apart, leaving them vulnerable to an enemy who won't stop until they're both destroyed.

From a *USA Today* bestselling author... Don't miss this heart-pounding suspense and swoon-worthy romance as Kenzie and Jasper discover their fight for survival—and for love—can only be won together.

Children of the Sea

Castaway

The Wright Heroes of Maine

Escaping with You

Running to You

Rescuing You

Finding You

Sheltering You

Protecting You

Capturing You

Defending You

Fighting for You

Anchoring You

Shadowing You

The Coventry Saga

Vanished in the Darkness

Redemption for Ransom

Betrayal of Genius

Traces of Virtue

Touch of Innocence

Inheritance of Secrets

Lineage of Corruption

Wreathed in Disgrace

Courage in the Shadows

Vengeance in the Mist

A Mountain Too Steep

The Nutfield Saga

Convenient Lies

Twisted Lies

Generous Lies

Innocent Lies

Beautiful Lies

Legacy Rejected

Legacy Restored

Legacy Reclaimed

Legacy Redeemed

Sleigh Bells & Stalkers

One Christmas Night

Amanda Series

Chasing Amanda

Finding Amanda

ABOUT ROBIN PATCHEN

Robin Patchen is a *USA Today* bestselling and award-winning author of Christian romantic suspense. She grew up in a small town in New Hampshire, the setting of her Coventry Saga books, and then headed to Boston to earn a journalism degree. After college, working in marketing and public relations, she discovered how much she loathed the nine-to-five ball and chain. She started writing her first novel while she home-schooled her three children. The novel was dreadful, but her passion for storytelling didn't wane. Thankfully, as her children grew, so did her skill. Now that her kids are adults, she has more time to play with the lives of fictional heroes and heroines, wreaking havoc and working magic to give her characters happy endings. When she's not writing, she's editing or reading, proving that most of her life revolves around the twenty-six letters of the alphabet.

www.ingramcontent.com/pod-product-compliance
Lightning Source LLC
Chambersburg PA
CBHW072012190726
48293CB00001B/256